Custom Made

A Brenner Falls Romance
Book 2

Kyle Hunter

More novels by Kyle Hunter

Circle Back Around
One December
Postcard from Nice (a novella)

The Provence Series

Prodigals in Provence
A Promise in Provence

The Second Chance Series

Marissa Rewritten (A Novella)
Julia Redesigned
Sydney Rewound
Eden Redefined

The Brenner Falls Series

Good Gifts
Custom Made
Embracing the Broken
Mistaken Destiny

*Thank you for making me so
wonderfully complex! Your workmanship
is marvelous—how well I know it.*

Psalm 139:14

Chapter One

Blair McCartney rubbed her eyes and slid her glasses back in place. One more time. She reread the bewildering instructions for the international fashion design contest, hoping for a spark of clarity. Her friend Lisa, currently living Blair's dream in New York, had sent the link the previous day.

Through the picture window of the small rental house in Brenner Falls, Blair spotted the red T-shirt of her six-year-old son, Jake. He ran back and forth in the small side yard, kicking a soccer ball, despite the summer heat.

A drawn-out sigh escaped her lips. She could submit the summer collection she'd created last year to the contest. Those designs lay tucked in a sketchbook under her bed. Or maybe one of her current ideas? Her gaze went across the cluttered living room to an unfinished storyboard studded with swatches of color, fabric, and notions. She'd already applied for a contest two months earlier, but that response could take months.

There must be an easier way to scale the walls of the fashion industry. For the last eight years since she'd finished her fashion design program in college, her dream remained a mirage on the horizon, always out of reach.

The door swung open with a loud clatter and Jake thrust in.

"Hey, what's your hurry, big guy?" Blair glanced toward the door to make sure he'd closed it behind him. No sense in letting the hot air in. Jake's cherub cheeks were red and moist with sweat.

"Mr. Walton yelled at me. He's so mean. I hate him."

She rose from the table and knelt in front of him. "What happened, sweetie?"

Her son's normally serene face twisted as he fought tears. "My ball went into his bushes, so I ran over to get it. I didn't hurt anything. All the bushes are dead anyway. He doesn't ever water them."

She bristled, nudged to remind Mr. Walton Jake was a child, not a hoodlum. She drew Jake into her arms and squeezed him for a moment. "Know what we should do, buddy?" she asked against his blond curls.

He squirmed, no fan of extended hugs.

She leaned back on her heels and grinned at him. "Pray that one day we'll get a friendly neighbor, okay? Let's ask God for it."

Jake sniffed. "I hope he'll answer fast."

Blair stifled a chuckle of silent agreement. It wasn't her son's first run-in with the old curmudgeon. She pinched the child-sized baseball cap from Jake's head. "Wash up for dinner," she said. "It's almost ready."

"'Kay." Jake took off running toward the back of the small house. The kid seemed incapable of walking anywhere.

She went to the kitchen of the house where they'd lived for almost a year, and absently gave the pot of chili a stir. A strange meal choice for July, but she and Jake both liked it. The sharp aromas of chili powder and green pepper floated through the air, and her stomach growled.

Blair's eyes roamed the chipped beige cupboards, formerly white, and a stained backsplash. A shaft of afternoon light spilled through the small window over the sink, adding a somber cast instead of cheer to the dreary room. The entire house had seen better days, but it was all she could afford. After they moved in, she unleashed her creativity in the house, or tried, with colorful curtains, pillow covers, rugs, and wall hangings. She'd partially succeeded in making it a cozy nest for her and Jake.

The best feature, despite its view of Mr. Walton's house, was a row of floor-to-ceiling windows in the living room. From there, she often glimpsed the sun sinking over a watchful row of lofty pines just beyond his house. At times, a sparkle of sun reflecting off the nearby river pierced through the trees. Wishful thinking, more likely someone's headlights. She and Jake lived several blocks from the river and walked along its banks when time and temperatures allowed.

A sizzle of burning rice snatched Blair's attention. She slid the pot to an unlit burner and pulled a bag of frozen vegetables from the freezer. They were often tasteless, but so easy. And she hoped to imprint Jake's young mind with a vegetable habit.

The cellphone on the counter buzzed. She glanced at it. Bad timing, but she'd catch up with Lisa, her longtime college friend, while she cooked. "Hey, Lisa."

"Hi, Blair. Did you get the contest link?" Her friend's voice comforted her, a connection with her old life and her persistent dream.

"Yes, thanks, Lisa. Looks complicated, but I haven't had much time to study it."

"Think you'll apply?"

Muffled voices in the background gave Blair the impression Lisa was still at work.

Blair pressed her lips together. It would take time to complete the requirements and send the contest application. The deadline was only weeks away. "I'd like to try. I don't have much time to get ready for it but can submit the spring collection I designed last year."

"Oh, that won't matter," Lisa said. "No one'll know it's last year's, as long as you reference next year's colors and a couple new style trends."

"I was thinking the same thing. I should have time this weekend. How are things in your world?" Lisa had followed the conventional route at a fashion house in New York doing errands for the monarchs of the industry. Inching her way up, she'd gotten a few tiny openings for her own designs.

"Pressured. Crazy. We have a catwalk coming up. I now understand why they call it a *catwalk*. The claws have been out all day." The women chuckled.

"Living the dream."

"Yeah, I guess so." Lisa's voice softened, as if sensing Blair's wistful resignation across the phone. "You'll get there, Blair. I know you will."

"I hope so. I'm taking the non-traditional route, but hey, look at Ralph Lauren. He wasn't exactly traditional, was he?"

"Exactly. And it is a grueling life, make no mistake."

"Well, I don't lack for grueling. That's for sure. Just a different kind." They'd finished college with the same stars in their eyes. But as graduation appeared on the horizon, so did a little red line to indicate Blair was pregnant. It was the moment her life plan took a drastic detour.

The two women caught up on news, while Blair surveyed the vegetables and tossed in a handful of cut herbs from the flower bed. She pulled ceramic pasta bowls from the cupboard, the phone still tucked between her shoulder and her ear. They talked mostly of Lisa's exciting life in New York, which consisted of roommates, her tiny but well-located apartment, and daily tasks working with up-and-coming names in New York fashion. Blair didn't have much to add, since her job at a clothing factory was a long shot from what Lisa did every day.

They disconnected, and she set the table. How different her life was from Lisa's. Blair refused to allow her dreams to disintegrate. The career climb of a fashion designer was steep under the best circumstances. In Blair's situation, it was Mount Everest. But she couldn't give up. It still burned in her bones and guided her decisions.

"Is it ready?" Jake ran into the kitchen where a two-seat table filled one corner. "You said I should wash my hands." He wiggled his fingers at her.

"Hmm, let me see those." Blair took each of his hands and covered his palms with kisses until he giggled and pulled them back. "They look perfect," she told him. "Now, sit and we'll have some chili."

"Yum. Can I put Fritos on top? And cheese?"

"But of course. It's the McCartney recipe, isn't it? Over rice?"

Jake grinned and nodded, his tight fist grasping the fork.

Before they ate, Jake offered a child's prayer for the food. "And help Mr. Walton be happy," he added. "And please give us a new neighbor soon. Amen."

Blair stifled a smile at Jake's heartfelt prayer, but her eyes stung too, since Jake had prayed for the old man to become happy. To be blessed.

At moments like these, her misgivings about her fumbled route to fashion design floated off her like dust and blew away on a winter breeze. If she never achieved even one of her dreams, she wouldn't trade her precious boy for all of them. Each time she looked at him and her heart swelled with emotion, it confirmed the rightness of her choice to raise him herself rather than placing him for adoption. It was a hard choice. Well, both options were brutal in their own way. She remembered that time too well. Because of her choice, both Jake's life and hers weighed squarely on her shoulders.

After supper, Blair cleared the table and Jake settled onto the living room rug with his stuffed dinosaur and plastic trucks. From the kitchen, she heard his noises, a growl from the truck motor, a roar from the dinosaur. As she rinsed the dishes, she yielded to a full-width grin.

She and Jake spent most evenings in the living room, him with a game or in front of the TV, and Blair at her sewing machine. After working all day behind a sewing machine at the factory, she continued each evening creating prototypes of her own designs, as well as purses, aprons, tote bags, or children's clothes to sell at the local market on Saturdays. She usually fell into bed exhausted at eleven or twelve, only to follow the same routine the next day.

Returning to the living room, she stared at the rectangular table along the opposite wall. Fabric swatches, sketches, straight pins, and boxes of sewing supplies covered its surface. Two headless mannequins stood in the corner, one still draped with half a spring party dress glittering with straight pins. She should finish up the projects she planned to sell at the farmer's market next Saturday, but her thousand-pound fatigue wouldn't allow her to move toward them.

Her gaze roved from the table to Jake to the couch, where soft cushions lured her. Back to the table. Back to the couch. She'd have time to finish tomorrow, wouldn't she? She'd also put off the fashion contest to the next day or so. Instead, she'd peruse a fashion industry magazine while savoring the animated, playful sounds of her son.

CR   CR   CR

Cooper Dawson flexed his fingers on the steering wheel. He stared out at the layered pink and purple horizon, then glanced over at his dog, Zipper, who snored in the passenger seat next to him.

Heaviness tugged inside him. He should be euphoric, having cut the ribbon, so to speak, the previous day. Windsor Fountains, a planned subdivision, was officially complete. The project he'd been married to for about a year was almost literally in the rearview mirror.

It should have been different. Miles should have been there to celebrate with him. Now it was time to go home, wherever *that* was these days.

His phone rang. Amber's name popped up on his dashboard screen, so he punched the response button. "Hey, sis. Was just about to call you."

"Where are you, Coop?"

"I left just over an hour ago, so I should be at your house in around thirty minutes."

"Great. I made fried chicken. Your favorite. Despite the fat content."

Cooper laughed. "Thanks, Amber. See you in a few."

"Um, Coop?"

"Yeah?"

"Are you doing okay? Are you all set to start this new chapter?"

12

He forced out a hearty, "It's about *time* I settled somewhere. I'm more than ready." Zipper awoke and let out a whine. He too was ready. Ready to see more of his master than he had over the last year.

"Is your house ready? If not, you can crash here as long as you want."

"Thanks. I'll just stay tonight. Tomorrow, I'll move back to the house and survey the property."

"Sounds good. See you soon."

Returning to Brenner Falls should be therapeutic, washing his mind of the daily reminder of his partnership with Miles. Of the business they'd planned since their teens when they realized they shared an interest and aptitude for architecture and construction.

Cooper punched his mom's number on the dashboard, hoping to flick away his rapidly sinking emotions.

"I wondered if you'd gotten on the road, son." Her warm voice held a coating of concern. Why was everyone worried about him? He was a grown man of thirty-four. Miles was everyone's loss, not just his. The whole family lived beneath the weight of shared grief.

"I'm about twenty minutes from Amber's house. So, within the hour, I'll be at her table eating fried chicken."

His mother laughed. The frequent sound he'd grown up with had always been like music to him.

"Fried chicken and green beans with bacon, right?" she said. "If I didn't know better, I'd think you were raised in the south, not in the middle of Pennsylvania. But I guess you acquired all kinds of tastes in your travels."

Yes, he had. Especially Indian. Yet another painful story.

"It'll be good to get a fresh start," she said. "I wish you lived closer but knowing you and Amber are in the same town is the next best thing."

"Maybe you and Dad should move to Brenner Falls."

His mom chuckled. "Visits will do fine for now, though you never know. When do you think you'll break ground on the new house?"

Cooper stuffed several fingers through his straight, too-long hair as his gaze found a road sign for Brenner Falls. He was almost there. "As soon as I can. I'm ready to get started on *my* project for a change. I have to get the land cleared first before the foundation goes in. Once there's something to see, you can come for a visit."

"And you'll stay in the little house you bought a couple years back until the new one's ready?"

"Yeah, that's the plan. Gotta go now, Mom. I'm at my exit."

"Be careful. Love you, Cooper."

"Love you too, Mom. Say hi to Dad."

Although losing Miles still burned a hole in his heart, he had Amber, Mom, and Dad. His anchors. And he had God, of course, who was his true anchor, though Cooper didn't lean on him nearly as much as he should. Might have helped him through the last year.

Instead, Cooper had worked like a machine, holding up the business alone. He'd finished the subdivision in record time, to the delight of the shareholders and pre-sold residents. No one realized he wasn't a prodigy, but only blockading his tears with hard work. He'd done it willingly, for Miles and his widow, Tarin, though not a single day had gone by without a fresh wave of grief for his fun-loving yet brainy older brother.

Time would heal and had already begun. A change of pace and place would help. Being near Amber would too. His little sister had lived in Brenner Falls for the last eight years, working as a physical therapist. Then four years ago, she'd gotten a tip for a building project there and passed it along to Cooper and Miles.

Miles had preferred to commute since Tarin was expecting their first child. Cooper had planned on staying with Amber, but as the project expanded, he decided to buy a little house and live there. He'd seen enough of Brenner Falls to know he'd like to settle there one day. Aside from the quaint setting and friendly residents, he'd fallen in love...with the river. That mesmerizing, calming river. He'd found it easy to visualize his dream house near it, waking up each day to sparkles of sun reflecting from its broad, majestic surface. A home where he'd plant deep roots, finding solace and security he wouldn't so easily lose. A home he'd already cultivated in his mind for the last three years.

Before he knew it, Cooper was in front of Amber's house. He turned toward Zipper. "Ready, pal?" Zipper's tail thumped in response.

Amber greeted Cooper at the door with a hearty hug. "Missed you, bro. I'm *sooo* glad you're here to settle." Her blue eyes sparkled, baring her sincerity. She bent to scratch Zipper's head. "Hey, old boy. Good to see you too."

"You're as beautiful as ever." And she was. Her thick dark hair hung in a fabric tie down her back, longer than he remembered. Why no man had snagged her yet was a mystery.

He grinned back at her and lifted his face to take a satisfied sniff. "And it smells great in here." He let his knapsack drop with a thump on the floor.

"Is this all you brought?" She frowned. "I thought you were moving back for good."

"The rest is in the car. No sense in unloading it twice."

"Ah, right. Of course. Well, how about chicken first?"

"Yes, immediately would be fine."

"Over dinner you can fill me in about your plans for this next chapter, including the dream house you want to build."

"The next chapter," he murmured to her back as he followed her into the kitchen, clutching a small bag of dog food. The next chapter of his life was anyone's guess. He prayed it would be brighter and better than the last one. It had to be.

Chapter Two

Blair's tires scraped on the gravel drive as she parked next to the house. "Bet you're glad to finish with the dentist for another six months, aren't you, big guy?"

Jake stretched his mouth wide. "See how glad I am?" He maintained his exaggerated grin as he slid out of the car.

"At least your big smile's all clean now."

To get Jake to his early appointment, she'd left work early. They'd dock her a couple hours' pay, but it was worth it to have time to catch up on sewing projects for the Saturday market. Having a free afternoon for *any* reason was a treat, especially a Friday.

One feature that drew Blair to Brenner Falls was the clothing factory. Though a sewing pool didn't resemble fashion design in the least, it provided inspiration, unlike her previous bank job, from which she returned home each night in tears. And who knew? The work might provide an open door one day. Brenner Falls had other advantages, like being less than an hour from her parents' home in Milton. Far enough to be independent, but not too far.

After her surprise pregnancy, she'd returned to her parents' home, staying in her old room for three years. She and Jake spent the following three years in a nearby apartment. It hadn't been easy to return, as though she'd gone backward. But with a baby on the way, she'd also been grateful. That is, once her parents had recovered from their shock and disappointment.

Blair unlocked the front door of the partly dilapidated two-bedroom house. Next door at Mr. Walton's place, a cleaning van backed out of the driveway. Strange. She'd never known the old man to hire a cleaner. A quick scan of the house revealed no sign of him, nor were there curtains at the window. The junk he normally kept on the porch was gone too. Dread mixed with relief. Had the old man died? Had Jake's prayer led to Mr. Walton's demise? She shook her head. That was silly. Only a fortunate coincidence. Jake would have no more run-ins with Mr. Walton.

Inside the house, she frowned as she noted the mess in the living room. Her efforts at neatness were futile, with a six-year-old's toys and her own sewing projects from one end of the room to another. At least it was their home, hers and Jake's. She loved their independence but recognized the importance of having her family nearby. Even if she *was* a misfit among them. For one thing, her parents adored Jake, and the feeling was mutual. For another, they kept Jake one weekend per month. That lightened her single mom load, and enabled her to catch up on chores and tasks tied to her dream. It was a win-win.

Blair appreciated the charm and growing energy of Brenner Falls. She'd found a church and made a few acquaintances. Not many friends just yet, except Leah. Her reserved nature and lack of time hadn't permitted more. Maybe with time.

She made good use of her free afternoon, applying for the contest, albeit with low expectations, and finishing several projects for the market. The lively bi-weekly market in the center of Brenner Falls offered her an outlet for earning a bit more income and designing her own products. According to her self-imposed quota for market inventory, she made headway.

Jake played happily outside without the threat of Mr. Walton's reproach. She ought to check on him. Blair slid her glasses up on her head and rose from her sewing machine. She stretched her arms to the ceiling and made circles with her sore shoulders. How long had she hunched over the machine? With a glance out the window, her eyes widened in alarm. Jake stood in Mr. Walton's yard speaking to a strange man and petting the man's dog. The man crouched at Jake's level for an animated conversation, possibly about the dog. It wasn't cool outside, but because of her worn but comfy tank top, she snatched a cardigan from the hook and slid into her Crocs.

"Jake," she called as she crossed the yard. The man and Jake halted their conversation and looked at her. She'd never seen the man before. Could he have rented the place so quickly after Mr. Walton's departure?

"Hello," she called to him, stuffing her hands into her sweater pockets.

As she reached them, the man straightened, topping her height by nearly a foot. He wasn't scrawny in any other way, either. Muscular arms displayed an impressive contour under his black T-shirt. He appeared to be in his thirties, with straight brown hair to below his ears, auburn highlights glinting in the sun. Clean-shaven, with a few faded freckles across his nose.

"Hi," he said. His warm smile knocked some stones from her protective wall. Eyes an unusual shade of dark blue connected with hers with a direct, no-nonsense gaze. "My name's Cooper Dawson."

Jake tugged on the hem of her cardigan. "Mommy, his dog is called Zipper. Isn't that funny?"

"Yes, it sure is." Zipper looked like a Golden Retriever, only smaller. His tail thumped the ground and his eager black eyes fixed on Jake as he stroked the dog's head.

Her gaze found Cooper's. "Uh, hi. I'm Blair. Jake is my son. Is he bothering you?" She'd extend the olive branch in advance in case the man was another Mr. Walton, though he didn't seem to be.

"No, not at all." Cooper waved the air. "He came over to meet Zipper."

"Zipper's really nice, Mommy. Mr. Cooper's nice too."

Blair chuckled at Jake's unguarded honesty. "I hope so, after Mr. Walton." Her attention returned to Cooper, who watched her with an amused twitch of his lips.

"Oops," she said. "I assumed you were moving in. The man who was here before often yelled at Jake, so Jake didn't like him too much."

Cooper winced. "Yeah, sorry to hear that. We didn't have much contact."

"Did he...is he dead?" Blair softened her voice and braced herself for the man's response.

Cooper laughed. "No, not at all. Alive and mean as ever. I'm the owner of the house." He hitched his head toward the dwelling behind him, obviously in much better shape than hers. Smoky gray siding still in good shape, antique red shutters, and a metallic roof installed in recent years.

"I was working out of town over the last year, so I rented it to him," Cooper said. "I finished my project and told him I wanted to move back in. He was only too happy to leave since his daughter had invited him to stay with her family."

"Oh, well, that's good for him." So, Cooper was their new neighbor. He seemed friendly enough, in answer to Jake's prayer. She couldn't stem a chuckle and nudged Jake. "I guess God answered your prayer, big guy."

Jake lifted an earnest face to Cooper. "I prayed that we'd get a nice neighbor. God answered my prayer and gave me a neighbor dog too."

Cooper laughed. "Sounds like a two-for-one deal. I'll try hard to be a nice neighbor." He winked at Jake.

"I like Zipper. Can I play with him sometime?" Jake asked Cooper.

"Jake, you can't bother Mr. Dawson."

"It's no bother." Cooper gave Jake a warm grin. "Zipper seems to like Jake too. He can come over and play with Zipper anytime. In the nice weather, he stays outside a lot."

"Thanks, Mr. Dawson." Jake beamed and continued to pet Zipper.

"You can call me Cooper. It's nice meeting you both."

"Likewise," Blair said, uncertain of what to say next. "And welcome back to town." After a beat of silence, she shrugged. "I guess it's time for Jake's dinner. See you." With a parting smile, Blair turned and led Jake to the house.

ജ   ജ   ജ

Cooper's gaze followed Blair and Jake as they crossed the lawn and disappeared into the house. Cute kid, full of energy and fearless too, despite his history with Mr. Walton. The old grouch. Maybe being with his daughter would sweeten him up a bit if it didn't end up sowing conflict in *her* household.

Jake had made a good impression on both Zipper and Cooper. Zipper let out a whine, looking wistfully after Jake as if he wanted his friend back. "Replaced me already, pal?" He scratched the dog's head and the animal's loyalty returned.

Blair—was that her name? Yes, Blair, his new neighbor had charged out of the house to check on her son who was talking to a tall, burly stranger. Cooper chuckled. What could one expect? She had Mama Bear written all over her. Definitely more guarded than her son. Yet, she held both a quiet dignity and fragile vulnerability about her. Being a man, he'd also noticed she was attractive, with smooth pale skin and thick blond hair that scooped just above her shoulders. Probably married, and a *Mr.* Blair would come home from work at about six.

At any rate, Cooper wasn't looking for a relationship. But he still noticed a pretty woman when he saw one. Especially one with wide hazel eyes and full pink lips.

He shook the image from his mind. Groceries. Yeah, he had to stock the house with the basics, most of which waited in the car. "Come on, Zipper." Cooper went to the back of the covered truck, drew out several plastic bags, returned to the house, and dumped the bags onto the wooden kitchen table. Basic food, cleaning gear, bathroom stuff. It would feel good to get settled in his own place again, at least until the new house was finished. That would take until next spring, barring delays. He wasn't in a hurry. He'd oversee the workers but also maintain a few architecture clients on the side. His priorities should be the other way around, of course, but he'd done more than his time.

A quick scan around the house brought a grunt of approval for the cleaning crew. Looked like a spotless but impersonal rental instead of a home. He'd have to work on that, though his tastes were simple. At least Walton hadn't ruined anything in the past year, no holes in the furniture or dents in the wood paneling. Bare windows stared coldly back at him. Amber would willingly help with that. She could give the place a cozy touch when she had time.

Cooper's groceries were basic. He was a meat and potato guy. Or had been. He stared at the jar of curry paste on the counter. He and Priya had broken up three years earlier and he hadn't seen her much since, though they'd spoken a few times on the phone. She'd moved on. But his taste for curry and tandoori and associated flavors hadn't. It was the one thing she'd given him that she hadn't been able to take back.

He sighed, surprised at a wave of stale pain that could still flow into the cracks in his concentration. The present didn't look at all like he'd imagined three years earlier. He'd done a passable job at anesthetizing himself with visions of his dream house and labor on the subdivision. With the completion of the latter, his thoughts meandered on dangerous ground.

One thing was sure. He'd have to do better at directing them. No more long threads of reflection about Miles, about Priya. Today was a new day, a new house. A new mission. The pain of the past would hover from time to time, but the future was okay, right? God had made that promise long ago, repeatedly. If only Cooper could push it into his heart and spread it through his circulatory system.

An hour later, he'd put away his clothes, put sheets and blankets on the bed, and got the place livable. Within days, he'd start clearing the land for the new house. His new mission would absorb his time, give him new optimism. Keep his mind away from pain and loss. Soil studies had been done, research for permits completed. Theoretically, he was on his way.

He slid onto the couch and punched Amber's number. She'd be getting off work. Zipper hopped up and curled up next to him. "Hey, little sis. Thought I'd see how your day was."

"Hi, Cooper. It was good. Couple new patients today. Are you getting settled in?"

"Yup. Did grocery shopping, put stuff away."

"Is Zipper happy?"

"Oh, yeah. He's always happy." He turned his head. "Aren't you, boy? He's right beside me. Today he met this little boy next door, and it was love at first sight." He laughed at the memory of Zipper's tail thrashing wildly as he wiggled his happy dance, which mainly involved his hind quarters. "So, he's already making new friends."

"Of course, he is. You will too. You've been gone for a while, but I'll introduce you to my friends. We meet over at The Grateful Fork sometimes. You remember that place, don't you? They have live music on Fridays."

"Vaguely. I was here less than a year before I left for Windsor. None of my first impressions stuck. Except that Victorian building across from the mayor's office."

"Ah, Seasons. The historic or semi-historic dinner theater. It's under new ownership and making some cool changes."

"Yeah, that's the one. I remember that for some reason. It's the architect in me, I guess."

"What are you making for dinner? If you have nothing planned, you can come over or we can go out."

Cooper frowned. He didn't want to become a burden to Amber. But he *had* just arrived. Hadn't found his footing yet. "I was thinking of making a veg curry. Potatoes and butternut squash, coconut milk."

"That's pretty exotic. Do you think about Priya when you make that?"

"Not anymore. I happen to *like* curry. Yes, she was the one who introduced me to it, but I like it. It's the only good thing that came out of our relationship."

"You don't mean that," Amber admonished.

"No, I don't. She's a good person. We just weren't meant to be together, I guess."

"Her parents might have been a challenge. Didn't they arrange a marriage for her?"

Cooper laughed. "No, I don't think Indians in this country do that much anymore. Not in her family, in any case. Some friends of hers introduced her to a guy from the old country and—"

"The rest was history."

He nodded without speaking, knowing it had been far more complex than that. Priya experienced such an instant connection with the new guy, she and Cooper concluded her culture was more ingrained in her than they realized. Better learn that sooner than later. "So, I gained a love of their cuisine, which I'll always treasure. Want to come? I'll cook for you."

"Sure. That sounds good. Just don't make it too spicy."

"No problem."

It had been a good decision for Amber to come for dinner. They cooked together, bantered, and reminisced. It filled his empty house when he hadn't quite been ready for one. They rebooted the close bond they'd had when he'd lived there before, and his thoughts stayed far from Miles and Priya.

Three hours later, Cooper hugged Amber at the door. "Oh, I forgot to tell you." He took a wooden dowel from the bookshelf and handed it to her. "I got you something."

"Aw, Cooper, you shouldn't have." She took the stick and looked at him quizzically.

"I was thinking about your sliding glass door. It's easy to break into those, but not when you put a stick in the runner. Use that at night."

Amber laughed. "You're my personal safety patrol. Okay, thanks."

He waved as she backed out of his gravel driveway. After her taillights disappeared around the corner, his gaze drifted to the house next door. A large picture window gave an unobstructed view of Blair and Jake in their living room. No Mr. Blair in sight, no additional car, but that didn't mean anything. She appeared to be busy with something, holding up what looked like a large piece of fabric. Was she sewing clothing? His mom used to do that for the three of them when they were small.

Jake crawled on the floor pushing a toy around. Cooper couldn't make out what kind—probably a truck or a tank—he could imagine the sounds the kid made to imitate them. He shut the front door before Blair had a chance to see him staring. Intruding. If she'd been suspicious before, she'd have reason to be if she caught him observing her small family and their quiet evening together.

Cooper turned back to his living space. Gradually, after a few hours, the familiarity had grown. A little. One thing was for sure. Until he could dive into his new build, he'd need more structure in his life. A full year of sixteen-hour days had left no room for lifestyle or leisure decisions. Now he found himself in open season. He'd have to drum up more business to fill his time and his brain, although financially, he was set for a long time. Even with what he'd given Tarin.

He grabbed his phone from the bookshelf. He'd promised to check on her. Felt it was his duty to Miles. "Hey, Tarin. Just wanted to touch base with you. I arrived yesterday in Brenner Falls."

"Hi, Cooper. That's good. Uh, I got the transfer of funds. Look, you didn't have to do that."

"That's the least I could do, Tarin. This was our business, Miles and mine, and we would have split the profits fifty-fifty."

"But you did all the work."

True, like a dog. He'd worked to exorcise his grief after Miles's accident. But there was no question about giving Tarin what she and Miles would have received. "It'll help, you know, with Joy Ann. With things she'll need. I like to think of it as Miles providing for you guys, like he would have if—"

There was silence, then a sniff on the phone. "Thank you, Cooper. I won't say it isn't helpful to us. In fact, last week I was looking for a full-time job and daycare for Joy Ann. The money will give me more flexibility in what I choose, and I can spend more time with her."

"There you go, then. Miles would have wanted it that way." Her response only reinforced the rightness of his decision to give half the proceeds of Windsor Fountains to her and little Joy Ann.

"Yes, he would." Her voice was soft. "I can't thank you enough, Cooper. What are your plans now?"

"I moved today into the little house I'd bought in Brenner Falls before the Windsor project came up. I'd rented it out over the last year, so I'd have a place to land. You may remember my sister Amber lives here too."

"Yes, I do remember that."

"I think I told you I bought a piece of property here last year, across from the river. I'm going to build a house there. Along with that, I still have a handful of clients, so all that'll keep me busy."

"Sounds great, Cooper. We're doing fine here. Joy Ann just turned three, so we had a little party with her cousins and my parents. It was nice. Your parents did FaceTime for a few minutes. They said they wished they lived closer. She doesn't seem to have any, I don't know, issues about her dad."

"She was so young when it happened."

"Yeah, for that, I'm glad she was young. I try to tell her how brave and wonderful her dad was, and I don't want her to forget him, but I'm glad she's too young to grieve like we do as adults."

"It's hard to find any upside, but I'm glad for her sake." His voice softened. "You'll both be fine."

"You will too, Cooper."

"Take care of yourself and call anytime you want. I'm not that far away."

"Will do."

He'd known about Joy Ann's birthday party but had been on the home stretch of the Windsor project. A lame excuse. Might have had more to do with Joy's resemblance to Miles and all the wounds that would have opened. He'd have to get over *that* and soon, because he wanted to stay involved in his niece's life.

But for now, it was his own life he needed to pull back together. His own life on the cusp of a new chapter, as Amber would say. He looked at Zipper, who'd awakened and stared at him, letting out a small whine.

"Right, Zip? We need a brand-new life, and we've got one here." Zipper's tail thumped a steady drumbeat on the couch. "Oh, you don't care? Okay, I guess you just need to go out."

Zipper responded by scrambling from the couch and plopping his rear next to the front door. Cooper pulled himself up with a groan. Despite his conversation with Tarin and the hovering temptation to think of the past, a breeze of hope swept through him. A new town that he liked. A new day tomorrow.

A new start.

Might be okay after all.

Chapter Three

"Happy birthday to you!" Blair's mother sang as she carried a glowing multi-layer cake into the dining room. Everyone around the table joined in. Jake wriggled in the seat of honor and adjusted his paper crown, which almost slipped off his head.

"Make a wish, Jake," said Stefanie, Blair's sister, four years her senior. Her husband, Brian, and daughter, Celeste, had driven from Pittsburgh for the party and planned to stay the weekend in Milton.

Jake squeezed his eyes together for several seconds before unleashing his breath on the candles. Cheers broke out.

Nine-year-old Celeste, seated beside him, poked his small arm. "What did you wish for, Jake?"

"It's a secret, Celeste," Brian said. "He's not supposed to tell anyone."

Jake returned a solemn frown. "I won't tell."

Blair's mother, Lois, brought a stack of dessert plates and set them before Jake, then sliced the cake.

"Just a small one for me, Mom." Stefanie placed her hands on her stomach. "I ate too much."

Blair had to agree. They'd all feasted on her mom's famous chicken divan. Though hundreds of variations existed, Lois McCartney's version topped them all. For dessert, another family favorite, chocolate buttercream cake with chocolate icing.

Jake and Blair had arrived at her parents' home that morning for Jake's celebration. Blair's other siblings lived too far to attend. The sisters weren't close, but Blair appreciated the sacrifice her busy pediatrician sister had made to be there. Too bad their son, Ethan, was away on an Explorer's Club retreat. At eight years old, he was the cousin closest in age to Jake. On the rare occasions when they saw one another, they played and giggled all day, whether inside or outside the house.

"Delicious cake, Lois." Blair's dad tucked into the last bites on his plate. He turned to Jake. "Time to open your presents, Jake-o." A stack of colorfully wrapped gifts sat on the buffet next to the dining room table.

"Yay, presents." Jake fidgeted in his seat. The metallic paper crown his grandma had made finally floated to the floor.

"I got an awesome present from Mom." Jake slipped from his chair to approach the pile of gifts.

"Yes, she told us." Lois sent him an affectionate grin. "A big boy piano. Now you can do a concert, which reminds me, we haven't ever heard you play. I hope we will one day."

"I upgraded his beginner keyboard for a nicer one, once I knew he was serious about it," Blair said.

"How are his lessons going?" her mother asked.

"Really well. His teacher is a friend from church. She sings and plays three instruments." Blair was thankful for Leah.

"She sounds very qualified." Lois raised her voice. "Everyone, Jake's about to open his presents."

For the next few minutes, Jake tore into his gifts. Oohs, aahs, and comments about each gift, filled the room. A frisbee, a popsicle kit, and a Lego race car set which Blair's younger sister, Audrey, had sent from Seattle. Blair would have to brace herself for more noise. Kool Kid night goggles... She wasn't sure how he'd use those, but he seemed delighted and tried them on. A metronome, a kids' piano songbook, a stuffed Chewbacca doll from her brother, Norris, and his family, who lived in Ohio. As usual, everyone spoiled all the grandkids, including Jake, during their birthdays.

"Boy, is that thing ugly." Celeste pointed at Chewbacca and scrunched her face.

"It's from Star Wars. Have you no respect?" Brian faked an indignant tone, and everyone laughed. "This one talks. Push that button on the back, Jake."

He did, and they all heard, "Wyaaa!" from the furry doll, which brought a fresh explosion of laughter.

"He's saying hello in Wookie language," Brian said.

Blair shot him a smirk. "Now I see how you spend your free time, Brian. You know a little too much about this."

Everyone laughed again.

A soft wave of belonging encircled her, a rare thing in her family. She looked around the table at her sister, brother-in-law, parents, and niece. She hadn't given them a chance in a long while. At almost thirty years old, it was about time she felt comfortable in her own family. She'd overlook the fact that they never asked about her design goals or progress. She'd have to let the water under that bridge ebb away.

"Look, Mommy! A jokebook for kids."

"Oh, no! Kids' jokes," Blair groaned and threw a napkin over her face.

"And believe me, they're corny," Stefanie said. "Perfect for a seven-year-old."

"Last one," Jake announced. "This one is from you guys." He lifted his face toward Stefanie and Brian.

"This is a serious gift to balance out the joke book." Stefanie watched as he opened the gift and pulled out a child-sized Pittsburgh Steelers sweatshirt.

Jake seemed more impressed with it than the other clothing gifts he'd received.

"Try it on, Jake," Stefanie urged. "I can exchange it if it doesn't fit."

"Or you can opt for the Eagles instead." Blair's father grinned. Football rivalry had started when Stephanie and Brian moved to Pittsburgh.

Jake slipped the sweatshirt over his head, and it fit perfectly. He returned to his seat. "Thank you. I love it."

Blair's throat tightened. Her little guy was becoming a young man. For a split second, she envisioned him at thirteen, then eighteen, handsome and filled out, playing sports, going camping. He had a wonderful future, and she had no regrets. Despite everything.

She blinked a few times and forced a smile. Not a time to become teary. Instead, she leaned over to Jake and gave him a quick hug, and pulled away before he could squirm.

"Um, there's one more gift," Blair's mother said, her voice suddenly timid. "It's from Nelson."

Blair's smile fell, and the room grew quiet. Her buoyancy popped like a balloon. "Nelson?" What did *he* want?

Her father placed a large box on the table in front of Jake.

"Who's it from, Mommy? I mean *Mom*. I'm a big boy now."

"Who's Nelson?" Celeste muttered.

The faces around the table tightened with sudden tension. In an instant, the room drained of festivity.

Blair would handle this. That man would not destroy her son's party. She turned to Jake with a bright smile. "Nelson is an old friend of mine. You haven't met him, but he knew it was your birthday." Her gaze scanned those around the table for corroboration. No one said anything. "You can open it." Her heart pounded in dread at what problems the gift would stir to life.

Jake's face showed uncertainty, as if he sensed the anxiety in the room, then tore into the box. "Look, Mom. A backpack. It's cool." Matching images from Lord of the Rings decorated the backpack, a water bottle, a neckerchief, and a baseball cap.

"That's great, Jake."

"Cool, put on the hat!"

"They all match." Everyone around the table exclaimed something a little too forcefully, likely to dispel the stiff atmosphere.

Jake put on the hat.

"Looks great on you, big guy." Blair patted his shoulder. "What a nice gift. In fact, all your gifts are great. What do we say, Jake?"

"Thank you, everyone. And thank you to Nelson, whoever he is." Everyone chuckled in discomfort.

"More cake, anyone?" Blair's mother asked with loud enthusiasm.

"I'll have some," Brian said.

Stefanie shot him a frown but said nothing.

Soon Stefanie and Lois rose to clear the table. Blair joined them, glad the awkward conversation was over. Or was it? She entered the kitchen and saw her mother's pinched face. "Thanks a lot for that, Mom. You may as well throw a grenade in the room." Blair couldn't stem her irritation.

"Doesn't he know *anything* about Nelson?" Lois hissed. "I thought you'd told him by now."

Blair crossed her arms as tension bubbled inside. "He doesn't know Nelson's his dad. I thought he was out of our lives for good, so I didn't see any point in talking to Jake about him *yet*." She'd planned on waiting until Jake started asking questions. "And *this* sure wasn't the time to bring it up."

Stefanie sidled up to her, a dishtowel in her hands. "But isn't he curious, at least? Surely, he must wonder. He's seven now. He'll have more questions as he grows up."

Blair let out a long breath. "I know. You're right. I need to tell Jake about him. I've had no contact with Nelson in years."

"That's because you rejected him and ran away to Brenner Falls." Her mother's voice held an edge of accusation. "He made his mistakes, but he *has* tried to contact you."

Blair pushed down the mounting frustration inside. How could her mother say that? "If you recall, he rejected *me*."

"He seems to have had a change of heart. Like last year when he sent you money for Jake."

"I don't know what his game is." Blair wished they'd drop the conversation, but it came up periodically, like a flu or a rash.

"His game is he wants to meet his son, Blair. You ought to give him a chance." Her mother pressed her lips together. "He has a right. Don't you think?"

"Ah, no. He does *not*." Blair's words shot out. "He gave up that right long ago." Nelson hadn't shown a sign of life for Jake's first six years. Why did he deserve consideration now?

Her mother sighed. "He could be a positive influence now that he's come around. He was afraid to be a dad before, but now he's matured."

Had she forgotten *everything* that had happened? "You give him an awful lot of credit." Blair couldn't stop herself from adding, "What, do you keep in *touch* with him?"

Her mother ignored her barb. "Along with that, it might help you not feel alone raising Jake. You're just out there in Brenner Falls holding it together by yourself."

She glared back at her mother, even though she had a point.

Brian entered the kitchen carrying an armful of crumpled gift paper. "What's this, a sorority meeting?" He stuffed it into the trash.

"No, Mom is trying to convince Blair to let Nelson have contact with Jake." Stefanie returned to the sink and turned on the hot water.

Brian stared at each woman, then harrumphed. "Not getting involved in *that*." He waved the air as he left the room.

"We're not talking about this anymore." Blair's tone meant business. "I don't want this to ruin Jake's special day."

"You're right," her mother said. "Think about it though, won't you, Blair?"

"I will. I promise." She'd learned the words that could effectively stop her mother when she wouldn't let something drop. But Blair had just made a promise. Would she keep it? Was it time? She'd decide when she wasn't furious.

During the ride home, Jake dozed, to Blair's relief. She wasn't ready to talk about Nelson, but the sooner she got it over with, the sooner she'd regain her sense of order and control in her life.

For now, she'd try to find the words. Yet as she considered how to go about it, her mind drifted back to that day. The day she'd told her college boyfriend, Nelson, that she was pregnant. Of course, her closeness with him had been inappropriate, but like the well-worn expression, one thing had led to another. She'd loved him. They'd talked about marriage. For those and other reasons, she excused her own behavior, the lowering of her standards.

She'd met Nelson early in her junior year and sparks had flown immediately. He was studying graphic design. His friends became her friends, all artists. She finally felt at home, unlike the previous twenty years in her own family. They accepted her, they *got* her. Her new friends didn't pressure her to pursue something more practical than fashion design. Rather, they cheered her on. After meeting Nelson and entering his world, she'd been happier than ever before. Her life turned vibrant, optimistic. Everything seemed possible.

Until her dreams splintered and crashed. Nelson didn't want to be a father, so he accused her of cheating on him. He had to know she'd been with no one else, but he'd chosen the easy way out. They were a committed couple, weren't they? His rejection broke her heart, but so did his accusation. He walked out of her life and left her with a problem he'd helped create.

Blair looked over at Jake, her little man at seven years old. As always, especially when he was asleep, her heart gave a squeeze. No regrets. Nelson was history, or at least the hurt he'd created. Should she finally allow him into their present?

They'd had no contact for years. Until a year ago. She'd been living in an apartment in Milton across town from her parents, working in the loan office of a bank. Each day seemed to pull her further from her dreams until she struggled with depression. Her mother called her one day and told her she'd received a letter from

Nelson. He'd requested that Lois forward it to Blair, wherever she was living. Out of the blue. Nelson.

In the letter, accompanied by a check, Nelson presented himself as a changed man. He'd grown, he claimed. He knew he'd hurt her and didn't deserve a second chance. In his heart, he didn't believe she'd cheated on him. He'd known she'd loved him. He'd simply run scared. He hadn't suggested they get back together but begged her to give him the chance to know his child. Seven years after the fact.

She hadn't responded. It had taken Nelson seven years to man up. He'd lost his chance the day he refused to recognize his son. She'd managed alone without him, along with help from her parents.

Yet, he'd remembered Jake's birthday. She didn't know what had changed Nelson's heart nor did she care. They were making out fine without him in their little family, in their new town. She'd tell Jake about Nelson. She had to do that. But she didn't have to let Nelson anywhere near Jake.

ʘ ʘ ʘ

Cooper's heavy boots crunched through the dead branches and crumbled dirt underfoot. He'd had his land cleared the previous week and the foundation crew would start the following day. After that, things would progress quickly, barring unexpected delays. He'd love to have started just as the ground warmed up after a wet winter. The Windsor project had kept him too busy. He hadn't had the mental bandwidth nor hours in his days to do more than make calls to block dates for the subcontractors.

Now that he was back in Brenner Falls and his schedule and head were clearer, he could focus on the house. Though he trusted his subcontractors, he'd still supervise and assure himself that things were done right. He'd never risk safety the way Miles had on that fateful day. Tracking its progress would fix his mind on the future instead of the past.

His favorite feature of his home, an unobstructed view of the river from the floor-to-ceiling windows. A balmy breeze floated off the river's surface and afternoon sunlight sparkled off the gentle waves of the river. That sight alone confirmed the rightness of his choice to return to Brenner Falls. "Thanks, Lord," he murmured, closing his eyes as a fresh breeze caressed his face. "For bringing me back here. For a new beginning." Like an unwrapped gift, yet to be revealed.

When he pulled into the driveway of his current home, Blair and Jake stood in the yard between the two houses. Cooper had left Zipper outside on a long leash, since he wasn't gone very long. Temperatures had dropped to a comfortable seventy-five. Jake threw a frisbee, but the dog seemed perplexed about what to do. Zipper always wanted to please, so he swung his tail and made a lunge, but stopped each time.

Cooper walked toward them. "Hello," he called.

Blair returned a reserved smile. "Hi, Cooper." She wore a peach-colored tunic with white cut-offs. A pair of glasses perched on her head, holding back her blond hair, as it had the previous week when they'd first met.

"Zipper never learned how to fetch," Cooper told them. "But I bet you could teach him, Jake." Actually, Zipper *had* fetched a time or two, but it rated low on his interest scale. "Here, let me untie him, and he'll probably do better."

"I told Jake he should start with something easier, like a stick," she said. "I imagine a frisbee is hard for him to pick up."

"Good point." Cooper squatted and scratched Zipper's head. He unlatched the leash and the dog pranced in a circle. Cooper spied a stick about an inch in circumference. "How about this one?" He handed it to Jake.

"Thanks, Mr. Cooper."

Jake looked cute in a Steelers sweatshirt, though the afternoon seemed too warm for it, especially running around after Zipper. As if on the same mental wavelength, Jake wriggled out of it and handed it to his mother.

"Are you hot, big guy?" she asked him. "It was a birthday gift, so he wanted to wear it." She folded it and tucked it under her arm. "We won't see it again until late fall."

"He had a birthday recently?"

"Yes, a few days ago, but yesterday we had a party for him at his grandparents' house. He turned seven."

Jake threw the stick. "Go on, Zipper. Fetch the stick. Go on, boy."

Zipper followed the stick. He sniffed it, then sat and looked up at Jake. Jake tried a couple more times until Zipper appeared to understand. He picked it up and carried it to Jake, who was elated. "Look, Mom. I trained him to fetch."

"Amazing, Jake!" Blair clasped her hands together. "You must be a dog whisperer."

"Huh?" Apparently, her son hadn't heard the reference. He happily continued throwing the stick to Zipper.

"Usually, he calls me *mommy*," Blair murmured. "But since yesterday, he changed to *mom*. He told me he's older now and wouldn't be calling me *mommy* anymore." She chuckled, her eyes still trained on her son, who she obviously adored.

"Growing up. It happens." Jake threw the stick again and Zipper complied. "Where do your parents live?" He hoped he wasn't being too nosy, but since Blair had mentioned it, he figured it was fair game for keeping the conversation going.

"I grew up in Milton, almost an hour from here. My parents have been there forever."

"I know where Milton is. Isn't that the headquarters of Chef Boyardee?"

Blair gave him a grin that lit up her face and sent an unexpected trickle of warmth through his chest.

"The very same," she said. "Although my mother always preferred to make her own tomato sauce. Milton's a small town with a big history. Lots of train history too, back in the day. Where did you grow up?"

"In a mid-sized town between Altoona and Pittsburgh." They watched Jake and Zipper for a moment.

When she said nothing further, he tried again. "You have brothers and sisters?"

"Yes, three. An older brother and sister, and a younger sister. I'm in the middle."

"That can be tough sometimes. I'm in the middle too. I have a sister who's been here a few years, which is one reason I came." Why did he bring up siblings? She might return the question and he'd have to talk about Miles, who he'd kept far from conscious thought for a few days.

"That's nice you have a sister here. Hey, look, Zipper's consistent now. I think he's got it."

He relaxed at the change of subject. "I never took Zipper for a quick learner, but there you go. Jake's got the magic."

"He's never had a pet, so he's in seventh heaven. What kind of dog is he?"

"Golden and Cocker Spaniel mix. Think you'll get him a dog one day?"

She shrugged. "I work full time and I'm a single mom, so my hands are pretty full. Though that could teach him responsibility too."

A single mom. *Don't go there, Cooper.* "One day, maybe. Well, he can borrow Zipper anytime he wants. No charge for the dog rental."

She laughed.

"How long have you been in Brenner Falls?" Was he asking too many questions? He hoped she wasn't feeling invaded. If she was, she didn't show it.

"Almost a year. We came last fall from Milton. I needed a change, and this seemed like a good place to live."

"I agree. It's just the right size, and the river's beautiful."

"Yes, it is." She slipped a lock of hair behind one ear. "Jake and I take walks along the banks on weekends when we have time in warm weather."

What did she do with Jake in the summer, or after school? Suddenly the complexities of single parenthood leaped into his mind, but he didn't voice his curiosity. It was safe to assume she was holding it together the best way she could. She must be a good parent, even if she was by herself. Jake was young, but seemed polite, conscientious, and determined already at age seven. Just the kind of son he would have wanted.

Cooper stifled the thought. "Jake seems like a nice kid. And smart. From what I can tell, you've done a good job."

Blair's expression sobered and he thought he detected the shine of tears in her eyes. "Thank you, Cooper. That's a nice thing to say." Her voice was soft, feminine. Her gaze slid to Jake. "It's hard sometimes. Especially when we first moved here. He had to adjust to the change, but he's doing fine now, after a full year of school here. He's a good boy. I'm blessed."

"Mom!" Jake's voice broke the moment. He ran to where she stood with Cooper. "Zipper's doing really good."

"Well," she corrected. "He's doing well."

"He knows what to do now when I throw the stick."

"Why do you call him Zipper?" Blair asked Cooper.

Cooper chuckled. "When he was a puppy, he was chewing on a jacket or something while he was teething. He got his lip caught in the zipper and I thought I'd have to take him *and* the jacket to the vet. I'd named him Flynn, but Zipper seemed more fitting after that."

Jake and Blair laughed. "Sounds painful for a little pup," she said. "He's probably embarrassed you told that story about his childhood." Her smiling eyes met Cooper's and for an instant, a spark ignited.

Cooper blinked then averted his gaze to the dog, who'd tired of playing fetch and gave a restless yawn. "Zipper doesn't know the word *embarrassed*, though he should. It's his supper time. That's why he doesn't want to play anymore."

Jake gave the dog a final scratch behind his ears then stood beside Blair. "Thanks for letting me play with Zipper."

"Anytime, pal."

"You two enjoy your dinner," Blair said with a wave. With one hand on Jake's back, she led him to her house.

His gaze lingered on them as they walked away. "Come on, boy." He led Zipper toward the house. "Keep your old man out of trouble, okay?"

Chapter Four

Fluorescent lights overhead bathed the cavernous factory in a cold antiseptic glow. Blair bent over her sewing machine, stopping for a moment to stretch her neck left and right. Up then down. With a deep breath, she refocused on the garment in front of her, but realized it was time for her break. She pulled off her headphones and the clamor of sewing machines—seven parallel rows of them—assaulted her ears. The noise drowned out all conversation, humming, and grumbling. Despite the din, her ears adjusted quickly. In her early days of employment at Simpson-Fink Textile Manufacturing, the noise rang through her head for hours after work.

Nearly one hundred people, men and women, did finishing work on garments that had been machine processed in the next room. There, huge metallic dragons, as Blair thought of them, cut large pieces of fabric according to a design which had been programmed. Other machines ironed them.

Though she'd been trained on other equipment, her skills remained strongest at the sewing machine. Little wonder since she'd known how to operate one since the age of seven. One day, she'd watched her mother assemble overalls, one for each of her children. Intrigued by the process, Blair asked a dozen questions until her mother shooed her away. Blair learned to sew and made most of her own clothes all the way through high school. Her fascination morphed into a life passion.

That day, her task was to sew ribbed bands onto gray crew-neck sweatshirts. Then someone else would sew the cuffs, someone else the band on the bottom, the label, the care label, and so on. She had to agree it was more efficient for one person to do a minor job repeatedly rather than tackle the entire garment, even if it made her feel like a robot. By the end of the day, at least twelve different employees had worked on each sweatshirt.

She stood and twisted her torso left and right, then snagged a small bag containing her lunch and a sketch book where she doodled designs during her breaks. On her way down the aisle between two rows of worktables, she greeted a few of her fellow robots. She'd be mortified if anyone in her college fashion design program saw her working on an assembly line. Her circumstances had detoured her, but it was temporary. She was determined.

Her lunch break flew by quickly. After gulping down a salad and yogurt, she sketched out a blouse idea that had hovered in her mind all morning. Puffed sleeves and a pleated V-neck bodice...

"That looks beautiful." A voice broke into her concentration. Lilly, a middle-aged woman with a kind face and gentle gray eyes, stood next to Blair's table. Lilly was the only person in the factory Blair could call a friend.

"Thanks, Lilly." No one else in the company, except for the taciturn woman who'd interviewed her, knew of Blair's training in fashion design.

"You're very talented. May I see?"

"Sure."

Lilly slid into a facing chair and took the paper from Blair. She studied the design for a moment then lifted her eyes. "What are you doing *here*, Blair? You should be in New York."

Blair offered a bland smile. "It's a long story. But you can probably guess, I don't plan to stay here forever."

Lilly returned the paper, and they chatted for a few minutes until lunch break ended. A thirty-minute break wasn't much to compensate for Blair's folded-up stiffness, but it still helped clear her mind. And Lilly's compliment warmed her as she gathered up her things to return to her post.

She noticed a wheeled bin the size of a small car inside the door to the machine room. In it, a stack of garments of various types and colors rose nearly to the edge. Was this tomorrow's task, or were they earmarked for the trash?

A supervisor walked toward her, a canned drink in her hand. Blair caught the woman's attention. "Excuse me, Sandy. What are these pieces here in the bin?"

Sandy leaned to look inside. She rifled through the pieces on top with one hand. "I think these are the irregulars. We've had too many of them lately since we have so many new employees who are still being trained." She shook her head. "What a waste."

"What'll they do with them?"

She shrugged. "I guess they'll give them away or sell them cheap."

"I'd like to have them." Over the noise, Blair raised her voice. "Can I have them or buy them? I can use them."

"I don't see why not," the woman responded. "Let me check with Hugo, and I'll let you know. Wait here a minute. He's in the breakroom."

Blair waited five minutes for Sandy, antsy because her own break had ended. The door to the breakroom swung open and the woman reappeared. "He said you can have them three dollars every ten."

So cheap. "That's great. I'll take them. I can have *all* of them?'"

"Sure. Take 'em all. Wait until after your shift. You can tell Hugo how many you took, and he'll deduct it from your next paycheck."

As Blair made her way back to her machine, she shook her head. There must be fifty to a hundred garments in that bin. She'd never been good at estimating numbers, unlike her uber-gifted siblings. Art was her thing. But even she knew that was a good deal. Those botched garments would serve as inspiration for new designs and save her money on buying fabric for experiments. At first glance, many already had sleeves, which would save hours.

Finally, she clocked out for the day and headed to the bin. She stuck her head into Hugo's office. "I'll be taking the irregulars now. Can I roll the bin to my car?" No harm in being careful, rather than risk someone questioning why she pushed the giant bin to the parking lot to empty it.

Hugo lifted his dark head from his desk that was covered from one end to the other with fashion flats, multidimensional drawings, and measurement specs. His eyes sagged behind his dark-rimmed glasses. He probably wouldn't leave anytime soon, despite the late hour. "No problem," he said. "You can give me the total number when you come in on Monday."

She smiled her thanks. "I'll let you know."

"Just leave the bin by the back door."

It took several minutes to shift the garments into her trunk and back seat, eighty pieces. Twenty-four dollars. She couldn't believe her luck, but also hoped she wouldn't regret acting on momentary zeal. As if her evenings weren't full enough.

She then drove to the home of Angela Perkins, where Jake spent his summer days. Blair had met Angela at church, and she'd been a godsend for childcare. During the school year, she'd picked Jake up after school and kept him until Blair finished work. When summer began, she offered to let him stay all day for the same rate, since she had a son almost his age.

Jake bounded out of the house and to the curb where Blair had parked. She waved at Angela, who stood in the doorway as he jumped into the car. What energy her son had. Blair only wanted to collapse on the couch with a glass of red wine.

"Mommy—I mean Mom, we made a puzzle today. It was cool. It had dinosaurs on it." His eyes were bright with excitement. Still her little boy, despite his birthday.

"Mrs. Perkins must know you like dinosaurs. You brought your stuffed one to church a few times when you were younger, remember?" It was only the previous year, but she'd encourage Jake's growing-up process.

"Yeah, that's how she knew. She got the puzzle for me, and she got one with dragons for Charlie. He likes them better than dinosaurs. She'll keep mine at her house. Then when it's finished, she said we'd put this stuff on it to make it, you know, solid like a picture."

"That's a great idea." She grinned as she drove. "You can work on your puzzle while you're there. When it's done, we'll find a place in your room to hang it."

Blair parked on the gravel drive and Jake dashed to the front door. She let him in and returned to the car. She cast a glance at the fabric filling her trunk and back seat. Where would she put them? The house only had two bedrooms and the garage was filthy. A task she'd neglected for the last year. She didn't even want her car in there, though last winter she'd caved in. She'd have to clean it the following day, which was Saturday.

For now, she'd start dinner. Fortunately, she'd remembered that morning to take chicken breasts out of the freezer to thaw. She turned on the oven to preheat and pulled a bag of noodles from the cupboard, then rolled the chicken breasts in breadcrumbs.

Minutes later, she checked the oven, which was still cold. "Oh, no," she groaned. Lately, the oven had been slow to heat up and had sparked a few times. She'd told her landlord about it two weeks earlier and he'd promised to come by to look at it. He'd never come and now it wasn't working at all.

Blair let out a long sigh and checked the stovetop which, thankfully, still worked. She cooked the chicken along with the rice. After dinner, she'd send another email to Don Mitchell, her landlord.

Another task for that evening...telling Jake about his dad. A wave of dread coursed through her at the thought, which she'd thrust from her mind every day since her mother had insisted she tell him. Though it was Blair's decision, her mother was right, she should tell Jake about Nelson. The sooner he knew, the sooner the weight of the secret would fall away from Blair's shoulders. She didn't want him confronting her as a teen because she'd never told him.

During dinner, Jake chattered about his day. "We went to this park where dogs run around. I wonder if Zipper can go there sometime. I bet he'd like it. There were a bunch of dogs everywhere."

"Sounds fun. Be careful of those other dogs, though. Sometimes they're friendly, like Zipper, and sometimes they get afraid and bite."

Jake frowned, as if the idea that a strange dog might bite hadn't occurred to him. Silence fell as he tore into his pan-fried chicken cutlet. Anxiety stirred in Blair's stomach. Might as well get it over with. "Um, Jake?"

He looked up from where he was making designs in the rice with his fork.

"I want to talk to you about something." She waited until his gaze met hers. "Remember when we were at your Nanna's house for your birthday, and you got a present from someone named Nelson?"

"Yeah. He gave me the backpack and everything. He seems pretty nice."

She swallowed. "Well, I wanted to tell you who he is." Where to start? Her mind grayed out, and she groped for anything to say that a seven-year-old would understand. "Nelson is your father," she blurted.

Jake stilled and his eyes widened. "He is?"

Blair nodded. "I've never talked to you about him before. There's a reason for that." Though it wasn't a good reason, she had to admit. She took a breath and shifted in her chair. "You see, sometimes people who aren't married still have babies. It's much better for them to get married first. Of course, God wants them to. But sometimes they don't. A long time ago before you were born, Nelson was my boyfriend. We were planning to get married one day, but I got pregnant with you before that. At the time, Nelson...he didn't want to be a daddy so he...he left me."

Jake's brow furrowed.

"It wasn't because of *you*, Jake. He didn't know you. We were young and he was afraid of being a daddy. That's why you've never met him. But since that time, he changed his mind. That's why he sent you the birthday presents." Now Jake would want to meet Nelson and their tidy, private life would fall apart.

Jake fixed clear blue eyes on her. So like Nelson's. Her heart thumped against her ribs. She imagined he struggled to pull those pieces of information into his current reality. "Will I meet him?"

Oh, dreaded question. "Uh, I don't think so. He doesn't know where we live." And besides that, she swore she'd never speak to him again. As she'd told her mother, he'd forfeited that right the day he walked away.

A tiny tug began inside. Was that fair? A better question was *why* was she terrified to see Nelson again, or to have him meet Jake? Was she simply still angry at him? Or was she afraid he'd try to gain custody? There was little chance of him wanting that or if he did, succeeding. At least that was her dearest hope.

"Do you have any questions, Jake?"

"Where does he live?"

"I don't know. Maybe Philadelphia. I'm not sure."

Jake was silent for a moment. Blair braced for his next question as the silence stacked in a heavy layer.

"Can I go play with my truck?"

Blair blinked and stared at him. "Sure. Looks like you've eaten enough."

With a grin, Jake slid from the table and before long, was growling out truck noises in the living room.

Blair let out a long breath and let her tense shoulders fall. She looked at the ceiling. "Thank you."

℞   ℞   ℞

Saturday morning was busy at Blair and Jake's house. Even before Cooper finished his second cup of coffee, he saw Blair through his window emptying the detached garage behind her house. Trip after trip, she brought boxes and old tools out to the driveway and carried them to the curb. It was a warm day for that kind of work. If she were preparing for winter, she ought to wait until September. But he couldn't tell her that if he wanted to maintain his status of *nice neighbor* and remain Jake's friend. And hers.

After some reflection, Cooper recalled the identity of Blair's landlord. Don Mitchell, an unpleasant man who owned about six or eight rental properties around town. Most of these, he rented to lower-income people and did little to upgrade the structures. The phrase *slumlord* came to mind. Mitchell had made a competing bid for Cooper's home back in the day, but Cooper had won the contract.

At first glance, Blair's home needed a coat of paint, some roof repair, a thorough gutter cleaning, and who knew what else? He guessed Blair had no choice but to add those chores to her own undoubtedly long list. Just a guess, but knowing Mitchell, probably an accurate one.

Next glance out the window—why did he keep looking out the window? It wasn't like he didn't have things to do. He had his own house to look after, since he wasn't fully settled yet, plus visit the property to see how the footings looked. They'd been poured the previous day. In fact, he was on the way over there, but Blair's activities kept catching his eye. She wore a turquoise tank top and faded cutoffs, showing well-shaped legs and a womanly figure, curvy but not too thin. He liked a few curves on a woman, not that he'd seen any in a long time. She'd tied back her blond hair with a headband. An expression of determination blazed across her face.

Now she was filling a bucket with soapy water. She stuffed a pathetic-looking mop into the pail and started sloshing it back and forth on the garage floor. Must be in disgusting shape if she was doing all that to a space meant for parking.

Before he could stop himself, he was out the front door. Perfect temperatures enveloped him as he crossed the yard to Blair's garage. "Hey, Blair. How are you?" he called to catch her attention.

She turned and let the mop rest in the pail. "Hi, Cooper." She swept one wrist against her brow. "I'll be better when I finish this chore."

"I'm sorry to break your concentration." He smiled. "I wanted to tell you I have a power washer. I'd be glad to loan it to you. In fact, I can run it for you on the floor and outside. It'll only take a few minutes."

"Oh, thanks, but I'm almost finished. It's so dirty in here and I've neglected it since I've been in this house."

"You've been here a year? I think that's what you said the other day."

"I moved here with Jake last summer. It was the only house we could find in my price range." She shrugged, as if acknowledging its sorry condition.

"I met the guy who owns it. Your landlord. Not my favorite person."

"Don Mitchell. Yeah, not mine either. I never see him or talk to him. Or I should say, he never talks to me. Whenever there's something to be fixed, I email or text him and he either ignores me or tells me he'll be over in a couple of days. Naturally, a couple of days go on forever."

"Yeah, I know the type." Cooper nodded, but his gut burned with anger on Blair's behalf. Mitchell had no right to take peoples' money for his dilapidated houses and not provide a minimum of maintenance. At best, it made the lodging unpleasant. At worst, unsafe. "Listen Blair, I'm a contractor, so I know my way around a house. If you have any urgent repair needs and can't get ahold of Mitchell, tell me, and I can probably fix it in about five minutes."

She smiled with hooded, unreadable eyes. "You're very kind. I couldn't trouble you like that. Anyway, he said he'd be here in a couple of days, and it is his responsibility to fix things. Like my oven that went out this week." She laughed and held up one hand. "Now, don't offer to let me use yours. You are a helpful neighbor. I need *him* to fix it, and I'll keep pestering him until he does."

"Let me know how that works for you." Cooper met her eyes for a moment then hitched his head toward the garage. "All done in there?"

"I need to let everything dry. I have things to store and don't want them getting dirty or wet."

Curiosity piqued his mind, but he wouldn't cross any more boundaries with Blair. "Right. I'll let you get to it. Enjoy your Saturday and the beautiful afternoon." He hoped she would, but he guessed that work never stopped for his neighbor. Did she ever soak in a tub, or take a vacation? Did she ever get her nails done, or have lunch with a girlfriend?

Why was he thinking about this?

Cooper waved and returned home, but his thoughts were still whirring, tossing up questions about what Blair's life must be like. Her reticence to accept his help was understandable. He was a stranger, her neighbor. She wouldn't want to be indebted to him, although he could easily do so many things she clearly needed. It wouldn't take him any time, but as it was, she'd wait for weeks or forever for old Mitchell to fix her oven or whatever else she needed.

Several minutes later, he pulled into a rutted dirt path on the edge of his property. He rounded the truck to the passenger side and opened the door. Zipper scampered out and began exploring.

The previous day, the site teemed with a beehive of workers pouring concrete and smoothing the footings. That day, no machine noises or worker conversations filled the quiet air. Instead, a peaceful silence hung over the canopy of trees and splinters of light beamed down on the clearing. There was a reason he wanted to build in a forest next to the river. At least he'd been on site to supervise the clearing, protecting his trees.

Cooper surveyed what they had accomplished so far, and satisfaction rumbled through him. He could picture it. A wide wooden deck would extend along the back of the house and look out over a private lawn flanked by towering trees. It would lend shade, privacy, and beauty to those spring or summer nights. When it was warm enough to cook outdoors, he could invite friends, or curl up with a special person, to the sound of crickets and crackling logs in the fire pit.

A special person. Huh. Lately, his thoughts touched on that topic far too often, then hit a wall. A wall Priya had helped create. One moment, he was preparing his future with her. The next, he found himself alone. He'd been invested in their future together. Right before the rug was pulled out, leaving him reeling in confusion.

It was around that time his mental blueprint for the new house formed, refocusing his pain into a more promising direction. But he couldn't picture enjoying his gorgeous custom home all alone. The panoramic view of the river, a brilliant sunset bleeding down into its still surface. He'd want to share that experience and his future with someone special. To someday be determined.

After Priya, he hadn't been in the mood to consider a new relationship. Then there was Miles. That event all but froze his heart to anything as hopeful as a new beginning, a new woman. The thought of a woman one day sharing his life was evidence he was healing.

He pulled his thoughts back to the present moment and returned to his meticulous inspection. He'd lay a slab rather than dig a basement. The work would go more quickly, be less costly, and stay drier during wet winters. Before the end of the week, they'd pour the slab. He'd spend more time on the site from now on. Less time to be distracted by his memories. And his neighbor.

Chapter Five

Blair scanned the newly cleaned garage, satisfied with her labor. Permanent stains still marked the concrete floor, but at least it was cleaner and would provide space for her irregular garments. A double stacked row of bins filled with bags lined one wall of the garage. It had been time well-spent, since her living room was already cluttered. Her collection would grow as she developed a system to work more efficiently. The thought made her giddy with possibilities.

For now, she'd grab an initial handful and see what she could do with them. She selected eight pieces from the top of a bin and carried them inside. She tossed them onto the dining room table and scanned them. Irregular garments that reminded her of herself. If she could improve these misfit mistakes for a good use, maybe she too, was salvageable.

Jake pushed back from the kitchen table after lunch and stood. "Mom, Joel invited me over to kick a soccer ball."

"That sounds like fun. Please be back by five, okay?"

"'Kay." He grabbed his baseball cap and dashed from the kitchen.

As she watched him disappear through the front door, a wave of gratitude flowed through her. Jake had taken time to make new friends. Although he was an outgoing child, during their early days in Brenner Falls, he'd reverted in age and clung to her like a toddler. Fortunately, that phase had only lasted a couple of months.

Much of the credit for that went to the children's department at church. They had a lively group around Jake's age, along with a couple of creative and dedicated adult volunteers. Once he felt comfortable and accepted, he blossomed socially.

She swallowed with emotion as she thought of the impact the little church had had on her and Jake both. She'd been a new, weak believer when she met Nelson and his gang of friends. During that season, her faith resembled the parable Jesus told his disciples about the seed planted but eaten up by birds before it could take root.

Thankfully, those little seeds had re-emerged and found purchase over the last few years. The Real Faith Chapel, as it was called, provided a soft landing and a structure to support her faith. The small church began two years earlier as an expansion of a larger church, Brenner Falls Community Church. She'd been at the Chapel almost since her arrival in town. It had grown, drawing new people of all ages and styles.

Lunch finished, Jake happily occupied, house quiet...*perfect*. Rare was the luxury of time to let her creativity run wild. Though her morning labor in the garage had drained her, anticipation for the new projects infused her with fresh energy.

Blair pulled the first garment from the top of the pile, a size large gray woman's sweatshirt with a front zipper. She saw the flaw right away, a botched neckline. Her aim wasn't to repair it, but to make it unique. In the same pile was another sweatshirt in a contrasting color. That piece looked unsalvageable. She stared at the sweatshirts for a moment as her training and vision kicked in. She'd cut bands from it to make a new neckline for the first one, then attach two triangular pockets to the front. Adding a few decorative buttons would turn it from an average sweatshirt to a stylish top.

She went to work cutting the condemned sweatshirt into strips. As she did, her thoughts wandered to her morning. To Cooper. She'd spoken with him three times, and each time he'd been willing to help her. She hadn't sensed he was flirting or motivated by an agenda. In an unpretentious way, he acted the part of a good neighbor, but possibly more, a friend. And she could use one of those. Maybe he could too since he'd arrived in town so recently.

The day they met, she'd felt protective of Jake and herself. Her life experiences had trained her to approach men with her armor intact. But from the start, she'd detected a sincerity in Cooper. Of course, it was too early to tell for sure. She could still be fooled.

Another hard-to-ignore detail. If she were honest with herself, she'd have to admit he exuded a manly presence and strength that drew her. It flowered by degrees each time they talked.

But she wasn't looking for anything. As if she had time or enough focus. No, she'd stay in her corner, eyes fixed on her goals. Her list of house needs was nearly endless, and she wouldn't impose on Cooper simply because he'd offered. It would be too easy to allow him to fix the many needs in her ramshackle house.

Too easy to get attached to him. To hope for something.

But if they could be friends—given that he was a decent guy, a positive male presence for her son, a neighbor she could count on in the event of a catastrophe—it was all good. As for the warm swirl in her stomach as his intense dark blue eyes linked to hers, she'd ignore that. She'd definitely try.

The afternoon proved to be productive once Blair harnessed her thoughts. She glanced out the front window toward Cooper's house a couple times but didn't see his truck for the rest of the afternoon. He'd said he was a contractor, so might be on a job site somewhere.

Jake returned home, gushing with energy and animated conversation. At times like this, when Blair was in full creative mode, it was hard to be an attentive parent. She gave him several minutes to tell her about Joel and his new puppy, his games, and the snack his mom had given them.

"That's wonderful, sweetie," she said. "I'm so glad you like being with Joel. Why don't you bring a book into the living room and have some quiet time until dinner? Mommy—I mean *I'm* in the middle of a project but almost finished. Okay?"

"Okay. I'll go see if Zipper's around first."

"I haven't seen him, but he might be tied up in the yard. If he's not there, come back inside, okay? We'll eat in about an hour."

She glanced out the window as Jake trotted across the lawn. Cooper was still nowhere in sight. Though it was Saturday, he might be working or out with friends. Or with a woman. Not her business.

Zipper sat on the porch, leashed to a post. At the sight of Jake, he leaped down to greet him, tail wagging furiously. Jake threw his arms around the dog to give him an extended hug, which drew a grin from Blair. At least Jake was easy. He didn't complain as she sometimes did in her head. Effortlessly, he added such joy to her life. She didn't want anyone or anything, including Nelson, to put that in jeopardy.

Her cell phone rang. It was Lilly, her friend from work. Blair frowned. The woman had never called her before, except once when she'd needed a ride to work. "Hi, Lilly. How are you doing?"

"Hi, Blair. I hope I'm not disturbing your supper."

"No, not at all. What's up?"

"I have a confession to make, and I want to apologize up front. I promise you, I meant well."

Blair tensed. "What is it, Lilly?"

"Well, remember last Friday when you were sketching in the break room?"

"Yes, I remember."

"After you left the room, I noticed you'd left the sketch behind. Must have fallen out of your notebook. I took it to give it back to you, but then I got an idea and acted on it without asking you. I saw right away you had talent, but figured the bosses didn't know. I thought you were probably too shy to tell them, so I took the sketch to Hugo."

Blair's eyes widened. "You did?"

"I wanted to help you because you're much too talented to be sitting behind that machine. I hope you're not angry."

"No, I'm not angry. I'm touched that you wanted to help me."

"Really? I'm so relieved. I did it impulsively, then I was going to tell you about it, and it slipped my mind for several days. It wasn't mine to give, so that was wrong, but my motives were pure."

Blair laughed. "You're a true friend. It might not do me any good, but it sure won't do any harm. Did Hugo say anything?"

"He looked at it for a long time and said it was *professional*. He said he'd give it to Gloria. She's in the design department. You haven't heard anything?"

"No, not yet. It's been less than a week, so I'll give it a couple more weeks. Then I'll ask about it. Who knows, it might shake something up."

Lilly might be the only one at work solidly in her corner. But if Gloria had one of her designs given by someone else, it could lead to something she couldn't have done herself. A small wave of hope carried a smile to her lips.

Might open a locked door.

ଔ   ଔ   ଔ

"Nice work, everyone. Go home now and enjoy your weekend." At five o'clock Friday afternoon, the exodus of vehicles from the worksite began with the sound of tires crunching dirt and gravel. Cooper chuckled at how quickly the place emptied out. When he'd hired his crew, he'd promised them they could leave at five every day, and they held him to it. He never squeezed any more time from them after a full workday, which made them eager to accept his projects. Plus, it was the right thing to do.

He surveyed what to most people would look like a house of sticks. For him, it was the start of a dream. A few days of framing yielded a basic form which brought that dream to life, at least in his imagination.

Having a project that stirred his enthusiasm was therapeutic, channeling his mind away from brooding over the past. Though brooding wasn't his personality, the last two years had given him reasons. He frequently had to push back the shadows of painful grief that either hovered in the corners of his mind or ambushed him out of the blue. He missed Miles acutely, and always would. But Miles wouldn't want Cooper to stay stuck in a state of mourning.

It had been a good day, a long one. The framing team had labored from early morning all week and were likely exhausted, ready for the weekend. For him, the thrill of seeing the walls go up only increased his energy. He wasn't a runner, or he'd head out to the path by the river. Maybe next week, he'd look for a gym and some other outlets, like a basketball team or a hunting club. He'd noticed an outdoor adventure center near his street. He'd love to get out on the river in a kayak or paddleboard. If he wasn't careful, he'd repeat the pattern of the previous two years and become a workaholic. He wouldn't let that happen. For starters, he knew the snares of that lifestyle. Along with that, Amber and his parents would be all over his case if he didn't maintain balance.

Amber. He hadn't talked to his sister in over a week, and she was probably miffed at him, or at least wondering if he was still in town. "Hey, Amber." She'd picked up on the second ring. "Just wanted to tell you I'm still here and in good health." He swung up into his truck and opened the window.

"Yeah, I was about to send the cops." Her voice held a gentle scolding. "I thought I'd see more of you once you moved to town."

"You will, I promise. We started framing this week. I wanted to put a lot of time on the front end to oversee the team and get a good start before winter sets in. You should see it, it's a beauty already. Well, you might not think so yet."

"You probably say that with all your buildings, but this is special because it's yours."

"You got that right, little sister. I'll show you some CAD drawings next time you're over. You'll love 'em. By the way, have you been using the dowel in your sliding door? I've been meaning to ask you that."

"Um, planning to. I'm not sure Brenner Falls is dangerous enough to warrant it." Amber chuckled.

"You never know. Use it? Humor me."

"Okay, I will. Hey, do you have plans tonight?" she asked. "I'm meeting some friends over at The Fork. Rather, The Grateful Fork. Everyone in town calls it The Fork. They have some live music, a bluegrass band, I think. Wanna come?"

He'd planned to work on a design for a new client but remembered his decision about not working too much. "Sure, why not? You're having dinner first?"

"We're going at six-thirty. We'll eat before the band plays. It'll be good for you to meet people, since you're new in town."

His outgoing sister would make sure he made new friends. "True. Okay, I'll come. What street?"

"Corner of Summit, then down a little alley where there are several restaurants."

"Gotcha. See you then." Cooper disconnected and within minutes, pulled into his driveway. He glanced at his neighbor's house. No sign of life. He wondered what time she got off work, and what kind of care she had for Jake. Maybe they were out doing errands.

Behind her house sat the cord of wood he'd had put there during the day. He'd also gotten one for himself. Having cleared trees from his land, it seemed a shame not to put the wood to good use. It would be too green to burn right away, but when he'd seen her house had a fireplace, he thought she'd appreciate some logs. Hopefully, she wouldn't mind, as hesitant as she'd been for help last weekend.

He hadn't seen her often during the week, since he'd put in a lot of hours at the site. He'd come back during the day a few times to check on things, have lunch, take care of Zipper. During those times, of course, they weren't home. In the evenings, he'd seen the house lit up, Blair and Jake moving around inside through the picture window. He still didn't know what she did for a living, but each evening she seemed to haul fabric around.

None of his business. He certainly didn't want her to see him staring, even if it was nothing weird, just curiosity. And attraction, which he wouldn't acknowledge. Wouldn't go anywhere, and he didn't need any more heartaches. They were miles apart in a lot of ways, even though only a few yards of ground separated them. His days overflowed with the new construction and getting adjusted to his new life in Brenner Falls.

"Hey, boy." Cooper gave Zipper a thorough scratch on his head and behind his ears. "Did you miss me? Did you get to see Jake today? I guess not." Zipper responded by closing his eyes and waving his tail like a flag. Cooper laughed. "You like that, I can tell. I'm sorry, but I gotta go out again later."

Cooper brought Zipper inside, fed him, and took a shower. He read his mail and straightened the house, though he hadn't had much time to make a mess. Waiting restlessly until time to leave, he also wished he could stay home. Felt strange going out with Amber and her friends for a social evening. He wished he was more enthused about a social event, knowing he needed one. Like a vitamin, he'd take it. It would be good for him.

Cooper got an overview of the town he only vaguely remembered as he drove around trying to find The Grateful Fork. He'd do well to take a tour in daylight. He'd likely memorize the city in about ten minutes.

Tucked down a partial street alongside other restaurants, he spied a hanging wrought iron sign, *The Grateful Fork*. It sat exactly where Amber had told him. He didn't immediately spot it because of his mental wool-gathering. Subjects such as what type of shingles he should use and whether he wanted an etched glass topper on the front door. Time to put all that aside and attempt to be social.

When he entered the café, laughter and banter encircled him. It was a lively and full crowd on a Friday night. He scanned the room and spotted Amber, who must have been watching for him. She waved both arms. He crossed the room and hugged her. She'd pulled her dark curls into a ponytail and her face glowed, making her look seventeen again.

"Right on time," she called over the din. They sat, and she turned to her companions. "Cooper, this is Johnny, his wife Tricia, Lindsay, and Manny." She pointed to each person around the table. Cooper nodded at each introduction, trying to appear friendly, though his previous energy had seeped away between the car and the front door of the restaurant.

As the meal progressed, Cooper unwound, deciding he was glad he'd allowed Amber to persuade him to do what most people did on a Friday night. He liked Amber's friends, and the food wasn't bad either. During dinner, he had a couple of decent conversations. Lindsay, an attractive, suntanned blond, asked him several questions, possibly checking him out. He'd never enjoyed being the new guy but preferred to observe quietly and come out of his shell when he felt ready. Once he did, he could be as extroverted as the best of them.

The server cleared the table, but a few minutes remained before the band would play.

"The owner of this restaurant is an older lady named Aggie," Amber said. "She's run the place for almost forty years, and I think it was her mother's before that."

"Food's good." Cooper didn't have more to say, but that much was obvious.

"What do you do for work, Cooper?" Manny asked with a chuckle. "I didn't get a chance to ask earlier since the ladies had all your attention."

"I'm an architect and contractor. I recently finished a year-long project in another town, so came back here to settle."

"And now he's building a house for *himself*." Amber looked as proud as if she'd built the thing herself.

"One that you designed, I assume." Johnny leaned his elbows on the table.

"Yes. I designed it a few years ago and have tweaked the blueprint since then until I found the right place and time to start building."

"Must be a good feeling to design your own dream house and understand what it takes to build it," Lindsay said with an eager smile.

"I'll confirm that," Cooper said, still enjoying the glow of the first full week of framing. "I spent so much time on my last project I decided it was time for my own home."

"What made you choose Brenner Falls?" Tricia asked. Her blond curls glowed beneath the overhead lamps.

Cooper supplied the same reasons he'd given to others he'd met since arriving. Amber, the river, the town's size and character, and its growth potential.

"Speaking of the town growing," Johnny said. "It's a great place for a contractor because it *is* growing, and fast. You'll have lots of work in years to come."

"That was one of my considerations as well," Cooper said. "I've been away from home for long periods but now I'm ready to work where I live."

"Otherwise, it would be hard to have friendships or raise a family." This from Lindsay. Was she sending him a message? He had the same theory himself.

"You should meet with Mayor Faulkner," Johnny said. "He can tell you about the direction the town is going and how your skills can work with his vision."

"I heard about the visionary mayor. Good that you suggested it." In fact, talking to Mayor Faulkner had occurred to Cooper before, but this was confirmation. No harm in meeting minds with the head guy of Brenner Falls.

Several guitar notes and a banjo twang cut into the rumble of conversation as the bluegrass band tuned instruments. Tricia leaned forward. "I hope you enjoy living here, Cooper. We still love it after fifteen years. If you need any names of professionals or ideas for settling in, let us know."

"Thanks. I might take you up on that." He nodded to Amber. "Especially if my sis gets too busy or runs out of ideas."

"Not too busy for you, bro. You just need to stay in touch." Amber nudged him with one shoulder as the first song began. The sounds of voices and instruments exploded into the atmosphere, making further conversation impossible. Everyone around the table shifted their chairs slightly toward the musicians. A wave of something almost unfamiliar drifted through Cooper. Peace. The absence of the weight of grief he normally carried in the background. Might not stay long, but he'd enjoy it while he could, and look forward to increasing amounts in the future.

Later, after they said goodbye to Amber's friends, she tugged him toward the door. "Want to take a walk around town or come back to my house to hang out?"

"Let's walk." Even though Cooper had been on his feet for most of the day, the gentle evening breeze called him. "It's a beautiful summer night. I need to get to know Brenner Falls." They shared a smile and left the restaurant. The quiet of the streets after the noisy concert made a startling but welcome contrast. The tension he'd carried around on and off for years was blessedly absent.

The sun had set, and its last pastel glow bled into a band of deep blue across the sky, sprinkled with glinting stars. Old fashioned-looking streetlamps spilled yellow puddles of light onto the pavement below. Cooper and Amber meandered from the restaurant down a brick sidewalk of the short alley and turned onto Summit.

"Your friends are nice." He sensed the possibility of friendships there. Something he hadn't had enough of since before Miles.

"Yes, they are. I've been friends with Tricia since her single days. She was one of the reasons I looked for a job here in Brenner Falls."

"I didn't realize that. Or remember it." Surely, she'd told him at some point.

"I knew her in college and came here to visit a couple times since. I liked the town so decided to move here. Kind of like you did."

Cooper gave her a slow nod. At one time, she must have felt as unsettled and disconnected as he did. But it wouldn't take him long to dig in. He didn't have a ton of social needs. A few friends to eat with, a man friend to talk real with, and maybe one day a woman. That would be plenty. He could wait. For now, his hands were full.

"I'm glad we're here together," he said. "I get to see you more and feel more connected."

Her face took on a wistful, faraway expression. He wondered if she was thinking of Miles, or simply the value of being near family. He felt both, but the realization brought depth of gratitude instead of pain, maybe for the first time.

"We'll always miss Miles," she said as if reading his mind. "But I'm glad we have each other."

He slid one arm around her shoulders and pulled her close. "Yeah, me too."

Chapter Six

Saturday morning dawned clear and bright. The lower-than-usual humidity in the air lured Cooper's attention outdoors. After spending the week at the work site, he'd do something different that day. He'd arrived in The Falls almost a month ago, but still felt like he was visiting for the weekend. If he was going to make The Falls his permanent home, he had to learn the lay of the town. The thought had occurred to him while searching for The Grateful Fork, and again during his stroll with Amber.

After a generous breakfast of bagels and scrambled eggs, he grabbed the leash and his sunglasses, and called to Zipper. "Come on, boy. We're going exploring." As he unlocked the truck, he cast a glance at the house next door, but saw no sign of life, which brought a faint wave of disappointment.

He drove toward town and parked in a strip mall on the outskirts. Zipper stuck his head out the passenger window and wagged his tail. Looked like he was excited about discovering a new place. *He'd* feel that way if he were a dog.

During his walk with Amber, he'd noted many examples of period architecture, mid-century and earlier. Now he'd observe them during daylight. He'd start down Brenner Boulevard, one of the primary thoroughfares of the small town. Along the street, shopkeepers opened their doors and set up sidewalk displays for the early customers. Several four-story office buildings stood dark and empty for the weekend, and a few restaurants prepared to open for lunch. Zipper trotted alongside Cooper, occasionally stopping to sniff something or investigate another dog in passing.

At the end of the street, the city hall building dominated the corner. Cooper planned to call the following week for an appointment with the mayor as part of his strategy to put professional and personal roots down in The Falls. Johnny's comment the previous evening at dinner had reminded him.

Cooper scanned city hall, likely built in the seventies. In contrast, an attractive Victorian stood across the intersection. Seasons Dinner Theater. He'd heard about the place and glimpsed it when he was in town the year before. Apparently, a historic landmark for the town, it looked as though it had recently had a facelift. Fresh flowers tumbled from hanging pots on the long, covered porch. Fluffy, budding bushes hemmed the front and sides of the building, which looked freshly painted in white and turquoise. The lighter color gave it a renewed, inviting exterior.

He crossed Brenner Boulevard toward Warren Street, another busy downtown avenue. As he did, his gaze fell on a wide grassy park buzzing with activity of a market or weekend festival. The clamor of conversations hovering among the displays drew Cooper's curiosity. He drew near and saw rows of vegetable and fruit stands, flower stands, and artisan displays, along with clusters of people everywhere. Energy and noise percolated in the air and aromas of grilled meat and sauteed onions wafted toward him from a row of food trucks.

"Let's check this out," he said to Zipper, who wagged his tail in agreement.

Although he'd stocked his fridge two days earlier, he couldn't resist a few farm-grown tomatoes, a bunch of asparagus, and a flat of strawberries. He accepted a plastic bag offered by the merchant, available for the uninitiated who had not brought their own canvas bags. He stopped at a booth containing watercolor pictures, to study some works which might accent his living room. Current or future.

"Look, it's Mr. Cooper. Mr. Cooper!"

Cooper turned and saw Jake running toward him. "Hi, big guy." Cooper grinned at Jake, suddenly realizing he'd adopted Blair's nickname for her son. "What are you doing here?"

Jake had thrown his small arms around Zipper's neck. The dog didn't seem to mind, nudging him with his nose. Jake stood and pointed. "My mom is over there. She sells stuff here every Saturday."

Cooper's heart leaped. "Every Saturday?"

"Yeah, come on and see."

ଔ   ଔ   ଔ

Blair said goodbye to the middle-aged woman who'd just bought sixty dollars' worth of merchandise. If only all her customers were like that, the morning would go quickly. Jake had momentarily disappeared from view, and just before panic set in, she spied him walking beside...Cooper?

Jake tugged Cooper's arm leading him to Blair's stand. He held Zipper's leash in one hand and a plastic bag of produce in the other. She offered a warm smile and couldn't snuff a spark of pleasure. He was dressed casually in flip flops and cargo shorts. A pair of sunglasses sat on top of his head.

At least that day, she was a bit more fixed-up than usual. Fortunately. Though she shouldn't be thinking that way. She wore a short skirt with a ruffle around the bottom and a pink sleeveless blouse. A refreshing morning breeze grazed the booth.

"Hi, Cooper. I didn't know you came to the market."

He grinned. "I didn't know there *was* a market until today. Seems to be a popular place." His glance panned the crowds and returned to her table where she'd artfully arranged colorful clothing, purses, and accessories on an orange tablecloth. "Jake said you sell things here every Saturday."

"Yes, when I can."

Cooper dropped his focus to the table. "Did you make these?"

"Yes, I design and make everything I sell here."

"Very nice." He fingered the stitching and buttons on a woven purse with multiple pockets. "I bet my sister would like this one." His eyes roved around. "And I'll take that too." He pointed to a frilly apron hanging from a hook behind her. "For my mom."

She chuckled. Seemed obvious that he wanted to help her. In fact, he'd left a load of firewood at her house the day before. For sure, it was him. "Don't feel like you have to buy stuff just to be nice." She smirked as she placed the items in a bag for him and took his cash.

"My sister and mom happen to love handmade things. I'm glad I saw your booth because I was wondering what to get them. For birthdays."

Blair saw through his game. "Well, everyone has a birthday sooner or later." Her gaze found his. "Are you the one who left the wood at my house?"

His smile fell. "Uh, yeah. Hope you don't mind. I saw you had a fireplace, and I'd recently cleared some land for a house. Thought you could use it."

"Thank you," she said. "I appreciate it, although I'm not sure my fireplace is safe. Last winter, I tried to start a fire with one of those fake logs, but it smoked, and I had to douse it with water. I didn't have the courage to try again."

"Was the flue open?"

She cocked her head and took on an indignant expression. He must think she didn't know anything about houses. "Of *course*. In view of the general neglect of the house, it wouldn't surprise me if something was stuck up there, or it hadn't been cleaned in eons."

"Or both. I can check it for you if you'd allow me. You can't burn the wood yet because it's green, but if you want a fire this winter, it should be checked."

She struggled with an urge to accept his offer, while a voice inside told her not to open a door to help and dependence. She sighed. "That's kind of you, Cooper."

"You accept?" His eyes caught hers, and for an instant, electricity crackled between them.

"If you're sure you don't mind. I'm mostly concerned about our safety, with the fireplace and oven." Her gaze wandered to Jake, who was still petting Zipper and trying to teach him to shake.

"As I am." He lifted his brows. "Concerned for your safety. Knowing what I know about Mr. Mitchell, we can't assume anything. In fact, I'm nervous for you in that house." A shadow crossed his face, and she wondered if he foresaw dangers she hadn't imagined.

Blair frowned. "I wonder if I should be more nervous than I already am. It's all I could afford at the time. Part of why I come here to the market is to earn a little more so I can give Jake what he needs and wants. I'd rather do that than spend more money on high-end housing."

"I understand. Do you have another job besides this?"

He wouldn't judge her, would he? He didn't know anything about her dreams and how far she'd fallen from them. "Yes, I work at a clothing factory."

"What do you do there?"

She took a breath and paused for a second, trying to decide how much to tell him. "I studied fashion design in college and would have moved to New York and followed the traditional route, working my way up in a fashion house. But at the end of my senior year, I got pregnant with Jake and my plans changed. When I moved here, I took a job in the factory and even though I only work at a machine on an assembly line, I figure it's a foot in the door." She shrugged, struggling to believe her own words.

"Sounds reasonable. At least, you're working in the same area. Then this can be your creative outlet." He swept a hand across the table.

"For me, the factory is a steppingstone, though I don't really have illusions they'll one day give me a design job. But it keeps me motivated to persevere. I don't know exactly how or when I'll get *there—*" she made air quotes. "But I'll keep plugging away."

Cooper leveled a stare at her. "Seems to me you're a hard worker, but also you have a vision, loads of creativity, and courage. Being a single parent isn't blocking you from pursuing your dream. I admire you for that."

"That's nice of you to say, Cooper." An understatement. He'd just given her a dose of hope. As though he, a near stranger, saw enough potential in her to believe in her.

"What about you?" she asked. "You said you're a contractor. Do you have projects here in The Falls?"

A prospective customer and her daughter approached the display, so Cooper stepped back. The woman asked a couple of questions, chose several items, and paid Blair. When she left, he said, "In answer to your question, I have a company and I design and execute building projects. Mostly single-family homes. I recently finished a development, which took a year to complete. That's why I wasn't in town when you moved here. I moved back and now I'm building my own house."

"How exciting." Seemed to fit the man, from what she knew. "I assume you designed your house?"

"Yes, and I finally have the time to build it. I still have a few clients, but my primary focus in the coming year is my own house."

Cooper watched Jake and Zipper for a moment. Zipper finally understood and offered his paw.

"Mom, look at Zipper," Jake burst out. "Look, Mr. Cooper. He learned how to shake. I taught him."

"That's great," Cooper said. "You're gifted with animals. Remember, the other day you taught him to fetch too." They watched Jake and Zipper for a moment.

"Have you ever thought of selling things online?" Cooper asked. "You might make a little more that way, though you'd have to have a fair amount of inventory."

"Yes, I've thought about it." Though not enough. Too intimidating and too much work. "I even drew up some plans for a website, started a Facebook page. But then life happened. Everything needs to be updated now." She shrugged. "I never got back to it. Besides that, I know so little about marketing."

"I'm sure you could learn." He leaned against one of the posts holding up her awning and a gust of air ruffled his hair. "In fact, didn't you learn a software platform in design school? Like I do when I design a building."

She nodded. "I learned InDesign and a few fashion-specific programs. But the whole blogging, social media, marketing thing…it's a little overwhelming to me."

"Just take a little piece at a time. My sister was like you, unsure of the process. She got some help from friends, took a class."

"I don't doubt I'm *able* to learn." If she had ten extra hours in her week, for example. "I don't know where I'll find the time."

Cooper frowned as if he just realized how packed her life must be. "Oh, yeah. There's that." He cocked his head sympathetically. "Take baby steps?"

"And you can help me with that too, right?" She smirked. "Mr. Helpful?"

He laughed. "You know me already. I'd rather help with things I'm good at. Like fixing your chimney and oven."

What a relief that would be. And he was willing. "You're starting to convince me about that. Though I *so* don't want to take advantage of your kindness."

"I get that, and I appreciate it. But don't worry, Blair. I'm offering. It won't take me long. I'd like to help."

He sure sounded sincere. She gave him a grudging nod. "Okay."

"When do you want me to come check out that chimney and oven?"

"Tomorrow? It's Sunday evening, so that may fit our schedules best. For sure, I'll be more relaxed with no chores to do. But you'll have to stay for dinner." Seemed bold, and yet the right thing to do. Along with that, she liked talking to him.

"Deal. See you around five?"

"Perfect. You need directions?"

Their eyes met as they both laughed.

"Okay, see you then. I'll let you get back to work." He turned to Jake. "Gotta go, buddy. See you tomorrow, okay?"

"Bye, Mr. Cooper. Bye, Zipper."

Cooper gave them both a parting smile, took Zipper's leash, and wove through clusters of shoppers until he was out of view.

A melodic run of guitar notes rippled through contemplative silence at the end of the church service. Blair closed her eyes and soaked in the peace, not only the soothing sound, but the rich message she'd just heard. As she had many times, she silently expressed her gratitude for having discovered Real Faith Chapel. She'd arrived with Jake nearly a year earlier, like an unanchored sailboat, adrift and alone. The little church had given her a place to land. A new family, in some ways. Roots for her new life. Best of all, she knew she was getting back on track in her faith and allowing those neglected seeds to flourish.

When the last note died out, Pastor Todd already stood on the stage. He lifted his hands and gave a benediction. "If anyone here today is new, welcome. We're glad you're here. Please stay after and let us get to know you. There are refreshments in the back corner. Have a blessed week."

People stirred, and a low rumble of conversation filled the air. Often, Blair helped with the refreshments on a rotating schedule. That day, she was off, so her gaze wandered the room for people she knew. Seemed like each week, a few new people visited, and some stayed.

Blair greeted several people she knew only by sight. She spotted her friend Leah Albright across the room. She wove her way to where Leah stood in a cluster with two other women. Too bad Leah wasn't alone. Blair was still shy about approaching new people, especially those already deep in a conversation. Leah's gaze lifted, as if she sensed Blair's approach. A smile spread across her face. "Blair, come join us."

Leah had a gift for noticing people on the outskirts and drawing them in. Thanks to Leah, Blair had fast-tracked to feeling more at home in Brenner Falls. She had a few acquaintances, some with friend potential.

"This is my friend Blair. She's a fashion designer." Leah touched the summer scarf draped across Blair's shoulders. "Your style gives you away, Blair. Always so creative and elegant." She included the other woman. "This is Cynthia. She's been here a few times. And this is Robbie, who's visiting."

Blair said hello, then fell silent as the conversation resumed. Minutes later, the group dispersed, and she was alone with Leah. Thankfully, because she had something important to ask her. A question had trotted around in her mind since her conversation with Cooper the previous day.

"Leah, I know your brother set up a website for you when you started teaching music."

"He did an amazing job," Leah said. "Lots of people in town have known me all my life, but when I launched my business, I had to get the word out. And that's how modern people get information, even if they have known you since you were in diapers."

"Yeah. That's exactly what I was thinking. So, you know I sell things at the market. I'm not thinking I can make enough merchandise to sell online, but I'm beginning to think if I could just update my website—"

"A fashion blog!"

Blair's mouth opened, and she cocked her head. "Um..." She recovered her words. "A fashion blog? I never thought of that. I don't really have time to blog, although I follow a few fashion blogs when I have free time. Which is like, never." She stared at Leah. "Why would I *want* a fashion blog?"

"Well, you want to get into the fashion industry with your own designs, right?" Leah's clear blue eyes widened with enthusiasm. Her glossy, shoulder-length chestnut hair glinted in the morning sun. "You could do brief articles on fashion trends and things, but also show some of your *own* designs. That'll draw people to the site, where they'll be able to see your unique style."

"I'd love to do that, but I feel so overwhelmed already." Blair dropped her head and stared at her hands. Leah's vision sounded ideal. But then, there was reality. "I can barely put food on the table, barely have time to sleep as it is. How am I going to do that?" It was true, yet she had asked Leah first, hadn't she? What had she expected?

Leah's smile fell. "I didn't realize. It'll be a challenge and probably a long process before you see results. I won't lead you to believe otherwise. But if you want to attain your dream..." She shrugged. "Having a website is essential, but people need to know you're there. You can't avoid online, unless you plan to move to New York one day instead."

Suddenly, puzzle pieces clicked into place. Blair sank into a nearby chair. She'd blindly pursued the traditional path, knowing in her gut that with a child and a full-time job, it would be an impossible climb up an unforgiving mountain. Her gaze found Leah's. "I might have to give up part of my dream. The traditional way seemed, I don't know, more legitimate."

Leah hastened to sit beside her. "No, Blair. Don't give up. New York isn't the only way to do this. Don't you know about fulfillment houses that execute designs others have created? They make masses of clothes and send them back to the designers who sell them directly or distribute them to stores."

Blair blinked. "I *should* know about them. I work for one. I'm sure I've read about them before but didn't apply it to myself." She let out a sigh. The new information flooded through her unprepared mind. Along with overwhelm, a spark of hope ignited. Maybe there *was* another path to her dream. But it would take time. She'd have to find it. "It may be the only way for me."

The realization settled hard in Blair's stomach like a lead weight. Her mental picture of a job in a New York fashion house was blurry on a good day. Now that image faded further from reach and nearly disappeared.

Leah touched her arm. "Blair, that's *good* news. You don't have to work under other people. You can be your own boss, run your own company. Wouldn't that be cool?"

Blair let out a humorless laugh. "Cool for you, maybe." How could she embark on anything so enormous? Were her designs even good enough to have manufactured and sell to an online public? "It's a lot to take in."

"I understand. Listen, there's Nathan over there." Leah waved to her boyfriend, Nathan, the current owner of Seasons Dinner Theater. "Nathan's in marketing and he can guide you through the process. I'm sure he'll have ideas for you."

Okay, maybe this would be less terrifying if she had some baby steps, as Cooper said, in the form of guidance from a professional marketing guy.

Nathan crossed the room and turned the chair in front of the women to face them. He sat and leaned his elbows on his knees. "Hi, Blair. Good to see you."

Yes, he looked like a marketing guy, according to Blair's stereotype. Neatly dressed, short brown hair, but with eyes so kind and attentive, her shoulders dropped a few inches. Tension spun out of her like air from a balloon.

Leah touched Nathan's forearm. "Nathan, you might remember Blair is an aspiring fashion designer. We were talking about options available to her one day through an online presence and eventually a fulfillment service. Do you think you can give her some guidance for that, for how to begin?"

Knots of tension unfurled inside her. Leah's words *options, begin,* and *one day* sounded much less daunting than running her own company. She could barely run her own household.

"Mom, there you are!" Speaking of household. She heard Jake's little boy voice before she saw him. He skipped toward her and plopped into the next chair. She slid one arm around his small shoulders.

"Hi Miss Leah, hi Mr. Nathan." He turned back to Blair. "See what we did today?" He held up a crayon drawing of the twelve disciples. They all had identical beards and robes, but a variety of hair colors. Brown, black, green, purple, and blue. Apparently, Jake had been observing the members of the congregation. At least the disciples in his drawing didn't have tattoos.

"That's amazing, Jake," Leah said. "You're a musician *and* an artist!"

"That's very nice, sweetie." Blair studied his picture, though her thoughts from her conversation with Leah ricocheted in her head, almost causing pain. "When you draw pictures of the scriptures, it stays in your mind even better. Jake, do you want to get some cookies at the snack table, or sit quietly for a minute or two? I'm finishing a conversation with Leah and Nathan."

"I'll go and come right back." Jake flew down the aisle.

"What a wonderful son you have," Nathan said with sincerity. "He's grown a lot in just the few months I've been here in the church. You must be so proud."

"Oh, I am. I'm blessed." Blair's gaze followed Jake to the table where he charmed the older woman supervising the snacks.

She returned her attention to Nathan. "Okay, where do we start?"

Nathan and Leah both laughed. "Sounds like you're taking the challenge," Leah said.

Blair knew that was her only choice, that or staying behind a sewing machine at Simpson-Fink Textile Manufacturing. Baby steps, Cooper had said. Baby. Steps.

"Let me know if you want me to walk you through the initial stages of an online business," Nathan told her. "I could meet you at Sophie's Coffee Shop or after church one day."

After promising to think it over, Blair and Jake said goodbye and drove home. Blair's new information and possibilities continued to storm in her head. She'd have to push that aside for a while. Not only should she step back and regain perspective, but she also had to prepare for a dinner guest. Her first since arriving in Brenner Falls. She still couldn't believe she'd impulsively invited Cooper to dinner. But it seemed the right thing to do, given the tremendous help he'd be to her that evening, help she didn't have to find the money to pay.

Cooper. Warm pinpricks of anticipation and a shade of nervousness surged a wave in her, one she hadn't felt in years. *Don't go there, Blair.* He was a neighbor. A friend. A handsome, kind friend. Nothing more. She'd enjoyed their conversation the previous day at the market, though she suspected he was just humoring her. Probably thought she was a dreamer, head in the clouds, like everyone else in her life did.

Speaking of clouds, her full plate was now stacked *up* to the clouds, with the unavoidable challenge of an online business. Then there was Nelson, who always hovered in the back of her mind. She had more than enough complications and sure didn't need any more.

Chapter Seven

The August sun streamed into the window that afternoon, raising the temperature in the kitchen. Blair mopped perspiration from her brow. Why did she invite a dinner guest when her oven was *broken*? Should she pre-cook the meal on the stovetop so the unit would be cool enough for Cooper to repair it? Or should she let him work first, but risk being tied up in meal preparation while he waited?

Was it the inconvenient circumstances of her oven tying her knickers in a knot, as her grandma used to say? No, it was Cooper. A man she found attractive was coming for dinner.

She'd never been nervous when they'd chatted in the yard. Because it was just the yard, not dinner. Enough already. She was being stupid, ridiculous. Or completely out of practice with basic hospitality. "Blair, stop being a goober," she muttered into the quiet kitchen. Time for an executive decision.

Brown chicken thighs on the stovetop in advance. Once Cooper diagnosed and repaired the oven, she'd let the chicken braise while she served the salad. Having decided on her method, she relaxed. At five o'clock sharp, she heard a knock on the front door. She ignored her thumping heartbeat and went to let him in.

Cooper's broad shoulders filled the doorway. He wore a close-fitting blue T-shirt and khaki pants and held a sizeable toolbox in one hand. "Hi Blair."

Blair took a breath. His apparent lack of awareness of how he looked in that blue shirt made him even more appealing. His smile said nothing but *friendly neighbor, nice guy*, though she might have detected an observant spark in his eyes when he scanned her face. She coaxed away her silly nerves and decided to act like a hostess instead of a pre-teen. It was *nice* to have company. Especially his.

"Hi, Cooper. Looks like you're prepared." She nodded toward his toolbox and stepped back to let him enter the foyer.

"Hope you and Jake have had a restful day," he said.

"More or less." Jake's airplane noises drifted from the living room. "Went to church this morning. After that, caught up on a few things. Jake was happy you were staying for dinner."

"You didn't have to invite me, given that your oven's broken." Cooper offered a disarming grin. "But I appreciate the gesture and I don't plan to turn you down now." Their eyes met for a moment. "Um, I thought I could work on the oven first, get that out of the way. I hope I can, at any rate."

"That would be perfect." She turned toward the living room. "Jake, Cooper's here."

Jake scrambled to the wide arched doorway of the living room. "Hi, Mr. Cooper."

"Hi, Jake. What are you up to in there?" Cooper hitched his head toward the room.

Blair realized he still stood there holding the toolbox. Though, judging by the size of his arm muscles, it likely wasn't too much of a burden.

"I have this game, it's like a miniature air hockey, but I can do it by myself. Maybe you can play it with me later."

She'd have to curtail her son's sociable chatter this time. "Jake, we'll see. Might not be the best time. Cooper wants to try to fix the oven first before we eat." She gave him an apologetic frown.

Jake let out an exaggerated sigh. "Okay. Got it." He trudged back to the living room.

She lifted her eyes to Cooper's. "You're welcome. Follow me."

Ê Ê Ê

Cooper followed Blair, thankful he'd escaped playing air hockey with Jake. She looked cute in long denim shorts and a tie-dyed T-shirt. Might be one of her designs.

He entered the tiny kitchen. Though worn and outdated, she'd made valiant efforts to add cheer and comfort. A colorful print valence hung at the window over the sink and a matching tablecloth adorned the corner table.

"Did you check the breaker?" he asked.

"Yes, that's the *first* thing I thought of." She gave him a smug smile.

"Smart girl." So, she had the basics down. Little wonder she didn't know what to do after that. It could be one of at least three different things. And it shouldn't be her personal headache to get her oven fixed when she was renting. A hot layer of anger roiled in his stomach. He wanted to punch Don Mitchell, her worthless landlord, for the distress Blair felt. She didn't need this on top of everything else.

Focus, Cooper. He set his toolbox on the floor and turned on the oven. After a few seconds, he waved one hand inside it. Cold as a tomb, sure enough. He knew what to look for. He'd seen a wide variety of appliance issues over the years, so he searched in the toolbox for his multimeter. While he worked, he was conscious of Blair sitting quietly at the small table a few feet away.

After running a few more basic checks, he stood. "I think it's the thermal fuse. When it gets overheated, it blows the fuse. It's possible that faulty wiring caused it to blow, but it's not an uncommon problem. The fuse is replaceable, but I don't have the part with me. I'll have to get one in town or order it."

Blair stood and clasped her hands together. "How much would that cost?"

"Between twenty and twenty-five dollars, but I might be able to find one at cost. Remember, I'm a contractor and I know all the right people."

Her tense expression softened. "How handy."

"This should be your landlord's cost. You said you already contacted him, and he ignored you, right? You could send him the bill and deduct it from your rent next month."

"Yeah, I thought of that. I should be bolder with him."

He leveled a serious stare at her large hazel eyes. "As a renter, you have rights, Blair. We need to find out what they are."

"Yes, Colonel." She smirked. "But it sounds like a fight to me. I'm not timid, just tired and overwhelmed. One more thing to do, you know?"

Compassion squeezed Cooper's gut. A woman like Blair deserved so much more. Her choice to be a single mom was a difficult one, to be sure, but the inaction of a negligent landlord was simply wrong.

"I'll replace the fuse this week," he said over his shoulder as he washed his hands. "Then if you have trouble after that, we'll troubleshoot. I haven't forgotten about the chimney, but I don't think I'll have time to do both tonight. I can look at it inside, but another day come back with a ladder and look from outside."

"I really appreciate it, Cooper. Otherwise, we'll spend another winter with no fire. That would be a shame because Jake and I both enjoy them."

"And it can cut your heating cost."

She straightened her shoulders. "Okay. Now that you're finished, I'll put the chicken on the stove. We can have our salad in about ten minutes while the chicken cooks." She leaned against the counter as he dried his hands on a tea towel. "I've been getting along okay with just the stovetop, pulling out every recipe I have that doesn't have to be baked. It's forces me to be creative."

"Something tells me being creative isn't a problem for you."

She seemed pleased by his comment. "Most of the time, that's true. Would you like to relax in the living room with Jake while I get this started? Shouldn't be too long."

"Maybe I'll try miniature air hockey." He raised his eyebrows playfully and got another smile out of her. Now, he'd go see what his buddy Jake was up to.

Blair served dinner at a larger table in one corner of the living room. Spread over it was a boldly colored checked tablecloth and a matching ceramic centerpiece. He guessed color was her superpower, though her clothing shades were lighter, maybe to coordinate with her blond hair. Her wardrobe suited her, unique and somewhat Bohemian. Not that he was an expert on women's clothing, but he *did* have a sister and he was an astute observer. Especially when the style gave away clues about the woman.

On the other side of the couch was a long table and two dress forms, and other tools of Blair's trade. Dozens of sketches, chunks of fabric, and color samples littered the table. The whole creative mess brought a grin to his lips.

Blair's chicken fricassee, rice, and green beans hit the spot. He was a decent cook, but a home-cooked meal he didn't have to prepare tasted even better. "Oven or no oven, this was delicious."

"Thanks. It's simple fare." She shrugged. "It's nice to... I'm glad you could come over. And not just for the oven, of course."

Her face colored and something warm stirred inside him. An urge to take her hand, to feel its softness, came over him. Cooper tightened his fists where they rested on his thighs.

"You relax and Jake will help me clear the table."

"If you won't allow me to help, I'll have a look at the fireplace."

Cooper knelt in front of the stone fireplace, stained with ancient soot on either side. Looked like Blair or someone else had tried without success to scrub the soiled stones around the opening. He peered inside, scoping his flashlight into the blackness. Hard to tell from this angle and without daylight, but one thing was obvious. No one had cleaned it in forever and there were likely several things blocking it. A mental picture of her house in flames while Jake pounded at the window flashed through his mind, causing a shudder.

Blair and Jake had made quick work of clearing the table. She brought back a fresh set of small bowls—colorful, of course—and two containers of ice cream. "Didn't have time to make dessert." She placed them on the table. Jake followed behind her and added spoons and a scooper.

"I'm glad you didn't make dessert," Cooper said, just in case she was feeling inadequate. She'd already done enough. "I love ice cream."

"What kind do you like, Mr. Cooper?" Jake slid back into his chair.

"All kinds. Especially ice cream with chocolate and nuts. And fruit. And caramel. And mint. And just about everything."

Blair and Jake laughed.

"Well, I'm relieved we have at least two of your favorite flavors." She took his bowl and began mounding it with scoops of strawberry and chocolate chip ice cream.

"I make popsicles, but I didn't make any today," Jake told him. "I got a popsicle kit for my birthday from my Aunt Audrey."

"He likes making creative flavors," Blair said. "Last week he used orange juice and half and half for creamsicle."

"Another day we put chocolate milk and peanut butter in the blender," Jake said. "That was my favorite."

"Sounds great. Wonder where he gets that creative streak from." He grinned and pulled the bowl of ice cream closer. "Thanks. You gave me too much, but I'll manage."

The three of them dug into their ice cream. Perfect ending to a satisfying meal. "I looked at your chimney, and I think there's a blockage of some kind. A buildup of creosote and possibly flue damage. Maybe falling brick too. I wouldn't use it at all until it's cleaned."

"Huh. That'll be the day when old Mitchell has my chimney cleaned. That must be expensive."

"It can be. But it's dangerous not to. Not only can it start a fire in the chimney, but it's hazardous to breathe the buildup that's on the inside. I have a fireplace," he said when Blair's face showed alarm. "You guys can come over with your marshmallows and sticks anytime."

"Yay!" Jake wiggled in his seat. Cooper didn't mind the thought of seeing even more of the little guy.

"Cover your ears, Jake." Blair shook her head at Cooper. "He's already over at your place so often to visit Zipper. Now he'll be there all the time." She rested her chin on her hand. "I wonder if I'm allowed to have a fire ring in my yard."

"I wouldn't think so. It'll be in your lease. But I'm *allowed* on my property, so we can have one there instead."

"I'll mention the fireplace to my landlord but not hold my breath."

"Good idea."

"Mmm. I like strawberry, Mommy. I mean, Mom." Jake licked both sides of his spoon. "We had this in Sunday school last week. It was Jamie's birthday."

"Oh, that sounds nice." Blair scooped the last drops from the bottom of her bowl. "A party at church."

"Where do you guys go to church?" It was more than curiosity. He'd needed to get back into a church for over two years now. He'd lacked the heart, which had cracked and gotten lost. Healing might have gone faster if he'd found a Christian community sooner.

"We attend a small start-up church called Real Faith Chapel," she said. "They call it a church *plant* because a larger church in town started it and now it's growing. It's in the shopping center close to the Outdoor Adventure Depot."

"I'm still learning my way around, but I've seen the Depot."

"You should come, Mr. Cooper." Jake's voice rose.

"I'd love to one day."

"Come next week," Jake urged.

"Jake, don't pester Cooper. He'll come when he has a chance."

"That's alright," Cooper said. "It's high on my list to visit churches. I have some catching up to do."

"Can I go play?" Jake waited for only a few seconds before sliding down from his chair. He disappeared to where his game lay between the couch and armchairs.

Blair met Cooper's gaze and there was that spark again. It set off an undeniable churning deep inside him.

She swallowed and blinked. "Those were exactly my thoughts when I arrived in Brenner Falls. A new beginning. And catching up with God. Or rather, letting him lead me through the next chapter."

"Exactly." He let out a long sigh. Part of him wanted to tell her. Explain what had driven him like a storm for the last two years, almost leading him to an exhausted breakdown. But it wasn't the time. Might never be. "I came to Brenner Falls to start my new chapter, and want to bring God more into my life. I also need to stay balanced and not work too much."

"And you're working on your house now?" She took a sip of water.

At her words, his spirit shifted in a more hopeful direction. "Yes, it's by the river. I'd done a lot of home designs and knew what my favorite features were. I've had a blueprint in mind for about three years now, but tweak it now and then."

"Have you started building?"

"We started framing last week. It's going up fast. That's usually where I am if I'm not home."

"Remember, you said *balance*." She lifted one finger. "I heard you say it, so I'm holding you to it." She raised her eyebrows. "So, tell me, where are you from? What's your family like?"

Cooper crossed his ankle over one knee, careful with what to share. "I grew up in a stable Christian family. We kids got along better than most. My parents still live there, and we keep in touch. My sister, Amber lives here, which is the main reason I came. You should meet her someday." Hopefully, Blair wouldn't ask about other siblings.

"I'd like to. What does she do?"

"She's a physical therapist."

"Have you... ever been married? Sorry if that's too personal."

Cooper waved away her concern. "I was engaged three years ago to a woman named Priya. She'd been born in India, but raised in the US. The culture wasn't a problem between us, or at least I didn't think so." He stopped. How much did he want to say about the last few years?

"I guess that didn't work out." Her voice was soft.

He shook his head. "Her parents liked me, but they preferred she marry in her own culture. I thought that was baloney at first, until she met someone from India." Cooper kept his voice light. "So, that was that."

"That sounds hard. I mean, you were already engaged when that happened, right?"

He nodded. "It was hard at the time, but I'm glad she's happy. Then—" No, he was *not* going there. It would only elicit her pity and put a pall on their evening. "Then, some other hard things happened. Other losses." He shrugged to deflect any questions.

The air grew still. Blair said, "I'm so sorry."

After a beat of silence, he asked, "How did you get interested in fashion design?"

Her face brightened. "I discovered sewing when I was about seven. I saw my mom making outfits for us kids and I remember being fascinated by how all the pieces came together. The sewing itself isn't what interests me. In fact, that part can be boring, but seeing things come together, and especially designing them. Putting a unique spin on a garment... I love that. I have ideas all the time. I can barely keep up."

"Do you have any clothing designs you wouldn't mind showing me?"

Surprise sparked on her face. "You want to see them?"

"Sure, a few of them." Cooper leaned back and steepled his fingers. "I'm curious and I'm interested. I've never met a fashion designer before."

She squinted at him for a moment to be sure he was sincere and rose from the table. "Okay, you asked for it. I won't show you everything, just a sketch or two to give you an idea."

Blair went through a doorway leading, Cooper guessed, to her bedroom or office, though he doubted there'd be room in the little house for both. She returned with a three-ring binder and placed it on the table. "Here are a few sketches I've been working on. I have quite a few on my laptop too. I created one during my lunch break and a colleague gave it to my boss's boss without my knowledge. He might have given it to the woman in charge of designers."

"That sounds hopeful."

Blair shrugged. "It might not go anywhere, but who knows?"

"Might help you break in."

"You're *quite* optimistic."

He leaned forward, resting his elbows on the table. "So, show me what you've got in that notebook."

She opened a square binder with unlined pages. His gaze fell on a sketch of a lanky woman wearing a full skirt and some kind of flowing top with wide sleeves.

"That's nice. I can picture it on someone." His eyes found hers. "In fact, looks like something you'd wear. Though again, I can't claim to be an expert on women's clothing."

She smirked. "I wouldn't think so. But in some ways, we're both *builders*. You build structures and I build clothes."

"Do you start with a complete sketch, then work out the pieces to put it all together?"

"Yes. Just like you do."

They shared a smile. "I see the similarities." And he did. He started with a mental vision of the finished work and sketched it. A computer drawing followed, which became the blueprint. He'd break it all down into structural parts and materials to construct a home according to the vision. Blair was doing the same thing with clothing.

"So, what about the parts?" he asked.

She turned the page. "These here are the parts of this outfit. The panels for the skirt are here, the parts of the top, which are a yoke, the facings, the sides, a collar... Here are the sleeves..." She pointed to each piece as she explained. She flipped to another page, showing a sleek pair of pants with a short matching jacket.

"I'd never admit this to another person besides you," he told her. "But I'm finding this interesting."

She laughed aloud. "Your secret's safe with me. Many designers are men, in fact. Don't forget Yves St. Laurent, Ralph Lauren, Tom Ford, Georgio Armani, Karl Lagerfeld…"

"Tom Ford studied architecture as well as fashion, by the way. That supports your observation about the similarities." He enjoyed bantering with her over fashion and architecture.

"I'm impressed you know that. Anyway, it gives you an idea." She shut the notebook. The tour was over.

"Thank you for that glimpse into your creative process. Keep going in that direction. You have talent."

"I appreciate that, Cooper." She picked up the binder to return it to its place.

He glanced at his watch. Almost eight. He didn't want to leave but didn't want to outstay his welcome either. Hard to guess. Jake still played a few yards away, either puttering like a car or growling like a lion.

Blair slipped back into her seat, as if she intended for him to stay awhile. He relaxed, feeling an invitation to prolong their time together. He'd stay in tune with her body language, so he'd sense when she was ready to boot him out.

"You told me a bit about your transition to Brenner Falls," he said. "Do you feel settled now?"

She pressed her lips together. "Getting there. Daily life with a child is pretty consuming. It doesn't leave much time for exploring, socializing, or leisure. But Jake and I do things together. We walk by the river after the market. In summer, we go kayaking or I take him to the kids' climbing wall at the Adventure Depot. He spends one weekend a month with his grandparents. He enjoys it and it's a big help for me."

"I'm sure it is. Why Brenner Falls? Did you have friends here or family?"

She shook her head. "No one. There are a couple of reasons I came here, aside from liking the town. I found a job here. And it's not far from my parents, yet Jake and I have our own space. I like that." She shrugged. "I love my family, but it's nice to have our own town."

"I imagine so." He did, even though he'd love to be in the same town with his parents. Her situation might be more difficult.

As if reading his mind, she said, "I don't quite fit in with my family, so it's better this way. I mean, they love me, but I'm not sure they really understand me."

Cooper remained silent, sensing Blair had more to say.

"I'm the third in a family of four kids. My older brother, Norris, is a financial advisor at an investment firm. My older sister is a pediatrician married to a chemist. My younger sister is an actuary married to a programmer." She paused. "Then there's me."

Understanding dawned on him. "You're the lone artist growing up in a left-brained universe."

"Exactly. Add to that the fact that I got pregnant out of wedlock. Doubly unacceptable."

"So, that's why you feel like you don't fit in." He held her gaze.

She nodded. "I went back to my parents' house during my pregnancy until Jake was two. After that, I got an apartment in town and worked in a bank. A terrible fit, by the way." She lowered her voice to a whisper. "I don't want Jake ever to think he'd caused me to lose my dreams."

She glanced over the back of the couch at Jake. "Don't get me wrong, my parents did so much for me when I wound up pregnant with no place to go. Of course, I had disappointed them. There I was, about to graduate and pursue my dream and *boom*! Everything fell apart. They stepped right in and helped. But I was tired of being dependent on them. Tired of living in their world. Feeling like I owed them so much. I wanted Jake and me to experience *our* world. *Our* family. That probably doesn't make sense to you."

"Of course, it does." Must have been hard being a flamingo swimming in a lake full of mallards. She was exotic, beautiful, sensitive. And misunderstood. "Is Jake's father in the picture?"

Blair hesitated. "No, he's not. At the time, I thought we'd get married, but he ended up denying paternity. I haven't seen him since that time."

"What a bum." Cooper glanced over the armchair and could see the top of Jake's blond head. "As I've said before, you've done great all by yourself."

"Thanks. I tend to think it's true, by God's grace."

"You guys are still talking?" Jake appeared beside Cooper. "I thought Cooper was gonna come see my truck. But now I'm playing something else."

"It's time for you to get ready for bed, big guy," Blair told him. Jake moaned. "Say goodnight to Cooper."

Cooper rose from the table. "I should get going so you guys can get ready for the week."

"Goodnight, Mr. Cooper. Say hi to Zipper. Will he be out tomorrow afternoon?"

"I'll make sure he is. Goodnight, Jake." He watched Jake disappear down the hall and gave his attention to Blair. "It was a great evening, Blair." She stood too. "Sorry I couldn't fix anything, though."

"You sure tried. It helps to know what's wrong and what to do."

He moved toward the arched doorway. "I'll keep you posted on the fuse. Won't take long to put it in. The chimney's another story. I'd call the landlord and tell him it needs to be cleaned. Maybe tell him it's for your safety. I'll be back to look at it outside." He shouldn't be standing there telling her what to do as if she couldn't figure it out. She deserved a ton of credit, that was for sure.

"Thanks again for everything." She looked disappointed the evening was ending. At least he wanted to interpret her expression that way.

He retrieved his toolbox, and Blair walked him to the door. They said goodnight and as he crossed the yard to his house, he recognized the mixed messages in his head. The *don't get involved* warning rose up like a neon sign in his head.

But it might be too late.

Chapter Eight

Blair parked in the gravel driveway Monday afternoon after picking up Jake at Angela's.

"There's Zipper on his leash," Jake called. "I'll be right back, Mom. I have to go say hi, since he's all alone."

Before Blair could respond, Jake had slipped out of the car and dashed across the yard. Zipper jumped at the sight of him.

Usually, she spent her workday laser-focused on the precision of her tasks at the sewing machine. Accuracy and safety were priorities. But that Monday, another image entered her mind far too frequently. Cooper's dark blue eyes connecting with hers across the table. She couldn't deny there was more to Cooper than rugged good looks. More than helpfulness and compassion. She felt at ease with him. Despite his occasional know-it-all suggestions, he was unassuming, as though she'd known him longer than a few weeks.

As though he wasn't miles out of her league.

Evidence of her comfort with him, she dumped out all her childhood angst. Probably should have held back, but he was such a good listener, so understanding. And he seemed to have his own burdens, though he hadn't been ready to talk about them. Losses, he'd said. Maybe he'd trust her enough to tell her one day.

Her wandering mind was evidence only of her craving for adult conversation. She shouldn't read more into her thoughts. Although she adored Jake, sometimes she missed that adult input. Cooper was a helpful neighbor. That was all. A friendly guy. She'd be wise to guard her heart, especially since the last time she'd given it away, she'd learned a painful lesson: Don't assume anything. As for Cooper, he'd only be around until he finished his house, then he'd be gone. Somewhere up the river, he'd said. And he likely wasn't looking for a woman with a child.

Time to get her thoughts back on track. She wasn't a teenager, after all, but a thirty-year-old single mother who had dinner to make and clothing to create. With a shake of her head, Blair got out of the car, dragging a bag behind her from the back seat. She continued to purchase irregular garments even though she still had two large bins remaining in the garage. They might not always be available, so she'd stock up. A pile of completed projects filled the corner of her living room. Maybe she'd sell the best ones with her regular market inventory.

Blair glanced over at Jake, still cuddling Zipper, who was lapping at his face. She grinned as Jake's giggles echoed across the yard. After snagging a handful of mail, she unlocked the door and went into the kitchen. Fortunately, that morning she'd remembered to move a container of spaghetti sauce from the freezer to the fridge to thaw. Since the stove had broken, she surveyed the freezer daily, thankful for her habit of cooking in bulk and sectioning off part of each meal to freeze for later.

Her gaze went to the pile of mail she'd dropped onto the kitchen table, lighting on a letter from her landlord, Donald Mitchell. Her pulse hitched. He was finally responding to her complaints about the stove, though why wouldn't he email her or call?

Blair ripped open the envelope, and a sweat beaded on her neck. She'd forgotten her lease term was up and it was time to renew. And with renewal came a rent increase. Hopefully not too much.

Her eyes zipped over the form letter and her heart thumped against her rib cage. *Dear renter, next month your lease will reach termination unless you desire to renew. Current market conditions dictate an increase in your rent effective the first of next month according to the amount listed in the space below —*

Her eyes widened and she drew in a sharp breath. Two-hundred and fifty dollars more. For a shack without a functioning fireplace or oven. Was this even legal? Blair sank into the chair, stunned into stillness. How on *earth* would she do this? She was struggling as it was to buy groceries, deal with rising utility prices, insurance. Let alone what Jake would need in days to come when school started. School clothing, supplies, outings...

She buried her face in her fists, willing the flood of panic in her chest to halt before it overtook her. "Lord, please help me. I know you can provide for me."

Blair controlled her breathing and relaxed her tight throat. Once her pulse returned to normal, she snatched her purse from the chair and fished for her phone. She punched Mr. Mitchell's phone number and, of course, had to leave a message. "Please call me as soon as you can, Mr. Mitchell. Thank you." She disconnected. What were the chances he'd made a mistake? Almost none. She'd have to find a way to earn more money.

While she pulled together a hasty supper, her mind groped for solutions. Would she have to move? The last thing she wanted to do was uproot Jake after only a year, pack up everything again, and look for new housing. Add to that, she'd miss Cooper, though she'd already decided he wasn't a factor. At all. Maybe she could work out an arrangement with Mr. Mitchell.

After supper, Jake helped Blair clear the table, as she'd taught him. "You can go practice your piano now. I'll finish here. Don't forget your lesson with Miss Leah tomorrow."

"I like going to Miss Leah's for lessons." His eyes danced and he dashed from the room.

Blair's smile fell as he disappeared around the corner. Thankfully, her parents paid for his lessons, so she wouldn't have to make him stop. Other budget items would have to go, but what could she cut? Everything was essential. She could buy less food, but how? Get into a co-op or find a cheaper grocery store?

As she rinsed and dried the dishes, her mind continued to churn. The phone rang. The words *Mitchell Landlord* popped up on her phone screen. Both relief and nervousness filled her throat as she answered.

"Hello, Mr. Mitchell. I received news about the rent increase today. I thought rent only increased a certain percentage per lease period, yet my increase is well above that." She kept her voice level, though she could almost hear her heart pounding.

"Ah, no, Miss McCartney. That's not the case. There is no cap in Pennsylvania or laws regulating rent increases. As your letter states, increases are driven by the market."

"What does that mean? It's not like the stock market. It's *your* decision what you charge."

"The market in Brenner Falls, Miss McCartney." Irritation laced the man's voice. "Prices all over the Falls are increasing, due to the influx of population, the shortage of housing, the improvements, and higher taxes in town. All that plays a role in housing prices."

"I'm not sure I can pay the increase. But I can't find other housing so quickly. Can I change to a month-to-month arrangement until I'm able to find a place to move?" No, she didn't want to move. The very thought of it caused a fresh wave of despair.

"If you like, though, your monthly rate will be even higher. The price quoted is for a locked-in lease for a year. Anytime you pay month-to-month, it costs more."

Blair moistened her lips. What else could she say? A spurt of boldness pushed her. "If I renew my lease, will you do the required repairs on my house? It's not safe here."

"It's perfectly safe. Having a broken oven doesn't constitute a danger to you."

"But I cannot *use* my oven, Mr. Mitchell. I told you about this last week and you ignored me. A friend looked at it and said it needs a thermal fuse. That's not a big deal. You can send someone to fix it. I'm sure you have a maintenance person on retainer, don't you?"

Mitchell chuckled, the sound grating through the phone. "Sure, sure. I'll get it done. Be patient. My maintenance team is tied up with more important matters than an oven."

"My fireplace is also dangerously clogged. It's loaded with creosote and other blockages. It's likely never been cleaned."

Now, instead of trepidation, anger frothed through her, fueling her words. "Remember, I have a young child living here, and even if I were alone, you'd be required to provide safe housing for me if you're willing to take my money."

"As long as you don't use your fireplace, it is not dangerous, Miss McCartney."

She sighed in frustration. "My lease states that you are *required* to keep appliances in good working order and keep the environment safe. Your negligence is putting my son and me at risk."

"If you're not happy there, you're free to move. Don't use the fireplace. I'll put your oven on my maintenance crew's calendar. If you decide to renew, send me your newly signed lease before the end of the month with your adjusted payment. Good evening, Miss McCartney."

Blair's mouth fell open to retort, but the man had disconnected. She stared at the phone as anger swirled inside her chest at the man's insolence. At his *power* over her. He owned the place and could do, or not do, whatever he pleased.

How would she manage? She didn't want to find a new home. She simply had to pay the increase, one way or another.

She turned out the kitchen light and went to the living room, notepad and paper in hand. Time for a brainstorming session.

Could she sell more products at the market? It was already only a small help. Too soon to ask for a raise at work. The fashion blog didn't even exist yet. She needed *immediate* income. What *else* could she do? Her creativity wasn't kicking in yet.

The previous year, she'd made some costumes for Seasons Dinner Theater when they had their Christmas gala. They might need help again, and she could also ask at the children's theater in town.

Blair jotted each idea that came to mind. She wrote Fashion Blog in the top margin. The blog would grow with time, an investment in her dream. A definitive statement she wasn't staying behind a sewing machine on an assembly line. But it could take years to gain traction and she needed income immediately.

One thing at a time. From where she sat on the couch, she saw Cooper's truck pull up in front of his house. He glanced toward her house for a moment, then walked toward where Zipper danced on his leash. She'd love to be as carefree as Zipper. Or even Jake.

Her gaze skimmed over the pile of irregulars in the corner. Her sales at the market were steady, but she had to work hard to have enough inventory. She'd have to sell her irregulars. So far, she'd mainly used them to experiment with new styles as prototypes. She'd take photos of them, then sell them. Once she had her website up, she'd give her market customers the address. It would take a lot of work upfront, but she'd be the one in control, not Mr. Mitchell. He'd only get *one* more year from her. This would give her a clear deadline to start earning from her designs. She'd better get busy.

Blair rose from the couch with renewed energy and knelt in front of the pile of garments she'd adapted for prototypes. She flipped through the stack, and with a wave of relief, realized she'd be able to sell almost all of them. She had until Saturday to make many more.

One more thing she'd do, as long as Mitchell was stirring her inner activist. She retrieved her phone and tapped Leah's number. "Hi, Leah. I hope I'm not bothering you."

"Not at all. How are you, Blair?" Leah's soothing voice had a calming effect on Blair's tangled emotions.

"We're still on tomorrow for Jake's lesson. I'm calling about something else. Today, I got news of a big rent increase. I was thinking of ways to get more income and our conversation came to mind. I feel nervous about starting an online store, but there's no time like the present."

"Oh, Blair. I'm sorry about your rent, and only a year after your arrival. I understand how you must be feeling. I lost my job a year ago and started teaching music. It's grown slowly, but it's good to be my own boss."

"Yes, I remember that. It's encouraging to realize there's more than one way to build a fashion design career." Blair slipped her pen behind one ear. "And honestly, the traditional way can take years too."

"I believe it. I know it's daunting to start something like this, but if you don't start, you won't be competitive with the rest of your industry. Give Nathan a call and he can walk you through the first steps. He explains things pretty well."

That was good news. Blair would need a child's level explanation of how to run an online business. "I'll call him. It's time."

"Let me know if there's anything else I can do to help."

"You've already been a big help just by listening. And loaning me Nathan for some marketing assistance."

Both women laughed. "It's pretty handy to have a marketing guy and a website guy—that would be my brother, Garrett—in my corner. They'll be in your corner too. Don't worry about that old landlord."

Though online business options had hovered in her mind for years, intimidation and lack of time had held her back. But now, she'd decided, and she had friends to help. Another doorway had opened. She was no longer at the mercy of her employer or her landlord.

ରେ   ରେ   ରେ

For the second Saturday in a row, Cooper left his house with Zipper to explore Brenner Falls. His framing team had continued at the house all week. As it took shape, his anticipation shot up. Though he loved to help others have their dream home, it was finally *his* turn.

A glance at Blair's empty house told him she was likely at the market. She might find it creepy if he just happened to saunter past her stand for the second week in a row. He didn't want her to think he was becoming a pest, even if part of him wanted to be.

He'd leave her alone, though could check with her later to see how her oven was functioning. He'd installed the thermal fuse for her on Tuesday, but hadn't lingered because she had to pick up Jake from piano lessons. After that, their schedules must have been opposite since he'd only seen her through her living room window as she sewed projects until late each night. Not that he was looking. Though technically, he couldn't avoid it since he still hadn't gotten curtains. Aside from that, Blair had become a magnet for him.

"C'mon, Zipper." He coaxed the dog out of the truck in the same parking lot where he'd parked the previous week. Zipper seemed overjoyed to have undivided time with Cooper, trotting down the sidewalks of the town instead of being leashed up under a tree.

Cooper covered the same streets as before, minus the market. Brenner Falls wasn't large, so it didn't take long, but he got thirsty. He passed Sophie's, a coffee shop. He'd never been there, but they might have cold drinks. A post by the door was ideal to attach Zipper for a few minutes. "Be right back, boy."

Inside, several café tables, all of them occupied, filled the space. A hum of conversation hung in the air, as did the sweet aroma of freshly baked waffle cones and roasted coffee beans. A row of painted shelves on the far walls displayed packaged cakes and snacks alongside local art pieces. He took a bottled drink from a refrigerator case and joined the line behind three people. While he waited, he scanned the room. Near the wall, a blond head caught his attention. Blair? What was she doing there? And where was Jake? And who was the guy at the table across from her?

It hadn't occurred to him she might be in a relationship. Cooper frowned. Wasn't any of his business anyway. He shot them another glance and noticed the guy was showing her something on a laptop. Might be some kind of business meeting.

He reached the cash register and paid for his drink.

"Cooper!" He turned and Blair waved at him, a smile on her face. She motioned him over. A good sign.

He crossed the room. "Hi Blair." He nodded to the guy.

"Nathan, this is my next-door neighbor, Cooper. He fixed my oven this week. This is Nathan Chisholm. He's my friend Leah's boyfriend. He's a marketing whiz, *and* he owns the Seasons Dinner Theater."

"Hi, Cooper." Nathan stood and shook Cooper's hand. "You sound like a perfect neighbor, fixing appliances and all."

"Nice to meet you, Nathan. Seasons is a beautiful building. I like Victorian homes."

"Thanks." Nathan chuckled. "I inherited it last year from my uncle and I wanted to unload it as soon as possible. I won't bore you with the whole story."

"It looks great, better than the last time I lived in the Falls." A steep understatement.

"We've just finished a series of renovations and reopened last month."

"Cooper's an architect and a builder," Blair explained to Nathan.

"I'd like to hear the story of Seasons someday." Cooper turned to Blair. "I thought you'd be at the market today."

"I spent the morning there but wanted to meet with Nathan this afternoon to talk about online business and marketing. You'll be happy to hear I'm taking the plunge. Since Jake's with his grandparents, it's a good time to get up to speed." She turned her focus to Nathan. "The other day Cooper also encouraged me to get my online presence updated. I'm hearing this from every direction." She widened her eyes and laughed. "I'm scared stiff."

Cooper grinned. "You got this. And you know the right people to help you."

"I'd never try otherwise. Can you join us? We're almost finished."

"Thanks, but Zipper's tied up outside." He hesitated. "Uh, I hope your week was good."

Blair's cheerful expression fell. "It started out terribly. I didn't tell you when you came by with the fuse. I got a *huge* increase in my rent."

"That scumbag." Cooper grimaced. "Keep a record of every conversation you have with him. You might be doing that already, but it crossed my mind to remind you. Record all your requests. You might need to prove his negligence one day."

She nodded. "Already done. I have a file with his name on it. I considered looking for another place to live, but just couldn't face it."

"So, she decided to dive into online business," Nathan said and turned the laptop screen his way. "New branding. What do you think of the logo Blair came up with?"

Cooper had to admit, the drawing of a spool of thread becoming a full dress was creative and attractive. He offered an approving nod. "I'm impressed."

"Thanks. I know it'll take time to make money. For now, I'm trying to sell more at the market. I sold a lot of my inventory today, so I'm jazzed about that."

"That's great. Well, I'll leave you to your discussion. Nice meeting you, Nathan. Blair, tell me if you have any more issues with your oven."

"So far, so good." She crossed her fingers. "I was able to roast a chicken last night. I owe you twenty dollars for the part."

Cooper waved her statement away. "Just invite me next time you make a roast chicken, and we'll call it even."

He left the shop as relief trickled through him. Why was he so relieved that Nathan wasn't a date? He sighed. Blair had definitely gotten under his skin, against his better judgment.

Her increased rent filled him with irritation. Not only was Mitchell negligent, but he'd raised Blair's rent to a crushing level without fixing a thing. Cooper made a mental note to ask Mayor Faulkner what her rights were once he got around to meeting with the man. Work on the site had been intense, so he hadn't yet called for an appointment.

He had the means to help Blair financially, but there was no point in offering. He knew what she'd say, and it would damage the budding friendship they were developing. But how would she manage?

Yet, he knew she would. He'd seen the iron determination on her face, noted the steps she'd taken despite her fears.

At least she'd decided not to move. A wave of gratitude accompanied that thought. He still wanted to look at the chimney from the outside. And her roof and her gutters. Another excuse to visit Blair.

Chapter Nine

The next day after church, Blair followed Leah back to her house. After the women ate a light lunch, Blair worked at the dining room table with Leah's brother, Garrett, a website designer who ran his own business. He explained how online commerce worked and spent two hours helping her map out her site design and strategy. Finding a name wasn't difficult since she'd dreamed for years about her own label. She'd call it BlairWear Designs.

She'd taken advantage of Jake's absence that weekend to lay important groundwork for her business, though that term wouldn't fit for a while. At the market the previous day, she'd sold almost all her completed prototypes, her most profitable day ever. Having more merchandise might be the temporary answer to her increased rent.

By the time she drove to her parents' home in Milton to pick up Jake, she felt inflated with hope. Though her head was spinning with new information, she'd taken the first step.

On the drive home, Jake chattered about what he'd done over the weekend. When they arrived, Blair helped him unpack his small dinosaur print backpack. "Got any dirty laundry in there, big guy?"

"I played in the sandbox and with the dogs next door."

Blair smirked. "I take that as a *yes*, then. Be careful of dogs you don't know. Remember when I told you that?"

"I remember. Grandpa was there and told me it was okay."

"Alright, if Grandpa was there. What's this?" She found an envelope sticking out of an inside pocket of Jake's backpack. Jake shrugged.

She turned over the envelope and her pulse ratcheted up. It was from Nelson. Her mother must have snuck it into Jake's bag so he or Blair would find it. Nelson hadn't shown a sign of life since Jake's birthday party nearly a month ago. She'd been relieved that following her explanation to Jake, he hadn't brought up the subject of his father again.

Nelson had addressed the letter to Jake. It showed his full return address in Harrisburg, Pennsylvania. Just over an hour away. Apparently, Nelson assumed Jake knew all about him.

She'd read it first, then consider what to do. Should she open herself to the possibility of Jake meeting his dad, despite the pounding in her ribcage at the thought of it? Dread and terror shot through her. Jake might be fine, but Blair wasn't sure *she* could handle it just yet.

"What's the letter, Mom?"

"Um, it's a letter your Nanna put in your suitcase. I'll read it first, then share it with you, okay?"

"'Kay." Jake opened his mouth wide with a long yawn.

"How about an early night tonight, big guy? You've had a busy weekend."

For once, Jake didn't argue, but just nodded and yawned again.

Once Blair tucked Jake in and heard his prayers, she slipped into the kitchen with the letter in slick hands. The previous year, Nelson had addressed his letter to her. Motivated by panic and stale anger, Blair moved to Brenner Falls as soon as she could. No chance she'd let Nelson find out where they lived.

When she didn't answer his first letter, he went silent until last month during Jake's birthday party. Blair had hoped he'd drop the idea of meeting Jake, but no such luck. Instead, he became bolder, writing a letter to Jake himself. There was a time she might have been angry, but fear and guilt wrestled inside. Did Nelson have the right to meet Jake? Her mother had always liked Nelson and had been disheartened by his behavior when Blair got pregnant. For Blair, Nelson had cancelled himself from their lives when he refused his son.

But that was eight years ago. He'd apologized, hadn't he? Maybe she should allow Jake to meet his dad. But she had such a loving, healthy relationship with her son. Would she put that at risk by bringing an unknown parent into the mix? It was a big gamble to take. And Nelson lived close enough to want to take Jake for weekends or visit him regularly.

Blair's stomach tightened. She waved at the air as if forcing calm into her pounding heart and tried to silence the what ifs flooding her mind. But she could at least *read* what he'd written.

With trembling hands, she opened the envelope and drew out a single sheet.

Hi Jake, We don't know each other yet, but I'm your father. I'm sorry we haven't been able to meet. I'm sorry I wasn't there for your birth and the first years of your life. There are a lot of reasons in the past for that, and I regret all of them. I'd like to meet you sometime. I would like to become your friend. I work as a graphic artist for a big company in Harrisburg, which is the capital of Pennsylvania. I don't live very far from you. I hope you and your mom will allow us to meet one day. I'd really like that. Sincerely, your dad, Nelson.

Blair stared at the letter and some of her armor slipped. He sounded approachable. Even kind. Before their hostile breakup, he *had* been kind, gentle, funny. But he'd been scared and selfish too. And he'd abandoned her.

He might have included facts about himself for her benefit. What should she do? She folded her arms on the kitchen table and rested her forehead on them. With a deep sigh, she prayed. *Father, oh Father, what should I do? I'm afraid. I'm scared of losing the quality of life I have with Jake. I don't want Nelson to mess him up in any way. But what do you want me to do, Lord? Is my mom correct in saying he has the right to meet Jake? Am I wrong or selfish for wanting to protect the little boy you gave me?*

For wanting things just as they were with no risk, no need to trust?

She stayed in that position for nearly ten minutes when she sensed rather than heard a word come into her head. *Forgive.* She lifted her head and pressed her lips together in defiance. Forgive? No way...

Then she dropped her shoulders. Her eyes stung. *Lord. I'll try. Please help me.* She had no choice. Not only had he instructed her to forgive Nelson, but she'd seen those words in her Bible, words she'd tried *not* to apply to Nelson. God had forgiven *her*. She could do no less. But did that mean she had to let Nelson meet Jake?

One thing at a time. Forgive him. Another prayer followed the first. She moistened her lips. *Lord, I lay down at your feet the anger and hurt I've had against Nelson all these years. Maybe I'll never see Nelson, but I know you want me to release him from everything he did.*

She swallowed. Blinked a few times. *I forgive him for cheating on me, for not recognizing Jake, and for not honoring the commitment I thought we had together. I release him, Lord. I know you have great plans for Jake and me, and I pray your protection on Jake. On us. Thank you, Lord.*

Blair leaned back against the kitchen chair. Tears rolled down her cheeks. So many years later, she could still feel the pain of Nelson's rejection and the terror of facing pregnancy alone. She'd decided back then that she *would* do it alone and never let Nelson near Jake.

Now, she felt lighter, painless, as if she looked at herself from afar. God had provided, protected. He would continue to do so. Maybe it was *her* turn to take the next step in trust, as she'd done with her business. As he required in every area.

The lightness, the clean feeling stayed with Blair as she got Jake ready for Angela's the next day and as she sat at her sewing machine at the factory. God would carry them, as he always had. And now, having forgiven Nelson, nothing blocked the channels of God's guidance and blessing. She still didn't know what to do about the letter, but she'd share it with Jake and then she'd know.

After her workday, Blair stood by her front door in the baking sun, angling water from a hose onto the boxwoods, petunias, herbs, and zinnias. She planned to share the letter with Jake after dinner. Next door, Zipper lay in the shade of the porch while Jake scratched his ears and talked to him. Under different circumstances, she'd get him his own dog, but in the meantime, this was ideal. As she watched them, Cooper's truck pulled up. She waved at him. He exited the truck, greeted Jake, and patted Zipper's head, then crossed the yard to her.

"How's the online entrepreneur doing?"

She cut the water flow and let the hose drop in the grass. "Ah, you'll never believe it. I now have a domain name, a website, and a few nuts and bolts in my head for this thing."

"Fantastic." He looked genuinely pleased. His face showed a deeper tan, and a few new freckles peppered his nose. "Let me know when it's live. I'll take a look."

"Absolutely. Leah's brother Garrett is making the website. Should be ready in a few days. Leah and Garrett both go to my church. Want to be my first subscriber? Oh, I take that back. I'd be too embarrassed."

Cooper laughed. "Do you actually think I know *anything* about fashion? I'm your perfect subscriber. I'll cheer you on without reading a thing."

"That works." Silence fell for a moment as they shared a smile.

He held up a finger and jogged back to unhook Zipper. The dog sprang off the porch and pranced around the yard as Jake dodged and ran circles around him. Cooper returned to her side. "I know how we can celebrate your new business." He waved toward his truck. "In my truck, I have two things that will interest you. Or rather, one that'll interest Jake and another that'll interest me and possibly you too."

"I'm intrigued now."

Jake came to where they stood, and Zipper joined them.

"I have a fire ring—"

"Yay!" Jake jumped up and down. "You weren't kidding."

"I'm always serious in my promises, young man," Cooper said with mock gravity. "*And* I have a half a cow."

"What?" Blair's eyes widened.

Cooper laughed at the look on her face. "I bought a side of beef, and it's all cut up into steaks. I like to do that once every couple of years and keep them in the freezer. So, I'm inviting you and Jake to enjoy a steak with me tonight. We can eat, then sit around the fire ring for ice cream."

"Can we, Mom?" Jake pulled on the hem of her tunic.

"I don't see why not. What can we bring?"

"Nothing. If I recall, you made a wonderful meal for me last week. Now I'd like to do one for you." Cooper's blue eyes twinkled. "I have potatoes, salad stuff. Even ice cream."

""Fire and ice cream." Jake jumped again.

"Sounds perfect, doesn't it, Jake?" Blair looked down at her son, who appeared as though he'd just won the lottery. Sounded perfect to her as well. An evening with Cooper around a fire.

"I'll get cleaned up and you guys can come over in an hour, okay?"

"Perfect. I'll be happy to help with dinner if you're in need of a sous chef."

One side of his mouth quirked, and his eyes blazed an even darker blue. "I may just take you up on that. See you in an hour."

ભ ભ ભ

Cooper combed his fingers through wet hair and slipped into a pair of long cargo shorts and a T-shirt. He pulled off the shirt and selected a navy blue short-sleeve shirt with buttons. Still relaxed, but not as sloppy looking. He was casual to the core, but still knew how to clean up. Especially when he'd invited a woman to his home for dinner. Anticipation for the evening swirled inside him.

He had to admit to himself that too often, thoughts of Blair hovered in the wings of his mind, whether he worked at home or the crew at the build. He enjoyed talking to her, but sensed there was more. But what was he to her? She'd sent no negative signals so far. They saw one another randomly throughout the week. That was fine, since his intuition told him he might be opening a door to more hurt, just when he was healing.

Right on time, she knocked at his front door. He swept it open, and her beauty caused his breath to hitch. She'd changed clothes and wore a pink tunic with matching leggings, *and* a necklace and earrings. She'd left her glasses at home, giving him a full view of her wide hazel eyes and flawless skin. Hope led him to conclude all her efforts were for him.

She thrust a bundle of something green into his hands. "I couldn't think of anything to bring, so I thought you might appreciate some fresh herbs. This is basil and that's oregano."

He took the herbs from her. "You have time to cultivate herbs? How do you do that?"

She laughed, a lovely melodious sound. "They actually grow all by themselves. I water them. That's all."

"Thanks for these, though you didn't have to bring anything. You contribute just by being here."

She smiled and lowered her eyes.

"Where's Jake?"

"Playing catch with Zipper. He'll be in soon."

His gaze followed Blair's as she observed his simple home. At least it was neat, though plain. Still no curtains. As a designer, she might think he lacked basic taste. What he lacked was interest in embellishing a temporary dwelling.

"Your home is pleasant. Cozy."

"I'm still getting settled. I need curtains and a few other things."

"You'll just have to move everything to the new house once it's built."

"I'm saving décor for over there. I'll enlist your help when the time comes."

"Gladly. I like the open concept here." She waved one hand toward the kitchen-great room combination. "And it's not falling apart like mine."

He offered a sympathetic look. "We'll work on that." He moved toward the island in the kitchen. "Did you talk to your landlord about the chimney?"

"Yes, and his answer was to not use it."

"I expected that. Would you like something to drink? I have sparkling water, beer, diet soda."

"Water's great. So, put me to work."

He handed her a frosted bottle of water and a glass. "You can wrap these potatoes in foil. I already scrubbed them. I'll cut some tomatoes." He handed her a roll of foil and fished a knife from the drawer, content to be working alongside her, instead of chatting in the yard or hoping they'd cross paths in town.

"Sounds like things are looking up with your market sales." Cooper set a cutting board on the island a few feet away from her and sliced several tomatoes into chunks.

"It's better than before." Her eyes became animated. "At the factory where I work, sometimes they have garments that are damaged and don't meet inspection standards. Recently, I started buying them cheap from my employer. That's why I wanted to clean the garage, so I could store them there. So, I fix them, if possible, then add my own touches. I could add different sleeves, a different hemline, buttons, contrasting fabric, whatever I can do to make them cute and unique. Then I sell them."

"What a great idea." Cooper gave her an appreciative nod. "So, that gives you more to sell." He slid the tomatoes into the bowl.

"Right. My table's full of merchandise now, and that draws more people. My original idea was to use irregulars for prototypes. But when my rent went up, I decided to sell the prototypes I'd made." She frowned. "It's not really a permanent solution, though. My market sales fell last winter, and the market shuts down altogether from mid-December to early February."

"You'll have a solution before then." He hoped his statement wasn't an empty promise of a someday blessing. But given her determination, she was bound to come up with an idea between now and then. "Maybe by that time, your website'll begin paying off."

"Huh. It'll take a while."

"Do you have ideas for making money from it?"

"Garrett gave me a few. I could sell products from other vendors and get an *affiliate* commission. Nathan's very knowledgeable about marketing." She moved a lock of blond hair from her forehead with one wrist. "If I had a big enough following, I could have ads and get income that way. I've been observing the fashion blogs I follow. Lots of them use links from existing companies and products. I suppose I could do that initially, though ultimately, I want to sell my own collections."

"One step at a time."

The front door burst open. "Zipper's getting tired," Jake said. "He just sat down when I threw a stick for him to fetch." He stood near the island. His round face was rosy and moist with exertion, and his blond curls stuck out in all directions.

Cooper laughed. "I think that's his way of saying it's dinnertime. Would you like to feed him?"

"Sure, can I?"

"See that tall cupboard there? On the floor inside you'll see a big bag of food with a scooper inside. Give him a scoop and a half into his green bowl."

Jake followed Cooper's instructions. "Maybe he'll want to play some more after he eats." Zipper wolfed down his food as his tail wagged. "He loves it."

"We'll have our own feast in a little while." Blair finished wrapping the last potato. She took a fork and poked holes through the foil into each one. "Jake, is there something you can bring to do while the steaks cook? I don't want you to get bored, and it'll take a few minutes."

Good idea. Cooper enjoyed Jake, but craved time talking to his mother.

Soon, the three of them sat outside on the paved patio he'd installed the previous year. Thick steaks sizzled on the grill. Although Jake had brought over a couple of comic books, Zipper had recovered his energy and resumed entertaining him.

"How is your house project coming along?" Blair sat near the grill on a woven lawn chair. Did him good to see her enjoying the evening air without responsibilities hitting her on every side. A mild summer breeze flowed around them. Having seared the outside of the steaks, Cooper closed the lid of the grill. Smoke scented the air and swirled upward, dispersing into the leaves overhead.

"Framing's going pretty fast." He placed the tongs on the grill table and settled in a chair beside her. "It's amazing what they've done in three or so weeks."

"When will they finish framing?"

"There's a little more to do, but we should be able to put on the roof by next week."

"Wow, I know nothing, but that seems fast to me."

"I've hired most of these guys before. They're reliable and work fast."

"How do you know them?"

"From projects I did when I lived here before. Then I got references for additional subcontractors, and lined them up before I moved here."

"Sounds efficient."

"Unless something unforeseen happens, yes."

"Then we won't be neighbors anymore, I guess." She offered a wistful shrug.

"We'll still be friends, though. I'm pretty sure of that." At his words, their gazes locked. Warmth stirred deep inside him. "And it's close to here. I'll take you over there once there's more to see."

"I'd like that."

An idea sparked. "I can show you a mock-up drawing on my computer. Like we talked about the other day."

"Oh, yes. Your house prototype."

"Something like that." Cooper rose. "It's a few more minutes before I have to flip the steaks."

He dashed inside to his office and pulled his laptop from the desk. He returned and sat on the lawn chair next to her. "Here we are," he mumbled as he opened the program, then the image. They leaned toward the screen. A sweet floral scent wafted from her hair, setting off a hum inside him.

"Wow," she said. "*That's* the house you're building? How *beautiful*." Her gaze found his again, but their faces were nearly close enough to touch.

Cooper nodded, pleased at her response to the design, while his heart raced at her nearness.

"I'm impressed," she said. "I love this design. Those windows..."

"They'll look right out at the river. There'll be trees in front, for beauty and privacy, but I should be able to see the water even in summer when the trees are full of leaves."

"Can't wait to see it all complete." Her eyes met his. "I have the feeling it's not just a house for you."

"You're right." His voice dropped. "I've always wanted to build my own home, but this design came to me three years ago. It kind of represents..." He paused. "Stability." Along with hope and healing. His throat felt raw. Her expression softened even though she didn't know how much loss his words conveyed.

He rose to open the grill, blinking, though not from the smoke.

When he sat, Blair quietly stared at the screen. What was she thinking? Were her own dreams light years away? His heart tightened as he watched her.

"All done?" he asked. She nodded, and he took the laptop from her. He returned it to the house then hurried back to the small patio. "Almost ready." He sat beside her again.

Jake appeared between their chairs. "I'm hungry, Mom."

"Jake, you don't say that when you're invited—"

"It's okay," Cooper said. "We're a little late, big guy, thanks to work and stuff. But it's about done. Do you like steak?"

"I think so." He looked at his mother. "Do I like steak?"

Blair and Cooper laughed. "I don't think you've ever eaten any, except maybe at Nanna's house."

"Oh, yeah. I can't remember if I liked it."

"He can try a small chunk and let us know."

Cooper liked the way she said, *us.*

The sun slipped down in the sky, unfurling ribbons of pink and blue across the horizon. Cooper took the plate of steaks inside and, after setting the table, they settled in front of the large picture window. The same one that allowed him to view what Blair and Jake were up to each evening, though he wouldn't tell her that.

Turned out, Jake liked steak, and told Cooper several times. The salad, not as much, but that was fine. Blair gave him a small amount to try. "I'll clean up here and then we'll have our ice cream around the fire ring, okay, Jake?"

"Fire and ice cream," Jake chanted.

"Next time, we can do smores."

Blair helped Cooper clear the table amidst his protest. Finally, they settled with large bowls of ice cream around a sputtering fire, which lit all their faces with a dancing orange glow.

"Without the ice cream, I think we'd get hot around this fire," Cooper said.

"You're good at starting fires. Look at that." Blair licked her spoon as she watched the flames leap up.

"Can I have more ice cream?" Jake asked.

"No, sweetie," Blair said. "We'll have to leave pretty soon."

Jake let out a loud groan and took off after Zipper.

"Where does he get his energy?" Blair murmured.

She and Cooper exchanged a smile, and she fell silent, staring into the fire for a few minutes. He wished he knew what she was thinking. It was too soon to simply ask her.

Finally, she turned a serious gaze to him. "Cooper, I need your advice about something."

"Sure, what's up?" He tensed, not sure whether he'd be glad for her confidence.

She swept a glance at Jake. "It's about Jake's dad. I, um, didn't tell you everything about him. I told you he's never met Jake. For six years, he never contacted me. Not a word. Not to find out about his child or how I was doing, or anything. Then, out of the blue a little over a year ago, he wrote a letter to me and mailed it to my parents' house in Milton. He didn't know my address because we were living in another apartment by that time." Her chest lifted as she drew a long breath. "In the letter, he said he'd changed. He realized he was Jake's dad and wanted to meet him. He apologized for denying him before and wanted a second chance."

Heavy fingers of something dark crept through Cooper's stomach. Had Jake's dad already pulled Blair out of his reach, after six years of silence? He silently rebuked himself. Here she was asking for his advice as a friend, and his first response was selfish desire and jealousy. He blinked. "Did you respond to him?"

She shook her head. "No, I was still angry. I was determined he wouldn't get anywhere near Jake. Sure, he'd had a change of heart, but that didn't change the fact that I had to do everything alone for all those years. I had to face my family alone. I had to go through labor and delivery alone, as well as deal with a newborn. My parents were a help, of course, but Nelson—that's his dad—should have been there with me."

Cooper silently agreed. Anger sparked on her behalf. "Did you hear from him again?"

"I didn't hear anything for a year. In the meantime, we moved to the Falls. But for Jake's birthday last month, he sent several gifts to my parents' house, so I had to tell Jake about him." She looked back at Cooper, her eyes shadowed by the fire. "I'm ashamed to say I hadn't told him yet. So, a few weeks ago I did. He asked some questions, but then seemed to lose interest. I was relieved. Then last weekend, Jake came home after visiting his grandparents for the weekend. There was a letter in his bag to him from Nelson. My mom had tucked it in there. I read it. He said again he wants to get to know Jake."

She looked away and her jaw tightened. "God showed me I still had a lot of anger and he wanted me to forgive Nelson. I... I forgave him. I tried, anyway. And I prayed for wisdom about what to do next."

"Forgiveness is essential, for *your* sake," he said. Her gaze found his. "But it doesn't mean you have to see him, unless you decide that's what you want to do."

"I know. I feel lighter and better since forgiving him, but I still have to decide whether to let Nelson into our lives. My mother thinks I don't have the right to keep him from his son. I'm scared to death to have them meet." Her gaze traveled to where Jake sat on the front step, Zipper curled at his feet. "He's such a happy, sweet boy. I don't want to jeopardize that."

"It's a tough decision." How would he give her advice? If Jake were his, he'd want to do the same thing, keep him protected from potential harm and confusion. "Did you let Jake read the letter?"

She shook her head. "I was going to do it tonight. So, maybe tomorrow." Her eyes cut to his. "I'd much rather be here than at home with Jake and the letter." After a breath, she said, "I thought as a first step I could let Jake read the letter tell me if he wanted to see his dad or not. Maybe he's too young for that decision."

Cooper scrubbed one hand over his jaw. "If I were in Nelson's place, I'd want to have that chance." What was he saying? He was encouraging her to meet with her ex, to have Jake meet his dad. Yet, what if it was the right thing to do? "But you said let Jake decide, not Nelson. Like you said, talk to Jake first to see if he's interested. If you want it to go slower, you could have them write to each other initially before meeting."

"That's a good idea. It'll break the ice. We can do emails." She drew her knees up under her chin and encircled them with her arms.

He wanted to protect her from pain, from Nelson, from facing this stress alone. But that would only muddy her turbulent waters. He still didn't know what she felt for him.

Or if his heart could bear possibly losing her to Nelson.

"So, you think I should open this door?" Her eyes reflected a sparkle from the flames.

"Ask Jake first. Let him read the letter. If you decide to let them meet, I don't mind coming with you if that'll help. I can sit nearby, or you can introduce me as your friend. Let him think whatever he wants."

She swallowed. "That's quite a service. You're a special friend, Cooper." She reached out and took his hand. He squeezed back and couldn't stop himself from running his thumb along the edge of her palm.

She held his gaze and didn't remove her hand. "I'm touched you'd offer to do that for me." Her tone softened. "I need to think and pray more about this, but I'll tell Jake first."

"Keep me posted. The offer stands."

She pulled her hand away. "Thank you. And thanks so much for this lovely evening." She stood, and he followed. "It was wonderful, but we need to go. It's getting late."

The firelight bathed her face and arms in a golden glow. They looked at each other for a moment. He reached out and touched her bare arm. Maybe she'd consider it a gesture of support. Probably unwise, but he couldn't help himself.

Jake and Blair thanked him again and said goodnight. They made their way across the small swatch of grassy lawn separating their houses. Emptiness howled through him for a moment. His thoughts tumbled inside his brain. Had he really volunteered to be an accomplice in a potential reconciliation with Nelson? And he'd even offered to pose as a significant other.

What if he truly wanted to *be* one for her? It would be far better to back off to a neighbor-friend category. Then when Blair and her former love reconnected, Cooper wouldn't be destroyed all over again.

The danger to his heart had just multiplied to a critical level.

Chapter Ten

Jake had gone to bed twenty minutes earlier, so the house was quiet. Morning would come too soon, but Blair wasn't tired. On the contrary. All her senses tingled with energy.

She removed her makeup and scrubbed her face. It had been a long time since she'd done anything special to her appearance for a man's sake.

Sharing her burden with Cooper had been inappropriate, but the decision suffocated her, and she'd needed input. Though she had a few budding friendships in Brenner Falls, such as Leah, she'd always kept her background with Nelson under wraps, as though talking about him would make him an active part of her story.

Now, he'd emerged from a dormant cupboard of the past and suddenly, he was front of mind. A problem to solve. Despite forgiving him, a thread of frustration at his sudden appearance chafed at her. She didn't need a fresh problem, the past invading the peaceful life she tried so hard to create with her son.

Cooper's words had provided reassurance against her runaway fears. Helpfulness was his nature. But was she his project, a problem to solve, as she was for her family? And here, she'd given him a new issue. Maybe he had no feelings for her except compassion.

Yet when they'd said goodnight, he'd touched her arm, whisper soft. Had he meant something other than comfort and support? Whatever it meant to him, his tenderness had touched a place deep inside her. But it had also added kindling to the smoldering fire that had grown little by little since the night he came for dinner.

She turned out the bathroom light, but instead of going to her bedroom, she returned to the dark living room. She slipped into the armchair, enfolded in darkness. Her gaze roved through the window to Cooper's house, where a faint light still burned inside. The yard where they'd all sat only an hour earlier lay dark, except for a faint glow of coals and wispy spire of smoke from the fire ring.

Cooper appeared at the picture window and stared out. He held a glass of something, but his stance seemed pensive. Was he still thinking about what she'd told him, or was he merely planning out his next day's tasks?

Her eyes swept over his silhouette, his broad shoulders, his narrow hips, the curve of his muscular arms. Several times during their evening, she'd longed to feel those arms around her, to hide in his strength. She'd wanted to touch his face, the bit of stubbly beard that shadowed his jaws.

Everything she knew of him seemed solid, trustworthy. And a man of faith. Of course, she'd been deceived in the past. Men were fallible, weak, even when they tried hard to show the world the opposite. Cooper had failings, for sure. And secret burdens. Each time she watched him interact with Jake, warmth pooled inside her.

Cooper bent his head for a full minute, almost in an expression of mourning. Then he lifted his head and looked directly at her window. She shrank back into the chair. Silly, there was no way he could see her. He raked one hand through his hair, then dropped his arm, turned, and left. A minute later, the light went out.

He'd be getting ready for bed now, preparing to work the next day on his dream home. A home more beautiful than any she'd ever seen. It wasn't enormous, but full of artistic details—a stone façade outside and roof-height stone fireplace inside—a home like she'd never have. His dream home was in progress. *Her* dream home was simply imaginary, like the rest of her dreams.

Seeing his design had planted a longing inside her she'd been unable to quell. She'd hidden the intensity of her response, verbally admiring the mockup of the exterior and the digital tour of the inside. Her pain hovered as a concept—home—more than a structure. Belonging. Acceptance and love. Security without the daily angst of providing, making sure of every last thing, preparing for problems, disasters, the lack or shortage of necessities.

Blair sighed a soulful breath into the quiet room. There was so much she couldn't have. Not yet anyway. Maybe not ever. The love of a decent man, a comfortable, safe home where she could invite people, the ability to freely work on her dreams without having to punch a clock. No use even thinking about it.

She caught herself. *Lord, I am thankful for what you've done for me. All you've given. I'm sorry for letting my thoughts go down the wrong road, the road of lack and self-pity.* Were her longings wrong? Maybe not, but no good could come from dwelling on them.

℃ ℃ ℃

The workers finished the framing in record time. Drills, nail guns, and other noisy tools were quiet now. Laughter and conversation filled the void as the workers finished for the day.

Cooper moved the phone to his other ear. "Yeah, I'm sorry I disappeared yet again," he said. "Forgive me, Amber?" He sensed his sister was genuinely annoyed with him this time. He'd kept in touch a time or two by phone or text, but it had been a couple of weeks since their evening at The Grateful Fork with her friends. He'd begun to settle in, planned to hang out with her more often. But then, he'd zoned out because of the job, and Blair.

Blair. As if he didn't have enough preoccupation with the woman herself, this new situation had his gut tied in knots. He knew she'd eventually see the guy, Nelson, face to face. Jake's dad, her former love. Would a new spark arise between them? Would it be Priya all over again, telling Cooper how sorry she was? That he was a great guy, but not for her?

122

Good thing he hadn't let things go too far with Blair, despite his desires. Not too late to guard his heart. If it was meant to be, it would be. He could simply tell her how he felt, but it was too soon.

And too late.

"Are you listening to me, Cooper?" A thread of irritation scuttled through Amber's normally easygoing voice.

He chuckled. "Yes, sorry. There's a lot of noise here. I should have called you from home." But would his thoughts be any quieter, just because he'd be off the work site? "Let's get together soon. You free tonight? We can get something quick."

"I'm doing low-carb this week, so can you come by for salad?"

"I can, but I'll bring my own food. Salad doesn't feed a grown man working construction all day."

Amber laughed. "I guess you have a point there. There's a fair amount of protein in my salad, but you may want a burger too. I won't be offended. See you when?"

"I can come straight over if you don't mind a dirty brother. It'll save us time."

"No worries. I have experience with dirty brothers. They don't scare me."

They laughed.

Actually, Cooper was pretty clean, having started working later that day. He'd snagged an early morning appointment with Dennis Faulkner, the mayor of Brenner Falls. He was glad to meet the man and learn more about his plans for the town in terms of housing and other projected buildings. Brenner Falls had notched up in Cooper's mind as a wise place to settle. He'd known it was growing and on the move. Faulkner was a visionary, but also appeared to appreciate what Cooper brought to the town. Cooper's contribution hadn't yet begun, but he had a multitude of ideas, like the mayor himself. Having opened an amicable door to the town's leader had been a good move that would open other doors in the future.

"See you in a bit, sis." Cooper disconnected, then waved to the team as he headed toward his truck. He ought to unleash Zipper first but didn't plan to stay long at Amber's. He wanted to see her anyway, but also needed to smooth her feathers. After all, she was one of the main reasons he'd moved to the Falls.

Amber's cheerful blue and white home came into view. Several potted geraniums still bathed in the golden glow of late afternoon as he parked.

"That was quick." She opened the screen door and hugged him, then followed with an affectionate swat on his head. "And that's for abandoning me again."

He could tell by the way her mouth tipped up and the mischievous sparkle in her eyes that she wasn't angry. She'd changed from her PT scrubs into long shorts and a tank top. Her dark hair swung from a high ponytail, making her look ready for a college volleyball game.

Cooper's stomach growled, thanks to an enticing aroma that arose from the paper bag containing two hamburgers. George's had quickly become his go-to place for burgers, take-out or not.

"I hear you're hungry," she quipped. "Let's eat." She pulled the salad from the fridge and got them drinks. "How's the house coming along?"

They sat at the nook of her sun-soaked, eat-in kitchen, as a late summer breeze floated in through open windows, swelling the sheer curtains. As they ate, he filled her in on the house progress. "I hope to get the roof on by the end of the week."

"Wow, that seems fast." Amber sipped from a bottle of sparkling water.

"Yeah, that's what Blair said."

"And who's Blair?" Amber had stopped eating and peered at him with full attention. A curious smile tipped one side of her mouth.

"Uh, my neighbor. We're friends." Way to open a big mouth. He rubbed his napkin too long over his chin, hoping to hide the color that must be creeping up his warm cheeks.

"Hmm. If I had to guess, I'd say Blair is a very *interesting* friend, by the look on your face."

He threw a glance toward the ceiling. "Pesky sister." How much should he say? "Like I said, she's my neighbor and friend." And if he were smart, he'd keep it that way, back to waving across the driveway.

"And you're interested in her," Amber prompted. "I'm glad, by the way."

Cooper gave her a patient pause. "It's too soon to have this conversation. I'm not ready for a romance anyway. That's not why I came to the Falls." He took a swig of tea, knowing his bluster didn't match his heart. But it was for the best. "How 'bout I keep you posted, but otherwise, don't ask?"

Amber let out a defeated sigh. "Okay, fair enough. Promise to keep me posted?"

"I'll think about it." He gave her a fake grimace, then grinned. She threw a napkin at him.

As it turned out, Amber's salad was tasty and, as she'd promised, full of protein. He only ate one hamburger and would have the second one for breakfast.

"There's a new group you might like over at The Fork Friday night. Are you free? Country rock this time, I think. It's a local group, but I hear they're not bad."

"For a local group, you mean? Sure, I'd like to come. Six-thirty for dinner?"

"Yup. You know the drill." She gave him a tight squeeze at the door. "I'm glad you're coming, bro. And I'm glad about Blair."

He waved off her words. "See you Friday. Hope the rest of your week is good."

He hoped the same for himself. In the meantime, he'd push the mental noise about Blair and her ex aside.

ɞ   ɞ   ɞ

Blair leveled a serious stare at Garrett across Leah's kitchen table. She heard Jake's piano scales float in from the living room. "This is a lot to take in, Garrett. I hope I can keep up with it."

Leah's brother laughed. "You'll do great, Blair. Everyone has to develop a system to maintain it all. You'll get there."

She let out a breath. "I guess it'll sink in, eventually."

"Look, you've already got some content here. You've got some photos lined up. You can upload the pics and take some of your own. Post regularly. That's important." He cocked his head full of brown surfer curls. "You'll get a routine."

Garrett had given her the assignment of coming up with ten ideas for posts before meeting with him again. At least she didn't have to write them yet, just get the ideas. That had been easy. She'd write her posts on Sunday afternoons, the only moment of the week that life calmed down. She'd pick a day to post them. Then she'd be patient.

"You can even do some of your social media posts in advance and schedule them. They'll go out automatically."

Seeing her widened eyes, he added, "Nathan can guide you on that. I'm no expert in marketing, but I'm here for you if you run into any tech issues with your website."

"My website," she said reverently. "I like the sound of that."

"Mom, we're done." Jake's exuberant voice sailed through the air.

"He had a great lesson." Leah's soft voice followed as she entered the dining room. "He's about ready for the recital."

Blair's brow furrowed as she turned in her chair to face Leah. "Recital? Did I miss something?"

"I told Jake about it and gave him a paper with the details. He didn't give it to you?"

"No, apparently not." She scowled at Jake. "You didn't tell me about your recital or give me the paper Miss Leah gave you." She returned her gaze to Leah. "When is it? Sounds exciting."

"It's next Sunday. Jake's been working on his piece for the recital all summer. It's at two o'clock in the auditorium of the big church, you know, Brenner Falls Community." Leah ruffled Jake's hair. "I think he's ready. I told him he'd play his song in front of a few friends in an auditorium, and he didn't seem afraid at all."

Blair shook her head and reached out to squeeze Jake's arm. "Where'd he get *that* from? I'd be scared to death."

"I'm not scared, Mom."

"He can invite friends and family members," Leah said.

"Mom, can I invite Cooper? And Nanna and Grandpa?"

"Cooper? I guess so." A warm feeling spread in Blair's belly, despite the fact that she hadn't seen a sign of him in almost two weeks. Maybe he was sending her a message. Backpedaling to a safe distance.

"I guess we're done." Garrett stood. "I'm going to see Abbie."

"Thanks so much, Garrett. If you won't let me pay you, at least let me cook dinner for you and Abbie one day. And of course, Leah and Nathan. You've all been such a big help."

"That would be lovely, Blair," Leah said. "Not necessary, but we'd all enjoy it, wouldn't we, Garrett?"

"Yep. I'll tell Abbie. Gotta go."

After he scooted out the front door, Leah laughed. "I think he's in love."

Blair stood. "Seems to be. They look so cute together in church. Kind of cuddly." She looked at Jake. "Do you have all your music books, big guy? You left a couple of things here last time."

"I have one more I forgot." Jake dashed out of the dining room.

Leah watched him round the corner. "Who's Cooper? I haven't heard that name before."

Blair's face grew warm. "He's my neighbor." A neighbor who's handsome and helpful, but was currently avoiding her. And she didn't blame him. "And friend. He's a good friend to both Jake and me." Too much explanation. A dead giveaway. She was aware of Leah's eyes narrowing on her face, which must be blooming all shades of red.

"And...?"

"Oh, I guess I'm easy to read, just fill in the blanks." Blair laughed. Her secret was out, at least with Leah. "I like him. But I'd be nuts to start something, with how complicated my life is. And it's only a friendship." Especially now that she'd sent him running with her story about Nelson. Just as well.

"I'm ready, Mom." Jake brandished the colorful music book. "I need this to practice for the recital. Can I tell Cooper today?"

"Yes, sweetie. We can tell him when we get home if he's there." She exchanged a glance with Leah, who smiled smugly.

"I hope I can meet your friend Cooper at the recital, Jake," Leah said.

"If he can come. He's building his house, so he's busy," Jake told her.

Leah nodded, eyes wide. "Oh, I see. That's pretty cool. So, you guys need to show up about thirty minutes early. Your guests can come about ten minutes early to get seated." She turned to Jake. "And practice every day, okay?" She squeezed his small shoulder.

"I promise, Miss Leah."

When they arrived home, Blair and Jake both noted with disappointment that Cooper's truck was gone, yet Zipper was still on his leash. Jake ran over to play with the dog while Blair got started on a simple supper. When she called him in to eat, Cooper still hadn't returned home.

"Cooper isn't home yet," Jake said. "Do you think he's still at work?"

"I don't know, sweetie. Maybe he's meeting a friend for supper." Hopefully not a female friend, but what could she say about that? Nothing. *She* was the needy neighbor who'd just dumped her personal problems on kindhearted Cooper. He was probably out with someone less complicated. No children, no bio fathers hovering around. And no broken appliances.

As they ate stuffed potatoes and soup, Blair struck a casual tone, though her heart thumped against her ribs. "Jake, do you remember a couple of days ago there was a letter in your suitcase?"

"Yeah." He slurped the last dregs of his soup from the edge of the bowl.

"So, do you want to know who it was from?"

He looked up. A red soup mustache lined top lip. She snickered. "Wipe your mouth, Jake. You're too young for a tomato mustache."

He cackled and wiped the soup away with a paper napkin.

"So, back to the letter..."

"Who was it from?" He wiggled in his chair, likely eager to leave the table.

"It was from your father. He wrote it to *you*. Remember, I told you about him a few weeks ago, that he was the one who sent you some presents for your birthday?"

Jake grew still and nodded. "He wrote to me?"

"Yes. Do you want to read it or have me read it to you?"

"You can read it. I don't know all the words, but I'm learning."

"Yes, you are." Blair stood and reached for where she'd tucked the letter next to the toaster. Beads of perspiration broke out on her neck. Cooper's words rang in her ears. He'd promised moral support.

Blair read the brief letter to Jake, glancing at his expression as she read. His brow furrowed and when she'd finished, he didn't speak.

Her throat had gone dry. She cleared it. "Jake, I want you to know that you don't have to meet him if you don't want to. I won't pressure you either way."

Jake frowned. "Okay."

"How...how are you feeling about this?" she prompted when he didn't respond.

"He sounds nice, and he gave me nice presents. But I'm afraid to meet him." His eyes found hers. "What if he's not nice like he seems?"

Relief trickled through her, but she kept her face passive. "I hope he is, but I haven't seen him in a long time." Then she remembered Cooper's suggestion. "If you want to know him better but are afraid to meet him right now, you can write him a letter."

"I think I want to write him a letter. Can you help me?"

"Sure, big guy. I'd be happy to help you." Would that be enough to satisfy Nelson? Doubtful. Might buy her some time unless he lost interest. At least she'd have satisfied her duty to Jake and to Nelson.

Headlights flashed across the kitchen window. "Cooper's home." Jake's voice was gleeful as he got up to rush out.

Blair set a hand on Jake's arm. "Give him a few minutes, Jake. He's just getting home and has to feed Zipper." Her gaze went out to the yard. Daylight was fading quickly, but she spied his movements across the yard.

"Can I go invite him to my recital when he finishes with Zipper?"

Blair chuckled. She wasn't the only one getting attached to Cooper Dawson. "Sure. I'll go with you."

"'Kay." He bounded from the room.

"Your dishes, Jake?"

"Oh, yeah, I forgot." He carried his plate and bowl to the sink, seeming to have forgotten about Nelson's letter already. "I have to practice my song tonight so I can play it without mistakes. I'll do that after I invite Cooper."

Fifteen minutes later, Blair knocked on Cooper's door. He opened the door and a grin spread across his face.

"Sorry to bother you, Cooper," she said.

"Hi you two. It's never a bother. I'm just glad you caught me before I hopped in the shower. Everything okay?"

"Jake has something to ask you."

"Mr. Cooper, I have a piano recital on Sunday afternoon, and I'm allowed to invite friends. You're my friend, so do you wanna come?"

"What an honor, Jake. I'm free that day, so I'd be glad to come hear you play."

"I'm not very good yet, but I'll do my best."

"He's got a gift for music," Blair said. "But it's his first year."

Cooper turned a smiling face to Jake. "I'm sure it'll be great. I can't wait to hear it. Where will it be?"

She told him the name and address of the church. "It starts at two and doors open ten minutes before. We'll go earlier."

"How about I go with you when you go? I'll relax in the front seat and cheer you on, big guy."

"I'm glad you can come." Jake's attention drifted to Zipper, who chomped eagerly in his green bowl. He took quiet steps toward the dog. "Hey, Zipper."

Cooper's dark blue eyes found hers. "Everything okay?"

Blair pressed her lips together and nodded. "I read him the letter tonight over dinner. He liked your idea of writing a letter back. He's not ready to see his dad."

"That's good news, right?"

She let out a shaky laugh. "For me it is. It'll give Jake time to adjust to the idea." She bowed her head then, not wanting him to see the layer of tears welling up in her eyes. The enormity of her decision weighed inside her like a ship-sized anchor.

"Remember, Blair, I'm here for you."

She lifted her head and swiped tears with one wrist. He meant well, but this was her battle. Her mess. "Thank you, Cooper."

Chapter Eleven

Cooper pushed open the door to The Grateful Fork. As he did, boisterous voices and enticing aromas surged around him. The Fork seemed to be the happening weekend destination in Brenner Falls, if the crowd that night and during his previous visit was a sign.

He hadn't wanted to arrive before Amber, so he came at six-forty. As with the first time, she waved him over to their table when she spotted him scanning the room. This time, four of them sat at a long table for six near the window, affording a better view of the stage.

Amber pushed back from the table and circled it to give him a hug. He smiled at Johnny, Tricia, and Lindsay, then settled into the empty chair beside Lindsay.

"Manny got held up at work," Johnny said. "He sounded pretty beat when I talked to him a while ago, so I doubt he'll make it."

"How was your week, Cooper?" Tricia slid a menu across the table to him.

"Pretty good. The house is coming along."

"I'd love to see it sometime," Lindsay purred. An unmistakable invitation blazed from her blue eyes. She was a pretty woman. No argument about that, but Cooper was trying to cut down. To just one in particular. Or rather, none at all. He wasn't ready, despite agreeing to go to Jake's recital. Hard to say no to a cute seven-year-old.

"There's not too much to see just yet. Bunch of sticks. Most people can't visualize it unless they see the drawings." He shifted his attention to Johnny before she could ask to see them. "Hey, Johnny, I took your suggestion and went to see the mayor."

Johnny perked up. "Yeah? How'd it go? He's a nice dude, from what I've heard."

"True. He was open and approachable. He told me about his vision for the Falls."

"Hi, Amber, hi everyone." An attractive redhead holding an order pad stood at the end of the table next to Amber.

"Hey, Kelsey." Amber stood and gave the woman a hug. "I forgot to call you back. Life got crazy on me."

Kelsey waved the air. "I was going to call you for a breakfast date soon anyway."

Amber pointed at Kelsey's half apron. "Are you working here?"

"Just helping. Aggie's short-handed and was afraid with the band she wouldn't have enough servers. I enjoy being here. Beats sitting in front of a computer all day."

"Amen to that." Amber turned to the group. "Everyone, this is my friend Kelsey." Those around the table murmured a greeting. "And Kelsey, this is everyone." They laughed. "Well, I won't stop you from your work."

"So, are you guys ready to order?" she called out over the noise.

Cooper took a quick scan of the menu. A server went by with something appetizing on his tray. "What's that?" he asked Kelsey.

"Fried chicken sandwich with gravy. It's one of Aggie's best sellers."

"I'll take that, please. With fries." He'd cut out fat the following day to make up for the overload the meal promised.

Behind Kelsey, the front door opened, and a familiar blond woman came in. He tried to catch her gaze. "Amber, there's my neighbor and her son. Can we invite them to sit with us? They're kind of new in town." Though he was a full year newer than Blair and Jake.

Amber's attention went to the front door. "Of course. We have room since Manny couldn't come. That's the neighbor you told me about?"

He nodded but sent her a warning glare. Her lips tugged up at the corners.

Cooper stood to intercept Blair before a server seated them elsewhere. She wore a lime green flowered top.

When she spotted him, her face opened with surprise.

"Hey, big guy," he said to Jake. "Hi Blair. You're welcome to join us, unless you're meeting someone."

She glanced at the table. "Oh, I couldn't barge in on your group."

"Come, join us," Johnny called out behind them.

Amber hopped out of her seat. "Hi, I'm Amber. Cooper's sister. Please join us. We can get another chair."

"Nice to meet you, Amber. I'm Blair, and this is Jake."

"Let's sit with Cooper, Mom." Jake pulled on her purse strap.

"Well, if you all don't mind. Thanks."

Jake slid into the chair Kelsey added and Blair sat next to Cooper.

Amber introduced Blair and Jake around the table as if they were good friends of hers. Amber's friends asked questions and welcomed them.

Once the introduction died down, Cooper turned to her. "What brings you to The Fork?"

"It was a long, stressful week. Jake and I needed to get out." Blair sighed. "Plus, I didn't feel like cooking."

Tricia leaned toward them. "Blair, how do you and Cooper know each other?"

"We're neighbors," she said, raising her voice above the noise. "Or rather, we became neighbors when Cooper moved into the house next door to me. Jake and I have been here about a year."

"Do you like it here?" Lindsay asked.

"Yes, Brenner Falls is the perfect size for us."

"I have friends at church and my friend Charlie," added Jake. "And Joel."

Cooper leaned toward them. "Blair's an aspiring fashion designer. You should see her stuff. It's great."

This brought ohs from around the table and a volley of questions. Blair dove right in, almost sparkling as she talked about her dreams. He'd seen her obvious talent and wanted to brag on her, but also bolster her faith in herself. He was happy Amber's friends had put out the welcome mat for her.

They volleyed the next few questions to Jake, who wasn't timid. He talked about his piano recital and how much he loved Zipper. Those around the table, including Amber, seemed as charmed by him as Cooper himself was. The kid was plain adorable, inside and out.

Kelsey returned and took Blair and Jake's orders.

"You had a stressful week?" Cooper asked her, once the group interview had ended.

She offered a weak smile. "I'm glad it's the weekend. Though I always say that on Fridays."

"That's why The Fork is crowded. It's a good way to head into the weekend." Cooper downed a swig of iced tea.

"It's nice to meet new friends," she said. "There are nice people at my church, but I'm still getting to know them."

"I still need to visit one day." He'd let various tasks fill his free time after working at the property. Didn't take long to get off balance again.

During the meal, Amber plied Blair with questions about her work, her family, and Jake. Blair didn't seem uncomfortable with all the questions. For a couple of weeks, he'd done a good job backing off from her. And now, here they were again, and his defenses crumbled, as they'd done since the day he met her. Maybe Nelson wasn't competition, and Cooper had no reason to avoid Blair. At any rate, it seemed futile to try.

They all talked in animated voices about a housing development planned across the river while Jake worked quietly on his stack of fries. He lived in a grown-up world so much of the time and seemed to adapt to it without seeking attention or pouting. Soon, the band took its place on the stage and the crowd hushed. They tuned their instruments and began warming up the crowd.

On Sunday afternoon, Cooper drove with Blair and Jake to the Brenner Falls Community Church for Jake's piano recital. A handful of cars filled the parking lot.

They entered the building into a carpeted foyer, which he could easily imagine mobbed with members after a Sunday service. That day, couples with children both younger and older than Jake milled around, waiting for Leah. Some children carried small hard-shelled bags and others gripped the handles of violin cases. Cooper glanced down at Jake, who was quieter than usual, and clung to Blair's hand.

On impulse, Cooper squatted to the child's level. "You're going to do great, big guy. Just remember, everyone in that room loves you, whether or not you hit every note perfectly. Okay?"

Jake nodded, then threw his arms around Cooper's neck. When he pulled back, Cooper blinked the sting from his eyes. He stood and met Blair's luminous gaze, also glassy with tears.

"I agree with Cooper. You'll do great. And if you make any mistakes, it absolutely doesn't matter."

Jake nodded. "Miss Leah said the same thing. She said the most important thing was to have fun making music."

"She's right," Blair said. "We'll be sitting in one of the first rows and we'll cheer you on."

"Is that Miss Leah?" Cooper pointed to a woman who'd appeared in the foyer with a clipboard in one hand, a long skirt swishing around her high heels, and a gentle expression on her face.

"Good afternoon, everyone," she called to the crowd. "I'm sure you're excited to hear these talented children play the piano, flute, and violin. We'll be meeting in the chapel, just down that hall. You'll see signs. You can leave your children with me now and go to find your seats."

The parents separated from their children, who clustered around Leah. Her face lit up when she saw Jake.

"Hi, Miss Leah." Jake clutched his folder of sheet music in both hands.

"Leah," Blair said. "This is my friend, Cooper."

Leah turned a warm smile to Cooper. "I'm so glad to meet you, Cooper. Thanks for coming today to support Jake."

Blair bent toward Jake. "You're going to do great, big guy. Now, go along with Miss Leah and we'll be right there in the chapel. You'll see us." She pulled him in for a tight hug and released him to Leah. She straightened walked to the chapel with Cooper.

They found seats in the second row. A low stage extended across the front of the room and a baby grand piano occupied one end.

They still had fifteen minutes to wait. Cooper had to admit, he savored sitting next to Blair to watch Jake perform, as though he were Jake's dad, Blair's husband. Or at least her boyfriend. Probably looked that way to others, and he liked it, despite the tug of war his feelings waged.

"Did you invite your parents to Jake's recital?" He murmured in her ear.

"Unfortunately, they're out of town visiting my sister, Audrey. It's been planned for a while. They would have wanted to come, since it's his first one. They also pay for his lessons."

The rows filled up with eager parents and friends. "There'll be others," he said.

"I wish they *were* here. Jake would like that." After a moment of silence, she whispered, "The day I called her, she asked me if I'd found the letter in Jake's bag. I told her I had, and that Jake had decided to write a letter as a first step. I said I didn't appreciate her just putting it in his bag without asking me."

"She went around you. That's not cool."

"No, it's not. If Jake had seen the letter and acted on it without telling me…" Her jaw tightened. "She defended herself, of course. Said she didn't know if I would do anything about it."

"What did you say?"

"I told her he's *seven*!" A rasp of frustration laced her whisper. "Seven-year-olds don't get to make that decision for themselves. I'm his mother and I should be the one to decide what to do with that letter, how to present it and when. I acknowledged her feelings that Nelson should meet his son. I said if we do, we'll do it on *our* timetable, not hers."

A few pink patches of anger appeared on her cheeks as her jaw clenched. He felt a surge of anger on her behalf.

"I don't stand up to her often, because I know she has our best interest at heart. And often, it's just too stressful to oppose her, so I let things ride."

He laid a hand on hers. "I agree with you, but you're getting flustered. I'm sorry I asked that question at this particular time."

She closed her eyes for a moment, then met his gaze full on. "You're right. I'm getting flustered at the worst time. I should be used to this. That's one reason I wanted to live on my own. On my own terms, without the hovering." She shook her head. "Your question was innocent. I just get mad when my mother thinks *she* can decide what Jake should do about his father. It's …complex."

"You've had no relationship with him for all of Jake's life, so you want to handle it carefully." He gently pulled his hand away. "I'm glad Jake decided not to meet his dad yet. He only just found out—"

His words were cut by Leah's appearance on stage. "Welcome everyone."

Blair and Cooper fell silent and fixed their eyes on the stage.

Following the recital, Jake sat wedged between Cooper and Blair in the front seat of Cooper's truck. He jumped and wiggled like a jack-in-the-box.

"Man, are you wired." Blair laughed. "Settle down, big guy, or Cooper won't let us ride in his truck anymore."

Jake had made one minor mistake, but otherwise played well. It wasn't a concerto, but at his level, something to applaud. When he finished, he stood and bowed, a grin stretching across his face. Cooper and Blair jumped up and hooted as if they were at a football game. Not only were he and Blair united in a show of support for Jake, but other parents did the same, with cameras, video, and banners. It was fun to see parents supporting their kids' achievements. Blair filmed Jake's performance to send to her parents and siblings.

"Want to get ice cream, Jake? Can't let a good Sunday go to waste." He sent Blair a sheepish look. "Should have asked you first."

She looked serene. "We could do your idea, but reverse it. Dinner first, then ice cream."

"I have another idea. Before we eat dinner and ice cream, let's drive by the house I'm building. There's not much there yet, but it'll give you an idea."

"Yeah, let's do that. Mom, can we? I want to see Cooper's house." Jake renewed his jumping.

"I'd love to. Let's go."

Cooper steered the truck in the direction of the river. It took only a few minutes before he pulled into the work site. They clambered out of the truck, and he led them up a path to the partially built house, hidden behind a wall of trees.

"Wow." Jake walked up to the edge where the framing began. "There aren't any walls." They stepped gingerly along one edge of the structure.

Cooper smiled. "Not yet. This is called *framing*. Like a picture frame. It's around the picture, but it's not the picture. This part's almost done. We'll put a roof on, then walls. After that, plumbing, electricity, and so on. Once that's all in there, we can put walls inside. The last thing will be the outside surfaces, things like stone, tiles, shingles, stuff like that."

Blair quietly studied the structure, her gaze sweeping the framing up to the beams and joists.

She turned to him. "I'm amazed. This process is so fascinating. I'm imagining it according to the drawings you showed me the other night. I can't wait to see it all finished."

Her enthusiasm warmed him. "I see it day by day and can't believe this'll be *my* house."

They left the work site and headed to George's. Cooper insisted it was his treat, amid Blair's weak protests. He let out a happy sigh as the late August breeze floated into the truck window on the way home. If he could only capture that moment, the whole day, in fact, he'd keep it close to his heart forever.

ભ   ભ   ભ

"I'll pick you up early from Mrs. Angela's today." Blair tucked a sandwich, an apple, and a container of yogurt into the canvas tote bag she took to work every day. "I'll leave work early so we can go get your stuff for school. Remember, it starts next Monday."

Jake made no comment as he finished a bowl of cereal on the other side of the small nook table.

"Are you excited about starting school, Jake?"

"Yeah. I'll be in second grade. What are we gonna buy today?"

"You need some pants and a couple shirts. You're growing, big guy." Her little man was bursting out of his clothes, or soon would be. "Maybe some new sneakers too. Yours are getting ratty."

He finished slurping the last of the milk and set his bowl down. "I'm a big guy," he repeated with apparent pleasure. "I played the piano in front of *lots* of people and I wasn't even very scared."

"I was so proud of you. First, your courage to get in front of everyone and, of course, your piano playing abilities." She wiped down the counter and sat her canvas tote next to the front door.

The memory of the hours they'd spent with Cooper the previous weekend sparked a glow that hadn't worn off, though it was Wednesday. Starting with Friday night, in fact. When she and Jake had ventured alone into The Grateful Fork, the last thing she expected was a welcome from not only Cooper, but his sister and a few friends. Being part of a group of adults instead of alone with Jake, had supplied vitamins she hadn't known she was missing. And the way he bragged about her designs created a warm puddle inside. He didn't seem to consider her a flaky artist or a dreamer.

Then Sunday topped Friday, as she and Cooper showed their support at Jake's recital. Then they talked and kidded over sandwiches at George's followed by ice cream cones, digging up delight she'd forgotten could exist.

Thoughts of Nelson were like a fly dropping into an apple pie. If she'd told Jake about Nelson years ago instead of dodging it, his appearance would hardly be disturbing. At least she'd forgiven him, but that was only the first step. A late one.

She parked in front of Angela's house and Jake slipped out. "I'll pick you up at three, okay, big guy?"

"'Kay. See ya later."

A week had passed since Jake told her he wanted to write Nelson a letter. She ought to remind him, help him connect with the father he'd never met.

The last thing she wanted to do.

After work, Blair picked up Jake, and they spent the next three hours getting clothes, shoes, and school supplies. She'd put it off for the entire month of August, reasoning that she could do it all at once. Might be time efficient, but it had sapped any remaining dregs of her energy. As usual, Jake still had plenty of that.

"Mom, can we do the letter tonight?" Jake's question after dinner saved her the trouble of reminding him.

"Sure, sweetie. Let's clear the table and bring some paper." Here goes. The future would change forever with the affixing of a simple stamp.

They settled at the living room table with notepaper. "What would you like to tell him, Jake?"

"I don't know. Will you help me?"

"Think about why you want to write to him. We can start with that."

"Well, you said he's my dad, but I've never met him."

"You could tell him you want to get to know him through letters, something like that."

"I can tell him about my piano recital, my dinosaurs. I can tell him about school."

"Okay, that's good," she prompted. "Fill him in on your life."

"I want to do this myself."

She'd let Jake do it himself but knew he'd learn more about writing in the coming school year. He wrote one phrase then pushed the paper back to her. "I don't know how. Can you write it for me? I'll tell you what to say."

"Sure, sweetie." She looked at the paper and he'd written, *I am Jake.* He expressed what he wanted her to write. Of course, she'd need to add a letter of her own, though the thought sent a chill down her spine. For now, she'd concentrate on Jake's letter.

When he finished, Blair held up the letter. "Okay, I'll read what you wrote, and you can let me know if you want to change anything. *Dear Nelson, I'm Jake and I think you are my dad. Thank you for the birthday presents. I'm seven years old and I like dinosaurs and I play the piano. I had a recital last week. It was fun, and I only made one mistake. I am starting second grade next week. Sincerely, Jake.*"

She met his gaze. "Are you happy with that? I can mail it for you."

Jake nodded. "Can I go practice my piano now?"

"Sure, big guy." Jake slipped away from the table and dashed out of the room. Blair let out a breath and sat still for a moment. Jake's letter didn't invite anything but would surely trigger a response from Nelson. A correspondence to start with? One that could go on for years as far as she was concerned. She'd like to write a note saying Jake wasn't ready to meet him yet. Maybe that much would be obvious in his letter.

The letter she'd *like* to write might go something like this: *Nelson, it's a surprise to hear from you after all these years, during which you never seemed to have a thought about your son. (For instance, if he was healthy or needed anything at all.) We've done absolutely fine without you. It's very hard for me to give you access to my son, but he seems interested in corresponding with you. He is not ready to meet you, however, for reasons I totally understand. You're a stranger. Don't pressure him. If you have any negative impact on his life or hurt him whatsoever, I swear to you, I'll move from here and you will never see him again. Ever. Trust me on that.*

Okay, a bit harsh. But it felt therapeutic to write it. Excellent, in fact, as it provided a fresh surge of energy. Blair laughed aloud. She'd start over with a new letter during the weekend.

Oh, yes, Mama Bear was on call at all times.

Chapter Twelve

Cooper stared out at the rumpled gray sky. His jaw tightened as the steady sheet of rain slid down the picture window. It had begun overnight. He'd awakened to the percussive *plink plink* sound on the metal roof, even against the windows. Puddles had already welled up in the flowerbeds and on the driveway. So much for advancing on the house that day. Or the next three, according to the forecast. This would put him back, but he had to expect at least some delays. Things had gone far too smoothly since he'd broken ground.

He made himself a second cup of coffee. He'd let Zipper out, but the dog hadn't wanted to linger once he'd finished his business.

"Sorry, boy. Can't go out in the sunshine today."

Zipper sat by his feet and cast his doleful black eyes upward and Cooper scratched his head. No work on the house, but he could always catch up on clients he'd neglected, though there weren't many. He'd taken a hiatus to complete his house, but would still need to maintain some outside business. Not only would that help establish his reputation in a new town, but also keep income flowing. Once the weather improved, he'd spend as much time as possible on the site before winter, which lurked right around the corner.

He hadn't seen much of Blair and Jake. They were preoccupied with the new school year, as of yesterday, so that seemed a good time to pull back himself. Probably for the best, though he could still count on Jake to come see his buddy, Zipper.

Cooper settled at the desk in his office and opened his computer. Many overdue requests on the online form he'd set up appeared on the screen. He'd always made it a practice to respond within forty-eight hours, even during his busiest season. Not anymore. Time to get his act together and stop mooning over Blair like a teenager. He'd stay up late responding to everything that had come, apologizing for his lateness. He still had a business and reputation to maintain. The house remained in good hands with the competent team he'd hired, so he didn't need to be on site all the time. But watching it come together fed his heart, like a long-awaited promise.

Amber came to his mind. He hadn't seen her either since that Friday night. It would be his third time forgetting to call her, and three strikes would get him in big trouble. She'd be at work, so he'd leave her a message. At least she'd know he tried.

"Hey, sis. It's me. I know you're over there breaking someone's bones, but I thought I'd say hi. It was good to see you last week. Thanks for being nice to my friend Blair and her son. I think she had a good time. Call me when you have time. I'm home, of course, because of the weather." Usually, he was far more succinct. Part of his motivation in calling was curiosity about her impressions of Blair. He'd been surprised she hadn't called him first.

Cooper worked at his desk until noon, absorbed in drafting projects. He got up to make lunch as the phone rang. "Hey, Amber. How's your day going?"

"Pretty good. Didn't break anyone's bones, though." She laughed. "Maybe I need to explain to you what I do."

"I didn't want you to think I'd forgotten about you, which I did not. It was good to see you the other day."

"Yeah. It was nice to meet your friend Blair. She seems sweet."

He sensed a hesitation in her voice, and was about to ignore it, but curiosity got the best of him. "But?"

"No, nothing. She's nice. Is Jake's dad in the picture?"

"He's not." Not technically, although Cooper wished his existence was irrelevant. "She hasn't seen him in years."

"Oh, okay. Well, I can tell you like her. Um, this is blunt, but do you feel ready to take on a child?"

"Amber." Cooper's voice was quiet as he stemmed his irritation. "We're not even dating, let alone engaged. And if we were, then, yes, I can handle that. Do you have any doubt?"

"No, Cooper, you'd be a great stepdad. I just didn't know you were open to that."

"Well now, you know." He heard a faint edge lacing his own voice.

"I don't want you hurt or in a tough situation."

"I'll repeat, Amber, we're not even dating." And a fine job he was doing backing off like he'd instructed himself.

There was a long pause on the phone. "Okay, you're not dating. So, why is that, since you like her?"

Her question was valid. But there were things he couldn't tell her. "I'm giving it time." Time for her to figure things out with her ex, which suddenly didn't seem like such a good idea, since he might lose her if they reconciled. "I haven't known her long. A couple of months."

"Oh, I see. Well, I trust your judgment."

"Doesn't appear that way, but thanks for the concern." He kept his voice light. He knew she was just worried, more than simply nosy. Or was trying to determine if *he* had reservations.

"Cooper, are you mad?"

"No, I'm not. I know you want the best for me. I would think you'd be glad I was interested in someone, you know, after Priya. It's been three years."

"I *am* happy for you. Even though there's nothing going on yet. So, make something happen and let me know." She laughed. "I'm sorry. I take back my earlier question. I really liked her. And I can see your feelings for her go deeper than I realized. Cooper, if you're happy, I am too. Just be careful."

"No worries. It's going slowly, but there are some reasons." He hadn't meant to tell her that. Amber likely thought the worst. He hastened to add, "Nothing serious, just don't want to go into it now." That sounded even worse, but he'd let it be. Some of that was his issue.

Amber wisely didn't insist, and the conversation moved along to news from their parents and her upcoming trip to the Caribbean.

"When are you leaving on your trip?" Her response to Blair still nagged at him.

"In three weeks. I'll let you know, so you can water my geraniums."

"Sure thing. Aruba, you said?"

"Yup. Not in the hurricane belt, you'll be glad to know, Mr. Safety. We should do a hike along the river next weekend if you're free. We don't have to eat every time we get together."

Cooper laughed. "True. Eating's overrated, and a hike sounds like fun."

"Well, I've gotta go. Talk to you soon. And keep me posted...on things."

"I'll think about it. Bye."

They hung up. Nosy sister, as if he couldn't handle being a stepdad. Talk about jumping too far ahead.

Amber and Blair had seemed to hit it off famously, which made his sister's response even stranger. Unless she perceived the same dangers he did.

At any rate, it was his decision if and when he'd go deeper in his friendship with Blair. The jury was still out on whether or not that was a good or safe idea.

ജ   ജ   ജ

"I'm tired of rain." Jake zipped his hoodie to his chin and looked out the car window through gray streaks. Passing cars sprayed funnels of water as they drove by.

"It's only been three days, but I'm tired of it too." Blair couldn't wait to get home, put on sweatpants, and begin her weekend. The wet hems of her jeans clung to her ankles. "I think it may slow down tomorrow. That's what the forecast said."

"I hope so. Zipper misses me."

"I'm sure he does. You can go over there. I'm sure Cooper wouldn't mind your paying a visit, even if Zipper is inside."

Too bad she didn't have a valid reason to go to Cooper's with Jake. She hadn't seen him in over a week, even with rain falling. He likely had work to do at home, a business to maintain aside from his house. No reason to think he was avoiding her. Why would he? But an uneasy feeling stirred inside.

But she'd love to tell him about her conversation with Hugo that day at work. He'd summoned her to his office during lunch. He'd said only that he liked her design and had passed it along to Gloria. She wouldn't get her hopes too high. She could share it with Cooper next time she saw him. Or Leah.

After the memorable day they'd spent together, she missed him. His truck had sat in his driveway since the rain started Wednesday. A light shone from inside, but there was no sign of him. As though they'd built something that had already faded away.

She parked in front of the house. "Let's go inside first and put your things away before you go see Zipper. Or you can go over after supper."

Jake scrambled out of the car and waited for Blair to unlock the door and grab the mail. Once she was comfy in dry clothes, she headed toward the kitchen to start supper.

As she entered the room, something cold dropped on her nose. She looked up and saw a wide brown stain on the ceiling spreading out from the corner. "Oh, no." It wasn't dripping much, but rain had soaked through the roof and ceiling. Now, that was something Mr. Mitchell *had* to repair. She went to the pantry closet and rummaged for a pail.

"What's that for, Mom?"

"Look at the ceiling, Jake. Rain is leaking through the roof."

Jake's blond head tipped upward. "Will we have a flood in the kitchen?"

"I hope not. It's small now, but it's one more thing wrong with this house." Frustration filled her chest. One. More. Thing. "I'll take a picture of it and email the landlord. Again." And keep copies of everything in a file. And send another picture when the stain expands.

"Can I go see Zipper now?"

Blair frowned. "I'd rather you do it after dinner. It won't take long, and I don't want to wait for you to come back."

During a simple meal at the kitchen table, Blair listened to Jake describe his teachers and his classmates at school. Normally, she'd interact with him and ask him questions. That day, she was bone tired, and discouraged about the ceiling. It was an effort to say anything. Fortunately, Jake didn't seem to notice, and she enjoyed listening to him describe his new life in second grade.

It was unlikely, Mr. Mitchell would fix it, so she'd have to file some kind of complaint. She wouldn't tell Cooper, who'd kindly offer to fix it, and she'd be indebted to him once again. She didn't want to call on him whenever something happened. She preferred putting on a beautiful dress and letting him surprise her with dinner at an elegant restaurant. In other words, she wanted a normal romance with Cooper Dawson. Was that too much to ask?

She didn't like it when she slipped into self-pity. It was rare, since she knew she'd chosen her life eight years earlier. And she wouldn't trade her beautiful tow-headed magpie across the table for anything on the planet. But sometimes, problems came in multiples. Since Nelson's letter had come, in fact, she'd felt less resilient, almost as if a dark storm awaited just outside the door.

With a wave of guilt, she remembered she hadn't yet sent Jake's letter, written days earlier. The holdup was twofold. One, she dreaded opening the door to Nelson in their lives, even though she must. Though her forgiveness of him had been real, Nelson was a pandora's box. She had no idea what he might bring. And two, she wondered what she'd write in her own letter.

One thing she knew. It wasn't fair to Jake for her to procrastinate sending the letter, even if he seemed to have forgotten all about it.

"Mom, are you listening?"

Busted. "I'm sorry, babe. I'm really tired."

"I said I want to go see Zipper now."

"You can go. Say hello to Cooper for me."

"'Kay."

The front door closed, and silence surrounded her. She'd forgotten to remind him to take an umbrella, but it was only a few dozen yards across both lawns. The mail sat in front of her. Without getting up, she leafed through it and saw a letter from the Fashion Foundation.

Her breath hitched. Could be a response to the contest she'd applied for earlier that summer. But the turnaround was so fast, it was likely a refusal. Her frequent survey of the contest website had yielded no information, hopeful or otherwise.

Blair's heart thumped against her ribs. The negative news she expected would simply put an additional pall on her day, but her curiosity pushed her to open the letter.

She scanned the first two lines of the form letter, and she let out a gasp. She was a semi-finalist! One of seventy, but still. Normally, they'd post the results online. The letter explained that to equalize access for those in countries with poor internet connections, they also sent the responses by mail. Whatever the reason, this news was exactly what she needed to perk her up. And the same day as her conversation with Hugo. Was God telling her something?

She skimmed further. If they chose her to be a finalist, she'd have to go to New York. In the case of the second contest, she'd have to go to Milan. How on earth would she do that? Well, she'd cross that bridge if she came to it. Applying for a contest in the first place without the scaffolding of a fashion school program was a feat. Her achievement could very well hit a wall right there, a semi-finalist along with sixty-nine others. There were only ten finalists, and that number would be further cut to three. Was there any reason to be thrilled? Not yet. But it lifted her mood considerably and reminded her that her dreams were still feasible.

The front door swung open. "Mom, Cooper came to see the ceiling."

Blair's head jerked up, and she stood just as Cooper filled the tiny kitchen. "Hi, Cooper. What a surprise."

He looked good—no, gorgeous—standing there in a T-shirt and gray sweatpants, just like her. She swallowed the sudden dryness in her throat and pointed to his chest. "Looks like we have the same fashion designer."

His eyes warmed to hers. "Looks that way. So, what's up with the ceiling? Jake tells me you have a leak." His gaze had already strayed upward. His smile fell and his brows gathered.

He was tall enough to touch the surface. "It's soft, like I expected." He looked back at her. "When did you first notice it?"

"When I got home from work today. It dripped on my face. It might have started yesterday, but wasn't this big, so I didn't notice."

"Of course, you'll have to notify the landlord. But make sure you take photos first."

His voice held an authoritative edge. Blair bristled. "Um, already done, chief." She batted her eyes. "I'm not a dumb blond, you know."

Surprise showed on his face, then a sheepish smile. "Of course. I never thought you were. It's just habit."

"I know, from your worksite. Don't get me wrong, I appreciate your coming to look."

"You're taking photos of every bit of damage you see in the house?"

"Yup. All in a file." She crossed her arms. "Anything else, chief?"

He smirked. "No, that should do it. At ease, corporal."

They laughed.

He checked the level in the pail. "There's not much more I can tell without getting on the roof. I think initially, we should leave that to Mr. Mitchell to see what he'll do—or not do. If we tamper with it, we won't be able to force him to do anything at all. If he's really in violation, which he is by now, we want to be able to force him to keep his part of your contract. Meaning the lease."

Blair nodded. "I'll keep sending him updated photos of the damage and see how he responds. If he doesn't, we have grounds to do... I don't know what. I'll take a look at my lease and see what he's required to do."

"There are resources. State government numbers you can call for legal support and things like that. I asked Mayor Faulkner about it at the tail end of our meeting. He'll have his housing deputy give me a call."

"The mayor's your fishing buddy?" Blair grinned. Didn't surprise her at all that he'd already connected with the head of government.

Cooper laughed. "Not quite. I met him for the first time the other day because I wanted to find out his vision for Brenner Falls and how I could fit into that as a builder."

"Ah. Good idea." She paused. "I'm guessing you couldn't work on your house this week because of the rain."

"You guessed right. At least we were ahead, but winter's coming. Not much I can do about the weather. I did some work at home today on other clients' projects."

"I have some interesting news myself. Remember that design my friend turned in at work? The boss spoke to me about it today. He gave it to a woman in the design department."

"See? You're getting there."

Blair shrugged. "Probably won't lead anywhere, but it's a seed planted."

"You never know."

He didn't add anything else, as if something were on his mind.

"Do you want something to drink or some ice cream? I remember you have an emotional attachment to good ice cream."

Regret crossed his face. "I'd love to hang out with you guys, but still have quite a bit of work to do tonight. I've gotten behind but I wanted to see what you were dealing with here." He shoved his hands in his pockets. "I could fix it, but it's a perfect item to add to Mr. Mitchell's list of sins. Not that I'd want you to live in a flooded house either, of course."

"Yes, of course." She smiled. "Well, it was nice to see you, as always."

His blue eyes caught hers for a long second. "Yes, it was." He moved toward the door. "And let me know if it gets a lot worse or if you feel in any danger, okay?"

Blair nodded. "Sure will. Thanks for coming by." She opened the door for him.

Her earlier elation sagged. Why hadn't he wanted to stay for a bowl of ice cream? Maybe he did have lots of work to do, but it seemed he was avoiding her in other ways. Was he backing off after their memorable weekend? Sending her a message? Maybe she'd read him all wrong since the beginning. The helpfulness, the invitations, his willingness to listen. Those could all be qualities of a great friend, and didn't necessarily mean anything more.

Blair sank into the kitchen chair as heaviness settled inside her. She understood she'd created a fantasy in her mind. Now she had to see reality.

Chapter Thirteen

After Cooper left, Blair took another photo and added it to the folder. While she was online, she researched roof leaks to become more knowledgeable in case her landlord gave her any resistance.

According to her research, a roof leak could be caused by the condition of the shingles themselves, the boards underneath them, or even a blocked gutter that caused water to surge beneath the shingles. She frowned. Was it her responsibility to clean the gutter? It likely was since she was also responsible for mowing the lawn. She hadn't touched her gutters since she'd lived there. They might be full because of the many trees surrounding the property.

That didn't mean the roof wasn't in disrepair. But Mitchell would ask her if she'd cleaned the gutters regularly and use it as an excuse to make her pay for any repairs. He'd do it if he could. Wouldn't be too hard for her to sweep the gutters out before he responded. They weren't very high. She could do it the next day since the rain was due to stop.

By midnight, she still hadn't fallen asleep. Thoughts and questions about the roof, Cooper, Nelson, and her stalling career ricocheted around her brain until the wee hours. At least the next day was Saturday.

Blair awoke the next morning to the sounds of Jake's motor noises in the living room. She glanced at the clock, which read eight fifteen. With heavy eyes and a slight headache, she stumbled to the bathroom, then the kitchen. "Good morning, big guy. You're making noise."

"You're still sleeping?"

"Not anymore." Coffee. She reached for the pot and filled it full. She'd need it that day. But at least the sun spilled through the kitchen window and the sky blazed cornflower blue overhead. Finally, no more rain.

Which reminded her of the roof leak. She looked at the ceiling and saw the stain had spread only slightly, but still looked like motor oil. Only a few drops of rain lay in the bucket.

After breakfast, her head felt clearer, and her mood lifted. The questions she'd wrestled with the night before hadn't disappeared but seemed less overwhelming. She could always write a letter to Nelson as a first step and tell him about her fears before sending him Jake's letter.

"Are we going to the market today, Mom?" Jake appeared in the kitchen doorway, still dressed in his military camouflage pajamas.

"No, not today." Thankfully, though, she needed the money. But she also needed a break. *And* time to clean the gutters. "I sold so much stuff last week, I need to make more before we go back." There was that too.

"Okay. Maybe I can go play with Joel today since it's not raining."

"That's a good idea. Just wait a bit. It's still early. And I need to get your breakfast."

After Jake left the table, she reread the letter from the contest. Nothing else was required. They'd notify her if she made it to the finals. At least she was in the running.

A perfect almost-autumn morning greeted Blair as she left the house, clothed in well-worn capris and a T-shirt. Jake still played in the living room. Cooper's truck was gone. Zipper wandered on his leash from the porch to the driveway, where he circled before sitting, waiting for his master to return.

She opened the garage, still filled with bins of irregulars from the factory, and spotted a small ladder leaning against one wall. An ice scraper would work to scoop leaves and debris from the gutters. She pulled one from the trunk of her car.

Gutters followed the roofline on only two sides of the house, so it shouldn't take her too long. She stood on the middle rung of the ladder to survey the task before her. As she suspected, the gutters overflowed with pine needles, leaves, and twigs. That could have led to a clog. She scooped it out and let debris fall to the ground. She'd bag it later. Blair shifted the ladder over every couple of feet as she worked.

The opposite side of the house took little time, as she scooped out a gutter, which stretched in a long, straight line. If she kept at it, she'd finish before lunch. The side by the front door was straight for a few yards, then pitched up a gable. She could almost reach it. Her last segment.

She jammed the ice scraper into wet leaves and mud. The first chunk came out easily, flipping out and showering to the ground. Then her tool dug into something solid, throwing her off balance. She tried to right herself before the ladder toppled over, but it had leaned too far. Blair screamed as she fell and hit the ground. Air left her lungs and the ladder jangled down next to her. Pain shot through her left wrist, where she'd tried to break her fall, and through her right ankle. There'd be a purple bruise on her left hip as well. Cradling her wrist, she curled in a ball. Tears leaped into her eyes, and she squeezed them shut. The noise of scraping gravel rose to her ears as she prayed for help.

ᘓ   ᘓ   ᘓ

Cooper's truck was still a distance from the house when he saw Blair's ladder pitch over and her with it. His heart pounded as he swung the truck into her driveway behind her Toyota.

"Blair, Blair! Are you alright?" He ran to where she'd curled up in a fetal position and knelt beside her. Her eyes were open, thank God. "I saw what happened. Don't move. Where does it hurt?"

Tears rolled down her cheeks. He'd never seen her cry, and it undid him. A lump throbbed in his throat.

"My wrist." Her thin voice accompanied a wince. "And my ankle."

"Did you hear anything snap?"

"No, maybe a sprain..." Her words halted. Her eyes shut.

"Did you hit your head? Your spine?"

She shook her head.

"I'm going to lift you up very gently, okay? I'll drive you to urgent care. You'll have to sit in the truck. Can you do that? Can you put one arm around my neck?"

Blair nodded, her large hazel eyes wide with pain and fear, her face chalky pale. She slipped her right arm around his shoulders. He slid his other hand beneath her knees and eased her upright. She cried out as she touched her right foot to the ground.

"Here, lean on me. All your weight. I'm going to get your knees, okay?"

"Jake... is in the house. Bring him..."

"Yes, I'll get him. I'll put you in the truck first." He wished he had a bigger vehicle. What had been fun and cozy the day they'd gone to the recital would be tight and bumpy today. "I'm going to carry you, Blair. Just relax."

She made a faint protest, then relaxed against him, resting her head on his shoulders. If only he'd left the passenger side open. Despite the circumstances, she felt good in his arms, light and pliable. The floral scent of her hair floated around him as he held her close.

He struggled to open the door, but Jake appeared beside him. "What happened? Mom, are you okay?"

He heard panic in the boy's voice. "Jake, I need you to open the passenger door for me. Your mom's going to be alright. She fell off the ladder just now and might have sprained her ankle." And who knew what else? His stomach clenched.

Jake opened the door and stood aside like a tiny soldier, yet with a stricken expression on his face. "Are you going to the hospital?"

"We're all going to urgent care. It's quicker. There's one just across town. You can get in first, okay?"

Jake scrambled into the truck and Cooper eased Blair in after him, striving to avoid hurting her as she settled into the passenger seat. He saw her delicate wrist was swelling and a purple bruise bloomed there.

"Thank you, Cooper," she murmured.

Fortunately, not many people sat in the waiting room at the urgent care. When Blair's name was called, he helped her hobble on her good foot to an exam room. While they waited for the doctor, Jake stood beside the exam table where Blair had collapsed. She reached out to touch Jake's head.

Several minutes later, the doctor came.

"Hello, Blair," the man said. "I'm Dr. Crispin. What do we have here?" He leaned forward and peered through dark-rimmed glasses at her wrist, then her foot.

Cooper glanced at Blair, hoping to save her from the exertion of explaining. "Do you want me to describe what happened?" At her nod, he explained to the doctor what he'd seen and what Blair had shared with him. Jake sat in silence, but swung his feet under his chair.

"Thank you, Mr. McCartney. You were there when it happened?"

"Name's Dawson. We're neighbors. I saw her fall as I came home. She was up on a ladder cleaning gutters." He narrowed his eyes, and raised one eyebrow in a fake grimace. She rewarded him with a weak smile.

The doctor examined her wrist and her foot, touching different places as she winced. "Did you hear a popping noise as you fell, Ms. McCartney?"

"No."

The doctor touched her ankle again. "Does this hurt you? What about that?" At certain moments, she let out a whine.

The man took his clipboard. "Looks like you have a sprained ankle and wrist. It's known as a grade two sprain, so isn't the worst or the mildest. You'll need to stay off your foot and not use your hand for at least a week. We have crutches you can borrow, though initially, you'll only use one of them with your uninjured hand. Bring them back when you don't need them anymore. You'll also need two or more weeks of physical therapy for your ankle. For now, you'll have to elevate your foot and ice both wrist and foot for several days, several times per day."

"That's a lot to remember, Doctor," Blair whispered.

"I'll help you," Cooper said.

Dr. Crispen turned to a nurse who'd hovered nearby, tapping into a computer. "Get her some extra-strength ibuprofen for now." He scribbled on a small pad. "This prescription is stronger for pain. They're not too strong but should help. Miriam at the front desk can fit you for the crutches."

During the brief interview with Dr. Crispin, Jake sat close to Cooper, wide-eyed and quiet. Cooper laid his hand on Jake's shoulder and the child pulled closer to him. Cooper listened to the doctor's instructions, determined to keep Blair accountable for following them. He sent up a prayer of thanks that it wasn't worse. That she hadn't hit her head, broken her leg, broken her pelvis as she hit the ground.

The thought of those outcomes almost made him queasy.

As they drove home, Cooper glanced over at Blair. She was more alert than before and returned his gaze. "Thanks, Cooper."

"I'm so relieved it wasn't worse. You won't be able to work for at least a week, if not more. Do you have sick leave?"

She nodded. "I haven't taken any yet. I should have a week built up, maybe more." She turned her face toward the window. "I don't know what I'll do without being able to make things for the market. I'll get behind."

"It's okay, Blair. You can catch up later." He'd try to get a smile from her. "I won't let you get thrown in the street or eat peanut butter sandwiches for a month." He looked at Jake and winked.

Jake returned a solemn expression. "I like peanut butter sandwiches."

"Well, it's not steak, you have to admit."

Jake considered his words. "No. Steak's a little better."

"Cooper, we're not your responsibility, you know," Blair said. "I don't expect you to—"

"Enough said." He held up one hand. "It's just who I am, and you'll have to accept it. I'm looking out for you. If you don't think you need *any* help at *all* right now, just let me know."

She chuckled and shook her head, then leaned back against the seat as if he'd pulled a load from her shoulders. At least, he hoped she felt that way.

"You're impossible. But thank you. I'll owe you a lot of home-cooked dinners."

When they arrived at the house, Cooper carried her in and set her on the couch as if she were a fragile china doll. He propped her crutches against the fireplace nearby. "Jake, can you get a couple of pillows and a blanket?" he asked and turned to Blair. "Bet you're hungry. I'll make up some sandwiches and bring them over. No arguments."

Once he had Blair settled, he dashed back to his house. "Sorry, Zipper. Can't play today. I'll send Jake over later." At least he'd done some grocery shopping the day before. He whipped together a few ham and cheese sandwiches with pickles, chips, and whatever else he could grab that might be suitable lunch fare. He slipped everything into a plastic bag and headed next door.

Once he was back in Blair's living room, he spread everything out on the coffee table, then enlisted Jake's help to gather some drinks.

"This looks wonderful, Cooper." Blair offered a delicate smile.

"You're in less pain, I can tell."

"The meds are kicking in. I guess the pain'll come and go. It's going to be so hard to get dressed, get a shower, take care of life. All the things I took for granted before."

"Well, I can't help you get dressed, but I'll do what I can to help." Blair blushed and darned if he weren't blushing a little too. Why'd he say that?

"I don't know how to thank you."

"We'll just start by thanking God." So, he did. Cooper took her good hand and Jake's. He offered a prayer of gratitude for the mildness of Blair's injuries considering what they could have been, as well as thanks for the food.

The sandwiches hit the spot after the morning's excitement. Cooper wiped his mouth and pushed his plate aside. "Timing's bad, Blair. I was planning to come to church with you guys tomorrow."

"I think you should go anyway," she said. "You'll like it. It's really down to earth and the people are nice. Go, Cooper."

"Okay. I can take Jake. On second thought, you might need him to fetch things for you."

"I think you're right. It's okay if he misses tomorrow. I wish we could be there to introduce you to people, though I don't know everyone."

"I met Leah the other day at Jake's recital, and I met her boyfriend at the coffee shop. So, there's two I know already."

"Nathan. I forgot you'd met him. So, you won't feel alone."

"Doesn't bother me to be alone." No, he was used to it now. "I'll go be with God. And I'll drop in after to let you know how it was. Maybe I can even summarize the sermon for you." Their eyes met and the familiar spark ignited. Seemed stronger every time. "You have my number, right? Call me if you need anything."

"I will."

"I'll let you guys rest. Please don't hesitate. Blair." He made sure she was looking at him. "Please. Don't. Hesitate."

"Okay, okay, mother hen." She laughed and waved him away. "But you're a great mother hen, by the way."

He smirked. "Just what a guy wants to hear. How about a more masculine image, like knight in shining armor?" He grinned at her.

"Definitely like that."

The following day, Cooper learned Blair was right about her church. He liked everything about it. The grassroots feel of the service, the friendliness of the members, the inspiring challenge of the sermon. He'd slipped in the back row and stayed there until the end, listening intently, scoping, observing, and simply enjoying being back in a house of worship. After the service, he'd planned to disappear like a phantom, but spied Leah in the aisle talking to Nathan. She'd played the violin with remarkable talent during the service.

Cooper approached them. Leah stared at him a moment, as if trying to place him. "Cooper, hi! Is this your first time here at church?"

"Yeah, the service was great. Blair invited me some time ago, and I was planning on coming today with her and Jake, but unfortunately, she had an accident and couldn't come. I thought you should know, so you can pray for her and maybe visit."

Leah's face paled with alarm. "What happened?"

Cooper recounted the events of the previous day while Leah frowned, and her eyes crinkled with regret.

"She'll be on bed rest for at least a week. I can look in on her, because I live next door and my schedule's flexible, but I'm sure she'd love to see you too."

"Absolutely," Leah said. "I'm so glad you told us, Cooper."

"We can mobilize some folks here to help her out," Nathan said.

"And take over food." Leah swept her gaze back to Nathan. "She won't be able to cook."

"Definitely not," Cooper said. "Like I said, I can go over there and check during the day once in a while."

He didn't want his watchfulness for Blair being usurped by the caring people of the church, but more help wouldn't be a bad thing.

On his way home, a wave of satisfaction hit him, for being in the right place to help Blair. He'd seen her fall and was able to help her, and now the news of her needs had gone to her faith community. He loved it when God used him to help people, though normally, Blair didn't need his help as much as he'd originally thought. In fact, she was darned competent in most things.

He thought of Miles and his spirits sagged. If only he'd arrived at the right time for him. Maybe that's what drove him to help and protect. He'd been incapable of either when his brother had most needed him.

Chapter Fourteen

"Jake, what about your lunch?" Blair struggled to sit up on the couch. Less than forty-eight hours and she was sick of lying around like a sack of flour, her foot elevated on several cushions. A few days to go. With crutches, she could at least make Jake's sandwich before he left for school. He'd gotten his own cereal.

"I can do it, Mom. I'm a big guy."

She had to smile. In a short amount of time, he'd begun taking more responsibility for himself. He'd brought her ice every couple of hours and helped her pack her wrist and ankle. He even walked straighter. Or was she imagining that as much as she imagined herself shriveling up? She wasn't used to being helped. And helpless. And she didn't like it one bit.

The previous day, Cooper had stopped by briefly after church. He claimed to enjoy the service, as she'd predicted, and apparently his few words to Leah and Nathan had mobilized the community on her behalf. She spent the evening on the phone as people she hadn't even met called her to tell her they were praying for her. Each time, her throat tightened, and her eyes stung, a wellspring of gratitude for these dear people she hardly knew.

Then the casseroles started coming. By six that evening, she had three meals, enough for the entire week. Lydia, Abbie, and Jannelle, the pastor's wife, each brought a foil-covered Pyrex pan but didn't stay long. Falling and almost breaking her head open was one way to get to know the people at church.

Jake ran into the living room, fully dressed for school.

"Did you make your lunch, big guy?"

"I made a sandwich and put in an apple and some cookies that lady brought over last night."

"That's great, Jake." She glanced at her watch. "You don't have much time before the bus comes. C'mere." She pulled him in for a hug and held on a little too long. Her little boy was growing up fast. She pulled back and smoothed golden curls from his forehead. "Have a great day, sweetie. Do you want to come home on the bus, or go to Miss Angela's house? I call her and let her know."

Jake hesitated. "Well, we started this game the other day and we're almost done with that puzzle. But I can come home if you want."

Blair's heart sank. "Oh, no, that's okay." She forced a smile. A couple of additional hours alone. She'd manage. At least Jake enjoyed being at Angela's. "So, I'll tell her what happened, but that you still want to go." If she really couldn't manage by herself, she'd tell him to come directly home for the next few days.

After he left, his dinosaur backpack on his shoulders, she leaned against the two pillows wedged behind her back. Her eyes followed him through the window until he was out of sight.

The silence of the house shouted from all sides. Usually, if she had time alone, she filled it with sewing projects. On a normal day, she loved having solitary time to focus without interruptions. What would that day bring, since she couldn't even walk, let alone catch up on her work?

She'd find a way to be productive, maybe do a blog post or sketch ideas with her good hand. Maybe the fingers on her left hand would work, though she doubted her injured foot could press a sewing machine pedal.

Priority one, a shower. Though she dreaded the difficulty of this routine act, she simply had to do it. It had been two days, and she had to wash her hair too. The previous day she'd mentally prepared herself but hadn't had the courage and ended up collapsing on the couch in a cloud of self-pity.

"You can do this, Blair. Even if you take all morning." She'd downed her pain meds, which took the edge off, though didn't eradicate the discomfort. She reached for one crutch and hauled herself up, which took several minutes. Once she was upright, it was easier to hobble to the back of the house. Walking on crutches wasn't elegant or comfortable, but she was thankful to have them.

Blair half sat on the bathroom counter, her weight on her good foot, as she gingerly removed her pajama bottoms, followed by her panties, then her top. A process that took nearly ten minutes.

The shower didn't have a grab bar, but the water felt good. Taking a shower on one foot and washing with one hand wasn't for the fainthearted. She frequently clutched the wet glass with her right hand for stability.

By the time Blair reached the safety of her couch, tears of frustration threatened to spill over. Breathing deeply, she relaxed into the cushions, but realized she hadn't brought her devotional books and laptop with her. With a heavy sigh, she pulled herself up again.

A few minutes later, she collapsed again onto the couch, her foot throbbing. A quick glance at the clock on her phone showed it wasn't yet time for pain killers. She braced herself for a long week.

Blair adjusted herself to an upright position and pulled her Bible from the coffee table. She hadn't read it in a few days, and the fact that she'd missed church left an additional void. She opened the book randomly and ended up in the Psalms, which usually brought her comfort. That particular Monday, she needed some.

After skimming a couple of chapters and feeling the warmth of connection spread through her, her eyes landed on a verse in Psalm 139 that caused her to stop. *O Lord, you have examined my heart and know everything about me. You know when I sit down or stand up...* Or even fall off a ladder. He knew it before it happened. Why didn't he protect her? She remembered Cooper's prayer. He *did*. It could have been so much worse.

As she read the Psalm, one she'd never read before, her throat tightened, and tears gathered in her eyes. *I can never escape from your Spirit! ... You knit me together in my mother's womb ... your workmanship is marvelous.*

Marvelous. She blinked. God called her marvelous, even a misfit like her. Marvelous. How could that be? She'd messed up her life, hadn't she? When she thought about Jake, she couldn't imagine that she'd messed up *everything*. If she'd had to choose all over again... How often that thought came back to her. Yet, despite the certainty of her choice in raising Jake, it was what came before that always pulled her down. She'd always known in her head that being an artist was a good thing, a gift, the way God had created her. But she couldn't get her heart to buy in during those years of feeling like she didn't fit into her own family.

But God called her *marvelous*. A masterpiece. Custom made.

Blair allowed those truths to settle in for a minute then bookmarked the Psalm to read it again. To study it. Maybe it would sink in over the next few days.

Her gaze roved to the other side of the room, where countless sewing projects awaited her. With Jake's new school year launching, her evenings hadn't been as available. She told herself she'd catch up once he was settled. Now, that would take even longer. She'd have nothing to sell at the market next week, if she could even walk by that time. The loss of one more Saturday might mean not having enough to pay her increase in rent.

Just when things were going her way, with the contest, the market, and possibly a positive response to her designs at her workplace. She'd called that morning to let them know she'd been injured and had to be out all week. Though her case was legitimate, a fear hovered in her mind. Would they determine they didn't need her after all? No sense in dragging into the mix a problem that didn't even exist.

She opened her laptop and scrolled to the attractive *BlairWear* website Garrett had designed for her. Across the banner, several women strode in confidence, like runway models. They weren't her designs, but stock photos to catch attention. For branding, as Nathan had told her.

Foreign territory. Her pulse sped up as intimidation engulfed her. *Take your time, Blair. Just get to know it first.* She'd work on one of the blog post articles on her list. She opened a fresh document and stared at the blank page. She already had an outline to follow, one she'd made as an assignment from Garrett the week before. After a few moments of staring at her outline, she typed a few words. Stared at the white expanse, typed a few more, tapping mostly with her right hand. She tried her swollen left hand and found her fingers could offer a small contribution. She started with a *Welcome to BlairWear* article for the front page. Garrett had also created an *About Me* page.

At noon, a knock on the front door jolted Blair from her absorption in her website. From where she sat in the living room, she spotted a thatch of dark brown hair, the top of Cooper's head, through the panes of glass on the door. A flush of eagerness filled her. She wasn't sure he'd come and was *so* glad she'd showered.

"You awake, Blair?" He called softly as he pushed open the front door, which Jake hadn't locked. "Lunch is here."

"Come in, it's open." Blair closed her laptop and set it on the coffee table.

He came into the living room, a paper bag in one hand, wearing jeans and a gray T-shirt with dirt on one sleeve.

"Hi, Cooper. Did you get back to the work site today?"

"Yes, can you tell? I'm covered with sawdust and sweat. How are you feeling?" He set a bag on the table, then settled in a chair next to the couch.

An enticing aroma of something fried filled the room and triggered a hungry growl. Blair pushed her glasses on top of her head. "I'm comfortable if I don't move much. I got a shower, so I feel *much* better, though it wasn't easy."

"I guess you called in at work. They were okay with you being gone?"

"Not much they or I can do about it."

He poked at the bag. "I should have asked you what you like. We can play twenty questions after lunch. Favorite sandwich, soup, all that."

She laughed. "You don't have to bring me food every day, though it's really sweet that you did. Some women from church brought by casseroles last night. I think as soon as you told Leah about my fall, word got around and a few of them went home and started cooking."

"I'd still like to check on you and see if you need anything."

"Don't get me wrong, I'm *glad* you're here. I need some company and I happen to like yours."

He looked bashful for a moment. "Well, that I can do, keep you company once in a while." He opened the bag. "I brought fried chicken this time. Figured you'd be tired of sandwiches. This'll change things up."

"I love that, even if it's messy." Her stomach rumbled again. "Smells wonderful."

As they ate, she asked him about his house, how much was completed, when he could start choosing things like rugs and tiles. She was interested in those things, but also wanted to avoid talking about herself too much.

"Ah, I see your interest," he said. "Decoration. Makes sense. I like the bones, but you like the skin." He reached for another piece of chicken.

"Clever. I'm interested in how it'll look when it's finished. Lamps, cupboard finish, wall color. I know that's probably the last thing you think about."

"I'll let you help me pick all that out when the time comes. I trust your design sense." He rubbed his oily fingers into the paper napkin and pushed the chicken box aside.

"Thank you, though I'm sure you have a pretty clear idea of what you want. Looked that way to me in that design you showed me." She licked her fingers and wiped them. "That was so good. You knew what I was in the mood for when I didn't even know."

He chuckled and cleared away the trash but didn't seem to be in a hurry to go anywhere. "Do you still have ice cream?"

"Yes, it's in the freezer. Perfect ending to this lunch."

He disappeared for a few minutes. "Butter pecan okay?" His voice carried from the kitchen.

"Perfect."

He returned with two bowls and spoons, and they dug in. "What are you working on?" He hitched his head toward her laptop.

"When I realized I couldn't do sewing projects I remembered my new website needs attention. So, I figured I could probably start writing some blog posts. I tried out my busted wrist, and my fingers work okay."

"Your site's going to be more important than it seems right now for getting your name out there in the fashion world."

"Yeah, that's what Nathan said. I'm finally letting go of my New York fashion house dream." She licked the back of her spoon and set the bowl on the coffee table.

"That was your dream? Why?"

Blair shrugged. "That's the approved route to the world of fashion design."

"I'm surprised, since so many people are entrepreneurs these days. Why would you want to work for someone else?"

She had no answer. "I'm not sure. It always seemed the path forward, but I missed the normal entry point when I decided to raise Jake."

He scratched his chin. "Aren't there many ways to get a foot in? I'm not saying it's easy."

"I *am* considering the *indie route*." She made air quotes. "But I think part of me wants the … legitimacy, I guess." She shrugged, having admitted something she was only recognizing herself.

Cooper fell silent then laid a hand on her arm. "You're legitimate, Blair. I've seen what you do. You don't need some fashion kingpin to give you a seal of approval."

His words stroked a bruised place inside her. She'd felt illegitimate all her life, in her family, then in her current pursuit of a goal out of reach. "You think I can succeed independently?" His hand still rested on her arm, spreading warmth up to her elbow.

"Not a doubt. It might take a long time in either case, but I think doing it yourself gives you more control and you'd own the final product."

"Maybe you're right. In the last week, I've had some good signs. First, the guy at work who validated my design. I told you about him. They have a design department, but that doesn't mean there are positions available."

"Would you want a design position?"

"It's the same goal I wanted to achieve by going to New York, only I could stay here in the Falls."

"That's *definitely* a good thing, for you to stay here."

"I agree."

He pulled his hand away from her arm. "You said *some good signs*. Any others?"

"I applied for a design contest a couple of months ago. A few days before I fell, I got a letter in the mail saying I was a semi-finalist."

"See, Blair, you're getting recognition. What's next?"

"Nothing, really." She let out an awkward laugh. "There are seventy of us who are semi-finalists, and they'll choose ten to be finalists, then three after that. So, I'm not packing my suitcase just yet. But it still felt good to read that letter. It was the same day as my ceiling leak, so God knew I needed encouragement."

He drained his water glass. "Would you like more water? And a fresh ice pack?"

"Yes, to both. Thanks." He vanished into the kitchen. Every day that went by, he surprised her with kindness, interest in her work, sacrificial time spent helping her with things. He had a house to build, had lost almost a week during the rain, but here he was, eating ice cream with her, encouraging her in her work.

He returned carrying two full glasses. An ice pack draped over his wrist. He set them on the table.

Blair shifted on her pillow, tired of sitting in one position. She held out her arm and he wrapped the fresh ice pack around her wrist.

He returned to the armchair. "I told you we'd play twenty questions. Here goes. First date."

She laughed. "I thought we were talking ice cream flavors. I'll see if I can remember." She'd been sixteen and couldn't remember the name of the guy. "Some school dance, I think. We went out a few more times, then he got interested in someone else."

"Can't imagine that." Cooper rested his chin on his fists, elbows on his knees, and stared at her with those fathomless blue eyes.

"What did you like about Nelson?"

Blair took a breath. Did she want to talk about Nelson? Cooper shared about his ex. She could too, despite the current crisis he'd created. "In college, I'd started meeting other people in my program, and some of their friends were artists in different fields. I felt like I'd found my people. Nelson was in that group. He's a graphic artist. We were attracted to each other right away and ended up dating for two years."

Cooper's brows went up. "Two years and he still had the nerve to deny his own son?"

"Surprised me as much as you." She cocked her head, remembering. "He was funny, kind. He had a lot of good qualities, so yeah, I was shocked when he not only cheated on me with a friend of mine, but abandoned me when I got pregnant with *his* child."

"Loser."

His indignation on her behalf made her smile. "Yes, but he seems to be realizing what he lost."

"What's the status? Did you send Jake's letter?"

"Not yet, and I feel guilty about it. I'll do it in the next day or so." She hated how that subject hovered endlessly in her mind.

"I've had second thoughts about what I told you," he said. "I'm not saying don't let Jake meet him, but I think you should take your time. Maybe even see an attorney before you do anything else. Find out what your rights are and how you can best protect yourself. Just in case."

"Just in case... That's what keeps me awake at night. Once I open the door, I can't shut it. I don't know what kind of guy he's become."

"We can Google him. Or do a background check. That won't answer too many questions, but might make you feel better."

"Jake wrote a sweet little letter then seemed to forget about it. Now I need to write one." She sighed. "I need to get it over with and trust God with what happens."

"Even after you send the letter, *you* can control what happens."

She lifted her head and their eyes met. For a moment, the air hummed between them. "I hope so. Didn't want to talk about this today, but it helps."

Zipper barked outside, breaking into the intensity of the moment. He barked again. Cooper rose to glance out the window. "I have to go. Looks like I'm getting a delivery. Something for the house."

Disappointment pooled inside her. "It was really nice to see you, Cooper. Come over anytime. Next time, don't bring anything. I'll share a casserole with you."

"Sounds great. We can continue with our twenty questions." He grinned. "When's Jake coming home?"

"About five. He's at the home of a lady who keeps him after school." Her hands flew to her mouth. She'd forgotten. "Oh, I don't know how he'll get home. I forgot to call her."

"I'll get him. What's the address?"

"Oh, I couldn't ask you to do that."

"Blair, what's the address? Can't be too far from here."

"It's not. It's on Acorn." She jotted down the address. "I pick him up at five."

Cooper nodded. "Five it is. See you soon."

No time would be soon enough.

Chapter Fifteen

Cooper's house finally bore a faint resemblance to the dream he'd cultivated through the barren years after Miles's death. The vision that had given him a reason to go on during the darkness.

The exterior walls were in place, as well as the roof. Time for plumbing. He didn't stay long at Blair's yesterday. They'd shared lasagna and he plied her with a few more light-hearted questions, while avoiding his own heartaches. He didn't need to burden her with that.

Before her accident, he usually spent all day at the construction site. But knowing Blair might need help, and by her own admission, company, he shifted his schedule to spend an extended lunch break with her. He told himself it was primarily for her benefit, but knew he craved her company and delighted in being of help to her, even if she didn't always want it. These days, she accepted one small service at a time. As she did, the magnetic draw toward her became even stronger. He may as well give up his high-sounding claims of protecting his heart. Resisting the flow of his emotions took too much out of him. Maybe *she* was what his heart needed most.

That day at lunchtime, he hurried home, took care of Zipper, and crossed the small lawn to her house, anticipation welling up inside him. He hoped he wasn't being a nuisance. He knocked on the door and was about to push it open but heard a faint voice inside. "Wait, it's locked."

Jake must have locked it that day, which was probably a good idea, but meant she had to hobble up and let him in. She unlocked the door, leaning on one crutch. Her red-rimmed eyes met his.

"Are you having a rough day?" he asked gently, reaching out to stroke her cheek with the edge of his hand.

She blinked rapidly, and a few tears squeezed out of her eyes. He couldn't help himself. He stepped forward and gathered her into an embrace, leaning her crutch against the wall. Her arms went around his waist and her head buried into his chest as she melted into him. She felt warm and soft in his arms, but it kindled a fire inside him. With her head inches below his chin, his heart thudded against his ribs. It would be so natural to kiss her, to lift her chin... Cooper swallowed and slowed his breath. As much as he ached for it, he wouldn't take advantage of her vulnerability.

She stayed in his arms for another moment, then pulled back, smiling up at him with luminous eyes still glossy with tears. "Thanks. I needed a hug."

"What's up?"

She waved the air dismissively and reached for her crutch. "Just me being weird. My thoughts went down a tunnel this morning."

He followed her through the wide arch into the living room. She walked better, though still used one crutch. She settled on the couch, sighing deeply with the effort. He sat across from her and folded his hands across spread knees. She must have already put a casserole in the oven. An enticing aroma of oregano and rosemary filled the air.

"I'm not sure what started the spiral." She reached for a tissue. "But I started thinking about the direction of my life and felt hopeless. I wondered, what if I don't make it as a designer, what will I do instead, and what if I can't afford to give Jake the life I want for him? And so on. I'm embarrassed to say I was feeling sorry for myself, and it snowballed from there."

Cooper ran one hand through his hair. "It happens to all of us, Blair." Happened to him on a regular basis. He'd become adept at corralling his thoughts. Mostly. "Take one day at a time, and remember God has you. That goes for you and me both. Otherwise, our thoughts'll take us way off course."

She pressed her lips together. He stared at them for a moment, then his gaze found hers. The air crackled between them.

"I know." She offered a lopsided grin. "Thanks for reminding me to fall back on what I know is true. You came at just the right time."

Relief trickled through him. "I'm glad. I was afraid I was becoming a pest."

"I enjoy your visits, Cooper." Her voice grew gentle. "I wait for them."

She waits for them. Her words stirred hope inside him.

"If I'm overstepping, let me know. I like to look in on you and see if you need anything, but it's fun getting to know you better too."

"Likewise." Her gaze found his. Those beautiful hazel eyes rimmed with thick lashes. He was glad she'd stopped wearing her glasses as often, although she looked cute wearing them too.

"How is your blog going?"

"Actually, pretty well." She perked up. "I started writing posts, and the ideas kept coming. So, I did three of them to start. I'll space out the others. I studied other blogs to get more ideas. I used to skim them, but now I'm dissecting them to see what they do, why, and how."

"That's smart. See, you're still moving toward your goals."

"I feel better, despite my meltdown. I'm not used to being handicapped. The simplest things are hard."

"You're doing better, though." He sniffed the air. "If lunch is ready, I'll bring it out."

"Should be hot by now. It's been in my *perfectly* functioning oven at least forty minutes. Something Greek, I think."

Cooper rose before she finished talking. "Be right back."

He brought in the meal with a pair of oven mitts, then went back for plates, silverware, and drinks. Whatever else happened between them, he'd treasure those moments spent eating and talking together while he could. She was walking better already and would probably return to work the following Monday. Steam billowed up from the plates as he placed a slab of Greek chicken and pasta casserole on each one. Alongside, he spooned out some salad from another bowl.

He placed his hand over hers and prayed for the meal, then opened his eyes. "I was thinking again about your housing situation and got an idea."

She blew on a forkful of pasta, but her eyes rose to his. "I'm intrigued. What's your idea?"

"There's a process to making a complaint against your landlord. If you email a complaint and several other renters do too, that might force him to do better at taking care of you all."

"How would we convince other people to complain when we don't know them?"

He sent her a wily grin. "We can compose an official-looking letter. Not traceable to us, of course. We find out who rents from Mitchell, since his property is public record. If they have issues, they might not know how to complain."

"So, the letter supplies links so all they have to do is write in."

"Bingo." He leaned forward." We could even drop by and visit each one, once your foot is better."

"I'd rather send letters. I like that idea, if you're sure it's anonymous and Mitchell can't trace it to me. I'd get evicted."

"No, we'll make sure it's completely untraceable. I'll pull together some ideas for the letter, if you want, and add your input."

"I'm not interested in revenge, but would love to force Mitchell's hand in doing the right thing."

"We'll get to it, then. By the way, have you tried walking without crutches yet?" He finished off his salad and took a gulp of water.

"Yes, this morning." She blew on a steaming forkful then set it down. "I got ready today without them and felt like I'd won the

Olympics. Physical therapy starts next week. My wrist is on the mend. See, the swelling has gone down." She held up her arm. It was slender and beautiful, like before.

"I noticed. That's great."

Silence fell. Cooper's gaze wandered to the clock on the mantle. Time was going too fast.

"What time do you have to go?"

"In a few minutes. Not in a hurry, though. I have an idea for you."

Her finely chiseled brows lifted, accompanied by an expectant smile. "You have lots of ideas for me today."

"Let's brainstorm what you'll do to the clothes on that chair." He pointed to a pile of garments. "You can't sew yet, but if you go through the stack and *plan* the work, you'll be ahead."

"I always plan before each piece, but planning in bulk is a good idea. Even if my hands and feet don't work yet, my brain still does."

He rose and grabbed a few garments. "Okay, let's start with this one." He lifted a pink dress. The sleeves bunched up as if the sewing machine had gone rogue. "There are three like this. Messed up sleeves."

"Three the same? That's great. I'll do the same thing with all of them. I'll replace the sleeves or—" She tilted her head to one side, staring at the dress. "I could remove the sleeves and make them sleeveless." She reached for a notepad from the side table.

Next on the pile was a pair of linen drawstring pants. "Looks like these are coming apart." He handed them to Blair, and she examined each side with an expert eye.

"I can take in these seams and make it a smaller size. That's an easy fix. Any others like this?"

"One more. Okay, that's five projects all planned. And it only took five minutes." He enjoyed being able to take part in her passion, as well as help her expedite her work.

Cooper held up an off-white dress with some kind of stain right in the center. "I think you'll see the problem with this one right away."

"I can try to dye it. That's all I can do with that one."

"You dye things too?"

"Sure, why not? You have *no* idea what I can do with a piece of cloth." Her tone was almost flirty. It tantalized him.

"I can just imagine." He matched her tone.

Blair's cell phone rang. "It's my mom. I'll call her back."

"You can answer it. I'll get going now." Cooper rose.

She answered but held up one finger. "Hi, Mom. I'll need to call you back. I have a friend over who's about to leave." She paused, listening. "Oh, I forgot. I can't drive Jake to Milton this weekend. I'm not sure I can drive at all yet, but definitely not that far. You sure? Okay, um...make it early if you can. If I'm able to go to the market, that starts at nine. Thanks. I'll call you this afternoon, okay? Bye."

She disconnected. "I think I told you Jake spends a weekend a month at his grandparents' house. I totally forgot this was his weekend, but of course, I can't drive him. She'll pick him up."

"Good. I'll be around if you need any help with anything."

"I'm going to start leaning on you."

"No problem." He meant every word.

"Soon I'll be on my feet, literally."

Cooper took his keys from the table and slipped them into his back pocket. "Will you have enough things to sell at the market?"

"If I can work on these Friday, I may have enough."

"Do you need help getting there?"

"Leah's on call to take me and pick me up. We talked about it yesterday when she stopped by to visit. Thanks for asking."

"And thank *you* for lunch. Or for sharing it with me." He'd better leave now before he thought of six more services to offer, and it became embarrassing.

She struggled to rise.

"Don't get up. I'll let myself out. I hope your afternoon is productive and you stay hopeful."

"You've helped me with that."

They shared a smile and he turned to go. He'd almost reached the front door when he stopped. Jake would be with his grandparents. The wheels turned in his mind.

"Blair?" He returned to the doorway. "Do you want to come for dinner Saturday? Jake won't be here, and I don't want you to stay alone." Ulterior motives abounded. "In case you think I'm being selfless, I've gotten accustomed to eating meals with you and enjoy it. No sense in each of us eating alone, right?"

She chuckled. "You have a point there. I'd love to come. Leah's shopping for me this afternoon. I'll bring a veggie, okay?"

"If you insist. I'll still swing by tomorrow, though I can only stay about an hour."

"See you then."

He carried the sound of her soft response in his mind as he let himself out the front door and returned to his truck.

ल	ल	ल

Blair sat still listening as the front door closed. Cooper's truck roared to life, and he backed out of the driveway. Silence fell like a blanket over the room.

She still tingled from the shower of chemistry that had pinged through the room from the moment he arrived on her doorstep. From the moment he pulled her into his strong arms.

When she'd fallen off the ladder the previous Saturday, she'd imagined lonely, unproductive days. The last thing she'd expected was spending moments she didn't want to end with Cooper. He checked on her, waited on her, spent hours with her, when all the while he had his own house to build.

She wanted to believe his intentions went beyond those of a kind neighbor, a caring friend. And the hug…Blair grew hot reliving the moments locked in his arms, the care and warmth flooding her. The manly smell of him, hard work laced with fading cologne. She'd wanted the hug to go further, fighting the temptation to lift her face and invite him to the next step.

Shortly before he arrived that day, a spiral of hopeless thoughts had dragged her into a dark state. With prayers of defeat, devoid of faith, the heaviness had persisted. She scrambled for verses to challenge her self-condemnation, but her certainty that her life would fall short of her dreams remained. Cooper's touch and his words infused her with hope. Reminded her of truth. Maybe she'd just needed a friend. No, she needed truth *and* Cooper.

And Saturday dinner. Almost a date. Maybe that night she'd tell him her feelings for him. Hopefully, she wasn't risking his friendship, but trying to act normal around him was getting exhausting. Beyond fixing things and offering advice, she'd seen another side of him. A side that drew her.

Blair cordoned off her thoughts and called her mother. "Hi, Mom. Sorry I had to cut you off."

"How are you getting along, Blair? I would have come over to help."

"I know. But I have a lot of help. My neighbor's been checking in on me every day. A friend from church is getting groceries for me this afternoon and I told you I have six casseroles from ladies at church in my fridge."

Her mother laughed. "Sounds like you won't starve. I'm relieved to hear about all the help. It's nice to have a helpful neighbor, too. She sounds like a blessing."

You have no idea.

"I'll be glad to get Jake," her mother said. "I can come Saturday around eight-thirty, so you can get to the market. Or even Friday."

"Saturday's better. I'll have him ready by eight-thirty."

"I'm an early riser." A beat of silence filled the phone. "Blair, have you done anything about the letter Nelson sent to Jake?"

Blair sighed. She'd recovered from her anger toward her mother for interfering in the matter of Nelson. "I read the letter to Jake and asked him what he wanted to do." She paused. "Mom, I'm glad Jake knows about Nelson, but I need you to understand this is *our* situation to deal with. I can keep you posted, but not if you plan to take matters into your own hands." Though she'd forgiven her mother, a bolt of irritation still shot through her.

"I did apologize for putting that note in his bag." Her mother's tone was brittle. "What did Jake say about the letter?"

"Jake told me he was afraid to meet his father but was willing to write to him at first. I helped him write a letter in his words. I haven't mailed it yet because I'm not ready for Nelson to know where we live. Can I give it to you to mail for me from Milton?"

"Of course. Your feelings are understandable, but I'm glad you're open to the idea of Jake meeting him one day. I agree it's wise to go slowly."

"I'm concerned about the impact meeting Nelson will have on Jake. He's doing so well now, settling into Brenner Falls. I don't want anything to hinder that."

"I agree. I'm here to support you, but won't interfere again."

"Thank you." Finally.

"Would you consider meeting Nelson advance? That way, you can check him out."

"It's crossed my mind, but I'm not ready to see him."

"I understand."

"I'll send a letter of my own along with Jake's and give my email address. That way, we can correspond without revealing where we live."

"That's a good idea. I'll see you Saturday morning."

Blair spent the rest of the afternoon going through the pile of garments, making notes on each one, and writing blogposts. The following day, she'd try her foot with the sewing machine. If she could knock out the alterations by Saturday, she'd have something to sell and still have a hope of making her rent the following month.

She'd begun the day feeling blue, but God had used Cooper to turn her completely around. As a bonus, her productivity that afternoon went off the charts. To her surprise, she enjoyed writing blog posts and ended up writing two more by the time Jake returned from school.

For the next two days, minor glitches at the work site kept Cooper tied up. He stopped briefly on Thursday and said he couldn't come Friday at lunch. She sensed his disappointment and wondered if it equaled her own. At least she'd see him Saturday night.

Thursday afternoon, Blair took small steps around the house without crutches, and for short periods, managed fine. Her success tempted her to try the sewing machine next. The gentle pressure she exerted on the pedal didn't cause much pain, so she worked on her projects all afternoon, completing the stack. She even made several purses to add to her market inventory.

Though she stayed busy, Jake's letter to Nelson hovered in her mind. She had to write one of her own before her mother came the next day. A knot formed in her throat. As soon as her mother sent the letters, there would be no turning back.

After eight years, Nelson would reenter her life.

Chapter Sixteen

Dear Nelson. Blair backspaced. *Nelson,* she wrote. Perspiration coated the back of her neck. Jake had gone to bed an hour earlier. Since that time, she hunched over her laptop, praying for words. She'd written and erased the first couple lines of her letter four times.

After a glance at the clock, her shoulders sagged. Once she'd finished the letter and was at peace with it, she'd be able to sleep. She'd entrust it to God. She prayed a fortress of protection around Jake's child heart. And her own.

Contact by email hadn't occurred to her at first, but it would give Jake and Nelson the means to correspond without meeting. And she'd be able to moderate the relationship without Nelson knowing where they lived.

Finally, she wrote something she didn't need to delete. After a good night's sleep, she'd reread it and either revise or print it.

Blair leaned back against the chair and read what she'd written.

Nelson,

It's strange for me to write to you after all these years. Last year, when I received your letter, I wasn't ready to speak to you. I didn't want to allow you into our lives, despite your claim to have changed and your desire to recognize your son. I want you to know I have forgiven you for your past behavior.

You haven't been part of Jake's life since the day he was born. I'm hesitant to let you meet him since I don't know you anymore. Jake and I have a nice life together, and I don't know what you'd bring into his experience, whether harm or good. You're an unknown, as you've chosen to be all these years. I understand you want to know him. I won't commend you for that since you're seven years too late. I felt it was fair to ask Jake what he wanted. His desires concern me the most, along with the possibility that you might be a positive person in his life.

I hope you understand my caution. I'm risking the well-being of my precious boy to an unknown person, father or not. I'm not ready to open the door and let you walk in. Not after eight years of nothing. When I asked Jake what he wanted, he said he was afraid to meet you right now but was willing to write you a letter. So, the letter in this envelope is from him. You and Jake may begin corresponding as a first step. The easiest way is by email. We'll see how that goes. Please understand, this is not revenge or anger, but protection of Jake and a desire to take things slowly.

I'll do whatever it takes to protect him and make sure he has the best life possible.

Blair

PS I'd like to request that you elaborate on your "change of heart" and what brought this about. Thanks in advance.

She added her email by her name. She committed it to God's will in prayer, turned off the computer, and went to bed.

The following morning, Blair awoke, relieved to have fallen asleep without tossing and ruminating for hours. After her shower, which was far easier than a few days earlier, she opened her computer and reread her letter. It was cautious, distant, appropriate. There was nothing she wanted to add or change, so she printed it and tucked it in the same envelope as Jake's letter. She addressed the envelope but left the return address blank, sealed, and stamped it, and set it on the kitchen counter to give to her mother.

A layer of calm settled over her. Was that confirmation she was doing the right thing? Or was she simply tired of agonizing about it?

"Jake, are you ready to go to Nanna's house? Here, let me check your backpack, okay, big guy?"

"I want to take my truck. There isn't room in my backpack."

"Doesn't your Nanna have trucks for you?" She kneeled in front of him and smoothed his unruly curls with her hands, then deposited a kiss on his forehead. She fought the compulsion to hold him in her arms for a long time.

"I like mine better, but I can leave it here."

Blair heard tires scrape the gravel drive outside. "Nanna's here, sweetie. I hope you have a fun weekend with her and Grandpa."

She opened the door for her mother, and they hugged. "How are you feeling, Blair?" Concern etched her face. "You must have taken quite a fall to be out of work all week. Let me see."

Blair showed her mother her wrist and her ankle. "They're much better. They were both swollen right after it happened. I'll do a few sessions of physical therapy starting next week. That'll strength the muscles." She met her mother's gaze and slipped the envelope into her hand. "Here's the letter. I added one of my own. It has my email address so they can correspond by email."

"It'll go out in today's mail." Blair's mother looked down at Jake. "Are you all ready, sweetheart? We're going to have a fun weekend."

"I'm ready, Nanna." He clutched the strap of his dinosaur backpack.

"I'll have him home Sunday after dinner." She laid a hand on Blair's arm. "Have a restful weekend."

With a last hug to both Jake and her mother, Blair waved them off. She took a breath before hurrying to prepare for the market as quickly as her sore foot would allow her.

Ten minutes later, Leah arrived. "You all set, Blair?" She looked cute, dressed in jeans and a mid-sleeved T-shirt, her shoulder-length hair in a high ponytail. Perfect for a Saturday morning. "I mean, you're sure you're up to this?"

"I'll be fine for a couple of hours if I stay seated. And it'll be good to chat with people."

"Call me when you're ready to come home, okay?" Leah had already taken an armload of bags filled with Blair's projects in one arm.

"I will. Thanks so much, Leah."

Leah dropped her armload into her trunk. Blair followed her, walking gingerly with her own smaller pile.

"I have a rehearsal later this afternoon for a musical we're doing at Seasons. We open next week, and there's still a lot to do." Leah backed up and headed toward downtown.

"I'd love to come see your show sometime. I've heard a lot recently about the revival of Seasons. Nathan must have done a significant makeover."

"Yes, earlier in the summer. He reopened in June. We're glad he's getting new people, not just the old timers who loved it before." Leah stopped at a light and turned to Blair. "He's gifted for it. What can I say?"

"And *you're* gifted for music. That makes you the perfect pair. How cool that you can do your passion and help Nathan with his business at the same time."

"After a series of terrible jobs, I feel more blessed than ever."

"That gives me hope." Both of them had done their time in dead-end jobs.

Blair's eyes wandered through the car window to the busy Saturday morning shoppers and crystal blue sky overhead. "It's *so* good to get out of the house," she said. "I'm touched by how much help everyone gave me this week. You, Cooper, the church women, everyone. And you're all so busy."

"Hey." Leah reached out and squeezed Blair's forearm. "We help each other. You helped with costumes last year when we did the Christmas show at Seasons."

"It was fun. Let me know if you need help again this year."

"Gladly." Leah turned on Summit and slowed down to look for parking. "Is there anything new with Cooper? He's really nice. And handsome, too."

Blair couldn't stop the hot flush that rose in her neck. "We're good friends at this point. I'll admit, I'm hoping it'll go further. He came over for lunch a few times this week to keep me company and check on me."

Leah's eyes widened. "He did? That's great, Blair. What do you mean you're just friends? He *clearly* has a thing for you."

"You think?"

Leah laughed. "Of course! Any guy who'll do that during a workday must be smitten."

"You're kidding! He's just a good friend who felt bad that I got hurt."

"Oh, Blair. You haven't been around men much lately, have you?" She grinned, then added, "But I was just as clueless about Nathan. I didn't know how he felt until he told me. I thought it was all on my side."

"Cooper invited me over for dinner tonight," Blair blurted.

"He did?" Leah laughed aloud. "No, Blair. It's *not* just friendship."

"Well, I'll find out tonight."

Blair called Leah three hours later. She was exhausted but satisfied with her sales. At least she'd missed only one Saturday instead of two. She drank in the early fall weather, laced with a hint of chill, and clusters of people to talk to after a solitary week.

The thought of Cooper stirred butterflies in her stomach. She'd kept those thoughts at arms-length during her hours interacting with market customers. Once she was home, she lacked such distractions and didn't have Jake, either.

She prepared a green bean casserole, then laid on the couch. She'd hoped to rest, but thoughts around Nelson's letter bounded in her head. That and Cooper's dinner invitation and wondering what Jake did that day. Anything but rest.

At six o'clock, Blair knocked on Cooper's door. She hadn't seen him in two days and after so many treasured hours of his company, it felt like two weeks. She wore pastels, which were her favorites. A lavender bell-sleeve tunic with large flowers across the front, along with white capris and matching shell jewelry. Of course, she'd spent an inordinate amount of time in front of the mirror.

Her heart thumped in her chest and picked up the pace when the door opened and he stood there, blue eyes hooking to hers, a wide smile of welcome. He wore a plaid cotton shirt, neatly stretched over his broad shoulders. The clean smell of soap floated toward her.

"Feels like I haven't seen you in ages." He took her casserole, but not before his eyes traveled over her with appreciation.

"Me too."

"Are you walking better now?" He set the glass pan on the counter and turned back to her.

"Much better." She took a few steps. "I won't do a pirouette, but I can stroll across the room. You'll probably want to nuke that casserole. I made it this afternoon."

"Got it. You didn't have to bring anything, since I'm sure it wasn't easy to be on your feet in the kitchen. But thanks. I made chicken this time instead of steak. Didn't want to be predictable."

"Your steak was wonderful," she said. "I'm sure the chicken will be too."

"You look good, Blair. All healed and, of course, beautiful."

A hot flush rose to her face. Maybe Leah was right. Blair recalled a few gestures and facial expressions that could support

Leah's theory. "Thanks. You're not so tacky yourself. And I *do* feel much better. I sewed some things over the last two days and went to the market this morning."

"How'd it go?"

"I lasted about three hours. I was good and tired when I got home but sold quite a lot. Made me feel better about missing last week."

"Because you went to urgent care instead." He smirked then peered into the oven. "Something to drink?"

Was it her imagination, or was he treading on the surface, maybe feeling nervous? Hope leaped inside her.

℥   ℥   ℥

After all the hours he'd spent with Blair that week alone, Cooper felt almost tongue-tied, like it was his first date with a new woman. *Pull it together, Dawson.*

"What can I do?" she asked. "I like to be helpful just like you do. And you can tell me how things are going at the house. Keep it in layman's terms, though."

"I'll try." That would break the ice for sure since he knew that area. "You're sweet to keep asking about the house, but it can't be that interesting for you at this stage. Once we get to tiles, curtains, and paint, that'll be another story."

She laughed, and her face lit up. The centerpiece, her large hazel eyes. He had difficulty looking away.

They chatted together about Jake, about the week, as she assembled the salad, and he removed the chicken and potatoes from the oven. He lit a couple of thick candles on the table and dimmed the light over the table. They settled at the table in front of the picture window, which allowed an unobstructed view of her house, now dark and empty.

He prayed for the meal. When he opened his eyes, she said, "Looks and smells wonderful. Do you like to cook?"

"Yes, but when I'm on a project, I come in so late I do what's simple."

"I do that about every day." She took a forkful of the marinated chicken breast. "This is tasty. If I weren't so tired every day, I'd cook more elegant meals. Experiment a little."

As if she'd read his earlier thoughts, she hitched her head toward the window. "Looks like you have a full view of my house. I hope you haven't seen me walking around in my pjs."

"As a matter of fact..." He smirked, hoping to hide a flush of guilt on his face for the times he *had* observed her quiet evenings with Jake. "Gotta tell you, the leopard print onesie was really memorable."

They laughed.

"That'll be the day." Blair continued laughing softly and served herself some roasted potatoes. "My priority all winter is staying warm. Besides my house's other sins, it's drafty in winter, so I put on layers, and it doesn't matter what they look like. Mismatched and all."

"Remind me to look for that this winter, since it'll likely set a new style trend." He wiped his mouth. "I try not to spy on my neighbors, unless I see them falling off a ladder."

"That's a scene I don't plan to repeat. Although..."

He cocked his head and waited.

She set down her fork. "I think some good came out of it. I sketched some new designs and got ahead on my website. But in another category, I learned about myself." Her voice softened. "How I see myself."

"And?" He leaned forward on his elbows and observed her across the candle's mellow light.

"God challenged my view of myself as a misfit. He told me I was marvelous." Her eyes became dewy. "In Psalm one thirty-nine he said that. He pointed me right to it. I hope my heart is changing. Toward my family, for one. I never felt accepted, but I think I projected that onto them. My parents were great during my pregnancy. Lot of parents would just say, *Get out of here. You've shamed us.*"

Cooper looked at her over his water glass. "Meanwhile, you did that enough to yourself. Maybe that's why you left Milton."

Blair crossed her arms on the table. "I never thought about that. Might have played a part."

"You don't need to be ashamed about the past. You're God's daughter and he promised you a *future and a hope.*"

Her eyes lowered. "It's coming. You've been an encouragement to me."

They exchanged smiles through the haze of the dim light. A moment of silence passed.

He slid his plate aside. "I wanted to tell you I finally heard from the housing deputy. Are you in the mood to hear about it?"

"Yes, sure. What did he say?"

"Seems there is an official complaint process which can push Mitchell to act. Sometimes there's mediation against the landlord. I looked up his name on public records and he has seven rental properties."

"So, what if all his renters complain, like we talked about?"

"He said complaints are handled individually, but could stack up against Mitchell if he doesn't do anything."

Blair steepled her fingers. "Hmm. Sounds like a win-win. Either Mitchell decides to mend his ways, or he'll be forced to."

"Hopefully."

"What's the next step?"

"I think we're ready to write that letter. I've done a rough draft but want you to give input."

She grinned. "Gladly. I'd love to see a stack of grievances against Mitchell. We'll set a time to do it next week."

"*There's* my activist." He held up his palm. She slapped it with hers.

The flame on the candle waned as it flickered light over empty plates. Cooper said, "I have ice cream. I still haven't learned your favorite flavor."

"I like all of them, just like you. But if you pushed me, I'd say cookies and cream."

"Good choice. I happen to have that."

He rose and cleared the plates before she could offer to help. She grabbed whatever dishes remained and set them on the counter next to the sink.

"I don't think I told you the latest about Jake's letter." Blair leaned one hand on the granite surface of the island while Cooper arranged the dishes in the sink a few feet away.

He didn't want to talk about Nelson. Not *that* night. But he wouldn't tell her that. He wanted her to feel safe processing her decisions with him, even if they punched him in the gut. And honestly, he'd rather be in the loop about Nelson.

"What's the latest?" He turned from the sink to face her, snagging a towel to dry his hands.

"I'll bring you up to date, then we won't talk about him anymore tonight, okay?"

"Whatever you want." He gave her what he hoped was an open expression.

"I wanted to write him a letter too, not just send Jake's by itself."

"That's smart. After eight years, you certainly need to set some ground rules, maybe ask some questions. What did you say?" He leaned one hip against the island and crossed his arms, facing her.

Blair pressed her lips together, as if she was nervous. "I told him I was hesitant to let him into our lives, but I was willing to allow Jake an email correspondence with him initially. I didn't promise anything, but I said we'd see how it went. Using email means I don't have to give him my address. I gave the letters to my mother this morning to mail from Milton.”

“So, they can get to know each other gradually, and you can control Nelson’s access to Jake.”

She let out a breath. “I’ve second-guessed myself every step of the way.”

He offered a sympathetic grimace. “I can appreciate how hard it must be, though I’m not in your shoes. I wouldn’t want to be.”

A different question involving Nelson pushed up like an annoying weed. A question that had chafed his mind chronically since hearing about the man.

Cooper’s heartbeat clanged inside him. “Blair, there’s a question I *don’t* want to ask you.” But he *had* to. Had to know her answer before becoming serious about her. As if he could turn back his feelings. As if it weren’t already too late. “Are you...*open* to reconciling with Nelson?”

Her eyes widened. “You mean romantically? No, definitely not.” She let out a laugh.

At her abrupt response, Cooper’s shoulders relaxed, and he released the breath he’d been holding.

“It was hard enough for me to just *write* to him.” She paused and stared with a quizzical expression. “Why did you say you *didn’t* want to ask me that question? It’s never been my goal.”

He kept his gaze locked on hers and took a step toward her. He could smell the floral scent of her perfume and ached to touch her. A smile tugged and he softened his voice. “I’m hoping I’ve given you enough clues to figure that out, Blair.” *Please figure it out. Put the man out of his misery.*

If not, he had a clear idea how he might help her.

Her lips and eyes opened with understanding. She held his gaze. “There are lots of reasons I wouldn’t reconcile with Nelson. For one, I have feelings for someone else.”

Her words sliced through him. His breath faltered. "Someone else?"

A beguiling smile emerged. "Someone named Cooper Dawson."

It took half a second for her words to hit home, for joy to spurt through his chest like a fountain. "Blair…" Her name came out like a prayer. His lips spread to a grin.

Cooper slipped his hands around her waist and gently pulled her, closing the space between them. Finally, he'd do what he'd longed to do for weeks. With gentle fingertips, he stroked her smooth cheek. "I so hoped you felt something for me."

She slid her hands up his chest and stared up into his face, softness and wonder in her expression. "How could I not, Cooper?" Her gentle voice caressed him, and her eyes were round. "Almost from the beginning, the first day we met."

"Me too." His voice was husky. "That first day, I saw this courageous woman, a wonderful mom, a hard worker, and beautiful, to boot. Then, over time, it grew into something deeper." He grinned then. "I confess, I watched you just a little through the window."

She chuckled, a sexy, throaty sound. "I kind of had my eye on your house too." She touched his face, feather soft. A tremor rippled through him.

He wove his fingers into her hair, his gaze sweeping her eyes, her face, her moist pink lips. Then he drew her face close and covered her lips with his, slowly at first, tasting her, like a long-awaited delicacy. She melted into his chest and slipped both arms up his shoulders and around his neck.

Her soft lips yielded to the increasing intensity of his kiss. She tasted sweet, of ice cream and surrender. A ragged groan escaped from his throat.

He pulled back and touched his forehead to hers, his arms like a pretzel around her. "You're amazing." Then he dove in to kiss her again.

Several moments later, he pulled back. "I forgot. You're standing on your injured foot."

He slipped his hands under her arms and gently lifted her and set her on the stool. She giggled. "There, that's better," he said. "And I can still reach you."

From her perch on the stool, she fit perfectly into his arms, molded against him, her arms looped around his neck. He pulled her toward him, satisfying the hunger that had built for weeks.

Nelson, Jake, Amber...they were distant discussions for another time in another world, far from Cooper's kitchen.

Chapter Seventeen

As Pastor Todd concluded his sermon, he stepped away from the podium. Overhead lights dimmed and delicate guitar notes filled the silence with a melodious but quiet song of reflection. Blair closed her eyes and drank in the music, the message.

She vibrated with awareness of Cooper's presence next to her, still in awe and unbelief of their new status. His voice rumbled in a solid baritone as they sang side by side. He slipped his large hand around hers and sent her a tender smile as his eyes roved over her face. If she were any happier, she'd probably fall over into a faint. She caught Leah's conspiratorial grin from the stage as she drew the bow across the violin perched beneath her chin.

When the noise of conversation replaced the solemn last notes, Leah approached them in their row. "Cooper, good to see you again. I hear you took good care of Blair while she was laid up."

"Yeah, I had to confiscate the ladder." He winked at Blair. "No, in all fairness, everything was slippery after all that rain. I'm just glad it wasn't worse." He stroked her back with one hand, a public gesture of affection that pooled more contentment inside.

"I feel so much better already," Blair said.

"I can tell." Leah grinned with an annoying double meaning, causing Blair to laugh.

"Cooper was a big help, and you were too, Leah."

Moments later, Nathan joined them and shook Cooper's hand. "Welcome back, Cooper. Hey, Blair. Good to see you standing on both feet. Leah said you're doing a lot better."

A couple greeted Nathan and Leah as they passed. She slipped her hand around the bend in his arm. "Nathan was new in town just a year ago like you, Blair, but he's gotten so involved here, he knows more people than I do."

"Trust me, that's not possible," Nathan said with a grin. "They asked me to pray about being an elder, but I felt a marketing role was a better fit. Turns out there was a big spot for me there."

"Using your skills for God. That's great." Cooper nodded.

"Your skills helped me too, Nathan," Blair said. "While I was at home, I wrote six or eight blog posts, and I studied those I read regularly so I could learn better how it's done. I've gotten about twenty subscribers so far."

"That's amazing, Blair," Nathan said. "Now you need to think of something you can give people for free when they sign up. For example, I noticed you like scarves. You could put together a small document and call it, *Twenty Ways to Use Scarves*. Something like that. Attach it to your site as a freebie for people who sign up."

Blair blew out a breath. "Major intimidation there, Nathan."

"Don't worry," Leah said. "Garrett'll help you. You just put together the content."

"It's *so* good to have skilled friends." Blair sighed in relief.

Abbie and Garrett joined their small group. "Great service, Leah," Abbie said. "The music was inspiring and amazing, as usual, along with the message." Her dark brown eyes sparkled with animation. "Do you all want to go somewhere for lunch?"

Blair glanced up at Cooper, then told Abbie, "Another time, we'd love to. Enjoy lunch and we'll see you soon."

"Okay, next time." Leah shot Blair a knowing grin, then the group dispersed.

Blair and Cooper left the small storefront church and slid into his truck. He didn't turn the ignition right away but sat quietly. His dark blue eyes locked onto hers as he turned and casually rested his arm on the back of the seat. "Thanks for that. " He stroked a finger along the back of her neck, causing a chill. "I wanted you to myself."

"You're not the only one."

She leaned toward him, and he swept soft lips across hers. Briefly, yet he said so much. Around them, noise rose from people retrieving their cars, talking to each other, and driving away.

He pulled back. "Lunch? Then we can walk along the river."

"Perfect day for it."

They had to make the most of every moment before Jake returned that evening.

For the next few hours, magic unfolded moment by moment. Cooper took Blair to an Italian trattoria on the edge of town. Neither of them knew many people in Brenner Falls, but being away from downtown felt deliberately private, intimate.

Cooper glanced around at the homey décor and the refurbished brick walls. "This place has tons of atmosphere." Their table, tucked alongside a mullioned window, afforded them a view of a canal where barely turning orange and red maples draped on both sides. "I found another place I want to take you about twenty minutes further. It's fancier than this. One day when Jake's with his grandparents."

"Sounds wonderful." An image flashed in her mind of her wearing one of her more elegant designs as she accompanied Cooper to a romantic restaurant. She'd long ago abandoned any hopes of that fantasy coming true. *Thank you, God, for this man you've brought me.* "I'm so happy to be with you, Cooper." It felt so right, even though it hadn't yet been twenty-four hours.

They joined hands across the table. His eyes roved her face and his lips curved in a way that turned her liquid.

"We won't think about Nelson or Jake or the house," he said. "Just us."

"I like the sound of that." *Us.*

After lunch, he drove to the river. Cooper pulled the truck into his lot alongside the worksite. "We'll park here and cross over to the path that runs north along the river."

"I love that area. I haven't been in a few months." Blair slid out of the truck. "Can I go look at the house for a minute?" She gingerly stepped between the trees along a pebble-strewn path. The house came into view, like a palace in the making. Since her previous visit two weeks earlier, when they'd come with Jake, it had progressed several stages. A roof and outer walls covered the framing she'd seen the last time. It was easier to imagine the completed home.

Cooper came over and stood beside her. "We caught up from the days we had rain, but then had a messed-up order of the plumbing parts. That cost us some time. But I've been in this business long enough to roll with it. Just have to stay flexible."

"When do you expect it to be finished?"

"By early spring, probably. I wanted to advance as much as possible to compensate for the winter months when everything'll slow down."

"What'll you do then? Work from home on clients?"

He gave her a sneaky grin that melted her bones. "I could hang around with my beautiful friend Blair. And her adorable son, of course." He bent his head and kissed her neck. "We could sneak into the kitchen while he's playing with his trucks..."

She giggled when his lips tickled her neck, glad for the privacy of the trees. Blair slid her arms around his waist and leaned her head on his solid chest, feeling at home, secure. Curling up in that refuge, she relaxed fully into him instead of feeling responsible for the entire world. His arms encircled her, and they stood a moment without speaking. Then he kissed her with tenderness, reverence. She melted into his kiss and his strong hands on her back.

He pulled away then and took her hand to lead her toward the river. "What'll you tell Jake about us? Mommy's dating the neighbor?"

They laughed. "No, probably not. He really likes you." She stepped over some tree roots as they found the path, which opened to a stunning view of the water. They crossed the street and Blair fell into step beside him on a dirt path. "I think he'll be glad. How to explain it, I'm not sure. I haven't dated anyone since Jake was born."

Cooper's eyes grew wide. "You're kidding. Have you lived with a bag over your head? Or just turned down every guy until they all declared a National Day of Mourning?"

"You obviously have no idea what it's like to be a single, working mother."

He sobered. "No, I guess not. No time for a social life, eh?"

"It's not that I didn't have time. I could have made time, found a sitter, but I was trying to keep my head above water. I had friends who were in my situation and dated. Some went online." She shook her head. "I just didn't have the energy, or the interest, really." It was true, but there was more. "I'd been deeply hurt."

He blinked. He knew what that felt like. "Makes sense you wouldn't want to risk another heartbreak anytime soon. I'm honored you'd take a chance on me."

She stopped then and touched his face where a few whiskers shadowed his jaw. "You've shown me who you are, Cooper. You weren't just trying to impress me. You were genuine in your caring, your good heart. I trust you."

"I'll try to be worthy of that trust." He clasped her hand, still on his cheek, and kissed her palm, a gesture she loved. A tingle ran up her arm.

She lifted her face toward him. "I trust you and feel safe with you." She sent him a wicked smile. "But I could also kiss you all day."

A chuckle rumbled up from his throat as he kissed her under the shade of low, leafy branches. A few joggers ran by, but she ignored them. They'd done a lot of kissing in less than twenty-four hours, but she still couldn't get enough. They'd calm down soon. Probably.

By the time Jake arrived that evening, Blair had to shake herself out of her dream state. How would she tell him about her new relationship with Cooper? Would he understand, be glad? Jealous? She'd never had to ask those questions before. Since his birth, she'd been his alone.

When Jake came home, she hugged him thoroughly. "Did you have a good time at Nanna and Grandpa's house?"

"Yeah! They took me out for pizza today and I played with clay all afternoon."

"Clay? That's cool. What did you make?"

"I made some dinosaurs and some little people who were afraid of them. But they became friends, and the dinosaurs didn't eat them. They ate fish and frogs instead."

"Oh, that's good. I bet the people were glad. Go empty your backpack and I'll see if you have any laundry, okay? You'll need to get ready for bed soon. School tomorrow."

"Oh, school. I forgot." He picked up his backpack and ran to his room.

Blair sighed. She too, would have to regroup. She hadn't had to work in a week and had savored the break, even in her injured state. Tomorrow she'd return and try to make up for lost time. She'd go to physical therapy and talk to Hugo about the design. Would it lead anywhere?

Amidst the random thoughts that shot around like asteroids in her brain was the memory of Cooper's arms and his lips.

Ⅎ Ⅎ Ⅎ

"You're in a good mood, boss," said Eddie, Cooper's project manager. "Must've been a good weekend."

Cooper couldn't stifle a grin. "You have *no* idea." He walked away, leaving the man chuckling.

"What's her name?" Eddie called after Cooper.

Her name was *Amazing*. And when she was in his arms, he had no further words. All he could do was look into those hazel eyes and dark brown lashes, at her soft lips, enjoy her subtle humor. He smiled to himself as he rewound their day together, walking along the river until dusk. They'd so completely lost track of time, buried in one another, that they'd had to hurry home so Blair could be there when Jake arrived.

He knew the glow would fade and change. They couldn't stay starry-eyed over the long haul, but it sure was fun for now. He'd forgotten what it could be like. She'd probably forgotten too since she hadn't had a romantic relationship since Nelson. Nelson who broke and trampled her heart and left her carrying his child. The thought still stirred a wellspring of anger.

By now, the man would have gotten Blair's and Jake's letters. What must he be thinking? At last, a response. A chance with his son. Well, Nelson would have to content himself with email for as long as Blair decided. At least she had the power, not him. She could be reticent to accept help, determined to do things her own way, but she came by it honestly as a survival skill. Nelson had forced her into it, and her family had played a role. It wasn't their fault that she was so different from them. Her developing sense of self took a hit when she was only a child.

He saw traces of insecurity in her, fear of not measuring up. Those things, he understood, but they endeared her to him as well. Made him want to champion her dreams and protect her from her fears. He wanted to help Jake grow into a strong young man, confident in life.

Cooper let out a long sigh. Was he moving too fast? Probably. Might not happen in the way or the speed that he'd like. That was up to God. But he had to admit, that was what he wanted. Sure, he and Blair would have conflict as they got to know each other. They'd encounter tough issues, disagreements even, but they'd talk through them, as any healthy couple would. They'd grow individually and together.

Cooper smiled at his glowing view of the future. *If it's your will, Lord.*

He had texted her during the day. *Hello, beautiful. I hope it wasn't too hard to return to work today. You're in my thoughts. Constantly.*

She'd responded a few minutes later. *It's a Monday, what can I say? And being gone for a week makes it harder to come back, but I'm here. I loved our weekend and can't wait to see you again.* She'd added a heart. Felt like high school, but he loved it. If he stayed in this goofy romantic state much longer, he'd start carving her name on the wood beams of his living room. Cooper laughed aloud at the thought.

Later when he pulled into his driveway, he saw no activity at Blair's house. He got out of the truck. Zipper pranced in rhythm with his wagging tail as if he hadn't seen Cooper in days instead of only a couple of hours. He rose on hind feet and pawed the front of Cooper's shirt. Cooper scratched his head on both sides. "C'mon, boy. I bet you want dinner." He unleashed him and they went inside.

As he prepared Zipper's dinner, his thoughts went to Amber, whom he hadn't spoken to since the dinner at The Fork. He'd been annoyed with her questions about Blair. He should call her and tell her the latest.

"Hey, Amber. Just wanted to say hi and remind you the phone works both ways."

"You're right, Coop." Her tone was contrite. "I'm always ragging on you about staying in touch as if it's your job alone. I'm sorry."

"Hey, no worries. I'm just busting your chops. It's fun."

"Glad you're having fun. So, what's new? The house must look pretty good by now."

"You should come by and see it sometime. Of course, it isn't finished, but it's at the point now where you could really imagine it. And with the CAD drawings, you can."

"I'd love to see it. I'll get off early Thursday, so I can stop by then, if that's good for you."

"Fine. And you're doing okay?"

"Yeah, nothing new. Everything's the same."

"Bet you're ready for that cruise. It's coming up."

"Yes, it is, and I'm ready. Kind of bored, actually. I need to spice up my life a little. Anything spicy in yours?"

"Well, now that you mention it. Blair and I are dating."

"That's great, Cooper."

"You don't sound too sure. But that's okay. *I'm* happy about it."

"I am too. Don't get me wrong. I just don't know her well. She seems smart and nice, and her son is precious. Well-behaved too, and mature for his age."

"You're right. And he loves Zipper."

"And I think you're pretty fond of the boy too. So, how did that come about? Did you finally ask her out?"

"She fell off a ladder last week and had to take time off. I stopped over a few times and our friendship grew. Last weekend we talked and turns out she feels the same way I do. So, there you have it."

"There you have it." She repeated softly. "Hey, I wanted to let you know that once I get back from my cruise, I want to have a fall party at my house. You and Blair can come, the gang from The Fork, some friends from church. We'll cook out if weather permits."

"Sounds great."

"Don't forget you promised to water my plants while I'm in Aruba."

"Will do. Date again?"

"A week from Sunday I fly out. The following week, I'll come back. Then the week after, the party. Got all that?"

"Yup. Got it."

When they hung up, Cooper had the lingering feeling that Amber wasn't happy about his news. But he was, so she'd just have to deal with it.

Chapter Eighteen

Wednesday after work, Blair picked up Jake at Angela's and headed to her physical therapy appointment. Having lost an entire week, she hadn't dared schedule it during the day.

She hadn't seen Cooper since Sunday, though she often scanned his property for signs of him, and they texted at least twice a day. He'd called her the previous evening, and they'd talked for an hour. Jake kept asking who she was on the phone with.

She'd mouthed the words, *a friend*, still unsure of how to explain their new relationship to Jake.

"Bet you're hungry, big guy," she called to Jake from the kitchen. It was nearly seven o'clock. She glanced up at the ceiling, where the ugly brown stain stared back at her. She should have sent another email to Don Mitchell while she'd been laid up, but she'd put it off.

After dinner, she sat at her computer. As she hit send and prayed for a response to her email to Mr. Mitchell, another message popped into her inbox. From Nelson.

Blair stared at the message as her heart thumped against her ribcage. The correspondence had begun. There was an email letter for her and an attached document for Jake. She read hers first.

Hello, Blair. I'm thrilled you and Jake responded to my letter. I'd almost given up hope of connecting with you both and didn't know what else to try. So, thank you. I'm humbled by the situation and grateful to have a second chance.

She frowned and stared at the screen. That wasn't what she expected to read. She'd been prepared to be defensive, clutching her well-worn role as protective mom and abandoned woman. She'd nursed her anger for so many years, it was the only feeling she recognized regarding Nelson. Yet his humble attitude had disarmed her. That didn't prove he wasn't playing a game. She kept reading.

You asked me about my change of heart. First, I deeply regretted what happened between us, even back then. I wasn't ready to be a father and basically ran away. I'm sorry I left you alone, I'm sorry I lost you too, but I'm glad you kept Jake. You had your own dreams, (which I hope you have kept), but they didn't lead you to give him up. I respect you for that.

A couple of years after our split, I dated a woman who had a little boy. I guess you could say he stirred a father instinct in me, and I mourned the chance I'd lost. It was an emotionally hard experience, one full of tears and self-hatred (and therapy.) I told my girlfriend about it, and she reamed me out. That's not why we broke up, but it didn't help that she knew what a spineless man I'd been. So, more time went by. A couple of years ago, I became determined to find my son. (Yes, I always knew he was mine, to my shame.) I only had your parents' address, so I tried that first. When I didn't hear from you, I decided to try again, since the letter wasn't returned.

I'm glad you responded this time and was happy to read a letter from Jake. I wrote him a simple letter which I've attached. With time, I hope he grows less afraid to meet me. I would love to meet him someday soon but won't push him.

I hope you are well, Blair, and the last few years have been good for you. I don't know if you're married or what, but I'd appreciate being part of Jake's life to whatever extent you allow me.

Thank you, Blair.

Nelson

Blair swallowed. Her throat ached as she reread his words. She saw no trace of the cocky guy she remembered from college days. The anger that had festered inside her and built her armor all those years ago weakened as she read his contrite words. He'd always been carefree, a magnet for fun-loving friends, talented in art, somewhat selfish, but fun and sociable. Time and failure seem to have sobered and matured the current version. At least it appeared that way.

Nelson's letter to Jake was brief.

Hi Jake, I'm so glad you wrote me a letter. I'm happy you enjoy school and you're learning to play the piano.

I play music too. I learned to play the saxophone when I was younger. I stopped for several years but recently started playing again. I draw pictures for my job, only I do this on a computer. Do you want to draw me a picture? I'd like to have one from you.

Please write to me soon.

Your dad

She'd forgotten that Nelson played saxophone in a band during college. He must have given it up after graduation. What else had he done during those years while she raised their son alone, struggling to pay for everything he needed? She didn't want to fall into the trap of seeing Nelson through rose-colored glasses, simply because he appeared to be repentant. He'd known Jake was his from the start, but never paid a penny for seven years, except once a year earlier. And it took him years to decide to find his son. She'd be wise to remember that and keep some of her armor intact.

She printed off the letter for Jake and created a file for herself for future correspondence involving Nelson. Depending on where all this went.

Jake sat at one end of the couch in the living room, leafing through a picture book.

"Jake, I have a letter from your father. Do you want me to read it to you?"

He nodded, and Blair sat next to him. She read the letter aloud but surveyed his face for any reaction. "What do you think of the letter, Jake?"

Jake shrugged. "He seems nice, I guess. He plays music like me."

"Your dad plays a horn called a saxophone. Do you have questions about anything?" Not that she knew anything other than what he'd written.

"Will I meet him?" His face turned up to meet her eyes.

"One day if you want to. You can write back to him whenever you're ready." She didn't want Jake to appear too eager, but would let him decide.

"Okay." Jake didn't seem fazed by the letter, though it was hard to know what he thought, unless it involved a new toy, a friend, or a piece of music.

Relief coursed through Blair at Jake's seeming indifference. Jake shut his book and started to wiggle off the couch. She laid a hand on his shoulder. "Hey, big guy, stay on the couch a minute. I want to tell you something." *Lord, give me the words.*

She slipped one arm around him. "You know how Cooper is a friend of ours, right?"

He nodded.

"Well, Cooper is..." She bit her lip. "Cooper is more than just a friend for *me*. He's my boyfriend now." She disliked the term, but Jake would understand. "Do you know what that means?"

Jake nodded. "Are you gonna marry him?"

Not so fast. "I don't know. But I like him a lot. You like him too, don't you?"

"Yeah. I like Zipper too."

"Yes, me too. Of course, my special friendship with Cooper doesn't change anything for you and me. You're my sweetheart and

I love you so much. Nothing will change that, even if I marry someone someday."

Jake appeared to consider this new information. Was he happy, surprised, worried? Blair had no idea how to interpret the calm set of her little boy's face. "Do you have any questions for me about it?"

He blinked a few times as he stared up at her. "No. He's really nice. He came to my piano recital."

"Yes, he did. And he took us out for hamburgers and ice cream." She drew Jake in for a hug. "You're my wonderful boy. Nothing will ever change that. But I like Cooper and I'm really glad you do too."

When she released him, Jake slid off the couch and put the book on the shelf in the corner. He left the room, and she exhaled. Then she pulled out her phone and called Cooper.

"Hey, I miss you," he said after he'd picked up on the first ring.

"Me too. Real life sucks sometimes." They laughed. She drank in the manly timber of his voice. "I prefer lazy weekends when we can hang out together by the river. Hey, I told Jake about us tonight. He seemed okay with it."

"You did? I'm so glad since I'm not going anywhere. I'll haunt your dreams and show up on your doorstep."

She giggled. "You'd better. Why don't you come over for dinner tomorrow night?" She fiddled with the tassel on the couch cushion. "I'd like to see you."

"Me too. I can bring pizza. That way, you don't have to cook."

"You convinced me. Jake and I love pizza."

"Makes three of us. I can't wait to see you both. Zipper misses Jake too."

"I'll let him know he owes Zipper a visit."

"Blair, we should talk about some kind of rhythm. I know you're busy. You have work plus a child to think of, and I don't want to be insensitive about that. You can tell me what kind of space you need. But I hope I won't only see you on weekends."

"I feel the same. I'd like to see you too, though I have to be careful. You can help me with balance. I appreciate your sensitivity to time and Jake." She paused. "Um, I got a letter from Nelson today."

"What did he say?"

Did she imagine a downturn in his voice? "He responded to Jake, but also wrote me a letter. I had asked him to elaborate on his change of heart. He explained it to me, and I felt a little better."

"Sounded plausible?"

"Yeah, could be."

"I'm glad his letter makes you more peaceful about everything."

If only it did.

"Don't trust him too fast."

She sighed. "I won't." She'd let his authoritative tone pass. He had a point, after all.

New complexities now wove through her already pressured life. A few weeks ago, it was just her and Jake. And her job and her dreams for the future. That was hard enough to juggle. Now, Nelson and Cooper had entered the mix. Thoughts of her links with each one crowded her mind. And Jake. How would he relate to Cooper? Would anything change between them? Would Nelson's contact with Jake change *her* relationship with her son?

☙ ☙ ☙

After the call, Cooper remained on the couch, absently scratching Zipper's ears. He suddenly understood Amber's concern. She had nothing against Blair, but foresaw a more complicated relationship than he'd have with someone like Lindsay. Lindsay had no children and no one like Nelson showing up out of the blue to claim fatherly rights.

Even if Nelson weren't in the picture, Blair still had a lot of responsibilities. Did she even have a babysitter if he wanted to take her out? And would that be just one more expense for her? How would they spend time alone to develop their relationship? Once a month when Jake was with his grandparents?

Though questions swirled around in his head, he didn't regret telling her his feelings. He'd have exploded if he'd waited much longer to tell her. But he'd have to accept all that she brought along with her, to be patient and understanding of her responsibilities to Jake. Not that he'd ever want to stand in the way of their closeness. He longed to date her and see where it went, but it would look different than it had in his daydreams.

He wondered if she was being gracious too soon toward Nelson. It wasn't any of his business, but he couldn't help himself. If Nelson expressed contrition, regret, humility, that was appropriate. The guy had done a despicable thing eight years ago, and it had taken him this long to recognize it.

The following evening, Cooper stood at Blair's door holding a large, fragrant pizza. He'd worked hard all day at the site and his appetite raged, but his desire to see Blair overshadowed it. When she opened the door, the sight of her almost made him drop the pizzas and gather her into an embrace. Which he did as soon as she'd led him two steps into the kitchen and put the pizza on the table.

After a lengthy kiss, they pulled away and stared at each other. "I missed you," Cooper whispered as his eyes traced over her face.

"Me too. We're going to have to work something out here." She smiled and something melted inside him. She leaned forward and brushed his lips tenderly with her own.

"Cooper, you're here!" A young voice caused them to pull apart.

For sure, Jake had seen them locked in an embrace. Cooper knelt to Jake's level. "Hey, big guy. How are you? Zipper was asking about you."

"I was gonna come yesterday, but I couldn't. I can go tomorrow after school."

"I'll tell him. Do you like pizza?"

His face looked like always until his eyes widened. "You were kissing my mom."

Guilty as charged. The best moment of his week. "Yes, I was. I hope that's okay with you, big guy. I really like your mom."

Jake shrugged and turned to the pizza. "Can we eat now?"

"That means you're hungry, I take it," Blair said. "Let's eat before it gets cold."

Dinner unfolded almost normally, except for Jake's occasional surreptitious stares at the two of them across the table. As if he were still processing the new status.

Jake talked about his day in colorful detail. Cooper enjoyed the interaction. He took part once or twice, but guessed she wanted to keep everything the same for Jake's sake. Cooper didn't want to butt in but didn't want to be invisible either. It was a balancing act, but he'd get the hang of it.

When they'd finished eating ice cream after pizza, Jake left the table and returned to a game he'd been playing earlier. He seemed to have taken his mother's new romantic relationship in stride. There weren't many dishes to do, but Cooper followed Blair into the kitchen, carrying whatever was left on the table.

"Does he seem okay to you?" he asked quietly as they stood side by side at the sink.

"I think he does. I'll see if he opens up to me at another time. Jake's pretty resilient."

"That's a relief. It's a new thing for him. Right after finding out about his dad, he finds me lurking around."

She turned to him, a grin on her face. "You're not lurking around. I invited you here, remember?" Her smile dimmed. "But you're right, that's two big changes for him in close succession. Maybe there's more going on inside his little head than he is letting on. But be assured, your involvement is a *good* thing. For me *and* for him."

He trailed a finger down her bare arm. "I hope to be a good thing for both of you. I want to be a support for you, but not overstep. I won't necessarily know the perfect boundaries. I've never dated a woman with a child."

"Please, don't worry. We'll talk about things as we go along. Just be yourself and Jake will adapt."

Sounded like good advice. If Blair and Jake both were taking their life changes one step at a time, he would too.

They sat on the couch together, a wise decision since Jake was used to having Blair in the room with him each evening. "Do you have a babysitter in case we want to go out one weekend night?" Cooper asked in a low voice.

Blair's full lips pressed together. "Not really. Since we've been in the Falls, I haven't done anything without Jake except on the weekends he goes to his grandparents. I can't think of anyone to watch him unless I find someone at church. But I *do* want to go out with you." Her earnest expression reassured him.

"It would be good to have a sitter available in general, but also my sister Amber is having a party in a couple of weeks. She'd like both of us to come."

"That's nice. She seems sweet."

"She's leaving on a trip to the Caribbean Sunday and wants to have a fall party when she gets back. Some people you met at The Grateful Fork will be there. She knows Leah, so she and Nathan may come."

"That sounds like fun. Maybe Leah knows someone I can ask to babysit." Her gaze wandered to Jake, who was building something on top of the coffee table with Legos. "Yet another change for my boy."

Chapter Nineteen

"I hope I look okay." Blair smoothed the front of a blue tunic dress she'd made the previous year. A cardigan for later that evening hung over one arm. "I haven't gone to a party in ages."

Voicing her insecurities made her look like she was fishing for compliments. She wasn't, but she wouldn't refuse a boost of reassurance. Especially as she and Cooper stood at Amber's door. Behind it, joyous laughter and thumping music drifted out. Would she fit in with Cooper's sister and friends?

It was a first on so many levels. The first time she and Cooper went out as a couple among his friends and the first time Jake had a sitter. Tension twisted in her stomach.

"You look perfect." Cooper leaned forward and placed a kiss on her nose. "I love your style." His fixed gaze and words infused her with courage. "What are you worried about?"

She shrugged. "It's silly—"

The door swung open. "There you are. No need to knock." Amber scooped them inside as the music enfolded them. Cooper's sister gave each of them a warm hug and took the bowl of macaroni salad Blair offered.

Blair scanned the room and recognized at least half of those she saw milling around the living room, including Johnny and Tricia from The Grateful Fork. Her nervousness slowly peeled away. Jake would be fine. Leah had helped her find a sitter, a sweet, bouncy teenager named Katie from the church worship team. She'd come over once during the week to meet Jake, and he seemed to like her. Hopefully, all would go well. She sighed. There were so many changes for her little boy. She pushed the thought away with a prayer. Adult time now.

She turned to Amber and dispelled guilty thoughts of Jake. Amber's wavy dark hair tumbled back from her pretty face, and a colorful scarf top flowed around her tanned shoulders. Despite contrasting hair color and texture, she and Cooper held a family resemblance.

"How was your trip to Aruba?" Blair asked, grateful for an easy conversation opener with Cooper's sister.

"Oh, it was *so* wonderful!" Amber clasped her hands together. "I highly recommend it. The snorkeling was unbelievable. Here, let me show you some photos." She led Blair toward an end table where her phone lay. She pointed to a framed photo on the table. "This one's my favorite," then scrolled through several more on her phone. A few women, including Tricia and Lindsay, joined them. Amber introduced Blair as Cooper's girlfriend, which sparked contentment inside.

Another woman who Blair vaguely recognized joined their discussion, and Amber hugged her. "Hi, Kelsey, so glad you made it. Do you guys remember Kelsey from The Fork?"

"Hi," Kelsey said. "Nice to see you again."

The photos triggered a conversation. Blair glanced across the room at Cooper, embedded in a cluster of men. He met her gaze, and gave her a thumbs up.

A few people went through the kitchen to the backyard to survey the burgers and bratwurst. "We'll join the guys outside as soon as more of the guests arrive," Amber said. "I have chairs out there, drinks, and cornhole."

"Cornhole?"

"You've never played cornhole? You have to try it. It's a beanbag game. Cooper's pretty good at it. We have badminton too."

Cooper joined Blair. "Looks like you've been inducted as an official member." He grinned.

Moments later, Leah and Nathan arrived. Blair crossed the room to give Leah a hug. "Everything go okay with Jake tonight?" Leah asked.

"I think so. He seems to like Katie." Blair bit her lip. "This is such a new thing for both of us."

"He'll be fine," Leah assured her. "Katie's great with children. She has a little brother and sister. It's *you* I'm worried about."

"I *was* a bit of a wreck before coming. Cooper probably thinks I've never been to a party before."

Leah laid a hand on Blair's arm. "It's natural to feel that way the first time you leave your child with a sitter. Especially at Jake's age. Most kids get used to it much younger, but don't worry. Jake's *not* fearful." She laughed. "I sound like I speak from experience, but I've observed Jake."

"You're right. Jake's never met a stranger."

"Here comes Nathan. He'll want to talk marketing, so brace yourself."

Blair laughed. Leah's words proved correct as Nathan gave her new ideas. "Sorry I shouldn't burden you at a social event," he said. "I'll email you those ideas. Blog's going okay?"

They chatted about her blog for a few moments, then went outside. In Amber's back yard an early fall chill laced the air, along with the aroma of grilled meat and smoke. Two men Blair didn't know surveyed the burgers and brats. Side dishes the guests had brought covered a long table along one side while folding lawn chairs filled the grassy space. After the meal, evening fell, and everyone returned inside for dessert.

With gratitude, Blair noted that the party had provided a collection of potential new friends and good food. A wave of joy filled her throat, as she took in the group and Cooper standing beside her. Being alone was overrated. After dessert, Nathan stood and clanged a wineglass with his fork. "Everyone, I have an announcement to make."

The room grew quiet. Leah stood next to Nathan. With a wave of anticipation, Blair predicted what they would say. "Leah and I want you all to be the first to know, after my mother, that is." A thread of laughter rippled through the group. "We're engaged."

A whoop of joy and congratulations rose, and the hugs began. Blair crossed the room and gave Leah a tight hug. "I'm so happy for you, Leah. You deserve every happiness." She meant every word. Leah had reached out to her when she didn't know anyone. She still didn't know many people. That is, until tonight. Hope flickered warmly inside, that she'd find friends and a life in Brenner Falls. "Have you set a date yet?"

Leah's face glowed with happiness, making her even more beautiful. "He only asked me last night, so it's very new. Probably next spring."

"Let's get together for coffee soon. I want to hear the details. Do you have a ring?"

"He wanted me to pick it out myself."

"Smart man."

Cooper appeared by her side. He shook Nathan's hand, hugged Leah, then slipped his arm around Blair.

Sunday afternoon, Cooper, Blair, and Jake hiked and picnicked by the river. Hopefully, the hours they spent together made up for Jake being without her Saturday night. Jake's interaction with Cooper seemed the same as before. An immense relief.

After lunch, Jake said, "I'm going to the edge of the river to see if there are any fish or frogs." He rose from the blanket.

"Okay, but don't get your feet wet," Blair called after him.

Cooper leaned over to steal a kiss. "Call me an opportunist. I'll take any opportunity I get."

They laughed and kissed again.

"I brought that letter for Mitchell's renters." He pulled a folded paper from his back pocket. "Want to hear it?"

"Yes, absolutely." She was eager to push their protest forward a notch.

"Here goes. *Dear Tenant, according to the terms of your lease, both you and your landlord have responsibilities. Here in Brenner Falls, you have the right as a renter to have safe and comfortable housing. If you have repair needs, your landlord will handle them. If he or she does not, you can file a complaint by email or call the consumer protection housing hotline. This may initiate action on your behalf. You'll find the contact information below. Keep this information handy should you ever need it.*" He looked up at Blair. "What do you think?

"That's perfect." She bent her knees and wrapped her arms around them. "It's got the right tone. Sounds like it came from the government."

"Kinda dry, eh? Do you want to add or change anything?"

"No, let's send it. I like it the way it is."

"And you can be the first tenant to complain."

"I'd be honored." She leaned toward him for another brief kiss.

Monday morning, temperatures dropped as the final days of September ebbed away. The first yellow and orange leaves swirled down as if to mark the end of summer.

After such an enjoyable weekend, Blair found it tough to return to her dead-end assembly line job. She tightened her thick cardigan around her shoulders against the chill in the big noisy room. Like a robot, her fingers guided fabric through the percussive needle as if by themselves.

When morning break arrived, she stood and stretched, but her mind raced. Time to speak with Hugo. She stuck her head in the doorway of his office. As usual, a haggard expression pulled at his face, but he greeted her with kind eyes. "Hello, Blair. What can I do for you?"

"Hi, Hugo. Sorry for disturbing you. I wondered if you'd had any news about the design you gave to Gloria. It's been a few weeks, so I wondered about it."

"I gave it to her but assumed she'd reach out to you."

"No, she didn't. Should I talk to her myself?"

He held up a finger. "Let me call her first."

Blair hovered in the doorway while he punched numbers on his desk phone. "Gloria, this is Hugo. You remember the design I gave you about a month ago, done by a worker from assembly? I thought it was worth showing you. You do?"

A thread of discomfort tugged. She waited in silence as Hugo listened to Gloria's response. "Ah. I see. I'll let her know."

He hung up. "Gloria liked your design. In fact, she plans to include it in the next season's lineup."

Blair's mouth dropped open. "She does? I'm glad she liked it, but why wasn't I notified?"

"I thought someone in her department would have told you."

The discomfort grew. "No one responded to me, and of course, no one has offered me compensation for my design. Don't you find that strange?" *And* dishonest.

Hugo's dark brows furrowed. "I don't know the process since that's her department. You should have been notified."

"*And* compensated." She stared at him. Her employer had stolen her design. She pushed down the roiling frustration, blocking words she wanted to say. No sense in risking her job, even if what they'd done was unacceptable.

"Why don't you speak with Gloria? She might have intended to talk to you about it and possibly arrange for you to provide more designs."

"Yes, I'd like to speak with her. Can I go to her office now while I'm on break?"

He hesitated for a moment. "Sure. It's worth a try."

Hugo was likely glad to pass Blair's frustration along to Gloria. She saw the woman's door open with an embossed plaque on the wall beside it. She knocked gently and waited until Gloria lifted her cold, unwelcoming gaze. Hair dyed red showed dark roots that matched black-rimmed glasses over her pale face.

"Excuse me for bothering you, Gloria. I'm Blair McCartney. I created the design Hugo just phoned you about. He said you'll be using it in the next collection, but I wasn't notified about this."

The woman leaned back with a bored expression. "Our designers aren't notified of anything. You work for the company, right?"

"Yes, I'm in the assembly room. I have a design degree, but there weren't any openings in the design area when I started. I thought I'd be notified and compensated for the design I created."

Gloria shook her head. "Our designers aren't compensated for their creations except in their salaries. They're employed as designers and their work belongs to the company."

"I understand that." Though it seemed unfair, even to the designers who agreed to those conditions. "If they have the title and salary of a designer, they aren't paid extra for their creations, which belong to the company. But I work in *assembly*. I don't have the salary of a designer, but I'm still not being compensated for my creation."

"Yet you are an employee."

The woman's flat statement stirred heat in Blair's belly. She struggled to compose her words. "So, you're saying that because I'm an employee, anything I create is owned by the company, even if I am not compensated in *any* way for the design?"

No response.

"I call that stealing," Blair ground out.

The woman grimaced, and a network of lines flared from her lips. "It's not stealing. Your work was available to use and you're an employee of this company."

"I think we're going around in circles," Blair said quietly. "You liked my design. I hoped it might be a door to eventually being promoted to designer." She paused. This could end up hostile. She'd lose the argument and maybe even her job. "I'm willing to work as a designer if you have any positions available. If not, I'm afraid I can't provide any more designs, knowing that you'll use them without compensating me."

Gloria didn't respond, as if the entire conversation wasted her time.

"Are there positions available in the design department?" Blair asked, despite the anger urging her to quit her job and walk out the door.

"Not at the moment. Sometimes we use contractors along with our salaried employees. We might be able to eventually offer you something like that."

"I'd work as a freelance contractor instead of in assembly, or in addition?"

"Whichever you prefer. And if a design opening becomes available, you can apply for it."

Blair's blood pressure sank slowly, and her heart's rhythm calmed. "Sounds like there are several options. When might a contract position be available?"

Gloria's splayed fingers said she had no idea. "I'll keep you in mind when something opens up."

"Please do. I work at machine forty-five and I'm here every day."

A cool smirk raised the woman's thin red lips. "I know where to find you."

℣ ℣ ℣

Cooper finished feeding Zipper and himself before calling Blair. He wanted to give her space to come home, get dinner on the table, and take care of Jake. He'd made efforts to avoid crowding her and sometimes felt like he was on a balance beam, not wanting to fall off in either direction. That was likely normal in the early stages of their relationship, but he hoped to progress beyond that soon.

"Hi, Cooper."

Blair's voice sounded flat, sapped of energy. It was a Monday, after all, but there was more behind it. He tensed. "How was your day? I sense something might have gone wrong."

"You could say that. First, how was your day?"

"Good. Plumbing's all finished in the house. Electric'll be done in another few days. That's my news. What's going on?"

She sighed. "Remember the design my colleague turned in? I went to the boss about it today since I hadn't heard anything."

Cooper's anger bubbled as Blair described her conversation with this Gloria woman. It sounded like stealing to him too, though he understood the company policy.

"So anyway," she continued. "Neither a design or contract position is available. I'm back to zero."

"No, you're not, Blair. You've still got your dream, which is to launch your designs. If you work for this company, they'll get all the fruit of your creativity. They'll own everything. So, even if they pay you, you won't get any further in your dream. You'll get more money, maybe, but that's all. It won't launch you to, well, anything."

Blair was silent for a moment. "I'm not ignoring what you're saying. I'm thinking. You're making sense. It's a long road, though."

"Yes, but it's the road you want. Being a full-time designer might be a more enjoyable job than what you have now, but it won't get your label out there with *your* name on it."

"If they offer me a contract job, that would be something. It could supplement my income."

"Your market sales supplement your income. Listen, I'm not trying to counter your ideas, Blair. I'll support you in whatever you do. I'm in your corner, but I think they'll continue to steal your designs and not give you credit for them. There's a reason gifted people become entrepreneurs."

"You're giving me a lot to think about. I feel better, even though nothing has changed."

"Maybe your perspective shifted a little. If I can help you feel better, that makes me happy." He paused. "Change of subject. Did you ever hear anything back from your landlord?"

"Nope. Not a thing."

"Did you write to him again?"

"Yes, I wrote twice about the ceiling in the kitchen and roof leak. I didn't expect to hear about the chimney, but I've kept records of everything."

"That's good. I wonder if we should call the helpline. They can tell you about other options. Do you want me to do it?"

"No, I can do it. It's my residence, so I should do it."

"I don't mind—"

"No, Cooper."

He'd overstepped. She'd already had a bad day. "Look, I'm not trying to take over."

She let out a chuckle. "Kind of sounded that way for a minute."

A heavy feeling coated his stomach. A few warning bells went off. "I apologize. I just want to help and—"

"Protect."

"Is there anything wrong with that?" He gentled his voice.

"I'm not a weak, helpless female."

Cooper sighed in frustration. "Is that what you think motivates me to want to help you? Blair, I have more free time than you do, plus I'm concerned about the house you live in. But if you don't want my help, that's okay."

"Thank you, really. I'll call the number tomorrow when I'm on break and see what they say."

The rest of their conversation returned to lighter subjects, but when they hung up, Cooper's disquiet remained. He stood from the couch. "C'mon, boy." He attached the leash to Zipper's collar, pulled a fleece over his own head, and left the house.

The cool evening breeze lifted his spirits slightly and tousled his hair. The sidewalks along the street huddled quiet and dark, except for pools of light from the streetlamps. While Zipper sniffed around and did his business, the conversation replayed in Cooper's mind.

Blair's response might have resulted from her frustrating day. That he'd urged her not to accept the status quo from her employer, then urged her to call her landlord, had been too much. Too much urging. He could see how she might think he was telling her what to do. Which he kind of was.

Clearly, he had to learn boundaries with Blair. And he had a tendency to tell her what to do, which understandably, she didn't appreciate. She'd been on her own for years raising Jake and had succeeded in making a home for him. Just because Cooper was dating her didn't mean he could take over.

But she could be more accepting of his help too. Was it pride, or was she saying, *Don't get too close too fast*? Was he going too fast? True, he had visions of a future with her and Jake. But maybe he should slow down. He had to learn how much was too much.

Lord, please help me know the difference between taking burdens away as an expression of love, and being controlling. I sometimes don't know the difference.

His phone rang. Blair.

"I'm sorry, Cooper." Her voice sounded breathy, and the hard edge had disappeared. "I appreciate your desire to help and protect us. You're so kind and I just snapped your head off. Can you forgive me?"

He smiled. There was the sweet Blair he remembered. "Of course. Look, I totally understand. I'm trying to learn boundaries. I really care about you, Blair. You and Jake. I care about your safety too. I'm a contractor and I know houses, so when I see something out of the norm, it concerns me, especially for you two."

"I hadn't even thought of that angle. I was frustrated by what happened at work today. Made me feel hopeless and disregarded. So, I got defensive with you, and I shouldn't have. You're so helpful and it makes me feel...sometimes I feel worthless when I can't do things for myself."

Cooper felt a punch in his gut. "Oh, Blair. That's the last thing I want you to feel. I want to take the *burden* from your shoulders. I want to make things *easier* for you, but in no way do I think you can't do these things yourself. You're so strong and capable and creative." He paused and heard her sniff. "And sexy and beautiful."

She let out a throaty chuckle, and he smiled in the darkness.

Zipper wiggled impatiently next to where Cooper stood about a block from his house. He started moving his feet again.

"Thank you for everything you are." Her voice was soft. "I care about you too. A lot."

He wanted to invite himself over for a hug and a kiss or two but held himself back. Holding back might be a useful thing to learn.

"I came over just now to tell you in person," she said. "But you didn't answer the door. I realized I'd blown it."

"Not at all. I'm walking Zipper. And needed some air." His feet crunched on the gravel driveway.

"Yeah, I have that effect on people."

He laughed softly. "Just got home."

As he finished speaking, her front door opened, and she emerged wearing a thick cardigan. She jogged across the yard to him and slipped into his arms. Cooper took a deep breath of her and buried his face in her hair. He tightened his arms around her shoulders, and they stood still for several minutes. He drew strength from her warm body against his. She lifted her face, and he kissed her. A tender touch became fierce as she pulled into him with both arms, as if to draw him even closer.

They pulled apart. "I guess that was our first conflict," he said. "It was totally worth the kiss-and-make-up part."

They exchanged grins. "I'm glad you think so." She tiptoed to place another feather-soft kiss on his lips. "But I'll try not to cause any more trouble."

Cooper watched her return to her house with a saucy backward glance before shutting the door.

Chapter Twenty

Jake finished his prayers and snuggled deeper under the comforter. Blair slipped her fingers into his blond curls and caressed his head. "You've had a lot of changes, big guy. You doing okay with everything? With Katie, with Cooper, with your dad?"

Round blue eyes stared out of his little boy face. He nodded. "I like Katie. And Cooper." And his dad was only a name on a letter so far.

"I'm just checking because you're the most important person in the world to me. You know that, right?"

Jake nodded again. "Is Cooper coming back over?"

"Sure, he'll come once in a while, and sometimes we can go over there. Would you like that?"

"Yes. I want to see Zipper. He misses me. I couldn't go today before dinner. Is it time to go to Nanna and Grandpa's soon? They said they have a surprise for me next time I go there."

"Oh, that's exciting. I wonder what it could be. I'll talk to your Nanna tomorrow and decide when you'll go. Get some sleep now. Tomorrow's a school day."

Blair leaned forward and kissed his forehead. "Good night, sweetie."

Once she'd turned out Jake's light and pulled his door closed, she returned to the living room. She dimmed the lamp and settled into the worn armchair, thinking about her almost fight with Cooper earlier that evening. He'd been trying to help her, so why had she been so defensive? She'd been afraid he'd start telling her what to do, acting like he owned her. He *was* a bit pushy sometimes, but it came from a protective and caring heart.

Her mind drifted to the first months of her pregnancy and the years that followed. She'd known she and Jake were on their own, despite the significant help from her parents. Not wanting to burden them more than necessary, she'd made independence her mission.

Her parents hadn't asked for those three years, and she had no right to push the limits of their hospitality and help. She'd made her bed, so to speak. She made good on her internal promise to be no trouble to anyone. That included Cooper.

If they stayed together and grew as a couple, they'd become interdependent. The thought frightened her a little, even though she trusted him. If she were truthful, she savored the fact that he cared about her safety so much, wanted to lighten her load, help her with things that would make her life easier. Why *wouldn't* she want that? It didn't make her weak.

Or worthless. Why had that word emerged unbidden from her lips? Was she worthless because she wasn't a superwoman, or hadn't become a fashion designer the world clamored over? *Lord, where am I getting my worth? And why is it in shambles? Is it because I haven't accomplished anything?*

But it wasn't true she hadn't accomplished anything. She'd raised a wonderful son by herself. *God, my worth is in you. You brought me into your family, and you see me as without fault, despite my failings. Marvelous in your eyes.* If only he'd bring that truth home to her heart.

The following day, Blair dragged herself to work, her motivation below zero. What was the use? Why was she there instead of at a post office or in a bank? It was all the same now. No greater opportunity existed behind a sewing machine than behind a desk. She'd been mistaken in thinking this job would be some kind of steppingstone. In reality, *she* was the one being stepped on.

No more. She'd keep her designs to herself and her hopes under wraps. Cooper had voiced her own suspicions. If they hired her in the design department, her unique creations would belong to the company, not to her. It would do nothing to advance her career as a fashion designer.

She released a long sigh as she parked in front of the nondescript brick building and clocked in. Maybe Nathan's marketing know-how could pump her with enthusiasm. But he would soon plan a wedding, besides the two jobs he already juggled.

Thoughts of Cooper, the care in his dark blue eyes, his arms wrapped around her last evening during their make-up kiss—sent a tingle through her bones. What a make-up kiss it was, so full of passion, she hadn't wanted it to end. He and Jake were sparks in her dull days.

Her mind went to Nelson. *Not* a spark. Rather, a dark reality hovering continuously on the edge of her mind. He'd written his letter to Jake three weeks ago. She should tell Jake to write his father a response. Nelson wouldn't forget, that was for sure. She'd remind Jake that evening.

Blair pulled a notebook from her purse and scribbled a reminder, along with a note to call her mother. Add to that a call to the housing hotline. That morning, Cooper had texted her a toll-free phone number he'd found, since she'd insisted that she wanted to do it herself.

During her lunch break, she made the call. This led to a menu, then another one. Finally, she had a person on the line. "Consumer Protection, housing division. Casey Johnson speaking."

"Hello, Ms. Johnson. My name is Blair McCartney, and I'm calling to find out what options I have if my landlord is not maintaining my property in a safe manner." Blair told the woman about the chimney, the roof leak, and a possible short in the oven.

"You have to give your landlord two weeks to make the repairs. If he or she doesn't do it, you can have it done, then deduct that amount from your rent. The landlord has no legal right to retaliate in any way."

Retaliate? As in, kick her out on the street? "What if it's something serious, like a roof leak?"

"You can get an estimate and send a copy to your landlord. Let him or her know that you have talked with us. If he doesn't fulfill the conditions on the lease under landlord responsibilities, you have legal recourse. You can file a formal complaint. And, of course, you'd have a legal right to break your lease and move elsewhere, if he doesn't make the repairs, since he'd be in breach of contract."

Blair sighed. "I didn't want to move. I have a little boy and I work full-time." Her voice trailed off as she pictured herself having to pack up boxes and look for another home, or else ask Cooper to fix the roof. There must be something she could do to push Mitchell to repair her house. "Do I have the right to stop paying rent until he fixes these things?"

"No, you don't. You'd risk eviction in that case. It would be better to enlist someone to do the repairs and deduct the expenses from your rent the following month."

"He'll just keep neglecting things until I move out."

"It's possible. But it may give you some immediate solutions. I can send you a document outlining your rights as a tenant. There may be free legal counsel available as well, depending on your situation."

"Oh, that's good news. Ms. Johnson, I'm curious. What's a worst-case scenario for a landlord?"

"Worst case? If he or she doesn't comply at all, a lawsuit might be filed. It's rare, because usually the landlord falls into line prior to that."

"And if not?"

"Again, worst case, the landlord could be fined or have his license to rent revoked. That's exceedingly rare."

"I guess so. I may have it repaired first and deduct it from my rent. It's good to know I can file a complaint if I have to."

"I'll email you some links and phone numbers, so you'll have several options."

Blair gave Ms. Johnson her email address.

"Thanks so much, Ms. Johnson."

So, she did have options. Would this make a difference?

"Jake, you need to write a letter to your father." Blair rose to clear the dishes from the tiny kitchen table after dinner that night. "He wrote to you a few weeks ago, and we forgot to write back to him."

Jake gave an exaggerated frown. "I don't know what to write. What should I say?"

"How about telling him what you did this week or something about school? Doesn't have to be long. He's probably wondering when you'll write back."

"Okay. If you'll help me."

"Sure. I'm going to call your Nanna while you're doing your music. After that we'll sit down and write something together on the computer. Okay?"

"'Kay." He left the room and soon she heard faint piano notes drift from his bedroom.

After she finished the dishes, she phoned her mother. "Hi, Mom."

Blair's mother chatted about her garden and shelving her dad installed in the garage. "How are your ankle and wrist?" her mother asked.

"Much better. I did a couple of weeks of PT, and I'll continue the exercises at home another couple weeks."

"Wonderful. I'm so thankful it wasn't worse. Your neighbor came along at the perfect time."

"Yes, he did." Up to then, her mother thought the helpful neighbor was a woman. "He's a good friend." Why had she said that? Why didn't she tell her they were a couple? "Um, he's...we're—"

"What about Nelson, dear? Have you heard from him? That's the second thing I wanted to ask you about. Let's see, he sent Jake that letter weeks ago and you told me Jake wrote back to him. What's the current situation?"

Blair blinked at the sudden change of topic. "After Jake's first letter, Nelson wrote back. I'm going to help Jake respond to him tonight. We'll send it by email, so he'll get it quickly."

"Oh, that's good. Did you learn anything else about him? Where does he live and what's he doing?"

"You know I wrote to him too, for one thing, to ask about his sudden decision to recognize Jake. He emailed a letter back to Jake, and one to me explaining himself."

"Oh?"

"He apologized and said he realized he'd behaved badly."

"That's nice."

"Nice? Mom, he abandoned me, and I didn't hear from him for seven years. Nice?"

"I only mean he's trying to make it right. Don't be bitter, Blair. He's making an effort. Now Jake can have a relationship with his father."

Blair shook her head in frustration. "Which is why I didn't ignore his letter entirely. I'm not bitter, Mom. I've forgiven him. But you seem to forget what I—what we all—went through."

"Do you mean with the pregnancy and birth?"

"I'm talking about my emotional pain at being abandoned and left alone with his child." Her voice had risen. Yes, she'd forgiven Nelson, but her mother was another matter. She gentled her tone. "Of course, you and dad were there, and I'll always be thankful for that."

"It was a shock at first," her mother said. "But we all got through it. We love Jake so much. It's hard to regret anything."

"Yes, that's true." Blair let out a breath as a layer of heaviness floated down into her chest. "Nelson lives in Harrisburg and works as a graphic designer. That's all I know about him, but I'll keep you posted. By the way, what weekend do you and Dad want to keep Jake? This weekend?"

"No, the following would be better. Your dad wants to finish the garage projects first, and I have a meeting at church."

Disappointment pooled inside Blair. She'd looked forward to a weekend alone with Cooper. "Jake said you guys have a surprise for him."

"Don't tell him, but we're taking him to an alpaca farm we discovered that's only a short drive out into the country. They have other animals too and some educational programs for children."

"That sounds great, Mom. He'll love it."

"So, not this weekend, but next."

"Yes. You can bring him by Saturday early so we can make a day of it."

"No problem."

Blair hung up without telling her mother about Cooper.

The moment had passed.

 C&3 C&3 C&3

Friday morning, light rainfall kept Cooper at his desk instead of at the work site. A good thing, since he was getting behind again on his design clients. The project had slowed that week due to permitting. He didn't expect any problems, but apparently their schedule was full. An unfortunate delay, but nothing he could do about it.

Blair and Jake were gone for the day, but they'd seen each other Wednesday evening. He'd invited them over to experience chicken curry, though he'd toned down the heat level. Jake had shot Cooper a suspicious glance when he saw the orange sauce in the bowl of chicken, but ended up enjoying it. Or so he claimed. He especially liked the ice cream after the meal *and* reuniting with Zipper.

At eleven, Cooper stood and stretched. Zipper came to the doorway and wagged his tail.

"Need to go out, Zipper?"

The tail swung faster. Cooper glanced out the window. Though gray clouds still rumpled the sky, the rain had stopped. He leashed Zipper and went outside. He circled the block, then returned to the house. As he approached, he noticed a dark blue sedan parked along the curb opposite Blair's house. Not unusual, except a man sat inside, as if on a stakeout.

His senses perked to vigilance as he watched the man. His first thought was Nelson, but the man didn't know where Blair and Jake lived. She'd made sure of that.

The man lifted a cell phone and peered at it. Cooper relaxed his shoulders. Probably a guy who needed to make a call or adjust his GPS. Cooper returned inside just as the rain pattered anew.

He settled in front of his computer with a cold drink. His thoughts resisted concentration. Must be in a Friday mood. Instead, he pictured Blair, and wondered about her day. Anticipation rose inside as he thought of seeing her that night and much of the weekend. He liked their routine, which was a bit like a family, the three of them having dinner a couple of times a week and spending afternoons together over the weekend. Jake had fallen right into the pattern and seemed not to mind Cooper hanging around more frequently. Their previous friendship had likely helped.

So far, their rhythm seemed to work with Blair's need for sewing time and Jake time. He wished they had more alone time, but they'd work it out over the coming months.

He phoned Mayor Faulkner's deputy to make sure he wasn't breaking any laws with the letter for Mitchell's renters.

The man chuckled. "Go for it, Cooper. You're not breaking any laws. There's enough useless mail in my box every day. One useful thing won't do any harm."

"You're right about that. My goal is to give people information they're entitled to if they're in this situation."

"It's available online, but people don't necessarily think of that. Hope it does some good."

"Me too."

"Just wanted to say Mayor Faulkner spoke highly of you, Cooper. Said you were just the kind of man needed in Brenner Falls."

"That's nice to hear. We had a discussion the other day about my goals for housing in the Falls. Safety's important to me, among other things."

"As it should be. Sounds like you and he are on the same page. The mayor supports that goal of creating good and safe housing to protect residents."

After they disconnected, Cooper swiveled back in his chair. Protecting. There it was again. Was it a strength and weakness at the same time? As long as he didn't smother or control, protecting was a worthy role. Especially after Miles.

He went to the front window. The blue car had left. After a light lunch, he sent Blair a text. *I hope you're having a good Friday. Looking forward to seeing you tonight.* He'd found a Tex-Mex restaurant in the next town over. On Fridays, it had a live mariachi band.

Cooper put in a good afternoon as the rain continued on and off. When the clock showed four-thirty, his concentration deserted him as he anticipated seeing Blair and Jake. Maybe he'd be able to catch some time alone with Blair over the weekend while Jake was at a friend's house. The thought brought a smile to his lips.

Right on time, he locked up as Blair and Jake came toward the truck, dressed in light jackets.

The blue car had returned. If he'd been a cat, all his hair would be standing up. While he watched, the blue sedan pulled away. He tried to get a glimpse of the driver without being obvious, since he didn't want to frighten Blair or let it spoil her evening. Seemed to be the same man he saw earlier, but apart from brown hair, he couldn't identify age or any features. He'd mention it to her later, so both of them could keep an eye out.

Chapter Twenty-One

The following day, sales at the market weren't as vigorous as usual. Blair hoped it wasn't a trend. That afternoon, she'd be able to relax and catch her breath after a tedious week. At least she could be with Cooper for a longer block of time than weekdays allowed.

Jake slipped out of the car. "Thanks for your help today, big guy," she told him. "Please grab that canvas bag and take it in for me."

"'Kay." He pulled the tote from the back seat and waited for her on the porch while she grabbed a few items still in the car.

"I'll get lunch on the table in about a half hour, okay? You can play and I'll call you when it's ready."

"'Kay."

Though she usually enjoyed the energy of the market, that day her thoughts had bounced in too many directions. The memory of her evening with Cooper and Jake brought contentment. They felt more solid as a couple. A family.

After Jake went to bed the night before, she and Cooper sat close together on the couch and talked. He'd held her hand, then he'd told her disturbing news that drilled a hole into her previous serenity. The same car parked on the opposite curb twice the previous day. A car with a man inside. It could only be one person.

How would Nelson have found out where she lived? And why would he have come without telling her when they were on email terms? Without asking her permission? Why the drive-by spy surveillance when he could have simply asked for a meeting? It was as annoying as it was creepy.

If it was Nelson. If it wasn't Nelson, that would be far creepier.

Thoughts of Nelson's possible presence triggered a full-blown anxiety attack. Cooper said again he was there for her. If the man in the car *was* Nelson, Cooper offered to be present when she talked to him, if she wanted him there.

After he told her the news, he pulled her against his chest and encircled her with his arms so tightly she'd felt his heartbeat. As she rested her head there, security and well-being engulfed her all the way to her toes, despite the news she'd just received. She hadn't resisted or resented his protective gesture, but leaned into him.

Really, she had nothing to fear from Nelson. If he only wanted to meet his son, she could handle that. But what if he wanted more? Overnight visits, partial custody? Cooper had suggested she see an attorney. The cost of that kept her from action, but she still needed to research her rights.

Cooper stood firmly in her corner. She wasn't alone to face Nelson.

And *God.* Whatever the circumstances, she'd never be alone. He'd known in advance everything that would happen, and he'd already supplied her with strength. How many times had he said, *Don't be afraid, I am with you*? She still felt so weak in her faith. It was easy to embrace faith when it wasn't tested. But in that case, it never grew. Maybe this challenge would spur her to apply it.

The muffled sound of a man's voice drifted through the front window to the kitchen where she prepared sandwiches. She dashed to the hall and peered out of the front door. Perspiration broke out on her neck and her heart thudded in her chest. Even after eight years, she'd recognize him anywhere.

Nelson stood in the yard about ten feet from where Jake stood on the porch, speaking to him. Before flinging the door open, she glanced at Jake, who responded calmly, standing straight and unafraid.

Blair stormed to the porch, anxiety and anger tumbling together inside her. "Nelson. What are you *doing* here?" She stood behind Jake and placed her hands on his shoulders.

Nelson hadn't changed much in eight years. The same clear blue eyes stared out from a more mature face with the beginning of tiny smile lines. Wavy brown hair was shorter now than in college when it had almost reached his shoulders. Blair's pulse pounded. How many times had she imagined this surreal moment of meeting Nelson face to face?

She felt little apart from anger. No attraction, no regret. He was a familiar-looking stranger.

"Hello, Blair. I'm really sorry to surprise you like this." Nelson's voice came out warm, familiar, like an old friend. As though he was simply passing through the neighborhood. He almost sounded sincere. But he'd always been easy to believe back then.

"Nelson," she sputtered. "There was a *reason* I didn't give you our address. You're violating the agreement we had, as well as violating our privacy."

Beyond where Nelson stood, Cooper emerged from his house with Zipper in tow, They locked gazes across the expanse of grass and driveways. Quickly, he attached Zipper and marched toward her.

Though she didn't fear Nelson, Cooper's appearance sent a thread of comfort through her. Regardless of how peaceable Nelson was, it wouldn't hurt for him to know she was involved with a tall, muscular man who lived right next door. A man who she didn't doubt would engage in physical combat to protect her and Jake.

He reached the porch and stood beside her, almost touching her arm with his. His fingers grazed hers. "Is everything okay, Blair?" Cooper's tone was low, but fire blazed in his eyes as his gaze swept hers. He returned a hard countenance to Nelson. The two men sized each other up.

"Cooper, this is Nelson. Jake's dad." To Nelson, "This is Cooper Dawson, my boyfriend." She curled one hand around his forearm.

Nelson managed an affable nod. "Cooper." He didn't reach out to shake Cooper's hand, likely in response to the ferocious look on Cooper's face.

He acknowledged Nelson with a curt nod.

"I'll stay if you want me to," Cooper told her.

Blair swallowed. "Um, I think we'll be fine." More loudly, she said, "Nelson is *not* staying long. We made no arrangement for a visit today. We'll, um, have a chat and he'll be on his way, but I'll come over in a bit, okay?"

Cooper nodded, his jaw clenched in severity. "I'll leave you then. But I'm not far and I'm not going anywhere." He met Jake's eyes and winked. He sent Nelson a parting grimace and returned to his house.

Blair's eyes followed Cooper partway across the yard, hoping to send a message to Nelson. She returned a cool gaze to Nelson. "We'll talk here on the porch."

If he were any regular visitor, she'd show him to the living room, but he was no regular drop-in.

"Jake, please go eat your sandwich in the kitchen. I know you're hungry and it's ready. I'll talk to your dad out here and you can join us when you're finished, okay big guy?"

Jake didn't answer his usual favorite syllable, but his widened eyes toggled a glance between his mother and Nelson. He went inside. Blair gestured to an Adirondak chair.

Blair sat on the edge of the chair beside his. "Why didn't you simply ask for a visit instead of showing up like a commando after eight years?" She couldn't hide the anger in her voice.

Nelson offered an embarrassed chuckle. "I'm sorry, Blair. I fully intended to do that. You said gradual, and I planned to respect that. But I knew it might take months for me to actually meet Jake.

I wanted to *see* him first. I thought if I could just *see* my son, I could be patient for the right time for us to meet."

"So, you stalked us." Frustration still simmered under the surface but started fraying at the edges.

"I didn't plan to get caught." He scrubbed one hand down his face. "I know that's kind of psycho. Then when Jake came outside, I wanted to talk to him. You know me, Blair. Not all my ideas are good ones."

True. Despite herself, his statement triggered a hazy memory or two and she fought the temptation to smile. She kept her poker face. Let him squirm. "That's the thing, Nelson. I don't know you anymore. I thought I knew you before and would have trusted you with my life. But you turned out different than I imagined." Her words emerged with a peaceful strength she didn't know she had. Her fear faded. Another force carried her.

His face sobered. Tears sprang into his eyes, and he swiped them away with his wrist. Maybe he *wasn't* faking it.

"I know, Blair. I know. Like I said in my letter to you, I hit bottom when I finally faced what I'd done to you. I know that doesn't help. If you think I deserve that self-condemnation, well, I agree. I've condemned myself plenty. But I'm here to take a first step. I want to thank you for letting Jake write to me. That meant the world to me. But it's not enough." Nelson shrugged. "I want to get to know him."

"I understand. But we have to do this in the right way. You can't just come by when you feel like it with no advance notice. The only reason I agreed to this at all is that you seemed sincere about wanting to know Jake. You seemed sorry—I hope that's not some kind of act—and you agreed to take things *gradually*. You've already violated that one. But you're here, so I'll allow you to speak with Jake. From now on, though, if you don't agree to do things gradually, there's no deal. Do you understand?"

"Yes, of course. I need to win back your trust, that much is clear. And our son is precious. Of course, you want to protect him. And that big guy next door seems to want to protect you too."

Blair stifled a smile. "Yes, that he will. He's special to both Jake and me and will stand up for us if there's a need." She met his eyes as if to level a warning, but she found a soft openness there. Blue eyes like Jake's. *Exactly* like Jake's. And the same lines of his chin. A stranger could see they were father and son.

Blair swallowed the dry lump that had formed in her throat.

Nelson held up one hand. "No need. I'm not here to threaten, bother, harass or anything. I have one objective, to know my son."

"You're not vying for partial custody?" She had to ask. "You shouldn't dream of that."

He blinked at her. "I want to be involved in his life and I don't know what that'll look like down the road. *He* has to learn to trust me too."

She pressed her lips together as a breeze of relief blew softly in her chest. Involvement in Jake's life. Pretty vague, but *she* could define what and when. *She* had the control. "How'd you find us?"

Nelson rested his elbows on spread knees. "Before getting Jake's email the other day, I got frustrated because I hadn't heard back from Jake in weeks. I was afraid it would be a one-shot thing, one letter, then fade to nothing. So, I talked to this guy at work about it. He's a friend and works in IT. He told me through the IP address, through the email, I could find out what town you were in. He helped me do that. Once I knew the town, it was easy to find the address. And like I said, I just came here this weekend to peruse the town and see if I could just get a glimpse of my son."

Blair looked away. "Should've been a private investigator. I'd have sent you a photo if you'd asked."

Jake came out to the porch and leaned on the arm of Blair's chair. "All done."

"You ate your fruit too?" Blair shifted her hips to give him space to sit with her.

He nodded.

"Jake, do you have anything you want to ask your father?"

Jake stared at Nelson. It was a lot to ask a seven-year-old, but Blair was at a loss to know how to conduct this strange meeting.

"Do you have a dog?" Of course, Jake would ask that.

Nelson grinned at him. "I don't have one right now, but I like dogs. I had one in high school. His name was Murdock. He used to go places with me. Do you have a dog, Jake?"

"No, but Zipper lives next door. I play with him a lot."

"Cooper's dog?"

Jake nodded.

Nelson's gaze met Blair's. "Cooper is...you guys are serious?"

The question caught her off guard. "It's kind of new..." Instantly, she regretted her words. Wasn't any of his business. "But yes, it's serious." Seemed serious to her.

Jake didn't appear to have another question.

"What's your favorite sport?"

Jake shrugged. "I like soccer, but I'm not very good at it."

"You have time to learn. Soccer's fun. Do you like basketball?"

"I don't know. I've never played."

"What subjects do you like in school?"

When Jake shrugged and looked toward Cooper's house, Nelson fell silent.

He turned to Blair "How long have you lived here in Brenner Falls?"

"A little over a year. It's not that far from my parents, so we can still see them. The town's a good size for us." She slid one arm around Jake's shoulders. It was okay that he didn't have more questions or want to answer any. Just being on the porch together with his dad could reduce the fear of the unknown.

"I had a good impression of the town as I drove around yesterday. It's about an hour from where I live in Harrisburg. Brenner Falls looks like a great place to raise Jake."

"It is. He's integrated nicely here. What took you to Harrisburg?" She shifted again, but kept her arm around Jake.

"I got a government job. Then later, I got a better position in a private company where I've been the last six years."

"Are you married?"

"No. I regretted so many times—" His blue eyes glinted, searching hers. "Haven't found anyone quite like you, Blair."

Was he looking for more than getting to know his son?

She didn't know what to say to that, especially as Jake heard and observed everything. "I guess you will one day."

"Do you keep up with anyone we ran around with at school?"

She shook her head. "No. They were mostly your friends, anyway. I keep in touch with my friend Lisa. You might remember her."

"I sure do. She told you to break up with me a couple of times."

"Yeah, she never liked you." After a beat of awkward silence, she said, "You'll be going home after this visit?"

"I, uh, guess you could say I met my objective."

Sitting on the porch next to Nelson felt both natural and bizarre. He offered a few facts about his own life, probably since she refrained from asking him much. Not yet. Not today.

Finally, he stood to leave. "Before I go, Blair, I need to talk to you privately about something."

Anxiety sparked inside. What would be the next step? She turned to Jake. "Say goodbye to your dad and wait for me inside, please. You can play a game or practice your piano."

Jake looked up at Nelson with a frightened expression he hadn't had before. "Bye." He scampered into the house, likely relieved.

They both stood and Blair stuffed her hands into her sweater pockets. Nelson said, "I'd like to have regular contact with Jake. Honestly, I don't know what that'll look like. He's not used to me or at ease yet, so—"

"You won't be alone with him. He's not ready. I'm not either," Blair blurted.

"No, of course not. We can do another visit like today one day. I'm thinking of brief visits, an hour maybe until he's more at ease. And I want to help you financially with his needs."

Her mouth dropped open. She hadn't expected that. Two responses came to mind at once, *we don't need your help* and *it's about time*. She said neither. "Okay. That would be appropriate. What do you have in mind?" She'd let him suggest a number, since she had no idea what a court would require, and he might come up with a higher figure than she would. Despite how helpful his support would be, part of her chafed against receiving help. Even from Nelson? After all his neglect? Her mind overrode her stupid pride for once.

He proposed a figure. "I've given it some thought. I hope that will help."

Yes, absolutely, it would. "That's fine. Thank you." Once they discussed how he'd pay her, he stepped from the porch.

"Thank you, Blair. You could have chased me off with a shotgun, but you didn't. I know Jake isn't comfortable with me, but I hope he will be one day. We can even make some short phone calls. Does he have a cell?"

Blair laughed. "He's seven. He doesn't have a cell, or a computer. He has toys. A piano. A bike." Though once he was older and more active, she'd get him a kid's version of a phone, just for emergencies.

"Well, here's my phone number." He handed her a business card. "When email feels complicated, let's talk on the phone. Then

I can ease into phone calls with him once in a while, now that he's met me. I'm not trying to invade your life or change it. I promise."

His arrival in their lives would change things, like it or not. "We've made a start," she said. "But remember, *gradual.*"

"I'll remember." Nelson took a few steps on the driveway. "I'll email you soon. Call me if and when you want to." He gave her a grin that brought a rush of memories, momentarily thrusting her into the past.

She said goodbye and watched as he drove away, holding onto the post of the porch. A surreal encounter she couldn't have imagined. After a few deep breaths she went inside to see Jake.

Ԛ   Ԛ   Ԛ

Cooper paced the length of his living room, trying to stay busy. He prayed and fretted intermittently. Finally, he went to his office. He'd have to settle down and release everything. This was Blair's issue, not his. She was capable, strong, and not likely to let herself get deceived or swayed in the wrong direction.

A few minutes into his design project, he heard a knock. He leaped up, dashed to the door, and flung it open. Blair stepped in and he encircled her. Her arms slid around his waist, and she let him hold her for a moment. He placed a kiss on her blond head and led her to the couch.

"He's gone?"

She nodded, looking drained.

"Something to drink?" He moved toward the fridge.

She smiled, nodded again, and collapsed on the couch. He returned to the couch with glasses of iced tea. "Do you think it went well?"

"I think so. As well as could be expected. Nelson came across humble. Contrite. Could have been a whole lot worse."

"How did Jake take it?"

"He didn't talk much, which was understandable. He asked Nelson if he had a dog." She grinned. "Nelson asked him some questions, but Jake didn't have much to say. I told him it was *not* okay for him to come without notice and spy on us. He agreed but said that he wanted initially to get a glimpse of Jake."

"That's odd." Cooper shrugged. "No, I guess I understand." His eyes searched Blair's face. "And for you, Blair? You loved him once and you haven't seen him in eight years. How was it for you?"

She hesitated, appearing to consider her response. "It was weird. Familiar and unfamiliar at the same time. Made me think of those time enhanced photos of people who've gone missing. But overall, it was okay. I wasn't traumatized because we'd already had contact. And he offered child support, which'll help me a lot."

"I'm glad for both." He took her hands. "For your calmness through it all as well as the support, which he owes you." He trailed a finger down her cheek. "You're very strong, Blair. You're doing a hard thing. But I'm here for you in any way you need me to be. I mean that." He grinned. "I'll even beat him up if you want me to."

Blair returned his grin and leaned into him. "I don't think that'll be necessary." She lifted her face, and he brushed her lips with his. He reached into her hair and pulled her closer, intensifying his kiss. Why did everything suddenly feel so fragile? At the thought, he pulled her closer with a groan, as if afraid to lose her to the uncertainties of her new situation. Having her in his arms responding to him with an equal hunger allayed his qualms. Mostly.

"Where's Jake?" he asked when they pulled apart.

"He had a play date with his new friend up the street. He was supposed to be there right after lunch but was late because of Nelson. I'm glad we can spend some time together."

"Me too." His eyes searched her face, his arms still linked around her. He touched her face, whisper-soft. She closed her eyes and buried her face in his hand.

He lifted her chin and kissed her again.

He hoped that was the last surprise Nelson had in store for Blair and Jake.

Chapter Twenty-Two

Sunday felt as normal as Saturday had been unreal. Blair, Jake, and Cooper left church together and enjoyed a casserole Blair had pulled from the freezer that morning. It was the last meal from those the church members had brought her during her week of recuperation. The three of them played Uno together and enjoyed bowls of ice cream, then Cooper went home to give Blair some much needed free time.

After he left, she caught up on laundry and some light cleaning. She hadn't had time or focus the day before. Memories of the strange visit from Nelson floated in and out of her mind throughout the day. It could have been worse, so she was thankful. Hard to believe she saw Nelson after eight years. Church and Cooper tethered her to reality.

"Jake, are you all ready for school tomorrow?" She went into his room where he was coloring.

"Yeah. We have Show and Tell. What should I take?"

"Are you allowed to take anything you want? What about your favorite toy or book?"

"I want to take my piano." Jake gave her an impish grin.

Blair smiled back at him. "How about a music book that *represents* your piano?"

Jake seemed to consider her words. "Good idea, Mom. Won't be as heavy."

They snickered together. "You can take your new book, the one Miss Leah got for you." Her thoughts went to Leah, who must be over the moon planning her wedding to Nathan. "Hey, Jake, are you feeling okay about your visit with your dad? You haven't said much about it."

"Yeah. He seems nice." He shrugged.

Of course, he wouldn't know what to say. "I know you don't know him very well, so it's normal to feel uncertain about him. That's okay if that's the way you feel."

"Yeah, kind of like that." Jake grasped a crayon in one fist and continued coloring.

"You can talk to me anytime about it. Maybe it'll be nice for you to have your dad in your life, kind of like a friend. And Cooper is our friend too."

"I like Cooper."

"Yeah, me too."

"You knew Nelson a long time ago, before I was born?"

"Nelson was my serious boyfriend when I was in college. I thought I was going to marry him, but we broke up." How much could a seven-year-old understand? She had to try, to make up for not telling him sooner. Her mind went to a couple of photos she'd saved. Though she'd avoided looking at them for eight years, she'd kept them, thinking one day when Jake was older, she'd show him photos of his father. Maybe this was as good a time as any.

"Jake, I have a couple old photos from back then. Do you want to see them?"

He nodded. "Sure, Mom."

She went to her bedroom and rummaged in a box under her bed. After a few minutes, she found them, two photos entombed in a shoebox full of newspaper clippings and the sparse mementos she'd kept from college days. In the first photo, her much younger self stared back, long blond hair curling down over her shoulders. She looked happy, in love, not suspecting what the coming years would bring. Nelson's face, grinning, handsome, his eyes glued to her as she sat beside him. As if he'd really loved her.

In the second photo, they stood with a group of their friends. Some of those couples had gotten married. Most of their friends predicted Nelson and Blair would.

A slight stab of pain and nostalgia made her catch her breath. A knot formed in her throat, then a rush of memories, of charred hopes, hit her like a wave crashing on the rocks. Life could turn out so differently than one would expect.

She pushed away her thoughts, ignoring the stale ache, yet thankful for how the following years had turned out with Jake.

Jake lay on his stomach, still coloring, when Blair returned photos in hand. "Here are two pictures of me with Nelson. Your dad." She set them on the bed. He took them from her and examined them.

"Your hair was different. You were pretty, Mom."

"Thanks, sweetie. We were both much younger back then."

"Nelson looks the same but his hair is short now."

Current-day Nelson fit a neat corporate picture, whereas college Nelson had fit the stereotype of the longer-haired, bohemian art student. Those days, that world...they'd all had to grow up. And she had much more quickly.

"I'll put these photos away then call your Nanna. She wants you to come visit her and Grandpa next weekend."

She slipped into the kitchen with her cell phone. Nerves jangled in her stomach at the thought of bringing her mother up to date about Nelson, because she'd never been neutral about him. If only she were on *Blair's* side.

"Hi, Mom. Am I catching you at a good time?"

"Yes, dear. We just finished the dishes, and your father is already parked in front of the ballgame."

"Should I still plan on bringing Jake this weekend? You said you and Dad had that surprise for him."

"Yes, next weekend we'll expect him. Bring him early Saturday morning."

"Okay, will do. Mom, we had a big surprise yesterday." Might as well dive right in. She'd need to hold her ground, though.

"Really? What happened? I hope no one sprained an ankle."

"No, not that. Nelson came to our house."

There was a long silence on the phone. Then, "Oh, Blair. How did that go, after all these years?"

"It was...shocking, really. Overall, it went okay. We'd begun emailing, so I didn't expect him to come. He dropped by without notice." Still made her angry when she thought of it.

"That must have been upsetting. Did you even recognize him?"

"Oh, yes. He looks about the same, just shorter hair." Unmistakably the same person. "So, we talked about Jake. He tried to talk *to* Jake, but of course, Jake didn't know what to say. Nelson's a stranger to him."

"Of course, he is. How did Nelson find you?"

"Some computer guy at his work helped him locate our town through my email address. He said if he couldn't meet with Jake yet, at least he wanted to see him. See where he lived, maybe what he looked like. I understand his curiosity but didn't like the way he went about it."

"Yes, seems a bit devious. But it went well, you think?"

"I think so. He wants to be a part of Jake's life, but I told him we'd do that gradually."

"Who knows, maybe over time, you'll decide to get back together. Stranger things have happened."

Blair frowned. There it was, the subtle pressure. Her mother's long-term hope. "Mom, I'm seeing someone. I'm in a relationship."

"Oh, I didn't know. When did that start?"

"About a month ago. I mentioned my neighbor, who helped me out a lot. His name is Cooper, and he's a wonderful man. He's very supportive of me." *Unlike everyone else in my world.*

"Well, I'm happy for you, dear. I don't know why you didn't mention it, though."

"I was about to the last time we spoke, but we got off on another subject." Maybe her mother was disappointed someone stood in front of Nelson.

"I always saw you with Nelson and, well, that didn't work. So, he's not married?"

"No, he's not. And I know you hoped we'd be together, but you keep forgetting how that situation played out."

"Blair, how could I forget? Why do you keep saying that?" Her mother's tone rose.

"Why do you keep thinking Nelson, who deserted me when I was pregnant, was such a great catch and I missed out by not marrying him?" She couldn't help the exasperation that laced her voice.

"I never said that. I know he did the wrong thing, but now he wants to make it right. Doesn't that count for something? Maybe it's time to forgive."

Blair stifled a groan of frustration. "I *have* forgiven him, Mom. I already told you that. But it doesn't mean everything is forgotten. I know you and Dad helped me a lot when Jake was born, and I'm forever grateful for that." Would she ever stop feeling the need to say it, to remind her mother of her endless gratitude? "But it doesn't change what I went through. My experience was hard." She could say so much more but knew there was no point. If her mother couldn't understand her frustration, her reticence to let Nelson into her life in view of past events, she never would.

"Listen, Mom. I need to get ready for work tomorrow. Just wanted to give you the news. Give my love to Dad, okay? See you Saturday."

"Um, okay. Blair—"

But Blair had hung up. Her eyes burned. And she felt like an orphan.

Later that evening after Jake was in bed, Blair checked her phone before turning in. A message from Nelson waited in her inbox. *Hi Blair, I wanted to thank you again for letting me stay and see Jake yesterday. It was good to see you too. It seemed like the years just disappeared. You look even better than when we were in college, if that's possible, since you were so beautiful then. I guess maturity and motherhood suit you."*

Huh. She wouldn't let *that* go to her head. Not from him, in any case. *By the way, that's not flattery. It's just my impression after not seeing you all these years. So, if you give me the name of the bank you use, I'll check if I can send a monthly draft with support for Jake. I don't need the account number, just the name and how you're listed on the account. I'll get that to you this week. I hope you have a good week, Blair. I'll write to Jake soon. Nelson.*

She grudgingly admitted he was doing all the right things so far but following up on child support the very next day was not something she'd expected.

She'd been grateful Cooper had come and stood beside her, offering moral support. At least Nelson knew there was a man in her life. Felt good not to be alone facing a challenge for once. She'd been thankful instead of offended. Since her injury, she had to realize some of her reticence to accept help was the armor she'd built around her over the years. She could do it all, thank you very much. She knew there was pride and hurt hidden there. And longing for the protective involvement of a good man.

With her phone in hand, it would be easy to hit reply and email Nelson the name of her bank. But he'd given her his phone number and she could just as easily text him. Then he'd have her phone number. He'd end up with it anyway, wouldn't he? Especially if things progressed gently and in the positive way they had begun.

Blair texted Nelson and gave him the name of her bank, writing only *thanks* afterward. After hitting send, she wondered if she'd trusted him too quickly. Assuming everything would unfold in as friendly a manner as it had begun. *Lord, I hope I'm not trusting him too soon.*

Chapter Twenty-Three

Saturday morning, Blair dropped Jake off at his grandparents' house. During her drive back to Brenner Falls, she anticipated her weekend with Cooper. Following her shift at the farmer's market, she'd be all his. And vice versa.

Her market sales were mediocre that morning, but she could make up for it during the holidays. Nelson's child support had lightened some stress from her still tight monthly budget.

At home, she caught up on household backlog. That night Cooper took her to a romantic restaurant in a neighboring town. She felt like a princess, wearing one of her more elegant dress designs, a layered skirt, and an embroidered bodice with slit sleeves. Seemed he couldn't take his eyes off her. He stared at her across the candlelight and told her several times how beautiful she was. Though she wasn't convinced, hearing it stirred pleasure deep inside. He seemed light, free from the burdened look he sometimes carried. Made her feel freer too.

Carefree hours without concerns of what Jake needed or wanted passed too quickly. After dinner, they returned to Cooper's house and talked on the couch while Zipper snored nearby. She leaned against his chest and his arm cradled her shoulder. Peace and well-being enfolded her. Nelson couldn't touch that. Finally, she'd learned mental boundaries, at least for that evening.

"Hey, did you send that letter to Mitchell's renters yet?" She tipped her face up to meet his gaze.

"I sure did. Last Monday. I don't know if anything will come of it."

"Yeah, maybe nothing." She'd put in a complaint to the email address she received and figured someone had contacted Mitchell. Nothing had changed.

"I guess things'll move slowly," she said. "We've done our part."

"We have. So, we'll be patient."

"I hope we don't both end up in prison for impersonating a government official."

Cooper let out a hearty laugh then kissed her brow. "Don't worry, my beauty. Something may come of it."

The following week at the clothing factory crept by without incident or interest. After her terse conversation with Gloria weeks earlier, Blair was again relegated to a faceless line employee and nothing more. Her company had stolen her design and planned to use it, profit from it, and she was helpless to stop them. Her outcry would echo through the uncaring ranks of the company. Since she had no copyright on the design, she had no power to fight back. And even if she did, taking her employer to court was a laughable scenario.

Thankfully, it was Friday. The weekend wasn't far.

"Jake, you have eight minutes before the bus comes," she called toward the back of the house. Sometimes she dropped him off at school on her way to work. Most of the time, she let him take the bus to build his independence and get to know other kids. He claimed to enjoy riding the bus, *like a big kid.*

"'Kay," he called back from the bathroom.

With the few minutes she had left, she'd check her fashion blog. As Nathan had advised, she posted new information weekly. She'd also created a document with photos on twelve ways to use a scarf as an accessory, and offered a free brochure to those who subscribed to her blog. Each day, a few people signed up. She had no idea how she'd ever make income from offering free information, but Nathan had assured her it was a first step to getting her name out there. She did understand *that* was important, for whatever would come later.

As she stared at the screen with the few minutes she had, her eyes grew wide with astonishment. The number of subscribers had shot up overnight. Against the backdrop of her discouraging employment situation, that gave her a boost of optimism.

She hustled Jake out the door, gave him a tight hug, kissed his brow, and hopped into her car. After her distraction with her fashion blog, she barely had enough time to get to work.

Once she was behind her sewing machine at work, she locked her focus for the next several hours. During her afternoon break, she checked her phone messages, surprised to see a voicemail from Nelson. She'd heard from him once since his email following his visit, and that was to write a new letter to Jake. She'd been fearful he'd overuse her phone number once he had it, but that hadn't been the case.

Blair listened. *Hi, Blair. I hope your week is going well. Listen, I have an appointment with some friends in Lewisburg tomorrow night and I'll pass right by Brenner Falls. I wondered if it would be okay if I swung by to take you and Jake to lunch. Then I'll continue on my way. Think about it and please let me know sometime today or early tomorrow if possible. Thanks, Blair.*

Seemed like a normal request on the surface. Was it? She didn't think they'd see him so soon, and it unnerved her that he was putting her in that position. Again. But maybe that was *her* problem. There was nothing necessarily devious about his request. She didn't want to see him that soon, but if he was passing by and wanted to see Jake...

Wanting to see Jake was normal, and it would be out of the question for him to take Jake by himself this soon. She'd have to go with them. Nelson was rushing the process, wasn't he? Or was this a normal request since he'd be in the area anyway, and she was the one making a mountain out of it? She wrestled as her thoughts went back and forth. She could simply say no, it was too soon. Why should she make things easy for Nelson?

The questions gnawed at her mind for the rest of the afternoon. She could talk it over with Cooper, but she still had to settle her issues with Nelson on her own. Then again, maybe Nelson didn't even have an appointment but was fabricating a means to see Jake. Or he was telling the truth, and it was completely innocent. She blew out a breath. She needed to make her *own* decision as an adult and Jake's parent.

By the time she arrived home from work, her stomach roiled with indecision. She should say no. But lunch with him would take about an hour and a half then he'd be on his way. He'd see his son, and they'd expedite the process of Jake feeling more at ease.

Neither argument felt entirely right. Making dinner and interacting with Jake distracted her for a while.

"Jake," she finally said. "Your dad wanted to take us to lunch tomorrow because he'll be in the area. What do you think? Be honest, you can tell me." Maybe Jake could help her make the decision.

"Sure, why not? He can take us for pizza."

Blair stared at him, deflated. He *wanted* to see his dad? Here she thought she was forcing something onto Jake before he was ready, but she was the one who wasn't ready.

Her brain still struggled but let go of the fight. "Okay, I'll tell him."

Unaware of her inner battle, Jake calmly looked at her and asked, "May I be excused?"

"Yes, after you clear your dishes."

As she wiped up the kitchen, her phone rang. Lisa from New York. "Hey, girl. It's been a while," Blair said.

"I don't have much time to talk but realized how long it had been since I called." Her friend's voice was breathless. "Things aren't going well here, and I'm ready to jump ship."

"Really? You mean work pressure?"

"Yes, loads of pressure. It's awful what you have to do to climb the ladder."

Would have been ten times worse for Blair with a child to think of. "I'm sorry to hear that, Lisa. You were living my dream, but it sounds like more of a nightmare."

"Nightmare is right. At least *this* week's been a nightmare. I have about ten minutes before they start cracking the whips again, so I want to hear what's new with you."

Blair blew out a breath. How to summarize? "Well, two huge things. First, I'm dating someone really great. Second, Nelson has suddenly shown up wanting to know his son after eight years."

"Oh. My. Gosh. That's huge, Blair. Both of those are *huge*. We need a much longer conversation so I can hear more details. I'm glad you found a decent man, though. I'm excited to hear about him. But Nelson? Does he even *deserve* this chance?" Lisa liked Nelson even less when he denied Jake's paternity. He was Lisa's theoretical arch enemy on Blair's behalf.

"I don't know. I'm giving him a chance to get to know Jake. He's been trying to find me for over a year. But we're taking it slow."

"How's Jake handling everything?"

Blair laughed. "You know Jake. He's kind of a quiet philosopher. He says in a few words what he thinks, then goes about his business. Hard to tap into any deeper emotions about it. Maybe there aren't any. He's never shown much curiosity about his dad, though I assumed he would once he was a teenager, or sooner. Maybe that's why I'm allowing this to happen now. First, Nelson's acted humble about everything. He seems to understand how badly he screwed up. If he simply wants to get to know his son, I shouldn't stop him, but I'm keeping it slow." Despite the lunch appointment she promised Jake.

"Sounds like the best possible scenario."

"I hope so. Hey, you need to come visit one of these days. Sounds like you might need a change of scenery."

"I do. And I want to see you. My last visit was too short. But I gotta go now."

They disconnected. Blair leaned against the kitchen counter and stared at the orange tinted maple leaves outside the window. Inside, she'd known the life Lisa led, the one Blair thought she'd wanted years earlier, was an illusion. What had seemed glamorous was a lot of work at slave wages, running errands for the design king and queens in the industry. She hadn't missed out after all. But what did she have instead?

A lump of lead still lay in Blair's stomach when her thoughts turned back to Nelson. A simple pizza lunch. What could it hurt?

She texted Nelson. *That would be fine, just for lunch. We'll be available at one. See you then.* No reason to be warm.

Should she see him at all? But it was too late.

ೞ   ೞ   ೞ

Cooper thumped on the horn, and the guy ahead of him eased away from the light. He wasn't normally impatient with slow drivers or traffic jams. As though an army of ants ran laps inside his blood vessels, every nerve was tense. His jaw hurt from clenching it almost unconsciously since yesterday when Blair calmly told him she and Jake were having lunch with Nelson. Nelson, who wasn't supposed to show up again for several weeks. The guy was already taking liberties. He'd stalked them, then dropped in by surprise, all innocence and friendliness after eight years of being a negligent dirtbag. And here he was again, less than two weeks later.

So much for *humble* and *appropriate* and whatever meaningless words Blair had used to describe him. Cooper had never taken her for naïve. Was something else going on? Did part of her *want* to see Nelson?

He rolled down the truck window and let the autumn breeze, flavored with chill, flow in. The edges of the leaves blushed orange, red, and yellow. The coming season in Brenner Falls promised to be an explosion of color and community events. Normally, he'd look forward to taking part in these with Blair and Jake. Why did things feel like they hung in midair?

Was he overreacting?

At any rate, Cooper was glad to be away from home. Anywhere else. He hadn't seen Amber in a couple of weeks. Seemed they couldn't quite swing the hang-out-together rhythm they'd envisioned when he moved to Brenner Falls. Maybe they should accept that they were both busy, but still loved each other. They'd do what they could. That day, he was going to fix her back door and install another deadbolt after she served him lunch.

A few minutes later, Cooper parked in front of Amber's Craftsman house, which she maintained with meticulous care. He shook his head, fighting the emotions rolling around inside, confused, hurt, and angry all at once. He'd peeled away from the house before Blair and Jake returned from the market.

You're overreacting, Dawson. They're just having lunch. Yet, it hurt that Blair hadn't asked him what he thought. He would have talked it over with her. Instead, she simply told him she was meeting Nelson for lunch on Saturday. Even though Saturday was normally *their* day, if other chores and appointments didn't block the way.

"Hi, Cooper." Amber let him inside and hugged him. "You're early. We can catch up while the soup finishes cooking. Chicken tortilla. Your favorite."

"Smells good. Haven't seen you since the party last month."

"Crazy. Well, I appreciate your willingness to fix my door."

"Of course." Cooper forced his tense shoulders to relax. "Your brother's a contractor. Why should you pay someone to fix anything?"

She stood on tiptoe and placed a kiss on his cheek. "You're sweet. Have a seat in the sunroom and I'll bring us some tea. Lunch'll be done in ten minutes."

He let her talk first. She had a new colleague at work, a man. They'd had some tension at first, due to insecurity and competitiveness on his part, she assumed. But now she found him attractive.

"So, do I need to do the big brother thing and check this guy out?"

"No point. Not sure he's a believer. I mention little things once in a while, but no, I'm holding out."

"You could give him a chance if he pursues you. Not sure why he wouldn't."

She swatted his arm affectionately. "You always say that."

"It's true. The men in Brenner Falls must be blind or stupid."

"Maybe I'm just picky. Ever think of that?"

"As you should be."

"What about you, Cooper. Is everything going okay with Blair?"

When he stared back, her eyes widened. "What is it, Cooper? You look like you want to kill someone. I know that look."

He laughed then. "Not yet." He scrubbed one hand across his face. "Trying to get a grip is all. So, the summary is Jake's dad is a dude who disappeared before his birth and hasn't shown any interest until a year ago. No support, no contact. Now, suddenly, he has this *epiphany* that he wants to be a dad to Jake. He starts writing to Blair and to Jake and they had a first visit two weeks ago."

Amber's hands flew to her mouth. "Oh, my gosh. That was the first time she'd seen him since before Jake's birth? And Jake had *never* met him?"

"That's right. He'd had some initial correspondence with Jake and Blair by email, then shows up unannounced."

"Was she angry?"

He shrugged. "I think so. I met him, so he knows there's another guy in the picture."

"Must have been a shock for her."

"Yeah, it was. But later, she told me he regretted everything, was humble, all that. Might be sincere, might be an act. We don't know yet. But today he was *in the area*." Cooper made air quotes. "So, he wanted to take her and Jake to lunch."

"Since he was in the area," Amber repeated. "And he met Jake two weeks ago?"

Cooper grimaced. "*Only* two weeks ago. She told me she insisted he go gradually with Jake, and he agreed." He shook his head. "Meaningless. Guy's pushing her already in his *humble* and *appropriate* way. She didn't ask my opinion. Just decided and told me about her decision afterwards." As though he didn't matter to her.

She leaned back against the wicker chair and sipped her iced tea. "You must be wondering where you stand with Blair if she won't ask your opinion."

"We've only been dating a month, but this is a big thing."

"I'll say it is. I'm sorry for your frustration. She probably feels the need to do it for Jake's sake, and it doesn't mean anything else."

Amber's statement made sense, but didn't lighten the weight inside. "He wrote to her a year ago for the first time. She got spooked and moved to Brenner Falls so he wouldn't find her. *That's* how strong her boundaries were for years. This time, he found her through her IP address and just showed up."

A buzzer sounded from the kitchen. Amber rose. "Come on to the table. Maybe my homemade soup and corn bread will calm you down."

He stood, and she laid a hand on his arm. "It'll be fine, Cooper. Relax. Maybe it's lunch and nothing more. Maybe Blair made an impulsive decision to go along with his request for lunch, for Jake's sake. Ever think of that?"

"Yes, I have. Jake's first for her, as he should be. But I don't like being totally left out of her thinking process." His tone dropped. "I thought we had more than that together."

Amber offered a sympathetic twist of her lips. "Maybe you do, but it's still early in the relationship. And don't forget, she's been on her own for years. Might be a reflex for her to decide by herself." She took an enamel pot from the stove and placed it on the table. "Give it time to grow, Cooper. She's probably confused and trying to do what's best for Jake. I put myself in her place and I can't even imagine."

She was right. He should give Blair the benefit of the doubt. He didn't have to like what was going on. Blair probably didn't like it either. If her kisses and open conversation with him the previous weekend were any sign, she was fully committed to their relationship. One lunch with her ex wouldn't change that.

"Thanks, Amber." He drew her into a hug. "Thanks for listening and for giving me another perspective. I needed to hear it. I guess after Priya, my jealousy meter is working overtime."

They sat, and Cooper's thoughts began to calm, grasping the logic of Amber's words. Despite that, his stomach still twisted as she served the food. What was wrong with him? Why did it feel like a small hurricane was gaining speed inside him?

Chapter Twenty-Four

It was late afternoon when Blair, Jake, and Nelson left the restaurant. He walked Blair and Jake to her car. "Thanks for giving up your Saturday afternoon on short notice. It was nice to see you both." They said goodbye and he drove away.

She drove home and unlocked the front door, more than ready to be alone and have time to reflect and regain her wits.

Nelson had taken them to Jake's favorite pizza joint in town, so that made Jake happy. Nelson had asked her questions about the years that had elapsed since college, as if they were old friends catching up. She asked a few of her own but couldn't help but wonder if they should be so amicable, so civil under the circumstances. Not that she wanted to be a harpy for no reason. Was Nelson getting off too easy? He *was* trying to come clean.

During lunch, she'd gradually relaxed, going from wound up to laughing at certain memories. His blue eyes found hers across the table several times in an almost flirtatious way. As if it didn't matter to him that Cooper was part of her life, waiting for her to come home from lunch with her ex.

Each time she'd thought about Cooper, guilt lanced through her. Then the wrestling match sparked to life. Hadn't this been an ideal opportunity for Jake to hang out with his dad in a more comfortable setting than the last time when everyone had been on pins and needles? Given her relationship with Cooper—her boyfriend for only one month—what *was* the appropriate thing to do?

A glance at the clock on the mantle told her to stop the mental current and start the meal. Cooper was coming soon for dinner. She needed time to sort things out in her mind, but Cooper would want to hear how it went, what she thought. Part of her wanted to put the afternoon behind her. She needed to see Cooper to anchor into reality. She should have ended lunch sooner, saying they had things to do. Always a true statement. Had she failed to enforce boundaries?

How had Nelson gotten past them so quickly?

ભ   ભ   ભ

Cooper knocked on Blair's door at six-thirty. The door opened and a beautiful, but concerned-looking Blair faced him. She went into his arms, and they stood still for a long moment. An appetizing aroma surrounded him, but he wasn't hungry.

She pulled back. "Are you okay?" Her chiseled brows gathered. She must have sensed his tension.

"Yeah. I'm feeling weird about all this Nelson stuff. I assume he's left town?"

She nodded.

"We can talk about it after dinner if you want to."

She let out a breath. "Yeah. Let's wait. We'll focus on dinner first."

He tipped her chin up and brushed a kiss onto her lips. He wanted to deepen the kiss, but his insides weighed him in place until he heard more about her afternoon with her ex. And what she was thinking.

Dinner unfolded with a cordial surface and a silent rumble of strain underneath. At least Jake seemed unaffected by his afternoon with Nelson, and he chatted like usual.

After dinner, the three of them cleared the table and left everything in the sink. Blair turned to Jake. "Jake, could you go play in your room for a little while? I need to talk to Cooper. When we're done talking, I'll call you for ice cream, okay?"

"'Kay."

Cooper and Blair sat close together on the couch. She turned to him. "I want to apologize for not asking for your input before going to lunch with Nelson."

He relaxed his jaw, grateful for her words. "You don't necessarily owe me that, Blair. I know you've been on your own for a long time. But I did feel kind of left out of the equation. I didn't know how to interpret that."

"I understand, and I'm sorry." She laid a hand on his arm. He turned his hand and grasped hers, rubbing its softness. "Even though it was *much* too soon for another visit, I thought it might be good for Jake to be in a different setting with his dad and with me present."

Cooper nodded. "That makes sense. I blame him for not being sensitive to the timing. He invaded your lives only two weeks ago." The rumbling inside came to life as he pictured her with her ex as they reminisced and stirred up old feelings. "Seems to me Nelson shows up and gets whatever he wants." She might not like him being hard on Nelson, but he had to call it like he saw it. Nelson didn't deserve all the time Blair had given him.

"I didn't tell you about the lunch because I thought you'd say I shouldn't go. I was confused enough as it was and felt I needed to make that decision alone. I mean, it involved Jake and me."

He stilled as her words hardened inside him, chasing the previous warmth. In other words, none of his business. "You thought I'd pressure you? No, Blair. I'd never do that. But I'll tell you what I think. Then what you do is up to you." He paused. "Despite that, I'd like to think my opinion means something, since we're in a relationship together."

"Part of me didn't want to bother you with my Nelson stuff. Part of me wanted to hear your thoughts." Her tone was subdued.

He looked away. "Made me feel like I'm just the guy who lives next door. Why should you ask me, after all?" His voice sounded petulant in his ears.

"Cooper, of course I care what you think." She laid one hand on his chest. "You're *not* just the guy next door. You're important to me." Her brow furrowed and she dropped her hand to wrap it around his.

Could have fooled him. "So, tell me how it went. If you want to."

"Of course, I want to." Her voice faltered, likely because of the aggravation that must still show on his face.

She described the events of the afternoon play by play, where and what they ate. "Jake seemed relaxed, more than before."

"How did *you* feel being with Nelson in a social context after all those years?" *That* was the question that weighed the most for him. He pulled his hand away under the guise of scratching his head.

She leaned back. "I admit, it was weird. I was nervous at first, then I got more comfortable." She shrugged. "I kept second-guessing myself whether we should have gone or not."

"Do you regret going?" His tone said it didn't matter either way.

"After seeing Jake's response, no I don't. It softened things between them. I hope this will be a good thing for Jake. It's important for a boy to know his father." Her eyes returned to his. "Jake's benefit was my motivation all along. I still feel like I'm walking on a tightrope. Sometimes I have no idea what to do."

Cooper's shoulders dropped, and he exhaled a long breath. "I don't envy your position, Blair. You're stuck between wanting the best for Jake and your negative history with Nelson. And he *is* persistent."

"I wonder what God wants too. Forgiveness, for starters. I'm pulled in too many directions, what's good for Jake, my past with Nelson, what *your* role is since you're important to me." She returned her hand to his arm.

"You told me not long ago that you weren't sure if you could trust him. You seem to have overcome that fear very quickly."

"What do you mean?" She withdrew her hand.

He shrugged. "It seems like you trust him now, because he acted nice and seems contrite."

"No, I don't fully trust him." A faint edge had entered her voice. "He hasn't done anything wrong but there's a lot of water under the bridge. That's not why we had lunch today, because I trust him and we're now good buddies. I felt it was okay because it was a public place where he and Jake could interact. What are you getting at?"

Cooper leaned forward, elbows on his knees. "I'm thinking first of the way he acted in the past, deserting you when you were pregnant, with no contact for years. All of Jake's early years, in fact. So, he seems sorry. But in the present, he takes the *liberty* to write to Jake without telling you first. Then he takes the *liberty* to drop in when you'd specifically withheld your address from him. *Then* he invites you to lunch just two weeks later."

"Maybe he's trying to make up for lost time."

"And now you're defending him. Aren't you seeing a pattern? I completely distrust this guy and you should too."

She paused and stared at him. "Are you telling me how to think? Because I can handle this. I've raised Jake alone for seven years and haven't done too badly."

Cooper sighed in frustration. "I'm just saying don't forget about his past and current behavior. He doesn't get a pass because he's being nice or humble. He *should* be humble after what he did. He doesn't deserve a medal. Give him *time* to prove he's trustworthy. In the meantime, protect yourself." Why couldn't she see it? Had Nelson duped her already?

"And if I don't, I'm sure you will." She crossed her arms and looked away from him.

He thrust his fingers into his hair. "Blair, this conversation is going the wrong direction. I'm not trying to control you. I'm pointing out his current behavior isn't beyond reproach. He may very well be a great guy, a great influence on Jake. But it's been two weeks. After *eight* years. That's all I'm saying."

Could she sense the frustration smoking off his skin, pushing him away from her? "We haven't been together long, Blair. But I have the impression that since Nelson showed up, you're not sure of us, you and me. Suddenly, you've had this grand reunion with your ex and the past is forgotten. Meanwhile, I'm left there not even asked what I think, though I thought we were a committed couple. If you're not sure of us or need more time to think about it, just tell me."

Her mouth dropped open. "Is that what this is about? You're jealous of Nelson?" She blinked at him. "No, Cooper, you're wrong. I've told you that already."

He so wanted to believe her words. Now that she'd spent time with Nelson, had something changed for her? She'd loved Nelson once. "Your words say one thing, but your actions say something else."

She tried to speak, but the words appeared to choke in her throat as she rasped, "This doesn't need to affect *us*, Cooper."

"It already has. You closed me out and went with him, even though you said you wanted him to go gradually. I see the contradiction, and I'm trying to understand it. But you're not helping me, because you seem not to see what's going on."

"I'm not *stupid*, and I *do* see what's going on." Her voice rose. "*Nothing* is going on. Why are you making a big deal of my lunch with Nelson?"

He pulled himself up as his insides went dark. "Have you heard anything I've said tonight, Blair? You need time to work this out. Nelson or me. Or neither." Frustration growled inside, mounting until the lid blew off.

He stood. "Take all the time you want." He grabbed his jacket from the back of the couch, then threw a last glance at her. "Your relationship with Nelson didn't work out too well the first time. But what do I know? I'm the dispensable short-term boyfriend." He went to the door.

She scrambled after him. "Looks like to me *you're* the one who wants space. You're fabricating something from Nelson's visit. Something that isn't there. I've told you everything that happened. By courtesy, since it didn't really involve you."

He shot her a stare. "You're right." He went to the door.

"Wait, Cooper."

He closed the door and went out into the chilly autumn night.

Chapter Twenty-Five

Blair bent over her knees and jammed her fingers into her hair. What had just happened? How could a simple conversation have gone so wrong? And it had, as Cooper had pointed out. Cooper's concern and protectiveness had just gone off the charts, but it seemed everything was fueled by jealousy. Of Nelson.

She heard the front door slam, his truck roar to life, and tires crunching on the gravel as he backed up and drove away. Tears sprang into her eyes, but her sorrow fought with anger. Did he only need reassurance of her commitment to him? Or was he asserting himself in her life, trying to control her?

Or was he right in saying she was too accepting of Nelson, too forgiving? Too trusting? He'd said several things that *were* true, and she'd known it. Nelson *had* taken liberties. Did that make him untrustworthy? *Why* had she been sure reuniting with his dad was such a good thing for Jake, when she'd spent the last seven years fleeing Nelson, to the point of moving to Brenner Falls?

Confusion swirled in her head. "Lord, please show me the real issue here," she prayed aloud in the darkened living room. A few tears rolled silently down her cheeks. "Am I wrong to give Nelson a chance, Father? I'm trying *so* hard to do the right thing for Jake, but in that, am I alienating Cooper? I'm trying to do the best thing for everyone, Jake, Cooper, trying to forgive Nelson, giving him a chance to do right by Jake. What do *you* want me to do? How do I understand this? How do I make things right with Cooper?"

Yet, Cooper's reaction bordered on irrational. What was driving him? She'd given him no reason to be jealous, had she? And if jealousy was a trait she was now seeing, maybe it was a red flag she should pay attention to.

ଓ   ଓ   ଓ

Cooper's heart hadn't hurt that badly in a long time. The need to get far away pushed him to the only place he knew to go. When he arrived at his lot, deep shadows of approaching night crowded in, matching his mood. His house loomed like a deserted clipper, casting phantom shadows across the gravel. He sat in his truck and stared out the smudged window into the darkness. What had just happened?

Not only had he said some stupid, anger-driven words, but Blair had as well. It was as though Nelson was a virus that had gotten under their skin, causing them to forget what they felt for each other.

But clearly, he'd overreacted. Nelson was her situation to handle, not his. Yet, he wanted her to care about him enough to ask. She was so used to doing things on her own, was there even room for him in her life?

All Blair had to do was provide him with reassurance. He'd almost begged her for that, just a word in his favor instead of toggling between him and Nelson. Up to the moment Nelson came along, Cooper thought he counted for Blair. Thought she might be falling for him, as he was for her. Maybe Nelson wasn't a virus after all, but a magnifying glass to reveal the fault lines in Blair's shallow commitment.

The thought left a leaden coating in his stomach.

Despite her protest, did she *want* to reconcile with Nelson? Is that what was driving her, making her suddenly trust him, though he hadn't yet earned it? She'd denied it, but hadn't he detected something alarming in her tone?

He swallowed and pain spread in his throat. What was driving *him*? Why was he sulking on his lot in the shadow of a half-built house, hurting like the dickens? Had he been passed over once again by the hometown boy, just like with Priya? Did he simply fear a repeat performance?

Yet, after everything they'd said, her reassurance hadn't come. Instead, cutting words that loudly sent the message that she didn't need him.

Fine, he didn't need her either.

It would take a while for his heart to agree, and in the meantime, frustration and loss stabbed him until he felt raw and bleeding inside. He longed to wash his mind of the entire conversation. They needed a break so she could figure out what she felt for him and what she wanted from Nelson. Not long ago, she'd wanted *nothing* to do with Nelson. Now, she was allowing him to break them apart.

Cooper thrust the fingers of both hands into his hair. Maybe tomorrow he'd see things differently. Maybe he and Blair would eventually work it out. But for now, he needed to focus on something else.

Finally, he'd done enough brooding in the dark. He got in his truck and drove home. By the time he got there, Blair's house was dark, though a light glimmered near the back. He was done looking over there. He unlocked the door and entered the house that felt as empty as he did.

ʘ ʘ ʘ

Jake trotted to the room where the children's service took place, then Blair went into the main sanctuary of the Real Faith Chapel. Of course, Cooper wasn't there. Before he started coming, she'd normally sat with Abbie, Garrett, and Nathan. That day, she avoided them, sat near the back, and hoped no one would talk to her. One continuous bruise extended through her organs, beginning with her heart.

Leah, who was her closest friend at church, was busy giving final instructions to the worship team on the stage. Good thing, since Blair didn't want to talk to anyone. Especially Leah, whose keen observation and compassion would lead her to notice Blair's despondency in an instant and dig the truth out of her. That would only cause an eruption of tears.

Though she couldn't sing during the worship set, the words and melodies soothed her. Then the message began. Pastor Todd got up and settled onto his wooden stool. A worn Bible flopped open over one knee. After greeting everyone and recounting a humorous anecdote from the week, he stared with compassion at the crowd. "It's been on my heart for a while to share a message about our identity as believers. Who we become. Who we are according to this." He held up the thick Bible with one hand. "What God thinks of us. You see, during our lives, we get all kinds of messages about who we are. Some messages hurt, and many aren't accurate, but that doesn't stop us from letting them shape our lives for years at a time, and not always in the best ways. I'm sure you know what I'm talking about, but I'll give you a few examples."

He told a few stories, positive and negative, to illustrate his point. "Here's the truth we need to remember. God reaches out to us and saves us. He adopts us and we're earmarked for eternity with him. That's fantastic enough, right? But that's not all. He transfers us to his kingdom then transforms us a little at a time. We're new creations, regardless of what we were before. Regardless of the mistakes we made, and continue to make."

God knew she was trying to straighten up, until recently, when it seemed she did everything wrong. Somehow, despite the ache radiating through her tightened throat, a tingle of truth brushed the surface.

"God can even use our emptiness," Pastor Todd continued. "Which, by the way, is a perfect fit for his abundance. This is true *before* we meet him, so he can draw us to himself. But it's also true *after*. Because we're still here on a fallen planet, we'll still sometimes experience emptiness. We'll get it wrong sometimes. So, he uses our emptiness and confusion to draw us in close to his heart. That's our daily reality. Or should be."

A few chains jangled out of place and fell as Todd's words soothed her shredded heart. True, God was bigger than her mistakes. Had she forgotten that? Yes, for years at a time. Still, her heart struggled to grasp that he'd made her new. He'd made her marvelous, he'd said. Seemed like wishful thinking.

Had she gotten it all wrong with Cooper and with Nelson? What was God saying about them? She blinked away the sting that began in her eyes and flinched against the fresh grief that rolled over her. *Lord, I didn't ask you enough for wisdom and direction when Nelson came back into my life. Now there's a clash with Cooper. I'm not sure how it all started or how he's thinking. Please show me what you want. Please work things out according to your will. I'm confused, Lord.*

One thing she wasn't confused about. She missed Cooper and wished she could slip her hand into his, as she'd gotten used to doing over the last month. His absence made her shiver, increasing the chill and the ache inside her.

She thought of Nelson, how adamant she'd been about firm boundaries, but as soon as he stepped over them in his friendly, humble way, she'd caved. Reminded her of caving in when he'd first urged her toward intimacy back in college. She'd never had good boundaries with Nelson. Was he only making up for lost time, time that he himself had sacrificed? Had he learned he could call the shots, as Cooper had implied? Or was he simply trying to get to know Jake and it was up to *her* to set the boundaries? Yes, it was up to her. Though Cooper's advice would have helped, ultimately, it was up to her.

Blair glanced at her phone as the service came to a melodic close. No text message from Cooper.

After church, Blair and Jake drove home. Cooper's truck wasn't in the driveway and Zipper's chain lay like a sleeping snake in the grass. Where had he gone? To visit his parents? To Amber's? He could be working at the house, though he normally didn't on Sundays. He was avoiding her, that much was certain. She opened her phone to text him, hovering over the keys for a long time. The details of their fight had become vague and tangled in her mind. He believed she wanted to get back with Nelson, but why would he think that? There was no basis for his fear unless he was vulnerable because of his breakup with Priya years earlier. He'd also alluded to another loss in his life, but hadn't wanted to discuss it at the time. Maybe there were things he hadn't told her that fueled his fears.

Finally, she typed, *I'm sorry for our argument and my sharp words. I hope we can work things out. I miss you.*

Blair dragged through the evening as her spirits dropped lower and lower. Cooper hadn't responded to her text or shown up at his house. Jake chatted over dinner, and she listened but couldn't find the energy to give full responses other than, "Oh, that's nice."

She didn't think Jake had heard their argument. They hadn't yelled or thrown anything, but the quiet, cutting words they'd both uttered had been far worse.

Jake took his plate to the counter.

"Thanks, big guy. Why don't you practice your music? Then we'll have ice cream and turn on a show if you want."

"'Kay."

Blair rinsed the dishes, then retrieved her phone. She hadn't called her mother in a few days. Was this a good idea, since she was so pro-Nelson? But she'd be calling soon if Blair didn't call her first.

"Hi, Mom. Are you guys finished eating?"

"Yes, we finished a while ago. Your dad is looking for a movie for us to watch. How are you doing?"

"Okay." They exchanged news, but Blair didn't mention Cooper. No sense in letting her know her new relationship was already on thin ice.

"Any news from Nelson?"

Trust her mom to bring up Nelson. Not Cooper. "As a matter of fact, he was in the area yesterday, so he took Jake and me to lunch."

"It's wonderful that he's back in your life, for Jake's sake, I mean. I always liked Nelson, except for what he did there at the end. That was inexcusable, but he's trying to make up for it."

"He's making an effort." She had to agree.

"Did he ever offer child support?"

"Yes, he did a few weeks ago. It's a big help for Jake's needs and bills."

"I'm sure it is. Honey, would you ever be open to reconciling with him?"

"Mom, we've talked about this before. I'm with Cooper."

"But you've known Nelson for years. You never know."

"Mom, I'm dating *Cooper*." By faith, since they hadn't spoken in twenty-four hours.

"Of course. You and Nelson have a child together, but you haven't known Cooper for long."

Blair sighed. Sometimes her mom could be like a dog with a bone. She raised her voice. "It's not the time to talk about this."

"Pray about it, hon. I'm just thinking of Jake."

"And I never think of Jake, do I? Mom, I can't just marry someone I don't love for Jake's sake."

"I know that, Blair. Be open, that's all I'm saying."

And Cooper? He was already convinced she wanted to go back to Nelson, despite her protests. And he'd already decided their conflict was irreconcilable to the point of disappearing. Blair shuddered as a fresh wave of pain gripped her inside. Tears erupted and trickled down her cheeks.

Maybe she was better off alone, like she'd started. Alone with her son.

Chapter Twenty-Six

Blair spread out the fabric with one hand and turned it beneath the needle, working mechanically though the weekend's accumulated despair weighed on her chest like a small elephant. In minutes, she'd finished the garment, then the next, while her thoughts were miles away. Suddenly, she stilled as a few thought fragments shifted, creating a stream of light in a blocked doorway.

By lunchtime, a headache pounded in her skull, but her hopes had lifted. She requested the afternoon off, sure she couldn't work through the tangle of issues, plus head pain, without a block of time alone, which she hadn't had in months.

She arrived at home, made a grilled cheese sandwich, and heated a bowl of the soup she'd made Saturday. Savoring the solitude, listening to the silence that wound a web around her, she replayed the previous two days in her mind. *Lord, help me see the core issue in all of this.*

Cooper thought she wanted to reconcile with Nelson, which hadn't entered her mind. He was overreacting, maybe because of what had happened with Priya. Meanwhile, her mother apparently hoped for the very thing Cooper feared. But what about the truth?

As far as she knew, Nelson simply wanted a relationship with Jake, and it had begun. She'd seen no signs of malicious intent, despite his clumsy efforts. Any prospect of reconciling with him romantically was out of the question. She needed to convince Cooper of that.

And convince her mother. Despite the legitimacy Nelson might supply in her family's eyes.

Legitimacy. Suddenly, the word sparked in her mind. She'd never felt legitimate in her family. Getting pregnant only underscored her belief she was a misfit, an irregular. Of course, after Jake's birth, everyone got past the shock and adored him. But she still felt like a subplot in her family, a problem to solve.

Did her mother pressure her in Nelson's favor because she thought being with Jake's real father would make Blair more legitimate? Worth taking seriously? Would it erase the mistakes she'd made? Or was that a subconscious and misguided belief due to her brokenness?

But hadn't her brokenness already been resolved by God himself? In her head she knew this, believed it. But all her life, she'd tried to prove she was okay. She hadn't proven herself yet in clothing design to the point of having a viable career. Could part of her motivation in even *that* arena be to prove to the world and especially her family that her skills were as useful and worthwhile as her siblings'?

Blair pushed her bowl aside and laid her head on crossed arms. What a snarl of wrong beliefs had guided her life. God had called her *marvelous* the day she'd been laid up with a sprained ankle. But he'd considered her marvelous since before she was even born. He'd been the one to gift her with creative design ability. Her creativity could give joy to others. It was just as valid as any ability her siblings, Norris, Stephanie, and Audrey possessed. Sure, she'd made mistakes in her life, but God had redeemed them, turned them into good. Jake, her little boy. She wouldn't trade him for any approved path she might have taken instead. God didn't call her irregular or misfit. He called her *marvelous.* Beloved. Chosen.

Hot tears of joy and relief squeezed from her eyes and dropped to the table. Pastor Todd's words came back to her, words she hadn't absorbed at church, but had returned like a boomerang. *We're new creations, regardless of what we were before. Regardless of the mistakes we made and continue to make.*

She lifted her face, wet with tears. She was a new creation who needed to march forward into the abundant destiny God wanted for her, instead of dwelling in the past. Instead of identifying with old labels she had for herself.

With budding understanding pushing through untilled soil, she rose from the kitchen table. In the next hours, she straightened the house and ran the vacuum. She even treated herself to a cup of hot tea while she watched through the kitchen window as orange and red leaves swirled in a downward dance. Blair took time to peruse some fashion design blogs, noting with satisfaction that hers continued to do well. A blanket of peace stole over her, despite her ongoing rift with Cooper. Despite the conversation she needed to have with her mother.

Too quickly, it was time to pick Jake up at Angela's house. Blair parked in front of the woman's house and waited for him. She looked up as he pushed through the front door. A homemade kite hung from one arm. She grinned and waved at Angela. As she watched Jake zigzag toward the car, fiddling with his kite, her heart swelled with love.

Jake. Technically, he was illegitimate, but no one cared. Everyone simply loved him, regardless of what came before. He was legitimate because of who he was and how he was loved. *She'd* felt illegitimate in some ways her whole life, but God poured out his love on her, not holding her to anything that came before.

℘ ℘ ℘

The crew just left after a long Monday and Cooper stood alone on the edge of the lot he'd called home for the last two days.

That place had been his refuge since storming out of Blair's house Saturday. He should go over there, should insist they talk.

But what if they argued again and the rift grew deeper? His gut told him that wouldn't solve anything, and they needed more time. *He needed more time, though he didn't yet know why.* Something rumbled underneath his reasoning, clouding his thoughts. *What is it, Lord? I think I'm the one making a mess, but why?*

He'd spent Sunday working away his anguish by himself and had stayed until late. He wasn't ready to see her. Knew he was behaving like a child, but couldn't help himself. Zipper, tied to a tree, had kept him company all day.

While he worked, he'd tried to convince himself that his short-term relationship with Blair was like others he'd had. A nice girl, but not the right one. In Blair's case, her heart wasn't his, so there was nothing else he could do.

Only *his* heart wouldn't get the message and move on. His thoughts went to Priya. She hadn't meant to break his heart those years ago. She'd simply met her soulmate, as she'd tearfully told him. Maybe that was why Cooper had assumed Blair wanted to be with Nelson. Had he put that on her when it hadn't even entered her mind? Because he had a history of being dumped in favor of the *soulmate?*

Darkness fell quickly and temperatures tumbled. He lit a lantern and it cast orbs of round light into the shadows. Yesterday, he'd felt some relief at the site, surrounded by trees while keeping the river in view. Sort of felt like camping, and it brought back a few good memories of his dad and Miles.

Settling into a lawn chair he'd brought, he breathed deeply. It would have been a peaceful evening if his thoughts weren't grinding around like a concrete mixer. Zipper sat next to the chair, lifting his chin with doleful eyes. Cooper scratched his head and behind his ears. "It's a mess, isn't it, Zipper?"

He leaned his head back and stared up at the trees, dark patches against the setting sun. "Lord, what's all this about?" he said aloud. "I've been acting like a little kid, escaping out here. But it's hard to go back and face more loss. I should simply ask her what she feels for me and then I'll know."

A soft breeze blew against his face. Lapping sounds of the nearby river reached him and despite his twisted emotions, a thread of peace came. A voiceless whisper. He listened, closed his eyes, and tried to settle the pain in his gut. Opening his eyes again, Cooper splayed his clenched hands and laid moist palms against his thighs.

He swallowed the dryness in his throat. "I've been assuming I'm the best man for Blair. Maybe I'm not. Maybe Nelson is. Lord, I pray that your wisdom and your will be done in her life. Maybe *he's* your will for her and Jake. He's Jake's father. I know in your grace you've forgiven him for what he did, deserting Blair. I want to give her and my feelings for her to you, Lord, and lay them on your altar, because she isn't mine, she's yours." He paused as words stuck in his throat. "Lord, I love her, and I know you can take that love away if she's not for me. I trust you, Lord. And help me learn I can't protect everyone. I think too highly of myself to imagine I can do that. You can, though. I want to lay hold of the fact that I can trust *you* to protect them and everyone else I care about. Please help me not to overstep, like I've done with Blair."

He stopped and listened to the cricket chorus that filled the forest with a night symphony. A curtain of understanding fell then. *He'd* been the one to sabotage his relationship with Blair.

But why?

Was he so certain she'd reconnect with Nelson that he saved her the trouble of breaking it off by doing it himself? How stupid was that when she kept telling him she had nothing with Nelson?

"Lord, something else is going on here. Why do I feel so afraid of losing her, that I destroyed the whole thing myself? It doesn't make sense."

He buried his head in his hands and steadied his breath. Pain shot through him as did the words *loss* and *empty* and *alone*. Each word brought a pang that drove the agony deeper like a rusty nail. It wasn't Priya. Or *only* Priya.

It was Miles.

The dam broke then. Heaving sobs erupted from a cavern deeper than he'd ever known existed, seemingly bottomless. Tears that seemed endless. "Oh, Miles, I miss you, bro. I miss you so much. Why'd you have to go and leave me, leave all of us?"

Flashbacks from childhood, from adolescence. Playing one on one basketball, working on building sites together. Starting their business and celebrating with their first client. Then, the grotesque visual image of Miles, twisted at an unnatural angle on the wooden floor of the half-framed house. An image Cooper would never forget.

More tears came, as though he struggled through a hurricane that wouldn't end. Seemed like forever until his tears subsided, until his shaking shoulders stilled. He felt emptied out, as though he'd had a short but violent illness that had gutted him. Tears streaked his face, moistened his jeans.

For another long period, Cooper sat still in the same position, his head bowed over his knees, sensing God's presence in a way that defied description. No matter what happened with Blair, God was there with love, acceptance, a future.

A sliver of lightness filtered into his grief. Had he ever grieved Miles like that? Had he ever cried such primal, raw tears before? No, he'd simply worked harder and harder, stuffing the tears down, thinking he'd dealt with everything in his own bone-headed way. All he'd done was bury the pain. Pain that had poisoned his fledgling romance with Blair.

A romance that he prayed still had a fighting chance.

Chapter Twenty-Seven

"Mom, do you have a few minutes?" Blair's moist hand clutched her cellphone. She leaned against the headboard of her bed that night, her knees curled up against her chest like a young child.

"Hi, Honey. What a nice surprise. I wasn't expecting a call this soon. Is everything okay?"

"Yes, we're fine. Did you guys have a good weekend?" She'd lay the groundwork first. Her heart pounded already.

"Nothing special. We went to the farmer's market Saturday. We both enjoy that. I talked to Norris yesterday for a while."

"How is his family doing? I should give them a call." Her siblings had been casualties of Blair's wrong beliefs. Might take years to restore those relationships. But first things first.

"He got a job promotion, so that's the big news with him. Shane made the soccer team. I'm sure they'd enjoy hearing from you."

"Yeah, I'll give him a call soon."

"Seems like Nelson's serious about reconnecting with Jake. It's nice that you all had lunch together."

"I think Jake is more relaxed around him. The lunch helped."

"That's wonderful news."

"Mom, I need to ask you something."

"Sure, honey. What's up?"

"Do you feel like I'd be more, I don't know, acceptable in the family if I had ended up marrying Nelson back then? Instead of raising Jake alone?"

After a lengthy pause, Blair's mother said, "You're already acceptable, sweetie. I don't understand what you mean."

"I know this sounds weird, but bear with me, okay?" Blair took a breath. "There are things I've never told you before. During my childhood, I felt like a misfit in our family. I was artistic instead of mathematical, like everyone else. Then, when I got pregnant, I felt even more like I didn't fit. Like I'd never measure up." Her voice had splintered away to a whisper. A metallic ball of grief lodged in her throat.

"Oh, Blair. I never knew you felt that way. We loved you for your uniqueness. You added such a special creative light to all of us left brainers."

"Really?" Blair sniffed. "You never told me."

"I thought you knew. I tried to cheer you on with your sewing and your clothing ideas. You were so gifted at an early age."

"You thought so?" How had Blair missed that? Had her mother never said it, or had Blair felt so persecuted, she wouldn't have heard it anyway?

"Oh, my goodness. You were a prodigy, Blair. I used to show photos of your designs to my friends."

"You did?" Blair swallowed a sob and snatched a tissue from the box on the bedside table.

"Yes, I did, and my friends were so impressed. They told me I had the next Coco Chanel under my roof."

Blair let out a soft chuckle and blew her nose. "Not quite, but getting there."

"I had no idea you felt that way all these years. And when Jake came along, we were surprised, of course, but then we were thrilled. We never thought you'd ruined your life or made an irredeemable mistake. I wouldn't trade those years you were at the house for *anything*. We love him so much, and we love you too. We got to see him walk, say his first words. Such a treasure."

Her mother's voice broke. "I can't believe you felt that way all these years up to the present time. If you'd married Nelson and he'd accepted his responsibilities, you would have been spared a lot of heartache and the difficulties of single parenthood. But that has nothing to do with being acceptable."

"I wanted to share this with you because I never have, and they've stayed with me all this time. I probably projected a lot of things on everyone in the family because I felt so different. And then, when you keep bringing Nelson up *all* the time, it makes me feel like, well, like you favored Nelson's needs over mine."

"Not at all. I thought it would be good for Jake to know his dad, honey. I wasn't trying to say what he'd done was okay. He created a crisis for you. So, if he's turning around now and wants to make it right, maybe it's time to let him do that."

She was right. Why not let a hard situation be redeemed, if Nelson was ready to make it right? "I understand, Mom. I think that's happening."

"I'm really glad. But I'll stop bringing it up. I didn't realize it was making you feel that way. You can tell me whatever you want me to know from now on, okay?"

Blair smiled. "Yes, that would be great, Mom."

"Now, what about the man you told me you're dating? What's his name again, and when can we meet him?"

"His name's Cooper." New tears spilled down her cheeks as she said his name.

"I'd love to meet him. If you care for him, he must be a very special man."

"He is. Very special."

After her call, Blair mopped her face from a deluge of tears. She'd climbed a brand-new mountain with her mother and the view filled her with hope.

Jake had been quiet for a while. She peered into the living room. "What's going on in there, big guy?"

He looked up from where he sprawled on the rug near the couch. "I'm coloring some big birds. They're tropical birds with big beaks. Wanna see?"

"Sure, I'd love to." She got on her knees and crawled on the floor next to him.

He stared at her. "You're crying, Mom?"

She kissed his forehead. "Yeah, just a little. I was just talking to your Nanna, and we got to talking about something sad."

He tilted his head and looked at her with wide, blue eyes. "What's sad?"

She waved away his question. "If I tell you, it'll make you sad, so I won't. Nothing too bad, though. We had a good conversation. And she told me to give you her love." She studied his coloring. "That's beautiful. I like the colors you picked for his beak and feathers."

"Can I have one like this someday?"

She laughed. "I don't know. We might start with a dog one day, though."

"Really?"

"Maybe, when you're a little older." She pulled herself up. "I have one more phone call to make, then I'll come and hang out with you, okay?"

"'Kay."

Blair returned to her bedroom and shut the door, eager to get it over with. Nelson answered after one ring.

"Hi, Blair. I didn't expect to hear from you so soon."

"I know. I won't keep you long. I thought it went well on Saturday with Jake. But I think we need a bit of space, maybe for a few weeks and go back to email. I think Jake and I both need that."

"I understand. I'm glad you think it went well." His voice sounded despondent. "Um, Blair, how was it for *you* to see me again?"

She didn't expect that. "I was more comfortable the second time than I expected. I feel like we can eventually become friends."

"Nothing more than friends? We're older now. *I'm* more mature, which is a good thing. You already were." He let out a soft chuckle.

"I love Cooper."

Silence filled the phone. Then, "Oh. I didn't realize you felt that strongly, or I wouldn't have said anything. Is that why you want to take a break from me?"

"We need time, all three of us. But don't worry, unless you step out of line, you'll see Jake again."

They laughed.

"I'm only partly kidding," she said. "Don't pull anymore surprise visits."

"No, no more surprises. No more short notice either. I'll behave."

Blair sighed. Nelson was making this easy. "That would be excellent. Not forever, just for a bit. That'll give Jake a chance to miss you."

"I'd love to see that. I'm not going to disappear, though. I'll just give you guys some space."

"Thanks, Nelson. I think you're turning into a decent guy."

He laughed aloud. "Coming from you, that's a huge compliment. I'll try to keep evolving in a good direction. And your idea of friendship... like that." His voice softened. "Take care, Blair."

"You too."

Blair disconnected and felt a weight roll off her chest. *Thank you, Lord.* Her life was mostly fine now. So much better.

She left her room and went down the hall toward the kitchen. "Want some ice cream?"

"Yeah."

"Please."

"Yeah, please."

Blair went to the kitchen and couldn't stop a glance through the front window. Though it was nearly seven, Cooper's truck wasn't there yet. She sighed. Every day that elapsed lessened the chance they'd reconcile.

But sadness and peace wound together. He was in God's hands.

෪   ෪   ෪

A peaceful hush ebbed into the early evening. Sounds of the river flowing across the street reached Cooper's ears as he drank in the sound and breathed the sweet earthy smell of freshly cut wood.

His experience that evening grieving Miles for the first time—real grieving instead of simply anesthetizing himself—had changed so much inside. The weight he'd carried inside for two years seemed to ebb away. He felt hopeful, almost weightless, having released the darkness. God had helped him limp into humble acceptance.

He'd still have moments, of course. He'd always miss Miles, but could remember him now without being driven by pain.

In the wake of his emotional release, he got a clear view of what a jerk he'd been to Blair. She'd been a victim of his insanity. He *had* to see her. Texting was out of the question. He wanted to tell her in person, feel her arms around him. That is, if she forgave him. She might have decided he was too much of a loose cannon, too controlling and obnoxious. She'd consider herself lucky that she'd made a narrow escape, and she'd be justified.

But he had to try.

It was nearly seven, so she and Jake would probably be home. His chest ached to see her again, to apologize, to beg her forgiveness. If she wasn't home, he'd wait on her doorstep for as long as necessary. A couple days late, but at least it was a plan.

Minutes later, Cooper parked and was relieved to see Blair's white Toyota. He slipped down from the truck and for a moment, stood staring at her house. Then he saw her through the window carrying a bowl to Jake. She looked up and saw him standing in

297

front of his truck. Their gazes met through the window as he walked toward her door.

He reached her porch as she stepped out. A rush of longing flooded through him, and his throat tightened. He had to stop himself from leaping toward her, kissing her until tomorrow.

"Blair." His voice came out like a broken sigh. All the words of confession and sorrow he'd planned fled his mind. So, he'd have to skip eloquence. "Please hear me out. I was on my way to beat down your door to tell you I'm an idiot and I'm sorry."

He stepped closer to her. Her eyes searched his face. He hoped she saw brokenness there. And change. He was almost close enough to take her hands, but wasn't sure of her welcome. "I created a problem with Nelson when there wasn't one."

"I know." Her voice was indulgent, sweet. "I kept telling you. Then you disappeared Sunday." Pain etched her sultry voice.

"I fell into my old stupid strategy of working through pain. I was at the site."

She moistened her lips. "You were? All this time?" Like a doe, her big hazel eyes stared unblinking.

He nodded, and shame filled him. "I should have been on your doorstep Sunday morning to take back everything I said. But I'm more stubborn than that." He shook his head. "I got it now."

"Don't you know what I feel for you, Cooper?"

He swallowed. "I wasn't sure, because all my insecurities and fears ran over me like a tractor. I got lost in that." He stepped toward her and took her hands. "But I know exactly how I feel about *you*. I love you, Blair McCartney."

"Oh, Cooper. I want to make sure *you* understand that I love you too. Not Nelson. *You.*"

Before she finished speaking, he pulled her into his arms. Her scent, like orange blossoms, rose to intoxicate him. "Did I already say I love you? So much." She nodded and a smile stretched across her face.

He kissed her then, not tenderly, but like a starving man who couldn't get enough. He *had* starved and withered every hour since he'd last seen her. She drew herself tight against his chest, wrapping her arms around his neck. A soft groan came from her throat as she responded with her whole being. He explored her face, her mouth with his lips. He wrapped his fingers through her soft hair and pulled her even closer. Finally, their lips parted, but they stood still locked together like a puzzle for several minutes.

Cooper's hands remained around her shoulders. "Blair, I need to tell you some things I haven't told you before. It'll give context to my behavior. Not an excuse, just context."

Apprehension crept into her eyes. "Okay."

"Could we sit in the truck for a few minutes? Would Jake be okay?"

"Yes, I'll tell him I'm just here talking to you."

She slipped through the front door and returned in seconds. They grasped hands and walked to the truck.

Cooper opened the passenger door for Blair and he settled into the driver's side. How would he start?

She waited silently for him to speak.

He took a breath. "I had a brother. Miles."

Blair stilled, as if sensing a change in the atmosphere. Her focus stayed on his face, as if she knew he was about to share something intimate and painful.

"Miles was a couple years older than me, but we were close. Ever since we were kids, we had the same passion for architecture and building."

Cooper swallowed against the ache that began in his throat. "During our teens, we hung around my dad's friends who did construction. We worked as gofers until we knew what we were doing, then they hired us in the summers. That's when we decided we'd have a business together. We both studied architecture and construction and built a company. For eight years we worked together, building a reputation, a clientele. Then one day about two years ago…" He'd never been able to say the words. Now he would say them to the woman he loved, and he knew it wouldn't kill him.

Blair's compassionate eyes glistened with moisture.

Cooper looked away through the windshield. "Miles was on a worksite after hours. I don't know why he did this because he knew better. He crawled out on one of the beams, maybe thinking he could reach something that wasn't supposed to be there. Or check on something. I don't know, but he fell."

"He didn't make it." Blair's voice emerged in a whisper.

Cooper shook his head. A long moment passed as he stared at his hands folded on the steering wheel. "About a year ago, our company won a bid to do a whole subdivision. I spent the entire year doing the job for both of us. I was running away from the grief by working too much. I did it for Miles. And his widow and my niece."

"How tragic. I'm so sorry, Cooper." Blair reached across space and took his hand. "I knew there was something. I should have figured that out. You avoided talking about him."

His gaze met hers. "Thing is, all that work I did to avoid thoughts of Miles just moved the pain to a hidden place, but didn't heal it. I didn't grieve in a healthy way, I just stuffed everything down. So, when Nelson came along, all the irrational fears of loss burst out and I overreacted."

"I understand."

He faced her. "That's why I try to protect everyone."

"I noticed. But it's sweet."

He smiled then. "You didn't think it was sweet when I bossed you around and treated you like you didn't know squat."

She laughed. "No, I did *not* think that was sweet. But so many other things about you are. I'm glad *you* realized that you can be a little bossy sometimes. Otherwise, we'd have to have a chat."

They laughed softly for a moment then he sobered. "I went there after our argument because I needed a peaceful place, but God dealt with me. Earlier tonight."

"Oh?"

"He showed me how I'd responded to losing Miles." He looked at his hands. "Then he helped me see what I'd done to you." His voice broke. "Then he told me he loved me and even if you didn't forgive me, or if you went with Nelson, I'd be okay. Even if I'd lost you, he was there."

She slid across the vinyl bench and circled his shoulders with her arms. "But you didn't lose me. I'm right here."

"Does that mean you forgive me?"

She offered a soft smile. "I have to forgive you. I want and need you in my life."

He met her gaze and lifted his brows. "You need me?"

She nodded. "Sure do. I need you and I love you."

"I need you too." If he didn't know that before, he sure knew it now. He pulled her onto his lap and kissed her for a long moment. "I love you so much," Cooper whispered against her temple.

"Both Jake and I missed you. After our fight, I could have kicked myself for not giving you more reassurance of my feelings for you. It was a delayed reaction, realizing that's all you needed to hear, and your jealousy of Nelson was a lack of confidence in my commitment to you. So, let me be clear. You *are* the one for me."

He grinned. "Music to my ears. So, where does that leave Nelson?"

"He knew he'd come on too strong, so we're back to letters for a while. But I think he's a decent guy."

"If you say so. I'm only your advisor if you want one. I won't tell you what to do anymore. Now, tell me again?" He raised his brows and grinned at her.

"I love you, Cooper."

He kissed her again and afterward, hung onto her for a long moment. He never wanted to lose her.

The shadows of evening snuffed out the pink bands across the sky. Cricket sounds filled the air and the autumn chill seeped into the truck.

"You never got your ice cream the other night," she said. "Would you like some now?"

"Absolutely. We can pick up from where things went sideways."

She gave him a soft smile. "I would say *as if it never happened,* but I have a feeling God used it for both of us."

That, he did.

Chapter Twenty-Eight

Half-naked trees lined the streets and milky clouds hung low overhead as Blair drove to work. A few orange and brown leaves released their hold and drifted to the sidewalks below. November was half gone and soon they'd be celebrating Thanksgiving. A rush of contentment filled her. Cooper's parents were visiting. He was planning a festive group holiday at his house with his parents, Amber, a few friends from The Fork, and *Blair's* parents.

Cooper. After their argument a month earlier, they'd bonded at an even deeper level. Jake still exchanged occasional letters with Nelson and slowly warmed up to his dad. Especially after Nelson got a dog and began sending videos. Smart man.

As Blair parked in front of the factory, her spirits sagged. Her personal life was back on track, but her employment situation stagnated. She pushed the heavy front door and punched her timecard. After slipping her personal items into her locker, she sat at sewing machine number forty-five. She stared down at the machine. One day at a time, she was losing her humanity. Eight hours per day, she imitated a robot.

To stave off despondency, she allowed her thoughts to drift to the previous weekend, when she, Cooper, and Jake had gone to Milton to have lunch with her parents. Her relationship with her mother had reached a new level of closeness and understanding. Blair finally discarded her long-term baggage she'd grown up with. Her image as God's redeemed daughter, marvelous in his eyes, took root more each day. She couldn't even describe the freedom and lightness that had taken residence inside her, as she became more optimistic, more joyful. Grounded in truth.

Cooper had changed too. He'd lost the melancholy expression he sometimes had when he didn't know she was looking, and was downright lighthearted. He laughed more and was more careful when making suggestions. Occasionally, he asked *her* advice.

Her parents seemed to like Cooper right away. She could tell by the grin on her mother's face, the endless questions she asked him, and the teasing and bantering from her father. Cooper was in, after only minutes. Blair wasn't surprised.

In her peripheral vision, she saw someone approach her sewing table. She looked up at a nameless woman who worked in the offices. She wore a skirt, blouse, and blazer, unlike the masses at their sewing machines. "Blair," the woman said. "Gloria would like to see you in her office in ten minutes."

Blair hadn't spoken to Gloria in two months since their first and only conversation about her stolen design. She didn't know if they'd used it or not. As a lowly machine operator, she'd had no way of knowing and no recourse.

A few minutes later, Blair left an unfinished garment hanging from the teeth of the presser foot. She went down the hall into another world, one where people dressed professionally and had their own desks and titles. She stuck her head in Gloria's doorway. "Gloria, you wanted to see me?"

The woman looked up unsmiling over dark-rimmed glasses. "Yes, have a seat, Blair."

Blair sat in a chair facing Gloria's desk and waited.

Gloria shuffled through a stack of documents on her desk and pulled out a sheaf of pages stapled together. "Here it is," she muttered. Her cool, shuttered eyes lifted to Blair's. "Last time we spoke, I told you of the possibility of a contract position. We still don't have any staff positions, but I can offer you a contract."

"When would it start? Immediately?" Blair wiped moist palms on her jeans.

"If you want. I'll tell you the conditions." The woman leafed through the pages. "You can read this over to get all the details, but the company will also provide you with an orientation. Basically, we'll let you know in advance the categories we need and when we need them. For example, we work two seasons ahead and might need a fall sports collection or whatever. You create designs and bring them to us. If we like them and approve them, you'll be paid per design for each one we accept. The amount you're paid depends on how much you design and how many of them we keep. It's freelance, so it's flexible. You work as much or little as you want."

Blair leaned forward. "How does payment work? Are contractors paid monthly, and is there a waiting period?"

"You're paid monthly for work you did two months earlier. It takes time to decide if we accept the work, whether it fits our collections."

"Would I keep ownership of the designs, or does the company keep those?"

"Your designs become our property as soon as we mutually agree that we want the design, and you agree to give it to us."

She'd expected as much. "Thank you for the opportunity. I'd like to read over the contract before I decide."

Gloria turned an unblinking stare to Blair. "Of course." She slid the sheaf of papers across the desk.

Blair stood and took it. "Thank you. I'll get back to you in a few days." She turned and left the office.

She returned to her machine, her thoughts spinning. A contract position was what she'd wanted, wasn't it? She could continue in the warehouse and do contract work on the side, but would she even have time to do both? Was she willing to sell her designs to the company and have them take credit, take ownership?

Cooper was bringing dinner that night after he picked Jake up following his piano lesson. She'd talk to him about it after the meal.

The workday ended and Blair sighed in relief. She drove to Angela's house. Jake ran down the walkway and slipped into the car.

"I hope you had a good afternoon at Miss Angela's house," she said. "Are you ready for Miss Leah? I heard you practicing your new song yesterday. Sounded beautiful."

Jake bounced up and down in the passenger seat. "I think I'm ready. Even if I'm not ready, she's nice."

"Yes, she is. Did you know she's getting married?"

"Uh-huh. Will she still be my teacher?"

"Yes, I'm sure she will. You've met Nathan. She's going to marry him."

Soon she turned onto Lansbury Street and parked in Leah's driveway. Often, she let Jake out for his piano lesson, and other times, she went in with him to say hi to Leah. This time, she joined him on the porch and knocked.

Leah, wearing faded blue jeans, fuzzy slippers, and a thick cardigan, let them in. Her smile and light blue eyes greeted them.

"You look ready for winter." Blair pointed to Leah's slippers, like stuffed cats on her feet. "How is wedding planning going?"

"We set a date in next May, so now the craziness begins. We've reserved a few things, but there's a lot more to do." Leah positively glowed.

"And with Christmas coming, you'll have even more."

"Exactly. I'm heading up the Seasons Christmas program again this year. I'll probably do some seasonal things at church too."

"I heard the Seasons event was great last year. Maybe we'll go."

"You *have* to go. You're making some of the costumes, so you'll go for free." Leah raised her eyebrows at Blair. "Everything's going well with Cooper?"

Blair couldn't stifle a wide grin.

"I think that's a *yes*. I'm *so* glad you guys worked things out."

Blair had told Leah the background about Nelson, and the complications that arose from it. "Cooper will be by later to pick Jake up. He offered, so I figured that would be helpful. I've already started bearing down on all my Christmas crafts to sell at the market, along with the costumes for Seasons." The finished projects went back into the garage in protective plastic bins, waiting for December.

"It's a busy time and bound to get worse. But it's all fun. We can put your web address in the back of the Christmas program, and you'll get some business that way."

"Yes, *Nathan*." Blair laughed. "You sound like your fiancé."

"He's tried to teach me. Not my gift, but that's okay." She shrugged cheerfully.

"I'm getting it more than I thought possible." For Blair, it would be a necessity, regardless of what she decided about the proposed contract.

In the car on the way home, Blair sang a song they'd learned at church. Gratitude bubbled up inside her, especially at the thought of how easily things could have gone south with Cooper. Instead, the last month had been, well, quite romantic.

A little over an hour later, Cooper and Jake arrived at the house. Cooper carried a stoneware pot filled with something aromatic, and Jake chattered about his lesson and Zipper's antics. Felt so right. Blair marveled in gratitude.

Dinner was a delicious tandoori dish Cooper had made. After he and Blair had finished the dishes, he pulled her into his arms and simply held her. "I can't get enough of this," he murmured into her ear. "I think about what I almost lost, and I never want to let you go."

She tipped her face up to his and her gaze found his. "I could say ditto, but that would be unoriginal."

He grinned. "And you're nothing if not original." He lightly kissed her. She savored his touch, the soft caress of his lips. *She couldn't get enough of him.*

"Let's go sit on the couch," she said. "I have something to talk to you about."

"Should I be worried?" He followed her into the living room.

"Absolutely not. I need your input."

"My input. She needs *my* input," he crowed. "It's about time."

They laughed and settled on the couch. Blair allowed Jake a limited amount of TV, so he had parked himself in front of it, entranced.

Blair told Cooper about the contract position she'd been offered that day. She snagged the document from the coffee table and handed it to him. "Here it is. What's your first thought?"

"I was going to ask *you*. You should tell me your impressions first." He waited for her to speak, leaving the paper in his lap.

"Well, I have two concerns," she said. "Time, first. I'd be spending time on making original designs. But since it won't be full-time or enough to pay the bills, I'd likely have to continue at the factory. And at the market. I don't think I can do all that."

"You have a point. And the second concern?"

"The second one is bigger." She turned her somber gaze to his. "They won't give me credit for the designs. They'd *own* them."

"Are you surprised? It's the same thing they did with your design months ago. It became theirs, though you didn't willingly give it to them."

"They stole it." Her voice softened, but anger stung inside. "They stole it and didn't compensate me, nor did they give me credit."

"And that's what they'll continue doing if you agree to the contract. I'm not trying to sway you, but that's the way I see it. And you *did* ask me."

He winked, and she returned a smile. "I'll support you whatever you decide, Blair."

"I can't do it." She fell back against the couch and sighed. "I can't do it for the money, sell my ideas like that. I'd rather do without. Cut corners. I'd rather try it on my own—why are you grinning?"

Cooper laughed. "That's my girl." He reached for her hand and lifted it to press a kiss there, then left their clasped hands on his knee. "Hey, it's not a terrible decision for some designers. But you're not that designer. You're a creative genius and you're going to have your own label."

She chuckled. "You're right." Something trembled inside at the realization of the decision she'd just made. Yes, it would be a longer road, but at least it would lead somewhere. And it was no longer a desire to matter, or for others to consider her *legitimate*. It was a validation of the gift God had given her, and free rein to do as he led.

"Remember, I didn't tell you what to do."

"No, you didn't." She grinned and held his gaze. "I made my own decision, and you were a good cheerleader." She set her other hand atop his. "Thanks, Cooper. That's so clear. I don't have doubts. But it'll be hard and long."

"Yes, it will. But you're not alone. Nathan'll give you the lowdown for marketing. I'll give you tandoori if you get hungry."

They laughed.

"Yes, tonight's meal was exotic and wonderful," she said. "We can thank Priya for indirectly expanding my palate." She cast a glance at Jake, who sat immobile before the television. "My son will be a gourmet eater before he's ten."

And maybe Blair would be a sought-after designer by then.

 CR CR CR

Cooper scanned the dark-gray shingles with satisfaction. For the last couple of weeks, he'd insisted on getting the roof on before winter, to protect everything they'd done so far. Drywall. Raw wood sub-flooring. Barring disaster, he'd be in the house by early spring, but didn't want a lot of repair work to do following a nasty winter. And in Pennsylvania, one never knew.

The team managed to complete the roof and shingles ahead of schedule. As he stared at the half-built home, he imagined it, as he so often had in the last month, with Blair and Jake inside. Cooking together. Enjoying the sunset on the deck out back. Listening to cricket songs mixed with the lapping of the river each night. He could no longer imagine his future without both of them in that house.

He hadn't forgotten the night he gave Blair to God, put her on the altar for his will. And he hadn't stopped thanking God for giving her back. He still needed to offer her each day, though, to avoid being too pushy or overprotective. She was *God's* daughter, after all.

If his fantasy played out, she could leave the decrepit house she rented with the dirtbag landlord in control. Two months later, the man hadn't yet fixed her roof. Blair, unable to tolerate the unsightly stain on the kitchen ceiling, had painted over it. The memory of it made him wonder if any of Mitchell's tenants had complained following the anonymous letter he'd sent. He could only hope it had done some good.

He wouldn't dally at the worksite that day for good reason. Two reasons, to be exact. Blair and Jake. It was Friday night, and he'd promised Jake pizza and a movie at the Brenner Falls Cinema. Finding a movie a seven-year-old and two adults could all enjoy had been a challenge, but they'd give it a shot.

Cooper hopped into his truck and drove the short distance to his house. As he approached his street, he noticed a small black cloud hovering in the sky. Alarm tickled in his veins. He got closer and his anxiety blossomed. And the cloud grew. There was a fire somewhere on his street.

When he turned the corner, he drew in a sharp breath. Blair's house was on fire, and she wasn't home yet. With a screech, he parked and snatched his phone from the passenger seat. He dialed 911 for the fire department first, shouting instructions to them with Blair's address.

He called Blair. "Blair, where are you?"

"I'm just leaving the grocery store with Jake. What's going on?"

"It's the house. There's a fire." He coughed as toxic fumes swirled in the air.

"Your house is on fire?"

"No, yours!"

"Oh, no! I'm on my way. Did you call the fire department?"

"Yes, they're on their way. How soon can you get here?"

"I'll be there in maybe ten minutes. Oh, Cooper. I can't imagine what happened."

"I can." He grimaced.

Cooper fidgeted, wondering if he should break down the door and bring some of Blair's things outside. He knew little about fire protocol, and wondered if breaking a window or door would make everything worse. Better to wait until the fire experts arrived.

The sound of sirens pierced through the silent afternoon. *Thank you, God.* That hadn't taken long. Looked like the fire had begun in the kitchen and had already spread to the bedrooms. With a jolt, Cooper thought about Blair's designs, and he hoped she'd made several copies or backed them up somehow. He should try to save her computer. She normally kept it in the living room.

What a thing to happen right after she'd decided to work for herself.

Sirens grew louder and became deafening. A fire truck swung into Blair's driveway, dwarfing the modest dwelling. Four men in fire suits and protective helmets jumped out and began uncoiling a massive hose. They didn't waste time applying water to the source of the fire. Shouts volleyed among them. During the mayhem, Blair pulled in behind Cooper's truck and leaped out of the car.

She ran to him, pulling Jake by the hand. "Oh, Cooper. My projects, my designs." She turned to Jake. "Go wait on Cooper's porch."

"Do you have a backup? Or copies?" Cooper asked.

"Garrett told me to get a backup subscription and it was on my to-do list. If I can get my laptop, that's most of it, but I have some sketches in the bedroom under the bed—" She dashed toward the house and whipped out her keys.

"Blair, don't!" Cooper charged after her.

She thrust open the door and was thrust backward by a gust of hot air. He reached for her and pulled her away from the doorway.

"No, my laptop has everything on it."

"I'll get it." The living room wasn't on fire, so he could safely slip inside and grab the computer. He pushed her back with one arm. "Stay here, Blair. Nothing is worth your life."

"Stop, Cooper. It's not worth yours either." She shouted behind him, but he was inside. Heat surrounded him like a hellish cloud.

"Sir, you can't go in there!" A firefighter's shout reached him in the front hallway. Cooper buried his face in his elbow against the fumes and darted to the right into the living room. If the laptop was right on the table, he could snatch it and run out.

The firefighter took Cooper's arm and pulled him out of the building before he could grab Blair's computer. Clouds of smoke billowed, hazing his vision. He coughed.

Once outside, he breathed deeply. Blair ran to his side. "Oh, Cooper. You shouldn't have gone in there. I shouldn't have said anything, but it was a reflex. You're more valuable than these designs."

He looked up at her and managed a smile. "Glad you think so. Maybe they'll contain the fire before it gets to your computer."

"I'll just do new designs. Let's go stand with Jake. We should get far from the smoke."

They jogged back to Cooper's house and joined Jake on the porch, all three of them watching the movements of the firefighters. A small crowd of neighbors stood on the curb, gawking as spires of black smoke twisted up from what used to be the kitchen. Gradually, the flames disappeared and only plumes of smoke remained. The other half of the house looked intact, but likely smelled like a barbeque.

"I must have caught it shortly after it started," Cooper said. He looked down at Blair and Jake. "At least you two weren't there. God protected you."

"Are *you* okay?" Blair looked up at him. She reached up to wipe soot from his cheek.

"I'm okay. I shouldn't have gone in, but glad I didn't have any bad surprises."

"Like a falling roof." She tightened her arm around his waist. "After all we've been through, I can't lose you now."

Her words touched a tender spot inside him. He pressed a kiss onto her brow. "I'm fine. Might have inhaled a bit of smoke, but I'll check it out with a doc if I have to."

Blair stared at her house. "I wonder what we'll do now."

Cooper extended a hand toward Jake, who sat in wide-eyed silence next to Zipper. He stood and Cooper drew him into the huddle. "Don't worry. The main thing is that you and Jake are safe."

Jake lifted his face to them. "Where are we gonna live, Mom?"

"You'll live in my house here," Cooper told him, then looked at Blair. "There are three bedrooms, two baths. You and Jake can stay here, and I'll stay with Amber until my house is ready in a few months."

When she was about to protest, he placed a gentle finger on her lips. "No arguments, okay? Can I be a little bossy for a minute? I promise it won't become a habit."

She nodded and offered a tired smile. "Yes, you can. Boss away." She let out a heavy sigh and collapsed against him, her head on his chest. He encircled her shoulders with his arms.

When he thought of Mitchell, Blair's landlord, anger burned inside him. There was undoubtedly some bad wiring in the kitchen, possibly in the oven, or this whole disaster wouldn't have happened. The fire officials would investigate and find the reason. Meanwhile, Blair and Jake were safe.

He pressed another kiss to Blair's head and squeezed Jake's shoulder. "Thank God you're both safe. That's all I've got to say."

During the week that followed, fire inspectors determined the cause of the fire to be kitchen wiring that wasn't up to code, as Cooper had suspected.

"It's amazing there wasn't a fire sooner," the inspector told Cooper and Blair. Cooper made sure the man knew Blair had made numerous complaints to her landlord about the oven, roof leak, and the fireplace. "We have photos and documentation of the damage and Ms. McCartney's requests. Mr. Mitchell hasn't done anything except raise the rent. A single mother and a child were endangered by Mr. Mitchell's negligence."

The inspector took notes.

Anger still simmered under Cooper's skin. He hoped Mitchell would get exactly what he deserved.

Following the inspection, Blair, Jake, and Cooper picked through the house room by room to see what was salvageable. Her computer was safe, but her notebook had burned in the blaze.

She silently examined each piece of furniture, clothing, shoes, sorting out what they could save. Fortunately, the firefighters had contained the blaze before it could burn all the contents of the bedrooms. Still, smoke odor permeated clothes, furnishings, and linens. Cooper found a restoration company which claimed they could remove odor from many items. At least most of Blair's finished projects for the Christmas market remained safe in the garage.

Amber welcomed Cooper back gladly, clucking over what could have happened to him, to Blair, and the house. "That was kind of you to give your house to Blair and Jake to live in," she'd said when he called to tell her the news. "You're welcome here, of course."

A week after the fire, Cooper parked his truck in his driveway behind Blair's car. He got out and knocked on the door of his own house, bearing a casserole Amber had made for them. Zipper wagged his tail, seeming happy to be home again. *Not yet.*

Blair opened the door and grinned, looking beautiful and peaceful, not like a woman who'd had a house fire a week earlier. In fact, she'd changed even before that, having lost the anxious, vigilant look in her eyes and the hurried daily tension. He knew he'd changed as well, and the impact on their relationship amazed him daily.

"I bet it feels weird to knock on your own door, doesn't it?" she said, a tantalizing tilt to her lips.

"A little, but I couldn't see myself barging in on you." He grinned.

She took the casserole from his hands and set it on the island. When she returned to his side, she took his jacket, then slipped her arms around his waist. They stood for a moment, glued together. "This is what it's like to live one day at a time, I guess," he murmured against her brow. "It's not too bad, is it?"

"No, it's not. I kind of like it." She stood on tiptoe and pressed his lips with hers. He drew her head closer with his hands and deepened the kiss. A guy could get used to this. Cooper's open layout didn't allow them as much privacy for a hello kiss as Blair's house had, but that was fine. Jake seemed to roll with everything that had recently happened. Thank goodness for a flexible kid.

"Hey, Jake," he called to where Jake sat on the couch working a video game on a tablet. He tried to include the boy whenever it was appropriate. He was growing to love the little guy almost as much as he loved his mother. "Are you holding down the fort over here?"

Jake leaped up and ran to him. "Hi Cooper. I'm holding down *your* fort." He giggled. Cooper leaned to slip one arm over his small shoulders and give him a squeeze. He'd only been doing that since the fire, and Jake seemed to like it.

Jake wiggled away and made a beeline for Zipper. "How's my friend, Zipper? I missed you, boy." He knelt and put both arms around the dog's neck. Zipper responded by thumping his tail on the floor and licking Jake's chin, which triggered peals of giggles.

During a hearty chicken and potato casserole with a side salad, they took their time around the table. A thick candle flickered light across the shiny wood surface as a tide of well-being lapped inside Cooper. Despite the circumstances. His eyes strayed to the picture window, as he had so many times before. This time, he saw only a grotesque silhouette, the half-burned house against the late autumn twilight. Wished he'd bought some curtains sooner to block that view.

He drew his attention back to those he loved around the table, and silently thanked God for the unexpected solution to Blair's housing problem. Didn't bother him to stay at Amber's house, as long as he knew Blair and Jake were comfortable.

"We can still do Thanksgiving here, if you want," he said.

"Of course, we can, if there's space. I just learned my younger sister is coming in from the west coast, and my sister from Pittsburgh. That's seven extra plus Audrey's newborn."

"A nice big crowd. May as well meet more family members. We'll get extra tables from somewhere." He grinned, glad Blair's family dynamics were on the mend.

"They'll love you." She reached across the table to take his hand, then reached her other hand toward Jake. "Not quite as much as we do."

Chapter Twenty-Nine

Five Months Later

"Blair, how do you want your steak?" Cooper's muffled voice reached her where she stood on the front porch of his newly minted home. She leaned against the wood railing, mesmerized by the view through the leafy branches of the calm, undulating swell of the river. She went inside and crossed the flagstone entryway under a lofty cathedral ceiling of knotty pine. The space opened to a full kitchen and dining area.

She couldn't help but admire the kitchen each time she walked through, all stone and granite with solid wood cabinets. State of the art, yet warm and stylishly rustic. Blair opened French doors and stepped down onto a wide wooden deck where Cooper stood at the grill, his broad back facing her. Smoke billowed up through the trees. She came up behind him and slipped her hands around his waist. "You called, Sir?"

He turned to complete the embrace. "I was asking you how you want your steak, but I guess it's going to be well-done now."

She giggled.

"You guys are too mushy." Jake chortled from where he sat scratching Zipper's head. The dog lifted his chin and closed his eyes in ecstasy. "Zipper and I are going to look for frogs."

"Wait, Jake. We're eating soon. We promise not to cuddle anymore." She lowered her voice. "At least not for a few minutes or so." They shared soft laughter.

"How's the salad coming?" He turned a slab of steak with a two-pronged fork.

"It's ready, though the river lured me for a minute. You weren't kidding when you described the beauty that first time you told me about this house." The computer rendition didn't compare to the completed home.

"Exactly why I wanted to be here."

Cooper had moved into the new house in March, a month earlier. He claimed he was more than ready to settle into his dream house, even if some of the final touches weren't yet complete. And it was stunning structure, as well as peaceful, spacious, and elegant. The man had *taste.* No wonder the vision had compelled him for years.

She and Jake still lived in his other house, which now felt like home. She'd even put curtains on the windows. Many of their furnishings, clothing, and books, had been restored and no smoke odor remained. She'd replaced other items too damaged to keep, like her couch and mattress. At least her sewing machine and computer had survived, enabling her to launch her business.

Despite her protests, Cooper refused to charge her rent. With that advantage plus the child support she received from Nelson, she was able to cut her work at the factory to part time. The extra hours enabled her to dive into her online business. In a few months, she'd be able to submit her first order to a clothing manufacturer. In the meantime, she kept learning how to set up the workflow, how to market, and how to run her own company. There was so much to learn, but she was in charge of her career, not the design divas in New York, nor her employer.

"Can we eat outside on the deck?" Jake asked Cooper, who plated the steaks and turned off the burners.

"Might be a little cool, big guy. Here, take these to the kitchen for me?"

"Sure." Jake took the platter of steaming meat in both hands.

Blair crossed her arms. "I agree. It's getting chilly."

"Let's eat."

The three of them settled around a dining table overlooking the backyard through a large picture window. "This seems to be our happy place, eating next to a big window." Blair grinned. "I'm pretty happy, at least."

"Me too," Cooper said with a lingering and thoughtful expression. "Makes me think of that first night we had steak at the other house. So much has happened since then."

The man spoke the truth. Not only had Blair's employment situation completely changed, but Cooper's had too. As he completed the house, he started bidding for projects nearby, thanks to Mayor Faulkner, who'd tipped him off. Later that summer, he'd begin creating a new subdivision across the river. Couldn't be any closer. For that, both he and Blair were thankful.

They ate ice cream around the table, then moved to the roomy living room in front of a wide stone fireplace with a knotty wood mantle. Candles inside glass columns flickered from the mantle and on the coffee table. Jake, who'd discovered games on his tablet, pulled it out and settled in on the love seat to play. Zipper curled up on the floor beside him.

"I wonder if my old house will be rented to someone else soon." Blair tucked her feet under her on the couch where she sat next to Cooper. After the fire, the damaged part of her house was repaired, but the building still stood empty.

"It's for sale," Cooper said. "Like the others Don Mitchell owned. I recently heard that from the housing deputy and forgot to tell you."

Blair's eyes widened. "He's selling *all* of them?"

"He has to. The court ruled against him because of all the complaints and the fire that could have cost your lives."

"Mitchell was forced to sell?"

"Not forced, but he isn't authorized to rent to anyone anymore. There's no point in having seven empty houses he's not allowed to rent. So, he's selling them. Even his own residence."

"Good riddance. I'm surprised the city stepped in that way. They stood up for the little guy. And *I'm* one of the little guys."

"But I'm the *big* guy." Jake looked up from his game and grinned.

Blair chuckled. "Yes, you are. And getting bigger all the time."

"Landlords aren't stripped of their role very often," Cooper said. "It's an extreme measure after loads of negligence and especially negligent endangerment. Having rental property is a business, but he wasn't conducting it in a fair and safe way, so the city finally shut him down. Mayor Faulkner wanted to run him out of town. Lots of people complained about him."

"Hmm. I wonder if our letter had something to do with that." She smirked.

"More than likely. So, they're for sale. I'm thinking of buying some of them."

Blair shook her head and laughed. "You're full of surprises. What made you think of that?"

"Well, he's selling them pretty cheap. He just wants to leave fast, I think. So, it's a great opportunity. I can fix them up and rent them out."

"Do you have time to manage rental properties, plus design and build an entire subdivision?" This was a side of him Blair hadn't seen before. Maybe once he had his own dream house off his plate, he became a tornado of productivity.

"No worries, I'll hire help. I don't ever plan to be a workaholic again. I'll manage a team for the new project, and I can engage a property manager too. For sure, I'll be a better landlord than Mitchell ever was."

"I can attest to that, since you're *my* landlord." She bumped his shoulder with hers.

He chuckled and shook his head. "Not your landlord. Your biggest fan."

She met his gaze and held it across the flickering glow of the candle. A smile tugged at her lips. "So, how long will you let us live in your house?"

Cooper stroked his chin in exaggerated pondering. "It depends."

Her eyebrows lifted, still teasing him. "On what? Market conditions? Whether or not I can clean my gutters without falling on my hind parts?"

They shared a laugh. Then Cooper's face grew serious. He ran a finger down her cheek. "Depends on how long it'll take you to agree to marry me. Then you guys'll move in here."

Her mouth dropped open. She lowered her voice to a whisper. "Is that a *proposal*, Mr. Dawson?"

Cooper took on a lazy grin, but his eyes smoldered. Softly, he said, "Not an official one. I have more class than to propose over a steak dinner at home. But consider it a heads-up."

She moistened her lips and her heart pounded. "Well, in that case, I'll be ready. And you won't have long to wait for my answer."

"Will I like your answer?"

"I think you will."

Then his lips were on hers and she knew the future had just begun.

I hope you enjoyed reading *Custom Made*. If you did, please consider leaving a review where you bought it and/or at Goodreads. It would help other readers discover my books and be encouraged by their inspiring truths.

You can also sign up to receive updates about new books at www.Kyle-Hunter.com where you'll receive a free novella just for signing up!

Discover more Brenner Falls Romance... Book 3

Embracing the Broken **(Book Three)**

Physical therapist Amber Dawson strives to make life better for others. She'd love to leave the corporate atmosphere of her current job. If only she could buy the charming, abandoned house on the edge of town and open her own practice.

Ben Russo overcame a troubled youth and works as an engineer for the town of Brenner Falls. He's convinced the dilapidated house is historic and wants to prove it. Not only does he love history, but the discovery might also help him climb in his career.

When Amber and Ben meet at a wedding reception, the negative impression is mutual. But they later discover the little house they both have their eyes on is condemned unless they can prove it's historically significant. If the house is demolished, neither one will get it, so they decide to work together.

As Ben and Amber delve into the house's past, they encounter intrigue they never expected, and an attraction to each other they can't deny. But as they hit roadblocks to saving the broken-down house, they also come face to face with their own hidden brokenness and the grace that heals it.

Then there's Book 4... **Mistaken Destiny**

After fourteen years away, Rick Russo never thought he'd come back to Brenner Falls—much less as a changed man. Following years of drug addiction and life on the streets, his newfound faith has given him a second chance, including reuniting with family and a role in the church youth ministry. But first, he needs a steady job...which he finds at The Grateful Fork, a restaurant favored by locals.

Kelsey Brewster has her hands full juggling her online job and caring for her sister, Molly, while their parents serve on a nine-month mission. The highlight of her week is taking shifts at The

Grateful Fork since food is her passion. She never expects to be drawn to a man with a past like Rick's.

When the owner's niece steps in to manage the restaurant, it goes downhill. As Rick and Kelsey fight to save it from her mismanagement, their friendship grows—as well as their attraction. But Rick thinks Kelsey is out of his league. Kelsey doubts her appeal since her close friends have gotten married, but she can't even get a date.

Rick pulls away from Kelsey, convinced he isn't good enough for her. As his ministry flourishes, he's forced to face the question: has he fully accepted the grace he preaches to others?

Just when Rick and Kelsey's relationship gets on track, a near-tragedy shakes Rick's confidence, leaving him questioning his calling—and his place in Kelsey's life. With the future and love on the line, can they trust that God is writing a greater story than they ever imagined?

More romantic stories by Kyle Hunter...

Romance in Provence Series

The Provence Series takes you with Bree and Lauren, best friends and business partners, to one of the loveliest regions of France. It's not always idyllic in the land of lavender fields and cliff-side villages. Join Bree and Lauren as each woman discovers her unique journey... and surprising romance.

Prodigals in Provence (Book 1) Bree's Story

A Promise in Provence (Book 2) Lauren's Story

Second Chance Series

In *The Second Chance Series*, you'll meet Marissa, Julia, Sydney, and Eden, four college friends who, twenty-five years later, renew their friendships as they find themselves empty nesters and single again. You'll love getting to know these women and following each one in her own book. (Women's Fiction.)

Marissa Rewritten (Book 1: a Novella)   A Writer Unblocked

Julia Redesigned (Book 2) Discovery in Florence, Italy

Sydney Rewound (Book 3) The Present Clashes with the Past

Eden Redefined (Book 4) Returning to College in Midlife

Stand Alone Novels

One December (A Romance in Paris)

Circle Back Around (A Return Home to Save the Family Business)

Postcard from Nice (A Novella set in Nice, France)

Read Chapter One of all books (and/or purchase at numerous storefronts or eBooks direct from the author) at
www.Kyle-Hunter.com

Kyle Hunter is the author of thirteen novels of inspirational romance and women's fiction. Her relatable characters will become like close friends you'll cheer for and learn from as you join them on their journeys. Story settings range from Europe to small town America. As characters face outward and inward challenges, the insights they gain are encouraging and relevant.

Kyle spent thirteen years in France, and she's intrigued by faraway places. Currently, she lives in North Carolina where she writes fiction, non-fiction (under the pen name K. B. Oliver), and the travel blog OliversFrance.com. She also teaches French to adults.